TRESPASS

OTHER BOOKS AND AUDIO BOOKS
BY SANDRA GREY:

Traitor

Tribunal

TRESPASS

a novel

SANDRA GREY

Covenant Communications, Inc.

Cover photography by McKenzie Deakins.
For photographer information, please visit www.photographybymckenzie.com

Cover design copyrighted 2010 by Covenant Communications, Inc.

Published by Covenant Communications, Inc.
American Fork, Utah

Printed in the United States of America
First Printing: October 2010

16 15 14 13 12 11   10 9 8 7 6 5 4 3 2

ISBN: 978-1-60861-052-5

Special thanks to . . .

My father, for a suggestion that was a catalyst for an idea

* * *

My husband, for support that shaped an idea into a story

* * *

. . . And Eliza at Covenant, for helping it shine

Troika:

A Russian sleigh drawn by three horses

* * *

A group of three, with one common goal or purpose

* * *

A special operative group of three, authorized by the Soviet Secret Police to administer swift punishment to threats against Stalinist Russia without the knowledge or permission of local judicial systems

"God must be out of Russia in five years."
—Joseph Stalin (circa 1935)

ONE

Before the sun set on one beautiful Paris spring day, Hans Brenner had managed to enjoy a relaxing evening meal with friends, inform his friend Rolf Schulmann that he'd joined the Mormon Church, ask the American nurse Natalie Allred to marry him, and volunteer to become the next political victim of the Soviet Union. Not bad for one day's work.

But the day wasn't over yet. The sun set too slowly to preclude the chance of any more drama before nightfall, and the automobile that idled nearby hinted that more adversity was on the horizon.

Hans faced the man dressed as a French chauffeur. "I remember you," Hans informed him. "From the airplane. You helped save Natalie from the Soviet intelligence agent Lieutenant Rostov—"

"I'm not surprised you remember." The young man closed the door behind Hans and returned to the driver's seat. He paused with his hands gripping the steering wheel and glanced through the rearview mirror. "You ready for this, comrade?"

"Do you realize what he's going to do to me?" Hans swallowed. "How could anybody be ready for this?"

"It's not going to be easy for you at first, sir. I've had to convince the Soviets I'm one of them, which means I'm not going to be your favorite person in a few minutes."

"I wasn't expecting it so soon . . ." Hans knew his voice was trembling.

The man was apologetic. "Major Matthews leaked the news of your whereabouts through an agent in the Soviet Köpenick district, and Lieutenant Rostov made his move. We had to act now."

"Is Natalie safe?" Hans interrupted, and he almost choked on the words.

"Matthews guarantees it."

"But why the white rose?"

"White rose?" The driver glanced at Hans, puzzled.

Hans let out a soft moan. "In the bouquet someone—I now assume Rostov's agent—handed Natalie less than an hour ago." Hans felt his palms sweating. "The white rose has special significance to the lieutenant since the death of his wife."

The driver swore softly. "If Rostov's on to us . . ."

"Please, let's just get this over with, all right?" Hans could hardly breathe.

The driver pressed on the gas, pulled the vehicle away from the riverbank, and carefully merged into traffic. As the *Île de la Cité* and its Notre Dame cathedral faded behind them, Hans's worry persisted, even intensified. Ever since he'd joined The Church of Jesus Christ of Latter-day Saints he'd wondered what it would feel like to receive an unmistakable prompting from the Holy Ghost. He wondered if this was it. "Listen—I can't go through with this plan if Natalie's in danger."

"You've got to trust Matthews. He said he'd keep her safe, and he will." The driver swung the wheel, exiting the boulevard and paralleling the railroad tracks.

Trust Matthews. One hand raked his black hair as Hans contemplated the suggestion. Major James Matthews was the American intelligence chief who had orchestrated the rescue that had saved Hans and Natalie from Rostov. And then Matthews had offered Hans an unprecedented chance to earn passage to the United States to be with Natalie. Yes, Hans silently agreed, he should trust Matthews.

The driver glanced once at Hans in the rearview mirror. "I've wanted to thank you for intervening in my behalf, sir—for saving me from that Ukrainian thug Vasik. He would've choked the life right out of me." The man hesitated. "Listen, Brenner, things are gonna get a bit dicey in a few minutes, and I just wanted you to know the name of the man you saved on the plane. Major Matthews doesn't think you need to know—but after what you did, I don't care what the Central Intelligence Group thinks." He took a deep breath. "I'm Reynolds. Alex Reynolds. And I wish I could shake your hand instead of doing this business the CIG sent me to do."

"Which isn't to give me a medal," Hans mourned.

"You know how Lieutenant Rostov works—always everything on *his* timetable, not ours."

Hans sneered. "And I'm supposed to put up a convincing enough fight that I end up in a wheelchair and you end up on the Soviets' approval list."

"In a nutshell." Reynolds looked uncomfortable.

Hans felt the same emotion, but his stubbornness was beginning to overshadow—and compensate for—his anxiety about what was about to happen.

"Look, Brenner, I can see from your scars that you've had more than your fair share of abuse at the hands of the Soviets. But you're a tough man; I can see that too. You're taller than I am and have twice the muscle. Doesn't make a bit of difference; I'm gonna have to clobber you rather convincingly in order to convince Rostov I'm one of them."

Hans growled "I'm no weakling. Think you're man enough to—"

"I know it, Brenner." Reynolds's answer was confident. "I'm tougher than I look, so make your struggle convincing because my orders are to help Rostov's Soviet thugs beat the living tar out of you."

"Believe me, I'll be convincing. Think you can do it?"

"I told you, I—"

"No, Reynolds—think you can convince the Soviets you're one of them?"

"I *have* to." Reynolds cleared his throat. "Everything depends on it. Major Matthews needs Rostov to trust me." His hands shifted uncomfortably on the steering wheel.

All this talk of beating and wheelchairs and Lieutenant Viktor Rostov was depressing. Hans felt the cold penetrate deep, where cold only goes when caused by fear. He was a brave man—at least he liked to think of himself as such. He'd faced enemies bigger and faster than himself and lived to tell about it. He'd been a lieutenant in the German army and led his Alpine troops to victory more times than he could count. He'd survived the war and a multitude of dangers since. He could take a little beating—or a big one, if Alex Reynolds felt that would earn Rostov's trust and help Alex infiltrate Soviet intelligence. Hans convinced himself he could do anything—if it meant he would earn his passage to America. And Matthews had promised him that Natalie would be there waiting for him . . . He clenched his hands into fists. *Trust Matthews . . .*

"Listen, Hans," Reynolds said, "I know how you're feeling. I'd be worried about my girl too." He glanced back at Hans. "But there's nothing you can do about your fiancée right now. Viktor Rostov is here"—Reynolds's hand waved toward a black Ford sedan that had pulled to a stop several dozen meters ahead—"and you know there's no turning back."

Hans nodded. But he didn't agree. His brain refused to erase the awful image it was creating—of Rostov . . . with Natalie . . .

The young American agent tapped the brakes, pulled to the side of the curb that separated the road and the train tracks, killed the engine, and dropped his hands to his lap. And then Reynolds said softly, apologetically, "Sir, it's time to get out of the car."

Suddenly Hans wasn't ready. He watched as the second vehicle emptied and its passengers approached his car, and he felt an unpleasant jolt of recognition. From this moment on he had only two choices: He could submit to this plan—*his* plan, actually—his brainchild, embraced by Major James Matthews of the American CIG—or he could break his promise to Matthews and make sure Natalie was all right.

"C'mon, Brenner." Reynolds turned, and Hans couldn't help noticing that the Beretta held steady in Alex's hand was rather persuasive. "Don't make this more difficult than it has to be. Remember, I don't want to use anything more lethal than my fists. I'll only shoot if you try to run. And then, I have to shoot to bring you down. Got it? Now get out of the car."

Hans got out of the car. Reynolds stayed close, and Hans felt the hard steel of the weapon press up against his spine. But Reynolds lowered his voice and said one last empathetic word for Hans's ears only: "Godspeed."

Three men approached Reynolds's car. Two were little more than attack dogs, Hans realized, and he dismissed them to keep his eyes on the one in the middle. As Viktor Rostov approached there was a controlled rage in the Soviet's stride that precluded any chance of an affable finale to this meeting. A business suit and the beginnings of a beard couldn't hide his military bearing, and his strong jaw was set, the whole image reminding Hans of a grizzly bear suddenly deprived of his long winter nap. Rostov's eyes smoldered with a determination that bordered on fury—Hans's last encounter with Rostov hadn't been resolved in Rostov's favor, thanks to Matthews's and Reynolds's intervention, so Hans could forgive the man his rage.

A train whistle sounded in the distance. As Rostov approached him Hans's first inclination was to raise his fists and knock the man's Slavic face and tailored suit into the middle of next month. But Hans forced his hands to stay at his sides. Instead, he demanded, "Where's Natalie?"

"She's no longer your concern." Rostov closed the distance between them and his own fist caught Hans squarely in the jaw. Hans's head whipped around, and through starbursts he saw a commuter train rounding a bend in the tracks less than a hundred meters away. Hans had only seconds to make up his mind whether to flee or face his destiny. If he stayed, he'd survive with bruises and perhaps a few broken bones. He'd be hauled away to the USSR to purportedly live out the remainder of his usefulness as an indentured nuclear scientist for the Soviet government. In reality he'd be sprung after six months by Matthews, Reynolds, and the Americans who eagerly awaited all Hans would gather on the workings of the Soviet nuclear program.

But if he fled, he would either arrive at Jacques Bellamont's apartment in time to save Natalie or he'd be shot in the back by Reynolds as he ran. Major Matthews considered Reynolds an imperative link between American and Soviet intelligence, and if Hans bolted, he knew Reynolds would have to at least try to disable him in order to keep that link in place.

Hans listened to the crescendo of the approaching train and saw the clear blue eyes of an American nurse in his mind, and suddenly the decision was easy. He bolted, sprinting toward the tracks. Rostov's henchmen leaped into action, racing after him. He heard Reynolds shout, and then he heard the shot. He felt something strike his collarbone, as if an invisible hand had swung a steel rod. He flung himself into the path of the oncoming locomotive and felt Death brush against his hip as he urged his body forward and past the train. His pursuers dived away to avoid disaster, and Reynolds with his Beretta did not try to follow.

Hans knew that when the train had passed, target practice would resume. He ran as he'd never run in his life. He realized he could make a cluster of buildings in the next few seconds, and he could hide there, catch his breath, and plan his next move.

But then he made a terrible mistake: He looked behind him.

He *knew* better. One should never turn to look in the last split second before safety. If he hadn't looked, perhaps he would've made it . . .

Through the moving darkness of the train he saw a shadow crouched low to the ground. Strange, he didn't hear the shot. Of course the train's passage was rather deafening, and the blood pounding in his ears only added to the cacophony masking the sound. But he always thought a bullet striking one's torso would make more of an impression on the auditory senses. He would think about the situation more another time. Right now, he suddenly just wanted to sit down . . .

He reached for the rough stone of a wall, the first of many that were to have been his sanctuary. His hand couldn't hold his weight but slipped like a dead fish away from the stone's surface. He felt the stone scrape away the buttons of his tunic, and as he slipped to his knees he had the strange, irritating thought that he would have to sew them back on.

He rested against the wall and thought about sewing buttons. His thoughts were becoming fuzzy, but he remembered beautiful blue eyes and auburn hair—a face that should have been familiar.

An auburn-haired nurse was sewing buttons for him. What a kind thing to do. The sound of a train faded and darkness around him continued to deepen. He wanted to find that pretty nurse . . . and thank her . . .

* * *

Some might consider the uncanny ability to sense danger a blessing. Jacques Bellamont, former guerilla fighter and Résistance leader, survivor of the terrible conflict between his beloved France and the German invaders, was blessed with that ability.

During the war this gift had been his ally, perhaps prolonging his life when without it he might have been destroyed. But now, with the war's horrors behind him and his future unfolding, it was seldom a welcome comrade.

He sensed danger now, at the moment that he began to climb the fifth flight of stairs, his hand grasping that of his young wife, Aimée. His wife's cousin preceded him, her auburn hair bouncing and her blue eyes sparkling with the joy that accompanies the end of a wonderful, eventful day. Just hours before, Natalie Allred had become engaged. Young and vibrant, Natalie's entire being seemed to glow with her delight—resulting not only from her engagement but also from her joy at finally reuniting with relatives she'd searched for since the moment she was assigned to Germany with the American Army Nurses' Corps.

As Natalie climbed the stairs she held to the railing and chatted over her shoulder with Aimée. The happiness that filled their voices at finally being united did nothing to still the unease that made Jacques's insides turn to stone. Something was wrong, and it was enough to slow his steps. He paused, feeling the old familiar call to arms that had protected him throughout the years.

He glanced upward past Natalie. He looked over his shoulder and saw nothing in the stairwell behind them. He wanted to discount the feeling, but he dared not. Once he'd done so and a friend had died because of it.

"What is it, Jacques?" His wife knew him well.

His gun was in the apartment. There was something reassuring about the cold steel of a reliable weapon in the palm of one's hand, and right now he would give anything to feel that old familiar comfort.

"Jacques? Are you all right?"

Again the maquis fighter glanced downward. The stairs behind faded into the dim half-light below. Anything could hide there—and his heightened senses told him something did.

Aimée whispered, "Jacques?"

"Stay here."

"What?"

"Both of you. Don't come with me. Get Madame Bouchard to let you in." He urged Aimée and Natalie toward a neighbor's front door. "Keep it quiet." He moved light as a puma back down the stairs.

He heard a sound. Soft, nonexistent to all but the most suspicious ears, it rose from the landing below and set his heart racing. He flattened himself against the wall and waited for any movement. He heard the footsteps now—slow, deliberate. He caught his first glimpse of the back of the intruder's head as his cautious footsteps brought him up the opposite-facing stairs. Soon he would reach the landing and turn, and Jacques's hiding place would be revealed. Jacques moved swiftly to the head of the stairs.

The intruder below turned, and Jacques launched himself through the space between them, contacting only a fraction of the sixteen steps before catching the man full in the chest. He felt pain between his ribs as he and the intruder crashed to the ground. Jacques saw a knife spin away from the man's hand and lodge itself precariously against the edge of the landing. His opponent groaned, struggled to rise, and recoiled as Jacques's knee buried itself in the soft flesh of his midsection. The man retaliated with a blow to Jacques's neck that knocked reason from his brain. Jacques faltered momentarily, just enough so that the man kicked free and lunged for the knife. Jacques lunged after him and flattened him to the concrete, the intruder's hand inches from the weapon. Jacques saw fresh blood on the blade.

He had no time to think of the obvious source of that blood. His hands seized the man's neck, years of guerilla fighting taking over all reason and dictating that he should quickly kill this man. It did not matter that the war was over. It was not over for Jacques.

His family was in danger. He could think of nothing else as his powerful hands tightened about the man's neck, squeezing life from him. He had to protect his family . . .

A memory tapped suddenly at the door separating fear and hatred from calm reason. In his fervor he almost didn't let it in. But somehow it slipped through, bringing with it a flood of emotion that numbed the edges of his hate. He remembered a German officer, a major assigned by the Nazis to crush the Résistance in southern France, befriending Jacques and saving Jacques's Jewish wife from deportation. His hands loosened from around the man's neck. Instead, he struck a debilitating blow to the base of his skull and the man went limp, unconscious against the cold concrete of the landing.

Jacques rose to his feet. He glanced down and noticed moisture seeping through a rip in his coat. He removed the coat, bunched it tightly, and held it against the wound in his side.

He glanced down the stairs, then up, and began to climb. He marveled that a body so strong only moments ago would feel so awkward now. He reached the last flight of sixteen steps and hesitated. His senses screamed at him that the fight was not yet over. Three steps and his scalp would be observable through the sights of a rifle held by anyone watching through the keyhole. Three steps that could be his last. His war-perfected senses shifted into high gear as he contemplated what to do. He glanced at the window to his left, his breathing becoming difficult.

He threw his coat aside and lifted the windowsill. He did not look at the ground six stories below. Rather, he leaned out and looked upward, forcing his eyes to focus as he attempted to discover a way to climb. Rain began to fall, soft and menacing, against his exposed skin.

He reached for the steel drain pipe and swung out over the street. The pain in his side sent spasms of agony through his arm, and his hold almost gave way. He clenched his teeth and focused on finding a toehold. He kicked off his shoes and managed to insert his stockinged toes into the spaces between the wall and the pipe. He didn't want the pipe tearing free of the stone, so he flattened himself against the wall and began to climb. His breathing became labored, and he focused his eyes on his goal and his mind on his wife and finally pulled himself onto the windowsill of the apartment one floor above his own. The tenant was a single, middle-aged Spaniard who kept to himself and drove a taxi. He was not home.

The window was open a crack and Jacques managed to get the fingers of his weak hand under the edge and pull it up. He slid into the room and fell in a soggy heap. He rested, his chest heaving against the agony in his side.

Finally he rose to his feet and tiptoed from the apartment. He hesitated on the landing while his eyes fought to focus. He closed his eyes for a moment, took a deep breath, and descended the stairs.

They would not be watching the stairs leading to the upstairs apartment. If they had a rifle trained through the keyhole on the landing, they would only be able to see the stairs coming up toward the door. He gambled they would watch for him from below. He crept closer, turned the corner, and faced the death that was guaranteed to follow if he were wrong.

No shots fired. He descended carefully, keeping to the wall and avoiding certain stairs he knew would betray him. He reached the landing and launched himself bodily into the door, knocking it entirely off its frame and slamming it and the hidden attacker behind it to the floor. A rifle discharged next to his ear, exploding through his consciousness and reverberating through every bone in his body. He recoiled in shock, but the job was done. The man did not bother to rise. He lay silent and still underneath the door. Jacques steadied himself against the doorframe, his breath ragged now as he struggled to remain conscious. He staggered beyond the still form and found a piece of rope. He dragged the man into the bedroom and bound his wrists to the heavy oak bed frame. He took another length of rope and stumbled down the stairs, conscious that his movements were anything but stealthy. He felt the burning under his ribs and fought for breath.

He did not see the first intruder where he had left him, on the landing below Madame Bouchard's door. He struggled back up the stairs to her apartment and saw Madame Bouchard's door standing open. He stared into the room where two women stood in the center of the parlor, clinging to each other. The first was his wife, and her eyes, wide and stunned, met his.

The second woman, her hair a disheveled mass of wiry white, began to scold and shriek, her eyes staring from her skull with a confused mixture of fear and frustration. She babbled incoherently and jabbed an accusatory finger first at her maquis neighbor and then at her parlor.

The room was in shambles. Destroyed furniture littered the small expanse, and a vase of lilacs had been shattered on the tile. Dark spots on the carpet made Jacques forget for a moment his own agony.

"Aimée . . ." Jacques swallowed, and tasted blood. "Where's Natalie?"

TWO

Natalie Allred paused at the door of the plane, her feet hesitating at the top of the steps and the roar of the twin engines of the Lisunov LI-2 deafening her from a distance of just a few feet. She felt a breeze move her hair and invade her lungs. From where she stood she could see over green tile roofs to the horizon.

She looked down and recognized the man standing at the foot of the moveable staircase. The recognition was accompanied by cold fear, but she forced herself to remain calm. She had known this moment would arrive.

Lieutenant Viktor Nikolayevich Rostov hid his emotions admirably; he deserved to be angry, she mused as she descended the stairs, because she and Hans Brenner had managed to slip through his fingers—until now, that is. He offered his hand, and obediently she took it. Her small hand lay numbly enveloped in his large one as he helped her down the remaining steps, and then she did not resist as he led her away from the plane.

"You look tired, Natalya."

She didn't answer.

He noticed her bandaged arm and the dried bloodstains on her clothes. His eyes flashed. "Are you hurt?"

She hesitated. She'd been thrown against a mirror and struck with a porcelain vase.

"If my men hurt you . . ." The threat was unmistakable.

"I'm fine."

"Have you had anything to eat today?"

She shook her head.

"I'll take care of you."

A tiny shiver whispered up her spine.

"You know why you're here, don't you?"

A Soviet's decree. U.S. and British approval. Lieutenant Rostov's claim that she was born a Soviet citizen. Natalie said nothing.

"In February of last year, at Yalta in Ukraine, this was determined." His hand still held hers. "I have proof you were born in Petrograd. You are a Soviet citizen, Natalya. Comrade Stalin wants you home, and your American president has given his consent. All who are Soviet citizens are to be returned to their country of birth."

"Viktor . . ." She took a deep, wavering breath. "Where is Hans?"

She saw a strange flicker in his eyes at the mention of her intended. He stopped walking, and she could see that he was struggling with something. "Hans Brenner is dead."

She felt the world slide sideways, and all she held dear suddenly seemed to hang precariously off the edge of a cliff.

"I didn't want to hurt you . . ."

Her sorrow exploded in waves of panic. "Don't lie to me, Viktor! I know you're lying."

"Natalya . . ." His voice held genuine regret.

"I know you wouldn't kill him. You *need* him—"

Rostov shook his head. "I was there." His words were gentle. "He ran, and my officer shot him—through the wheels of a moving train. An impossible shot. Hans Brenner fell within reach of freedom."

"No, Viktor, please no." It came as a sob from the deep recesses of her soul. "I don't believe you. I—I won't believe you!" She refused to consider the possibility that this man was telling her the truth. Because if he were, then her one remaining hope had just been destroyed—that Hans Brenner would somehow find her . . . and rescue her . . .

She did not ask where they were. She didn't care where they were going. They drove through small towns, past ancient cemeteries marked with crumbling stone markers, pink and white houses sagging into the earth, narrow streets, and an abandoned church, or a monastery, crumbling and stark against a setting sun. It was a stunningly beautiful vista and she hated it.

Rostov delivered her to a small cottage, into the care of a nameless couple and their teenage son. He didn't introduce them to her; only told her that she should not try to escape. He gave her anonymous jailors instructions, his unintelligible words sharp and almost menacing. And then he turned to her and said that he would be back for her. Soon.

Natalie stood at the door and watched him drive away. Her hand closed about the base of her throat, as much to restrain her flailing pulse as to hide it. She thought about the events that had brought her here, including the unfortunate agreement between Allied powers eager to mend wounds caused by the war. The same law that returned many to their Soviet roots forced her into a world of fear and uncertainty. Her unknown father had been Russian. It did not matter that she had been raised an American; she had been born on Soviet soil and was therefore caught in the Soviet net.

She could not get Hans Brenner out of her mind—the way he had saved her life on a deserted, war-destroyed Berlin night, his gentle kindness with her and the way she had missed him when he was gone. She remembered one night, seemingly ages ago, when he risked his life to search for her aunt. And then he had secretly, silently learned more about the religion that meant so much to her, and had changed his life.

The rough-cut, gentle German had finally gathered the courage to ask for her hand—and on that very same evening Viktor Rostov had stolen her away. The revulsion that consumed her at the thought of Viktor Rostov was more than she could bear.

THREE

Hans Brenner felt the explosion in his chest, ripping apart his lungs, his ribs and internal organs. The agony that consumed every cubic millimeter of his being was the most excruciating pain he had ever encountered—at least until the next moment he tried to draw breath. He moaned.

"You've been shot, Mr. Brenner. Twice, I think. Once in the shoulder and again in the gut. You've been operated on at least twice already. It's your own fault. If you hadn't tried to run . . ."

Hans knew that voice. He summoned all his courage and, without even opening his eyes, launched himself at its owner. His fingers curled, ready to choke away the man's life. He imagined Viktor Rostov struggling beneath his grip.

There was a moment of silence, and then Rostov cleared his throat. "You're a strong man, Mr. Brenner, but not as strong as those restraints. You'll have to forego killing me."

Hans collapsed back onto the pillow. He opened his eyes and glowered at the man who had once been his professor. His mind was beginning to clear, and it flew over the events he last remembered: the car ride, Agent Reynolds trying to impress Rostov in order to help the Americans infiltrate the Soviet Union, the train, gunshots . . .

Rostov sat in a chair next to Hans's cot, arms folded in front of him and his expression serious. "You almost died—back in Paris," Rostov accused. "Obviously you underestimated the incredible talent of my new young intelligence officer. Lucky for both you and me, he was an exceptional shot." Rostov hesitated. "Any worse and he might have killed you and therefore sentenced my daughter to death. For her sake I need to deliver you—alive."

"Where is Natalie Allred?"

"The American nurse?" Rostov blinked. "How should I know?"

"Where is she, Rostov?"

"You always think the worst of me." The Soviet officer sighed. "Why would you ask *me? It's you* I was after—not Natalya. I assume she is on her way back to the United States."

"Or she's here with you and I'm gonna kill you as soon as they remove these restraints."

Lieutenant Rostov stood. "I came as a courtesy to see how you're doing. I can see you're on the mend. I brought you this far. My men can accompany you the remainder of the way." He indicated two guards outside the door. "Now if you'll excuse me—"

"You'd better not be lying to me."

Rostov turned to go.

"Where am I, Rostov?"

"At a crossroads in your life," Rostov replied. "You're in Sverdlovsk in the Soviet Union. You're near your destination and you'll head to Novosibirsk as soon as you're well enough to travel by rail. I've completed my assignment, and I can't imagine I'll be seeing you again. *Dasvidanya,* Hans Brenner." Rostov tipped his uniform cap at Hans. "Good-bye. And thanks for my daughter's freedom." Lieutenant Rostov walked away. He did not look back.

* * *

Viktor Rostov called Moscow from the hospital. He began to worry when he was ordered to wait. He silently fretted while the operator transferred his call.

"Lieutenant Rostov?"

It was not the voice he was expecting. Surprised, he cleared his throat. "Comrade Krajnik."

If Krajnik was happy to hear from him, it was not evident in his voice. "We're awaiting your return to Moscow. Now that your war assignment in Berlin is over you will resume your teaching position at the university. You will retain your military rank under the new MGB—"

"What happened to Director Sushin?"

Krajnik ignored his question. "Has the scientist been delivered?"

"As far as Sverdlovsk." Why was he required to talk to a subordinate? "He will make the rest of the journey when—"

"Is the American woman with you?"

"Natalya Ivanovna is with me. Where is the director?"

"Do you have your gun with you?"

"Of course . . ." Rostov felt a flicker of dread.

"Use it."

For a moment, Rostov didn't respond. He removed his visor cap and laid it carefully next to the telephone base. He ran his hand through his hair. "I have permission to bring her home with me—permission from Director Sushin himself. Let me speak to him, please."

"Comrade Sushin is no longer in charge of the Moscow branch of the MGB. *I* am. The American woman is a liability to you and a danger to the Motherland. She—"

"Natalya Ivanovna is as Soviet as I," Rostov snapped. "Her American background is unfortunate, yes, but I plan to take the responsibility for her adjustment myself. With the proper environment, mentorship, and education—"

"Her 'adjustment'?" The voice grated. "Do you think, Comrade, that when you return to Moscow you'll have nothing better to do than 'adjust' the selfish mindset of a Westerner? Stalin needs you elsewhere— not tutoring a simpering, pampered American nurse. Besides, I understand she escaped your loving care once already."

"She will not escape again," Rostov nearly growled. "That time she had assistance from American intelligence."

There was a derisive snort from the other end of the line. "Zhukov believes the Americans had assistance from the inside—from among your own agents, Comrade."

Rostov's hands didn't usually sweat like this.

"Major James Matthews used to be your associate," the voice reproached. "How can we be sure you're not secretly collaborating?"

That was too much. Lieutenant Rostov rose to his feet, dragging the receiver with him. His voice would have chilled lava. "I am a loyal patriot, Comrade. My past association with the American major is not an issue. I'm a dedicated Party member and a loyal Soviet. I will not have you questioning my allegiance. Do I make myself clear?"

"As a crystal bell," the voice soothed. "And now, let me make myself clear: I have not changed my mind about the girl. She's as treacherous as a Christian and as dangerous as a German. We—"

"She is not a danger!" Rostov could barely control the fury in his voice, let alone the sudden panic that he might be required to put a gun to Natalya's head. Neither his anger nor his fear at losing the American nurse was helping his weak heart, he knew. Suspicion of foreigners permeated everything in Soviet society and policy. The understanding that had shaped wartime strategy with the Americans—it could never be referred to as friendship—had eroded to no more than gross mistrust of each other. He took a deep breath and forced himself to speak calmly. "I've been ordered to arrest her and bring her back to Moscow."

"You've been ordered to *arrest* her," the voice shot back. "There your orders are specific. The 'Moscow' part I believe comes from your growing fondness for the auburn-haired copy of your dead wife. This *Amerikanka* has bewitched you; you are incapable of lucid thought when you're with her." Suddenly Krajnik laughed. "No, you're right, Comrade Rostov; you should not shoot her. You couldn't do it! I will take care of the details myself. In the meantime, feel free to bring her to Moscow. We'll talk in person when you and your American sorceress arrive."

Rostov hung up the phone, disturbed at Krajnik's elevation to MGB director and worried at the sudden danger to Natalya. And it was true; he was fond of Natalya Ivanovna. She would never replace his Alyona, but she was more than he'd ever hoped for. It bothered him that he'd become so attached to her that her very presence endangered his reputation at the Kremlin, his status as a professor at the university, and most importantly, his daughter's life.

Fear for the safety of his seventeen-year-old daughter, Lucya, enveloped him. She'd been condemned and imprisoned in order to keep

Rostov in line. He still carried with him a photograph that spawned constant nightmares: one depicting his gentle daughter, in prison rags, forcibly boarding a train bound for a Siberian work camp.

He had completed his mission. Surely now they would return her to him . . .

But he could not bring himself to harm Natalya. She was not the political criminal the authorities claimed her to be. She would not be executed—he would find a way to protect her. He would convince the authorities of her usefulness—despite her unfortunate upbringing—and they would agree to spare her life.

And someday, perhaps she would forgive him for what he was doing to her.

* * *

"Lucya Viktorovna Rostova!"

Through the grimy courtyard tired heads lifted, eyes searched for the owner of that name. One figure stood, slowly, hesitantly, with a bundle clutched in dirt-stained hands and her face burned by the sun. A dirty handkerchief was wrapped tightly about her long blond hair. She moved forward, dozens of eyes following her careful progress through the bodies huddled together in the dirt. No one bothered to move out of her way, and yet the voice that had first announced her name berated her for taking so long. "What do you think you are, citizen? Model Soviet in the Great October Revolution Parade?"

She pushed herself to move faster, moving as quickly as the crowded courtyard would allow. She stumbled once as she tried not to step on another woman's legs. She sensed the woman's irritation and disdain, and she couldn't help but hear the whisperings of several of her fellow prisoners as she passed. She straightened her slender frame, lifted her chin, and tried not to let their words hurt her.

"Thinks she's the queen of America the way she walks."

"Look at her clothes; must be from some influential Moscow family."

"Someone takes care of her, that's for sure."

Yes, Lucya thought. *My papa cares for me. And soon, Papa will come and get me.*

"Wait till we get where we're going. No one's gonna care a bucket of slop where she came from when we get where we're going."

Her papa had told her in his letter that his assignment in Germany was finally completed. He'd promised that soon they would be back together . . . Maybe she would not be transferred with these women to another work camp after all.

"Look at that figure of hers. Look at those eyes! Wait till she has to work in the same camp as the men . . ."

Lucya felt her hands trembling, and she clutched her bundle closer against her body. Maybe Papa was here now! Maybe that was why she had been summoned . . .

"Look at the way she holds that bundle," someone sneered. "Filled with amber rocks to buy her release, you think? Can't wait to get my fingers in it when she returns."

Lucya forced herself not to listen. She followed the guard who had called her name, and he led her toward the foreman's hut. She couldn't contain the fear that accompanied her anticipation that today might be the day her papa saved her.

"Step inside, citizen." The guard held the door for her and then closed her inside the hut. She glanced about the room, desperate to see Viktor Rostov, tall and powerful, waiting to leap forward and take her in his arms.

He was not there. The foreman sat behind his desk, chewing on a foul-smelling cigar and dissecting her with his eyes. She lowered her gaze to her hands, which held tight her bundle.

"How old are you, citizen?"

She hesitated. "Seventeen."

He played with his cigar and contemplated both that information and her slender figure.

"What's your name, citizen?"

"Comrade Lucya Viktorovna Rostova."

"Remember, you are no longer my comrade." His voice was thick and wet, as if swimming in phlegm. "Your crimes against the People have lost you that privilege. You are now called 'citizen.'"

"Yes, sir."

"You received something from your father."

She looked up, just in time to lunge for something tossed in her general direction. She dropped her belongings but managed to catch the object. She clutched at the paper wrapping and it crushed in her hands, as if wrapped about something soft. Papa had already sent her dresses and warm winter wear. Would this be more of the same?

"Open it."

She fumbled at the twine and pulled off the paper. She held in her hands a red shawl, hand-painted with intricate flowers and leaves, cheerful in its simplicity. Her fingers played with the fringe as she read her father's note.

> *My beautiful Lucya. This was your mother's shawl. Wear*
> *it to keep warm and to remember how much I adore you.*
> *Until soon, your papa.*

Soon. The word warmed her soul and she didn't even mind that the officer insisted she hand over her papa's note. She was grateful he didn't also demand the shawl.

"Tomorrow you will be transferred, citizen."

Her heart skipped a beat. "But my papa's letter says soon he will—"

"That's for someone else to decide."

"But Papa is an important officer." She panicked. If she were transferred now, how would Papa know where to look for her? "He is Lieutenant Viktor Nikolayevich Rostov. He is negotiating my release . . ."

"That is all, citizen. Return to the courtyard." She was dismissed with one hand.

"But, sir . . ."

The foreman made a point of displaying his irritation. "Do you want me to return that shawl to where it came from? Shall I say it was undeliverable?"

"No, sir." She backed away, fumbling for the door handle. Then she turned and fled. Not until she had covered half the distance to the waiting prisoners did she remember that her bundle lay forgotten on the foreman's office floor.

FOUR

Natalie Allred lay with her head against the seat, staring out the window of the train compartment, her gaze far away as the window's scenery passed her by. Even though she tried not to think of it, she was acutely aware of the Soviet officer in the same compartment with her. Natalie was far from peaceful; the panic that had clutched at her throat since the moment Rostov joined her still affected her breathing, making her lightheaded.

Rostov stretched out his legs until his boots disappeared under the empty seat in front of him. He rubbed the stubble he was letting grow and then folded his arms across his torso. He closed his eyes, but they did not stay closed for very long. Soon he withdrew his feet and stood, one arm steadying himself against the train's motion while the other wiped at his brow.

Natalie watched him, rubbing her hands together nervously as he towered over her. She wanted to hate this man for what he was doing to her. It would be easy—even though Viktor had lost his beloved wife, his son had been murdered by the Germans at Stalingrad, and his daughter was now in terrible danger. Perhaps she should pity Viktor, but her fear kept her from feeling that emotion as her heart told her she should.

Yet she still didn't quite feel hatred for the man, either. He had threatened and blackmailed her, stalked and kidnapped her—all to force Hans Brenner to work for him. And now that she was finally in the Soviet Union as he had threatened, she had no idea what the future held for her, and the thought made her very afraid. The fear, it seemed, edged out the hatred.

The train unexpectedly lurched and then continued its rhythmic swaying. Rostov steadied himself and ended up grinding her foot with his boot.

"I'm sorry. Please forgive me." He turned his attention to the window. He frowned, cursed softly, pushed away from the window, and returned to his seat. She wondered what it was that worried him.

It didn't take long for Viktor to again spring to his feet. This time he left the compartment, and she could see him through the interior window, staring down the corridor as if waiting for someone. He continued to pace back and forth in the narrow corridor as the train swung rhythmically toward a destination that seemed to be troubling him tremendously.

Outside the window the scenery began to change, and as they approached Moscow, Viktor's unnerving behavior intensified; he returned to the compartment, sat and then stood, wrung his hands, stared into space, sank onto the bench at Natalie's side, stood, and left to pace the corridors again. If it were any other person Natalie might have put a hand on his arm, said something to soothe him, or tried to discover what it was that was causing his agitation. But the fact was, Natalie had never been so frightened in all her life. She'd never been in a situation such as this—a prisoner, hungry, exhausted, and trapped thousands of miles from home in a nightmare she couldn't escape.

But she was curious, and his anxiety heightened hers. What awaited them in Moscow that troubled him so? She took a deep breath to steady her nerves. It would be better to know the dark truth than to wonder about it.

"Viktor?"

He turned to look at her, and she was startled to see that he looked as afraid as she felt.

"Viktor, please tell me—"

He knelt in front of her and took both her hands in his, and the movement caught her entirely off guard. He wanted to tell her. She could see it in his eyes, as if he were pleading with her to understand without him speaking. And as the train began to slow he wouldn't let go of her hands. He was making her even more afraid, as if the thing that plagued him was so terrible, so devastating, that he couldn't bring himself to say it. He turned to look out the window as the train reached the station, sliding between platforms that muffled the sound of the wheels on the track. Anonymous faces flowed by—a smattering of old people, wounded veterans, and uniformed soldiers, but mostly women and children. The train crawled to a stop, gasped, shuddered, and lay still. Viktor's grip tightened on her hands, and then, through the window, she saw what he saw.

In the middle of the platform waited a grouping of soldiers, belted uniform hats over military haircuts, crisp tailored tunics worn long and belted at the waist over the tops of soft breeches and knee boots. They watched the train carefully. With them stood another individual, dressed in black overcoat, black tunic, and dark pants, with dark hair slicked back from his forehead. He and his men studied each disembarking passenger, each window, and every exit as the train expelled its passengers.

"Viktor . . . ?" The fear had found its way into her voice and she could not erase it. "Who are they?"

He turned then to look at her, and his eyes held a strange mixture of dread and compassion. "Those men are from the MGB—Ministry for State Security. They . . . work for the intelligence branch of the government."

"The intelligence branch . . ." Natalie murmured. "*You* work for the intelligence branch."

"This is not my doing."

"Viktor, why are they here?"

"They're here for *you,* Natalya Ivanovna. Please understand—I didn't want this."

"For me?" Suddenly it all became terribly clear: Viktor's anxiety, his distraction, and his tenderness toward her. He hadn't wanted this to happen. This hadn't been a part of his plan for her. Had someone warned him? She felt weak. "What are you going to do?"

Viktor rose to his feet. "You must stay by my side. Don't leave my side—do you understand?" He reached for his overcoat and briefcase and then took her hand. She had to will her legs to follow, and by the time she'd descended the stairs, stepped from the train to the platform, and faced the official entourage, Rostov had to support her.

The somber group faced them. The man in the dark overcoat approached and spoke to Rostov. She understood when he pronounced her Russian name, but the unfamiliar words terrified her. "Natalya Ivanovna Karagodina . . ." He spoke at length, and she could understand nothing but her name. He was near Viktor's height but as slender as a weasel and perhaps closer to Natalie's age. His dark eyes bored into Natalie's with a snake-like fascination that made her skin crawl. A woman might have looked twice as he passed by, but on the second look she would have shuddered, perceiving a cold disdain that darkened otherwise pleasant features. He accentuated his gloomy presence with his choice of ominously dark apparel, and the way he looked at Natalie made her want to crawl into a hole and never come out.

He reached for her arm. Natalie clutched at Viktor's sleeve and Viktor blocked the officer's hand with his briefcase. Viktor reasoned with the man in Russian—a long, angry tirade that did little to quell the officer's determination. Rostov turned quickly to Natalie. "Don't let go of my arm. *No matter what.*"

Speechless with fear, she nodded.

The officer spoke again, this time pointing to himself as he spoke to her. "Ivan Stepanovich Volkov." He then produced a folded paper and held it in front of her face. He continued to speak at her, and even though she had no idea what he was saying or what he was holding, his words contained a barely concealed menace.

Viktor reached for the paper. Volkov smirked at him and held it out of Rostov's reach. He spoke then directly to Rostov, disdain in his voice.

Waiting passengers sidled away to a fearful distance, and soon Viktor and Natalie, Ivan Volkov, and his policemen stood alone, as if in an arena, ready to do battle.

Suddenly Volkov lunged for Natalie, capturing her in a death grip that made her cry out in pain. Every policeman sprang into action, attacking Rostov and peeling her away from him. They forcibly detained him while Volkov dragged Natalie away. She buckled her knees, grabbed at Volkov's forearm and rolled sideways, twisting his forearm until he yelled. He lost his grip and she fell to her knees on the concrete. His face ugly with anger, he kicked at her and recaptured her arm. She pried at his fingers and refused to rise to her feet, and he tightened his grip, turned, and pulled her away.

As he was dragging her across the platform, Viktor Rostov called out, and his words seemed to reverberate across the space between them. Ivan Volkov stopped in his tracks. He turned and stared at Viktor. After a moment of stunned silence, he asked a question. Rostov answered, his voice calm and controlled, and Volkov dropped Natalie's arm.

Natalie scrambled to her feet and ran to Viktor. He threw an arm around her but kept his eyes on Volkov. Volkov seemed to be contemplating Rostov's words, and then he walked back across the platform, burning hatred in his eyes, to confront Viktor.

Volkov launched a tirade of Russian at Viktor, then turned to stare at Natalie, and the look in his eyes was meant to wither. He shook his head, as if incredulous.

What was happening? Whatever Rostov was discussing with this official was significant enough to confound Ivan Volkov. Natalie's heart flailed against her ribs as if it would burst from her chest, and she looked up at Viktor. She did not see the fear there that she'd seen while on the train; Viktor was now in complete control of his emotions.

Ivan Volkov snapped his fingers, and one of his policemen jumped to his side. He turned and delivered a lengthy list of instructions to the young man, who nodded at intervals. Then the policeman turned and quickly left, taking one of his comrades with him.

Volkov grimaced at Natalie and then strode away. Viktor followed, holding Natalie's hand firmly in his own. They walked off the platform, through a door, up a narrow, smelly flight of stairs, and into an empty office. Volkov said a few more words to Rostov, glared again at Natalie, and abandoned them there.

Viktor released her hand, and Natalie felt a curious sense of relief, as if his releasing her indicated that the situation had improved somewhat.

"What's happening?" Natalie whispered.

"Comrade Volkov has decided to listen to reason." He spoke without enthusiasm. "He'll be back in a few minutes and we'll be on our way."

A few minutes turned into more than an hour. Natalie's feelings crept back toward precrisis levels, with her distrust of Rostov again creating distance between them. She sat by a window that was grimy with ages of dirt and silently studied the train platform below. Viktor resumed the pacing he'd perfected on the train. Natalie fought back tears as she thought about Hans, and she wished that Rostov's declaration that Hans was dead might not be true. She clung to that faint hope as if to a sinking raft, and even allowed her imagination to take fanciful turns for the better: Hans would show up and save her from a life in Moscow; Hans would still marry her in the temple . . .

She was thrown back into the depressing present by the sound of Ivan Volkov reentering the room. This time he didn't even look at Natalie. He produced two documents, which he tossed onto a table. Rostov walked to the table, eased himself into a chair, and pulled one of the papers toward him. He read the few lines written there, hesitated, and then picked up a pen and began to write along the bottom half of the page. He wrote for several minutes; his pen flew across the page, but Natalie noticed that his hand shook. She looked up once and saw Volkov watching her again.

Rostov silently reread what he'd written, thought for a moment, added a few more lines, and then shoved the paper away. He reached for the second document and aligned it in front of him. He read the words written there, and then he turned to look at Natalie. For several moments he studied her, and his eyes held a frightening mixture of esteem and sorrow. Then he returned his attention to the document, lifted the pen, and signed at the bottom.

Rostov stood, and Ivan Volkov sprang into motion. He retrieved both documents and studied them carefully. He paid particular attention to the one filled with Rostov's neat handwriting, and then he placed them back on the table and motioned for Natalie to sit in the chair Rostov had vacated.

Reluctantly she complied. Volkov handed her the pen and indicated for her to sign.

Natalie stared at the unfamiliar Cyrillic. What was she being forced to sign? She turned to Viktor, hoping for some sort of explanation.

"Sign here, Natalya, below the paragraph I've written. Sign this second document right below my signature." That was all the explanation he would give her. He would not look her in the eye.

"What am I signing?"

"Important documents relating to your repatriation." His words were evasive.

"What do they say, Viktor?"

Rostov became impatient, his words suddenly edged with danger. "Sign them, Natalya, before it's too late."

"Viktor, I—"

"Sign them now. Your future depends upon it."

"Viktor!" She felt dizzy with alarm. "I have a right to know what they—"

"Sign them!" Viktor thundered, and Natalie began to cry. From the other side of the desk Volkov began to chuckle, as if the sight of a foreign woman being frightened out of her mind was in some way amusing.

Natalie couldn't get her hands to stop trembling long enough to sign the documents, and she pleaded with Rostov. "Please, Viktor . . ."

He leaned close, his arms resting on the desk on either side of her and his mouth inches from her ear. His voice was deceivingly gentle. "Let me explain it to you, Natalya Ivanovna: You will sign the documents in front of you *right now,* or you will be executed by Comrade Volkov this afternoon. Do you understand? Good. Now you will sign your *Russian* name—Ka-ra-go-din-a, Na-tal-ya I-va-nov-na. Just like that. If you sign 'Natalie Allred,' you will be executed this afternoon, as I explained to you."

She was crying so hard she could hardly see the documents in front of her, but she put trembling pen to paper and she signed. She wrote the unfamiliar name twice in handwriting marred by fits of violent trembling, and then she dropped the pen and buried her face in her hands. Rostov picked up the documents, placed one on top of the other, and handed them to Volkov. Volkov took them without a word, turned, and left the room.

Rostov said gently, "We can go now. Everything will be fine."

Natalie's shoulders heaved, and her throat constricted so violently that she struggled for air. She clutched at the base of her throat, bent over the table, and gasped air that seemed poison to her. She couldn't go home. She would never see Hans again. She was stranded here, in this awful country with this diabolical man, facing a future so frightening that it consumed her. "I—can't—breathe."

Viktor Rostov's arms went around her. His touch made her skin prickle and she didn't have the energy to pull away. How could a villain console his victim? Hate penetrated her soul, translating physically into nausea so awful that she began to dry heave. There was nothing in her system to expel, and so her empty stomach continued to lurch, over and over, as Rostov held her close.

"Viktor . . ." She could barely whisper. "Let—me—go—home."

"You are home, Natalya Ivanovna. You *are* home."

FIVE

That evening Rostov stood with her on the step of her hotel, across the river from a place Natalie had never thought she would see with her own eyes.

"Saint Basil's Cathedral." Rostov indicated the multi-colored onion shapes reaching for the sky. "Past the cathedral is Red Square. And there—the Kremlin, where I will work whenever I am not teaching at Moscow University."

The imposing architecture seemed to threaten the surrounding city. Towering stone bespoke influence and power, and the sheer size of the square that separated the buildings from each other made her feel smaller than she already felt.

Rostov leaned past her and pointed further to the east. "My apartment is over there, near the merchant quarter and shopping district. And over there, to the west, you can see the tomb erected to Comrade Lenin. Over there used to stand a cathedral and a chapel and the Resurrection Gates. They were recently demolished to make more room for the military parades." Viktor glanced at Natalie. "You're the religious sort—or at least you were. They would've intrigued you." He continued his visual explanation. "And that's a statue of two heroes who helped defend Moscow against Polish invaders in the early seventeenth century—"

"*Stop,* Viktor!" Natalie cried. "Do you think I care? You've forced me to come here against my will and you think I want a *history lesson?*" She burst into tears.

Viktor stood watching her outburst. Finally he said, "Natalya . . ."

"*No,* Viktor. I don't want a guided tour of Red Square. I don't want a tour of Moscow, or your university, or the marketplace. I just . . ." She gasped. "I just want to go home."

His demeanor changed. His face darkened and he scowled down at her. He spoke to her as he might reprimand one of his soldiers. "Natalya Ivanovna, you are a Soviet citizen. The sooner you accept that fact, the sooner you will heal. You will learn the things a Soviet citizen is required to learn. You will become a Party member and you will learn the language of your ancestors. And you will not speak to me again of going home."

* * *

Over the next few days he applied in her behalf to a residential cooperative, found a small room in a crowded community apartment for her, and left her at the door. She withered into a corner, wrapped her arms around her feet, and leaned into the crumbling, moldy wall. She was numbly aware of the goings-on of the apartment's residents, and her lack of Russian language skills and her miserable spirit kept her from doing more than observe. What else was there to do as an unwelcome stranger in a foreign prison?

Even without means to communicate, Natalie could tell that she was the topic of conversation. Apartment residents hovered near her open door, staring unabashed at the mysterious American woman who'd been thrust into their existence. The communal kitchen stove crouched directly in Natalie's line of sight, and every mealtime, five women fought for possession of a few square centimeters of its hot surface. They boiled water and stirred soup pots, sliced heavy black bread and poured tea. And they talked about her, glancing at her often throughout conversations laced with "Amerikanka."

Daylight faded and other residents retired to their rooms. She should climb to her feet, take three steps across the room and close the door. At least then she could imagine her misery was hers and hers alone. But she couldn't muster the will to do even that.

Past the kitchen lay the communal bath, and the stench from a seldom-clean toilet mixed with lingering culinary odors and tied her stomach in knots. By morning her midsection growled, then throbbed, and then began to feel as though it was consuming her internal organs. Through her debilitating agony she thought for the thousandth time of the food Rostov had left with her. How she hated accepting anything from him! But she finally crawled across the room and opened the box of supplies.

The box was empty. Food, money, blankets . . . Someone had helped himself while Natalie had slept.

She couldn't shake the darkness and fear that had engulfed her even to care for her own body. The second night she could not sleep. Would they take her shoes next? She curled into a fetal position, shivering on the dirty mattress while listening to the scurry of rats and the snores of residents. Through the paper-thin wall at her shoulder she heard a man and woman screaming at one another. Glass shattered against the wall.

Morning crept reluctantly over the dirty windowsill, and the women began jostling each other again at the stove. Again Natalie was observed with little more than guarded hostility, and not one of the tenants went out of her way to assist the American girl. The smell of bread taunted her. In her stubbornness and anger at Rostov, she hadn't eaten much since the night Hans Brenner kissed her good-bye. How long ago had that been? Her insides throbbed, her head pounded, and her soul hurt. Never had she imagined anyone could feel so sad.

She felt pressure on her arm, and she looked up and saw a piece of black bread held close to her face. "Eat."

The woman couldn't have been more than five years her senior. She crouched next to Natalie and insisted, speaking with a curious British accent, "Eat, Natalya Ivanovna, or you'll be dead by tomorrow."

Natalie took the bread. She studied her visitor; comely and neat, the woman wore a simple gray blouse and plain skirt. Her dark hair was mostly captured under a clean white scarf, and her blue eyes smiled at Natalie.

"You speak English?" Natalie murmured. It was a dimwitted thing to say, Natalie realized too late. Hadn't the newcomer just proved that she could? "Why are you helping me?"

"Your benefactor was worried about you. He sent me to help you."

Natalie bit into the hard bread and tried to swallow. "What do you mean, my 'benefactor'?"

The woman shrugged. "Your protector. Your friend."

"Viktor is not my friend."

The woman shrugged, and a hint of a smile played across her lips. "And yet you speak his name as if he were your husband."

Natalie choked, black bread grating like dry sand in her throat. Her eyes filled with tears. "You need to understand something: Lieutenant Rostov brought me here against my will. He's not my friend. If anything, he's my greatest enemy. I speak his name the only way I know how."

The woman's face softened. "He said you've suffered a great heartache. He wants me to help you, until you can speak our language and take care of yourself."

Suspicious, Natalie asked, "Is he paying you?"

The woman shrugged and said nothing.

"I—I don't need your help," Natalie murmured. "I certainly don't need *his* help, and I don't want people thinking he's my 'protector.'"

"Be grateful for it," the woman insisted. "Everyone needs the protection of influential Party members, and only a privileged few have it."

"Where did you learn to speak—"

"English?" the woman finished for her. "My papa insisted. I had a tutor, and then I attended the Foreign Language Institute here in Moscow. An American accent is taboo there, by the way. Oxford only."

"How do you know Lieutenant Rostov?"

"I was his student at Moscow University—briefly, before the war. Comrade Stalin had more need of me as a nurse than an interpreter."

Natalie studied the woman crouched beside her, and for the first time in what seemed decades, she yearned for a friend in this terrible predicament. "Your name—forgive me, I haven't even asked your name . . ."

The woman smiled. "Regina Igorevna Oryekova. We will have plenty of time to become acquainted; I work at the Kremlin Hospital, where you will work. Your benefactor has been able to secure a good position for you, Natalya. You will see what luck it is to have Lieutenant Rostov as a friend; and this room he secured for you is further proof of his goodwill."

"*This* room?" Natalie looked around, incredulous. "Proof of Lieutenant Rostov's goodwill?"

"It's a good room, Natalya. You have a window." Regina pointed. "And the kitchen stove will keep you warm in the winter! In the kitchen there's a gas water heater, so you'll have hot water on most weekends for baths. And you have a place to lay your head without a little babushka—grandmother—sitting on it." Regina giggled. Natalie stared at her in disbelief.

"And when you speak Russian, you'll begin to feel camaraderie with these people"—Regina gestured about the apartment—"that will fill your heart and make you forget your sorrows."

Natalie sat, speechless, staring at the woman. She contemplated Regina's words. Regina Igorevna had an easygoing way about her that intrigued Natalie, and she truthfully seemed interested in Natalie's welfare, even if she *was* being paid to help her.

"I'm supposed to give you this." Regina handed her a package wrapped in brown paper and twine. "It's a dress—and sensible shoes and a few personal items you'll need. The lieutenant wants you to look presentable when you visit the hospital with me."

Visit the hospital? Natalie panicked. She wasn't ready to step out of her self-imposed isolation and into a strange world forced upon her.

Regina nodded. "Time to get to know the doctor you'll be working with." Regina glanced about the Spartan room. "You're in need of a few things. We'll visit the shopping district someday soon, get more clothes for you—and blankets. Possibly a piece of furniture or two. You didn't bring much, did you?"

Natalie sniffed. "I didn't have much time to pack."

"You'll need a guide, Natalya Ivanovna—until you learn to find your way around, to navigate the streetcars and find your way to the shopping district and the hospital."

"I'm fine, Regina."

Regina laughed. "Forgive me for being blunt, but you'd get lost in a forest with three pine trees. You need me." Natalie was certain she heard a wistful tinge to Regina's next words. "And you can use a friend, Natalya. I can help you with that, also." Regina straightened and smiled at Natalie. "Eventually you'll need sturdy winter boots—and a uniform for work. Tomorrow we'll stop by the hospital, so you can meet your supervisor. And if we have time we'll do a bit of shopping and find a restaurant and try to fatten up that skinny body of yours."

Natalie felt Regina's kindness like creeping warmth inching its way up her limbs toward her frozen heart. "I'm not really hungry."

"You mean you're past the hunger stage and well on your way to starvation. Natalya, you'll die if you don't eat."

Natalie mourned, "I hope so."

"You don't really mean that." Regina's brow furrowed.

Natalie leaned her face into her hands and didn't answer.

Regina's deep brown eyes studied her closely, and her head inclined so that a dark curl fell away from her cheek. "It's really not that bad," she murmured, and her hand touched Natalie's cold wrist. "Life here isn't that bad, I promise. I'll help you, Natalya Ivanovna, and who knows? Maybe you'll grow to love our hot summers, gray skies, and frozen winters."

Natalie couldn't help a giggle, followed by tears that fell unbidden down her cheeks.

Regina's eyes showed her sympathy. "Maybe when the river freezes in a few months I'll teach you to skate . . ." She hesitated, her hand automatically finding her own midsection. "Or maybe I'll wait till after the baby—" She cut off midsentence and glanced at Natalie.

Natalie asked softly, "When are you due?"

Regina hesitated. "November. My husband will be home by then, and he'll be happy that we are having a baby." Her words sounded almost defensive. Regina glanced out the window, as if looking at something far away. "If it's a boy I will name him Edik—after my husband. If it's a girl, then Ina after my mother."

"Where is your husband, Regina?"

"He's a political officer for the army. Right now he is stationed in Kirov." Regina smiled. "But he'll be home by November. Wait and see."

* * *

Viktor Rostov arrived at Lubyanka just as Roman Krajnik was about to leave his office.

"You transferred my daughter." Viktor tried to remain calm. "Where is she?"

Krajnik stepped into the corridor and closed the door. He produced a key and seemed to study it for a moment before answering. "She is safe, Comrade. She has been moved to where she can be of most use to the Motherland."

"Where is she?"

Krajnik frowned. "Patience, Comrade. These things take time."

"She was supposed to be released."

"Ah, yes." Krajnik inserted the key in the lock. "And her father has preserved the life of an enemy woman who has no allegiance to Comrade Stalin."

Viktor felt the telltale signs of his anger and took a deep breath to steady himself. "I will prove Natalya Ivanovna a good Soviet, Comrade. Her talents as a nurse will be appreciated by—"

"They will be," Krajnik interrupted, turning to face him. "And your German scientist in Vladivostok will produce results. Or they will *both* be executed. And news of your daughter's location—your daughter's *freedom*—will depend upon the outcome of your choices. You may be certain of that."

SIX

Friday, May 24, 1946

Regina called for Natalie the next morning, her face rosy with enthusiasm. Her high spirits fizzled when she saw Natalie still wearing her same travel-worn clothes.

"You must wear the green dress the lieutenant sent you," Regina insisted. "He asked me to make sure you wore it."

"I don't have it."

Regina stared at her. "You don't have it?"

Natalie did not respond.

Suddenly Regina headed for the nearest resident's room. Without waiting to knock she thrust open the door and walked inside. She searched through clothing while a woman berated her. Regina did not respond.

She repeated the process in the next room, and the next. She found the item of clothing and thrust it into Natalie's hands. "The lieutenant will be disappointed if you don't wear it. And you must make a good impression at the hospital."

"I don't want it." Natalie shook her head. "I don't want the lieutenant's help. I don't ever want to wear that dress."

Regina studied her for a long moment. "You really don't like it?"

"It's not my style," Natalie lied. "But it would look fantastic on you. That is . . ." Natalie gave Regina a faint smile. "Once the baby's born."

Regina snorted. "The lieutenant would skin me alive."

Natalie changed into the dress. When Regina saw it she cried, "Oh Natalya! *Krasivaya!* Look at it—isn't it so beautiful?"

Reluctantly Natalie agreed. Rostov's gift was lovely.

Regina clasped her hands in glee. "Wait till the lieutenant sees you in this!"

Natalie's satisfaction with the dress faded. "I prefer he never sees me again."

Regina shoved her out of her stuffy room, past the kitchen stove and out of the apartment, down the stairs and through a deserted playground. She ushered her three blocks to a busy intersection, hectic with bicycles and a few carriages, pedestrians, streetcars, and occasional automobiles. Moscow's morning commute grated on Natalie's shredded nerves.

They joined a crowd of pedestrians at the curb. "Oh my!" Regina raised her voice to be heard. "You remembered your identity papers, didn't you?"

"They're not mine." Natalie pulled them from her pocket and waved them at Regina. "They belong to someone named Karagodina Natalya Ivanovna."

"Very funny."

Natalie didn't return her smile.

Regina advised, "No one's allowed on the street without his documents." Suddenly she pulled Natalie forward, and Natalie could feel the urgency in Regina's grip. "Streetcar's coming."

Natalie resisted the hand on her elbow. "It's just a streetcar ride, Regina—not an emergency evacuation. Everybody's pushing like the world's gonna end if they don't get on first."

"You want to get on that streetcar or don't you?" Regina demanded. Natalie looked where Regina was pointing, and her jaw dropped. She could hardly believe that the object moving toward them was a streetcar. It wasn't like any streetcar she'd ever seen. It was like a giant slug, brightly painted and sprouting appendages at doors and windows. Passengers clung to narrow ledges around the sides and backs, bodies bouncing with each jolt of the streetcar. The monster swerved toward Natalie and slowed to a dramatic stop. Natalie took an involuntary step backward and Regina shoved her forward again. "Go, Natalya! Get on!"

"How?" Natalie shot back, overwhelmed by the impossible task presented her. Regina continued to press her forward until hands reached from above, grasped Natalie by the arms and hauled her onto the steps. Regina crowded in behind her and the streetcar heaved away from the curb.

She could find only enough space for one of her feet, and the other swung precariously out over the road. A young man threw his free arm around her and pulled her in close, laughing good-naturedly at her predicament. Natalie's face became planted in his shoulder and she smelled old sweat and cigar smoke. She could hardly breathe. But at least she wasn't flying through the air and landing in a broken, sodden mass on a busy Moscow street.

At the next stop people descended, more entered, and they resumed packing themselves in. Passengers fanned out along the narrow ledge encircling the rear of the streetcar, hanging by their fingertips as the car began to move. Natalie and Regina were pressed farther into the car.

Her young benefactor spoke to her, obviously wanting to be sociable. Natalie stared at him and didn't understand a single word. She searched for Regina and found her wedged several passengers away. Regina wasn't going to be any help.

The young man again tried to draw her into conversation, and Natalie didn't even know how to tell him that she couldn't understand. His brow knit; he studied her for a moment, and then asked over the roar of the engine, "Amerikanka?"

She nodded.

He contemplated that revelation for a moment. The unfriendliness shown by Natalie's roommates underscored the mistrust of foreigners that permeated Soviet life. But this young man seemed to be mentally weighing a fear of Westerners against the exotic adventure of being in close proximity to one. Adventure triumphed, and a boyish grin split his face from ear to ear. He said something to another young man, and the two chatted back and forth, interlacing their conversation with periodic grins in her direction. Natalie forced a weak smile.

Regina pushed in behind her and shouted into her ear, "We've got to move forward or we'll be riding this streetcar till midnight!"

"Amerikanka?" Natalie's young man asked her as well.

"Nyet," Regina snapped, and she gestured for the young man to let Natalie go. Reluctantly he did so, but he planted a wet kiss on Natalie's cheek before Regina was able to rescue her.

Regina pulled rubles from her pocket and waved them over her head. Hands grabbed the money and passed it to other hands, and eventually two tickets returned to Regina the same way. Natalie watched the trusting exchange in silent, confused amazement.

Regina raised her voice for Natalie to hear. "We're passing through the old Arbat section of Moscow—we'll come here someday to walk past the mansions and pretend we're politburo wives out for a stroll." She grinned.

Natalie watched out the window. "Why do all the women bind their hair up in scarves?"

"You think we have water to wash our hair every night?" Regina gave her a wry smile and then wagged her finger at Natalie. "But you neglect your appearance and the head nurse will dissect you alive. Wash your hair every week—even when there's no hot water, understand?" She grinned at Natalie and then pointed. "Over there somewhere is what the Americans call the Spaso House."

"The what?"

"Home of the American ambassador. Keep moving forward!"

"What?" Natalie was overwhelmed, confused, and ready to scream. So much had been thrown at her in the last ten minutes that she could hardly keep it all straight, let alone hope to remember the details that would make her self-sufficient in this bizarre place.

"Oh no! This is our stop!" Regina shoved against Natalie's shoulder blades, pushing her directly into the wide back of a man in front of them. She kept pushing until Natalie had rolled past the massive form. The smell of unwashed flesh, musty clothes, and heavy perfume stifled Natalie, making her gag and choke as she fought her way forward. "*Go, Natalya*—before the conductor closes the door!" She raised her voice and hollered over the packed heads, "*Stoy, stoy!*"

Breathlessly the two of them thrashed their way toward the door, with Natalie feeling like a salmon swimming upstream. "*Stoy! Stoy!*"

"What are you saying?" Natalie shouted.

"You'll learn."

Natalie fought her way down the stairs and popped out the exit like a cork from a bottle. She wondered why she'd bothered to dress up at all. She felt as if she'd been squeezed until she was about to explode, pummeled into the most distressing shapes, and then ejected from the car with a force so violent she felt robbed of any dignity she might have possessed when they first got on. She brushed herself off and attempted to straighten her hair.

"And that, my dear American, is the streetcar. Let's do it again!" Regina grinned at her, even though her face was flushed, her eyes showing her fatigue.

"No!" Natalie grabbed Regina's arm, not wanting to run the risk that her strange new friend wasn't joking. Regina's giggle exploded into a full-fledged laugh before diminishing to a happy smile.

Regina indicated their surroundings. "We're in the outskirts of Moscow. A bit more relaxing for the hospital's patients. Surround them with scenery, feed them plenty of fresh fruit and vegetables, herbs and natural remedies, and they'll heal, right? This was the healing center for the czars." After the pandemonium of the streetcar it felt as silent as a graveyard to Natalie. Regina took her arm. "Welcome to the Central Clinic Hospital of the USSR—the Kremlin Hospital."

Natalie studied the massive concrete walls that hid the main hospital buildings from her view. They ascended to a height of at least ten feet and seemed to lean in toward the grounds, as if hovering to protect it from attack from the outside. "It looks like a fortress."

"Comrade Stalin is treated here. So are members of the Politburo, the MGB, leading state scientists and mathematicians, and military officers and their families." Regina and Natalie approached the enormous steel entrance gates, which were open but guarded by several armed military personnel. "There's also a psychiatric ward in here." Regina's voice caught, and Natalie wondered what about the hospital upset her friend—the hospital that Natalie was supposed to be grateful to work at.

The Soviet nurse produced her passport and indicated for Natalie to do the same. Natalie kept her eyes downcast as the officer studied their papers carefully. He glanced up at Natalie and asked her a question. Regina quickly answered for her, and Natalie caught the name

Rostov several times in the ensuing conversation. Finally the officer handed back her passport. Regina grabbed Natalie's elbow and pulled her quickly forward into the compound.

They walked down a path bordered with apple trees so old they looked as if they'd once provided apples to the czars. Oak and birch trees grew inside and beyond the confines of the walls. Natalie followed Regina up a flight of concrete steps that were pockmarked by weather and inadequate repair. They entered the hospital.

Regina seemed pleased to be playing the part of tour guide. "Just think, here you'll empty bedpans for the most influential citizens of the Motherland!" Regina's eyes twinkled. "You'll feed them and take their temperature, change their sheets and mop sweat from their foreheads." She sobered. "Seriously, here you'll find the most advanced medical care available in the Soviet Union. It's a privilege for you to be assigned here. Your benefactor is either incredibly influential or unbelievably lucky to secure you such a position."

Natalie didn't want to be here. Not only because she was here against her will, but because she knew there would be differences between the way she'd been trained and the way Regina and the other nurses, doctors, and specialists practiced medicine. She might be ostracized—seen as strange and perhaps even dangerous.

Almost immediately Regina grabbed her arm. "Olga Popova," she murmured, indicating a nurse striding toward them. "Head nurse over surgery." She lowered her voice and whispered, "She'll feed you black crow if she ever catches you breaking the rules."

"She'll feed me what?" Natalie asked, alarmed.

"Shh—" Regina giggled. "Just steer clear of her and you'll continue to breathe. Understand?"

Olga was a stunningly beautiful woman with a slender hourglass figure, willowy arms, and trim ankles. But she wore thick, sensible shoes and an unbecoming nurse's white frock, wrapped about her like a flour sack with folds of flour still in it. One dark ringlet lay against her high forehead, and the rest of her hair remained hidden beneath a white scarf. Her face carried a tinge of pink in a smudge across both cheeks, and her lips were set in a severe line. She locked gazes with

Natalie, and her blue eyes seemed to smolder as she continued past the two women and down the hall.

Regina stared after her. "She's a wonderful human being—once you get to know her." She smiled. "I'll take you to meet your new boss. Doktor Vlasov is the head cardiologist for the hospital. You'll like him. He's of a more amiable, sociable disposition than our head nurse."

She led the way through the hospital. Natalie followed, worried. If Olga was representative of the way she was to be received by the staff . . . !

Natalie heard someone call Regina's name, and they were soon apprehended by a portly fellow in his midfifties, with a balding head and bewhiskered face, a stethoscope about his neck and his white coat perfectly pressed. His beefy hands came up to capture Regina's face, and he kissed her forehead. Natalie wondered at the sudden flicker in Regina's eyes—like a deer caught in an auto's headlights. She listened as the two conversed, her Russian name the only intelligible sound.

The doctor finally turned and beamed at Natalie. He spoke to her in English, carefully pronounced. "You're the American nurse Comrade Rostov told us about." The man leaned close and took her hands in both of his. "I've wanted to meet you. I am Doktor Yuri Mikaelovich Komarov, head of the psychiatric department."

His hands, warm and plump around hers, urged her down the hall toward his office. Regina declined to join them. "I have someone to visit," she explained, and she glanced quickly at Dr. Komarov before walking away. Natalie felt an urgent desire to follow, but she couldn't extract her hands from their fleshy prison.

Komarov didn't seem to notice her reluctance. "Ah, America, America . . ." He ushered Natalie into his office. "How you must miss America."

Natalie didn't know why, but she took an instant dislike to this man. She looked into his dark eyes, sunk deep in flesh, and felt a tiny shiver run up her spine. He was acting courteous, even genuine. But under his civility she couldn't help feeling as if he were the proverbial wolf adept at donning sheep's wool. She forced herself to answer as Viktor Rostov had instructed: "I may have been raised in the West, but I am a Soviet citizen, just like you."

"Ah, yes." The man smiled, nodding. "You're wise to renounce Western connections." He indicated a chair. "We must get better acquainted."

She didn't want to get better acquainted. She sat in the proffered chair although every muscle resisted the act. Komarov pulled a chair around to face her, maneuvering his thick torso into the seat, and leaned forward toward her, his hands clasping about each other as he leaned into his knees.

He continued his intent smile. "You will forgive my office. It is simple compared to those in American hospitals."

She hesitated. Viktor had warned her to never speak unfavorably about anything in the Soviet Union—especially in comparison to Western luxuries. Why would this man, presumably a good Soviet, risk his freedom by making such a comparison? She shifted in her chair as a new thought surfaced: What if he was trying to bait her? What if he hoped to catch her in subversive and traitorous conversation? Were her feelings of dislike from the moment she'd laid eyes on Dr. Komarov a warning to tread carefully?

She had no tangible reason for distrusting him, but the strong aversion she felt was unmistakable. So she had to accept the probability that this man was dangerous—both to her physical safety and her mental stability. She wet her lips. "It's more than adequate."

His smile deepened.

As the conversation continued and the hands of the clock counted an excruciating hour, Natalie became more and more convinced that Komarov could have the same power of life or death over her that Rostov possessed—perhaps even more so.

Finally Komarov released her, apologizing that pressing business kept him from spending more time with her. She escaped from his office as if from an inferno.

Regina was waiting for her and wordlessly took her to visit the head of the cardiology department.

Dr. Vlasov shook her hand. She was drawn to him immediately. He was slender, barely her height, with a bald spot and tufts of white hair peeking out from his ears. He sported a neatly trimmed, salt-and-pepper mustache and had the kind eyes of a grandfather and the gentle hands of a friend. After Komarov she found him as refreshing as sudden relief from a migraine.

"I've heard so much about you, Natalya."

She must have shown more surprise than she intended, because he chuckled. "I'm Lieutenant Rostov's doctor. He tells me about you."

Her gaze wavered. Viktor had permeated every aspect of her new existence. She swallowed. "You speak with a . . . a . . ."

"Southern accent?" Vlasov laughed. "I've been speaking English as long as your heart's been beating, Natalya Ivanovna: four years at the University of Virginia, four years of medical school, my residency, and twelve years as a cardiologist in Georgia. Ahh . . ." He smiled at her, an amiable, genuine smile. "How good it feels to speak it again! Lieutenant Rostov said you were raised in South Dakota."

She nodded and tried to fight tears welling in the corners of her eyes.

"And you're also a Soviet citizen, it seems. Quite a shock, I take it." She could see the gentle sympathy in his eyes.

"Yes, sir." She was losing the battle with her tears.

Vlasov studied her carefully. "Why don't you and your friend come into my office? I was about to take a break. I have something you might like to hear."

She felt his empathy as physically as if he'd handed it to her on a platter, and it melted her defenses. She and Regina followed him into his office.

He had an RCA phonograph on one end of his desk, and he immediately turned it on. "Do you know how long I've waited to play this for someone I knew would appreciate it?" Vlasov selected a phonograph record from a box and laid it on the turntable. He rubbed his hands together gleefully. "You'll recognize this song, I'm sure."

He placed the needle, and then he jumped as the first notes of a solo trumpeter shattered the silence of the office at a decibel level that set Natalie's teeth on edge. "He was a famous trumpet man from out Chicago way . . ." shrieked the Andrews Sisters before Vlasov could lower the volume.

He chuckled, placing a conspiratorial finger across his lips. "Lieutenant Rostov gave this to me," he hissed. "It's about as Western as music gets, and I can't get enough of it!"

He told her he wanted her to take a few days—perhaps a whole week, and let Regina help her get situated at her apartment. He told her he was looking forward to working with her. And then he grasped her hand as she left, and for a brief moment, Natalie's sorrow ebbed.

Sunset painted the sky red as Regina and Natalie exited the hospital grounds. At the streetcar stop Regina confessed that Rostov had insisted she bring Natalie to see him after the hospital tour. "I know you don't want to," she apologized, "but he insisted."

"Are we traveling past the Kremlin?"

Regina nodded. "That's good news for me—I live across the square. Lieutenant Rostov will take you home to your apartment in his auto."

"I'll take the streetcar."

"By yourself? You're braver than I thought."

Miraculously, the car was barely full. Natalie swung up the steps and into the car along with Regina. She pressed toward the front as soon as they began moving, and Regina sank into a seat offered by a passenger. Regina rubbed at the back of her neck.

Natalie stood close to her. "You all right?"

"Tired, that's all."

"How long until we reach our stop?"

"Twenty-five, maybe thirty minutes."

"How many stops until ours?"

"You'll know it when we get there." Regina was too tired to converse. "No way are you going to miss Red Square."

"I know." Natalie persisted. "But how many stops? I—I want to practice counting them so I won't miss it . . ." She trailed off.

"I don't know, Natalya. I really don't know."

"Maybe you could give me a heads-up; y'know, tell me what to look for, say, a mile or so before we get there?" Natalie hastened to explain. "I want you to be able to rest, and I don't want to miss—"

"Okay, okay." Regina yawned. "Remember what I said about the Arbat section, the Spaso House and the fancy mansions and those Politburo wives out for a stroll?"

"Yes." Natalie listened carefully.

"When you get there you've got about three minutes to get yourself to the exit."

Natalie nodded. "Close your eyes for a while. I can wake you when we get close."

"Are you joking? I can't sleep in a streetcar."

"You've got twenty-five minutes," Natalie insisted. "Close your eyes, at least. Your baby deserves as much rest as you can get."

"You're my doctor now?"

"Absolutely." Natalie smiled at her. "And—Regina?"

"Keep talking and I'm not going to get any rest."

"Thanks for helping me today. I—I enjoy your company."

SEVEN

Regina finally rested, her hands clutching the metal bar of the seat in front of her and her forehead on her hands. She couldn't sleep deeply, but she drifted in and out of consciousness with the movements of the car. She glanced up once and saw Natalya standing nearby, her hand clutching the bar above her head and her eyes riveted to the scenery outside.

Regina was amazed by how much she liked the American. She'd accepted this assignment because she needed the money and extra ration coupons it would provide. With the baby coming there were expenses, and she needed this extra income while Edik was away. It seemed an easy enough assignment: look after the American nurse, teach her Russian, and help her acclimatize to her new surroundings. At least until Natalya overcame her aversion for the man who'd brought her here.

She thought about her husband, her darling Edik. They'd met before the war—soon after Regina's mother died, when her papa was still head of the Moscow MGB. Regina was a Young Pioneer and Edik was a young political officer stationed at the Kremlin. They marched together with thousands of other Young Pioneers in the Great October Revolution Parade in Red Square.

Edik went off to war. She began her medical training. She served as a nurse along the front and he was assigned to serve as a political officer in Stalingrad. In 1945 they were reunited—and they married in November, exactly seven years after they first marched together in Red

Square. And now, in a few months he would return from his assignment in Kirov. And they would finally be a family . . .

Like every *moskvitch,* she'd developed an inner sensor that alerted her to her particular stop. She raised her head, stretched her legs, and then pulled them out from underneath the bench in front of her.

She rose to her feet and braced herself against the bench. The streetcar had filled while she rested. She searched for Natalya and couldn't find her. Of course Natalya would've moved toward the front. Perhaps she hadn't wanted to disturb her until the last possible moment. How thoughtful of her. Regina worked her way toward the front exit.

She reached the conductor and indicated her desire to descend at the next stop. She could see the multi-colored domes of St. Basil's Cathedral loom through the glass and then she moved through the remaining bodies to the door.

Natalya was not there.

$$* * *$$

She caught a glimpse of Viktor Rostov standing at the Red Square stop, and Regina panicked. How was she to explain the American's disappearance? She was afraid of him; he had the authority to have her arrested—even banished to Siberia! At the very least he could have her dismissed from the hospital. She would lose her wages, her room, her ration coupons, and her privileges as a member of the housing cooperative. Worse still, a homeless person in Moscow could be banished from the city within twenty-four hours. She had no money to join her husband in Kirov—and even if she did, he'd written that his quarters were with the officers. There would be no place for a homeless, disgraced wife. If only her papa were still stationed at Lubyanka. She could appeal to him. But Igor Sushin couldn't help her now. If she lost her home in Moscow there would be no place for her to go.

The streetcar slowed and pulled to a stop. Regina gripped the handrail until her knuckles hurt. Rostov had a legal right to destroy her; she had lost track of a foreign woman—*his* foreign woman—and her disappearance might be construed by the MGB as an escape attempt. Natalya would be labeled a spy and arrested as soon as she was discovered. Rostov would be furious.

She could already see his eyes searching the crowd. He turned and looked at her, and Regina mentally cringed. She knew his temper. She'd seen it when a student didn't respect his authority or a subordinate didn't follow a directive explicitly. But in all the years she'd known him he'd always been so civil with her.

She told him what happened. At least, she told him what she knew. There'd been no indication from Natalya that she was going to run. She'd been standing right next to Regina in the streetcar. Regina had only closed her eyes for a few minutes . . .

"Where did she get off?"

"I don't know . . ." Regina moaned. "You know what it's like in the car. There wasn't a crowd, but it was full. I had people brushing against me in the aisle all the time—and I just assumed it was Natalya . . ."

Rostov looked as she imagined he had the day he discovered his wife strafed by enemy gunfire. "Regina, you've got to think. Was there anything she said to you—in the car, at the hospital, while you were walking—anything that might indicate where she went? Think, Regina! Think!"

"Professor—*izvinitye!* I'm so sorry I lost her. I was so tired . . ." She felt nauseous at the thought of what she had done, as if she might vomit onto the shiny boots in front of her.

He persisted. "Did she *say* anything, Regina?"

She searched through her panic to the last few hours; the streetcar on the way to the hospital, Olga Popova, Komarov's curious interview with Natalya, Vlasov's American music . . . She could think of nothing Natalya had said that raised a warning flag in her mind. "No, sir."

"Did she ask about a certain stop? A certain location on the streetcar's route? A building? Think, Regina!" He clutched her arms.

"Nyet! Izvinitye, izvinitye . . ."

"Regina . . ." He was visibly trembling, and Regina couldn't remember the last time she'd seen him so distraught. "Do you have any idea what could happen to Natalya if she's discovered?"

Regina moaned.

"There are people who want her dead, Regina—and one little mistake on my part . . ." His voice wavered. "They'll kill her. Do you understand?"

His mistake! He was blaming himself, not her. She began to cry.

He put an arm about her. "Please, Regina, if you can think of anything, now would be the time to tell me. I can find her quickly if I have any idea where she might be headed. If I don't find her, *they* will. Please help me know where to look for her."

Her whole body was tight with worry. She hadn't expected he would treat her with such kindness, and it made her feel even worse. Then she remembered something. "Natalya wanted to know how many stops—before Red Square . . ."

His expression urged her to continue.

"She asked . . ." Regina searched her memory. "She asked me to remind her of landmarks before the Square. She didn't want to miss the stop. She knew I was tired . . ."

"Regina," Rostov spoke gently now, leaning close as if afraid he might miss something. "Tell me which landmarks you mentioned."

She swallowed. "I told her to look for the Arbat section; you know, the mansions, the Spaso House, and the homes of the Politburo . . ."

He straightened. Something she'd said was of interest to him. He kissed her cheek, much as her papa used to do, and asked, "Can you make it home by yourself?"

"Of course. Do you know where she went?"

He nodded.

She was relieved. "Does that mean that I can keep my job?" It sounded childish, even to her.

He chuckled, smiled at her, but she could see his mind was already elsewhere. "Thank you, Regina . . ." He didn't finish, but turned and sprinted away.

EIGHT

The sudden rain drenched Natalie before she'd arrived at the stately Arbat quarter. It quickly dampened both the streets and her spirits, and she longed for a coat. She had only Regina's offhanded reference to an ambassador at the Spaso House to guide her. And she knew her time was short; she had no doubt Regina had already noticed her disappearance. But she had no idea if the Soviet nurse had seen her escape the streetcar at the Arbat quarter. And Natalie knew Regina would go directly to Viktor. She wrapped her arms about herself, chilled and miserable in her new green dress and sensible shoes, and felt again the gravity of her situation.

Natalie couldn't blame Regina; in fact, she'd grown rather fond of her exuberant new friend. It had bothered her to deceive Regina and leave her to face Viktor's wrath. She hoped Viktor would not censure her too harshly. It wasn't Regina's fault. Natalie would've escaped even with Regina hanging to her arm. But Natalie couldn't face Viktor Rostov. She *would* not face him!

Streetlamps flickered and turned on. It was not yet dark, but the rain amplified the impending night. She could see where work crews had begun to asphalt over the cobblestones, modernizing roads for an automobile age. But Moscow's streets were still ruled by buggies and bicycles, pedestrians, and the occasional public transport. Automobiles were the luxury of the government—especially here in Moscow.

She didn't know how to find the Spaso House. She didn't know what it looked like. She wasn't even certain she'd descended at the correct stop. She picked up her pace, shoes chafing as rainwater seeped in around her ankles and worked its way between her toes. The unpleasant truth was that Viktor Rostov or one of his agents could be waiting for her at the Spaso House whenever she managed to find it. She had no doubt he would catch on quickly, and she hoped against hope that she could get in the door and find a sympathetic ear—an *American* sympathetic ear— before he found her.

What had Regina said? The house was in an area of wealthy mansions, owned by politburo members and their families. As she wandered the unfamiliar streets she felt more and more confused and terrified. She didn't have the vocabulary to ask for directions to the ambassador's residence—let alone the vocabulary to get herself back to her apartment if she couldn't find the Spaso House. It brought back memories of the time in Soviet Berlin when she'd been searching for her cousin Aimée and had become lost. Hans Brenner had saved her life—and the brief memory of the man who'd captured her heart was almost more than she could bear. But even then, she hadn't felt this miserable and afraid. *Heavenly Father,* she thought, shivering in the rain, *please, please help me!*

Of course she couldn't read the Cyrillic letters of the street signs, and the only Russian word she could salvage from the overload in her brain was *Stoy!* Stop! In frustration she was about to retrace her steps when she saw something that warmed her straight through her soggy dress, waterlogged shoes, and wet hair. She saw an American flag.

There are few things that can reassure a person caught unprepared in a Moscow rainstorm. For a displaced American girl, the sight of an American flag is one of them. She ran toward the miraculous sight, through a modest park edged with rows of moist flowers and surrounded with maple trees and evergreens. She emerged in front of a columned mansion built in a style that reminded her of the palatial residences of the more affluent sections of Berlin.

The building was in desperate need of repair. But she could forgive its crumbling plaster and peeling paint, because the American flag flapping over the pavilion made it the residence of angels from heaven. High up on the second story balcony over the portico, someone was busy with the ropes that held the flag in place, and then the flag was lowered, a foot at a time, from its lofty pole. A few moments later and there would've been no American flag to guide her feet.

She mounted the steps and rested a few moments under the blessed roof of the portico. She listened to the steady hum of the rain and watched the water undulating over the irregular surface of the streets, and then she walked toward the massive front doors.

She lifted the heavy knocker and let it fall, listening to its hollow boom as it echoed somewhere inside. She recalled a scene from the movie *Hunchback of Notre Dame,* where Quasimodo shouts "Sanctuary! Sanctuary!" as he protects La Esmeralda from Claude Frollo and the fanatical crowds below. Natalie needed sanctuary—someone to protect her from Viktor Rostov and the horrors of a future here with him in the Soviet Union.

She took an involuntary step forward as the massive door opened, as if she would rush inside. The Asian man who stood framed in the entrance stared back at her as if he couldn't decide from her appearance if she were an intruder or a guest who'd misunderstood the date of a party.

"P-p-pardon me . . ." she gasped. "Sir, I'm looking for the American ambassador—excuse me, I don't know his name"—she couldn't keep the chattering of her teeth from affecting her voice—"but I must see him. Please."

The man continued to stare at her, and she wondered if he had even understood her plea. Trembling, she tried again. "*P-pazháloosta* . . . please help me . . ."

"General Smith is not available." The man's English was impeccable. "He's at dinner with an important guest. You'll have to return later . . ."—the man cleared his throat—"with an appointment."

"No!" She wished she could force her way past the man and into the vast expanse of the interior. "You must let me in! Y-you don't understand . . ."

"You must have an appointment," the man insisted. "Go home and come back when you have an appointment with the general."

"Please, sir—I'm an American citizen . . ."

His gaze wavered. "What is your name?"

"N-Natalya—I mean, Natalie Allred . . . and I have nowhere else to go . . . My life is in danger . . ."

"Of course," the man said suddenly, and she was momentarily taken aback.

She stammered, "I'm here to request asyl—"

"Come in, please." The man stepped away from the door.

It was as if between one breath and another, the sun had miraculously come out. Wordlessly she followed the servant into the home.

The man indicated for her to wait. Water from her dress trickled onto marble as her eyes took in the second floor balconies supported by massive columns and protected by ornate balustrades, rising toward the soaring ceiling. She felt like she was standing in the center of a gothic cathedral. She stared in awe at the largest chandelier she'd ever seen, shimmering gold and bejeweled with dozens of sparkling crystals which must have weighed over twenty pounds apiece. It would've been a heavenly sight—if she hadn't been so preoccupied with her own dire predicament.

The servant returned with a luxurious white towel, almost as large as she, and placed it decorously about her shoulders. He asked for her shoes and replaced them with soft blue slippers. He produced a smaller rag, which he used to whisk away moisture that had dripped on the floor. And then he left her with only the chandelier for company.

She dared not sit and destroy the plush velour of the armchair nearest her position, nor step onto the thick Oriental rug spread beneath the chandelier. So she stood where she was, and after she'd mopped up and squeezed as much water as she could from her dress and hair, she huddled in one spot, shivering, worrying, and waiting.

She could hear the murmur of voices and the chink of silverware on fine china, and her stomach became a tight little ball of grievances, mixing anxiety with hunger. She closed her eyes and tried to ignore the pain.

She heard footsteps approaching from the dining room—different from the soft shuffle of the servant who'd attended her. She opened her eyes and straightened, slipping the towel from her shoulders and holding it behind her back as she turned, hoping to look a little more presentable now that she'd dried a bit.

Her hope turned to dismay when she saw Viktor Rostov approaching her across the marble tile, and she felt her legs turn to rubber and her feet suddenly fuse to the floor. "No-o-o . . ." she lamented in a wail that didn't even reach as far away as the chandelier.

"My dear Natalya . . ." There was something in his eyes that frightened her. He removed his suit coat and placed it about her shoulders. "You're drenched. Soaked through to the bone! What in the world were you thinking, coming all this way on foot?"

She was speechless, and she struggled with the sudden tears that accompany sharp disappointment. It was as if her last avenue of escape had been blocked by this man who seemed to always stand in the way, no matter what she tried.

Suddenly he wrapped her in his arms and pulled her close. He had a strange edge to his voice that shocked her almost as much as his next words. "You should've *told* me you wanted to come here, *malen'kaya*." The Russian word meant nothing to Natalie.

Rostov continued. "I would've brought you in my car and spared you the dreadful walk in the rain. Ah, Natalya . . ."—his voice caught— "How you scared me!"

She heard another voice, muffled through Viktor's shoulder, also approaching from the direction of the dining room. "So this is the girl you told me about, Lieutenant. My goodness—what the deuce happened to her?" It was a deep, rolling voice, with a strong, friendly American accent, but because the man's arrival came on the unfortunate heels of Viktor's, she no longer felt as relieved to see him as she'd thought she would be. But she pressed against the arms that held her, twisting until she was free of Viktor's embrace and able to face the man entering the room.

General Smith was a smartly dressed businessman with a studious face and a receding hairline. Natalie wondered if the lines about his eyes and mouth might be from laughter rather than age. He carried himself with the air of a military officer, but something about his commanding presence hinted at genuine affability.

Lieutenant Rostov spoke before she could open her mouth. "Natalya"—he sounded almost apologetic—"meet my friend and comrade, General Walter Smith, U.S. Ambassador to Moscow. We've known each other since before the war. General Smith, this is Natalya Ivanovna Karagodina."

The last flicker of hope she clung to died like the flame at the end of a candle.

"You're soaked to the skin, Natalya!" The man stated the obvious in a voice that boomed through the arched rafters above his head. "I'll have Chin and Tang prepare the guest room. You can take a hot bath and rest for as long as you like. I'm sure my wife will have something to fit you." He saw the despair on Natalie's face and hurried on. "My good friend here told me about your predicament. It's no fun being hauled away to a strange country—especially against your will. Have you eaten anything? You must be famished. The cook will bring you up a plate. I can see the transition has been difficult for you. Rostov is anxious to help you any way he can. He's going to work with us to make your future as comfortable as possible—under the circumstances."

"Sir—" She knew before the words left her lips that they would be useless. "I came here to ask—to ask—"

"For asylum?" The man shook his head, his gaze sympathetic. "Impossible."

Even though the kind look in his eyes was meant to soften the blow, she was devastated.

"Natalya, you're a Soviet citizen. Lieutenant Rostov has proven that to me, beyond any doubt—"

"No, I'm an American." Her voice rose along with her desperation. "I served my country during and after the war—"

"There are many repatriated Soviet citizens with dual citizenship." The general's interruption was gentle. "You're not as alone here as you might think. You should connect with other repatriates of dual American-Soviet citizenship. Get to know them and spend time with them. Viktor has told me how melancholy you are. You miss your mother in the States. You miss your fiancé—I am so sorry for your loss, by the way—and because of the role Lieutenant Rostov played in your repatriation you're obviously not on the best of terms with him." Smith gave her shoulder a paternal squeeze. "I would feel the same way as you, if I were in your shoes." He dropped his hand. "But you're here because President Roosevelt signed an agreement with Joseph

Stalin. I know it's difficult. As an ambassador I deal with people like you all the time. But if you could just think of your experience as an opportunity—"

"An *opportunity?*" Natalie had a hard time getting the words to leave her dry mouth.

"Yes, Natalya. An opportunity! Think of yourself as an ambassador—like me!" He nodded encouragingly. "You have an opportunity to influence this country for good. The Soviet Union is at the threshold of incredible growth and progress, and you can be a part of that!"

She turned her face away, fighting frantic fear.

"Of course, you're not required to sever all ties elsewhere, my dear; I can make sure the embassy courier posts a letter for you, if you'd like. I know how difficult it is to have faith in the Soviet mail system—begging your pardon, Lieutenant—so I can see to it personally that your letter gets in the diplomatic pouch with embassy mail."

Natalie took a deep breath and composed herself. "Where are my shoes?"

The ambassador blinked. "Your shoes?"

"Your servant took them from me and gave me these slippers."

"I'm sure he was concerned that your feet might not be comfortable in wet shoes."

"I would like them back."

"Why?"

"Because I'm going home."

The ambassador cleared his throat. "Natalya, I just explained to you: *Moscow* is now your home."

"I'm going back to my apartment."

For a moment the general looked bewildered. "In this rain?" He made a general gesture in the direction of the front entry. "You're wet enough as it is. Allow my wife to lend you a dress—although the one you're wearing is striking . . . a shame it would ruin the upholstery—and then stay the night with us and we'll discuss your future."

"Will my future entail a return flight to the United States?"

"Unfortunately, no."

"Then we have nothing to discuss. I need my shoes, please."

"I'll take her home," Viktor said.

Shaking his head in disbelief, the general motioned to the servant standing in the doorway. "Tang, bring this young lady her shoes. Make her rest for a few days, Lieutenant. Make sure she eats something before she dries up and blows away. Certainly you have influence enough to get her extra ration coupons. Does she have a position?"

"At the Kremlin Hospital."

"Beautiful." The general was impressed. "You do have influence, it seems." General Smith turned kindly eyes on Natalie. "Don't worry so much, Natalya. You're young and strong—and very lovely. You have many wonderful years ahead of you. Moscow is a magnificent place for a young woman like you. Do you like theater? My wife and I go every week. You and the lieutenant should come along. Theater is quite popular in Moscow! Ah, how I love Moscow . . ."

Natalie looked him in the eye. "You will live here, then, after your tenure as ambassador is over?"

Smith's gaze flickered ever so slightly. Then he smiled. "My fondest wish. However, as a public servant I'm required to go where my country sends me . . ."

"It seems you and I have the same problem, sir," Natalie said softly. "Only *your* obligation takes you toward home, while *my* duty forces me far away from mine."

"A sad state of affairs, I know." The general did not lose his composure.

Tang returned with her shoes. He must have placed them very near a fire somewhere because they were toasty warm, and only slightly moist near the soles. He knelt and removed her slippers from her feet, and then placed a foot in each shoe. It was a simple gesture of kindness, but one that, coupled with the dried shoes, warmed her to the center of her bruised heart.

General Smith asked, "Will you be sending a letter in the diplomatic pouch, Natalya?"

She hesitated, contemplating whom she might possibly contact. Certainly her mother in South Dakota. But she didn't know yet what to write that would soften the news of her situation. Rolf Schulmann? He'd always been a good friend. Would Rolf and Marie be married by now? If she knew where they were, Natalie was certain she'd find a listening ear in the two of them. But could they really do anything to help her? What could a former Nazi officer do to negotiate her release?

She had a sudden spark of inspiration: She could send a letter to Major James Matthews, stationed with the U.S. Central Intelligence Group in Frankfurt. He'd been the main reason Viktor's first attempt to abduct her and Hans Brenner had failed. *He* could help her. That is, if she didn't mention her unfortunate citizenship . . .

"Yes, sir. I'd like to send a letter." She glanced uncomfortably at Viktor, then back at the general.

"I'm assuming you didn't come with a letter ready?"

"No, sir."

"Tang will help you."

She imagined Viktor Rostov looking over her shoulder as she wrote, censoring her every word. "I'd prefer to return—at a later date."

"Not a problem." Ambassador Smith smiled at her. "Bring it whenever you'd like and Tang will include it in the pouch." He turned to go. Problem solved. He was washing his hands of her.

She felt melancholy settle over her like a depressing fog. She allowed Viktor to lead her from the chandelier room, through the vestibule, and out of the Spaso House. She saw his car and driver approaching from the rear courtyard of the residence and she understood how Viktor had managed to surprise her.

As they drove, rain continued to fall, thundering across the roof and pounding the windshield. It pummeled useless wiper blades as it hurried in frenzied waves down the glass. She stared at the windshield and did not say a word.

She expected a lecture. She expected a warning, or threats, or perhaps even violence. She expected any emotion other than the one she was feeling from Viktor. He seemed sad, and his silence cut her to the core.

And when they reached her apartment complex he got out of the car and opened her door for her. He helped her from the car. But he did none of the things she'd anticipated. "Natalya." His voice sounded hoarse, deeply emotional. Water poured across his face as he said simply, "I'm glad you're all right."

Then he left her there, standing on the curb in the rain, her mind reeling and the shock of her situation like an atom bomb exploding in her chest.

NINE

Natalie met Dr. Vlasov in his office for her first day of work at the hospital. Stored away were the records and the RCA phonograph. Vlasov was as congenial as before but focused on the job at hand.

"Are you ready to work?" he asked, his kind eyes peering into hers.

"Yes, sir."

"You seemed like a little lost kitten the last time we met."

Natalie looked away. "I've come to terms with a few things since then."

Vlasov nodded. She could see that he understood.

"Now to business: No matter what Nurse Olga insists, I think you need to learn your job in your language. So I'm going to be speaking a lot of English with you. Hope you don't mind."

She was relieved. "Not at all."

He walked her through her responsibilities. He introduced her to several of his long-term patients, and she assisted him with a simple procedure. He seemed pleased with what she knew.

"It's been years since I've worked with an American nurse. Things are done differently around here—just in case you haven't noticed— and sometimes it's like pulling teeth to get the local nurses to understand what I'm asking them to do."

"I guess we're trained differently."

"Do tell. You realize what they use to anesthetize the patient for minor surgeries around here?" Vlasov rolled his eyes. "*Vodka!* They make the patient drink a bottle of the stuff and then they start cutting away." Vlasov grinned. "The patient's so happy he never feels a thing."

* * *

Natalie spent the period of her training trying not to think about her predicament—trapped in a foreign country with no way to escape. She tried not to think about the man she'd meant to marry, or the Soviet officer who'd turned her dreams to nightmares, or how hungry she was, or how she detested boiling water before she could quench a chronic thirst. And she tried not to think that what she was doing was what she might be stuck doing for the rest of her life.

One morning Vlasov presented her with a tray of syringes and a list of room numbers. He left her to the task and went off to perform a surgery. "The operation's on a member of the Politburo," Vlasov confided with a wink. "If I make a mistake they'll probably have me shot." He walked away, leaving Natalie wondering whether or not he was joking.

She read the room number on each syringe and dutifully injected the fluid from that syringe into the resident of that room. Often there were several syringes with the same room number, and because everything was labeled in Cyrillic she had several moments of near panic. She remembered Vlasov's parting words with a shudder: *If I make a mistake they'll probably have me shot.*

When she got down to the last syringe, she paused. From her limited experience, the most influential Party members had their own rooms while others stayed in rooms with as many as twenty beds. This patient was obviously someone of importance—or at least influence. So much for the socialist ideal. She prepped the needle and walked into the room.

In the doorway Natalie froze, the syringe ready in one hand. She stared at the patient in the bed. "What—what are you doing here?"

Viktor Rostov met her gaze. His head and upper torso were propped with pillows to almost a sitting position, and his arms lay quietly at his sides. He gave her a faint smile. "My heart."

She moved into the room and forced herself to approach the bed. "Are you all right?"

"Would I be here if I were?"

She colored slightly. "I mean, how do you feel?"

"Better, now that you're here."

She took a deep breath. "I'm supposed to give you—"

"I know. I've done this before, Natalya."

She reached for his sleeve, gingerly rolling it upward in an attempt to not touch his flesh.

He watched her as she administered the shot. "Do you like it here?"

She didn't know how to respond. The hours were grueling, but they kept her at the hospital and away from her terrible apartment. The cook fed the nursing staff once in a while, which was appreciated, because she ate almost nothing anywhere else. Dr. Vlasov appreciated her efforts and didn't mind that she didn't speak Russian very well. And Regina was becoming a good friend. "It's all right," she murmured.

"I'm glad."

She turned to go.

"Natalya . . ."

"I—I have more patients." She fled from the room.

She took a moment to calm her breathing and compose herself. She knew Viktor had requested her as his nurse, and it made her furious that he would manipulate her into a position where she would be required to attend him every day. It made her uncomfortable to be alone in the same room with him, even as his nurse. She knew he was deeply in love—or obsessed—with her, and that fact alone made this situation difficult.

But Regina was right—he'd been kind to her since their arrival in Moscow, and he'd protected her—perhaps even saved her life on several occasions. And she, in her acute misery, had never acknowledged that assistance, whether to herself, to Regina, or to the man who'd offered it.

Later, she passed the laboratory and noticed Dr. Vlasov at his desk in the corner. As she approached he raised his head from his charts and gave her a kind smile. He'd been her favorite doctor since the moment she arrived at the hospital, and whenever she had the privilege to accompany him on his rounds she'd been amazed at the kindness and care he showed each of his patients.

His bedside manner was not the end of it; he treated Regina with respect, when other hospital staff scorned her for deciding to have her baby. He showed deference to Natalie, and she had grown to trust him and appreciate his advice.

She could go to him with her concerns and her questions, and he would listen to and gently tutor her. If something weighed heavily on her mind he was far more capable of discerning the cause and the cure than the head psychiatrist, Dr. Komarov. Or, perhaps it was that Vlasov was more genuine in his friendship, and this gave Natalie reason to trust him more.

Now she approached him with another concern, and he promptly set his work aside to attend to her.

"Doctor, the patient in room—"

"Lieutenant Rostov?" Dr. Vlasov laced his fingers together and gave her his full attention.

"Did—did he suffer a heart attack? He told me about his heart . . ."

Vlasov shook his head. "Not a heart attack. But his heart is more susceptible to heart attacks than many people's. He's suffering from acute angina pectoris. His health has been compromised by it for several years."

Natalie turned the term over in her mind, trying to remember back to her medical training. She hadn't been trained extensively in the diseases of the heart, and it embarrassed her to have to request an explanation.

But Dr. Vlasov seemed to understand. "You're under a tremendous amount of stress, Nurse Natalya—Lieutenant Rostov is also—and that stress, in conjunction with his sorrow over the loss of his family, has accelerated his medical condition. His heart does not receive the oxygen it needs when his emotions are high, or he overexerts himself, or he exposes his body to extreme cold. No," Vlasov patted her shoulder, his gesture sympathetic, "he hasn't had a heart attack. But he's at high risk for one, if he doesn't take better care of himself. He asked for you, of course. He . . . admires you very much."

Natalie didn't respond, but her fingers clutched at her skirt.

Dr. Vlasov noted her concern. He said kindly, "Perhaps your presence here is keeping him alive."

"Dr. Vlasov, I—"

He raised a hand to stop her. "I know your affections were once elsewhere. The lieutenant knows this, also. And you'll see, Natalya, Viktor Rostov is honorable. He won't violate your memories of another man."

Natalie didn't respond, but she felt her frustration and anger at Viktor rising dangerously near the surface. He had destroyed her life. He'd torn from her the greatest chance for happiness she'd ever known, and she didn't think her resentment would ever go away.

And even as she had that thought, something whispered that she needed to forgive him. She fought against the feeling. Not only did she have no desire to forgive Viktor; she couldn't imagine how to do it.

TEN

Saturday, June 8, 1946

In Great Britain, a clear June morning means only a little precipitation. This was just such a clear morning. After the shower subsided, Londoners folded their umbrellas and wiped off their chairs. They shook out their blankets and guarded their tiny claims of curb and grass with English stubbornness and English pride. In London, June 8, 1946, was the official Victory Celebration, and the World War II Victory Parade along Whitehall finally began.

One solitary figure stood in the crowd across from the Saluting Base. Of above-average height, he wore a long wool overcoat, a hat still moist around the brim, and leather gloves that enveloped hands tucked loosely into pockets. His light brown hair was clipped short, and his eyes, blue as the skies of his German homeland, darted to the left and the right as he searched the enthusiastic crowd for the person he'd come to meet.

This blued-eyed man was as much a war hero as any marching before the king, but that fact remained forever buried. Because he'd been labeled a Nazi, he would never acknowledge with a salute a crowd of two million on London's famous Whitehall, or receive a ticker-tape parade in New York City. But in a perfect world he might also be receiving a hero's applause next to the king, the queen, and the prime minister for the part he played in the recent war.

But this was not a perfect world, and Rolf Schulmann had seen much during his thirty-seven years to confirm that fact. He didn't need praise or recognition, nor did he want it.

"Now I remember why I steer clear of Great Britain this time of year."

Rolf Schulmann turned and faced the man he sought. Major James Matthews swept his hat from his head and twisted it in his pudgy fingers, squeezing moisture from its fabric. "I apologize for being late." He locked hands with the German. "Good choice of a meeting place. No one will ever overhear with the hullabaloo below."

"How's your wife?" Rolf leaned close to ask. "Your daughter?"

Matthews raised his voice to be heard over the noise. "Nellie's expecting in December, and my wife extracted a promise from me that we'll spend Christmas in California with the happy newlyweds."

"That's good, Major."

"How's married life treating you, Goodwin?"

Rolf smiled faintly. He still hadn't accustomed himself to his alias, and hearing it from his superior officer was still mildly disconcerting. "It's wonderful."

"Are you comfortable? Is the cottage to your liking?"

"Perfect."

"Natalie is in Moscow."

Rolf looked at him silently. He felt his pulse accelerate as he waited for Matthews to continue.

"Your French friend, Jacques Bellamont, told me she'd disappeared," Matthews explained. "And then I received a letter from her—sent through the embassy's diplomatic pouch. I was supposed to watch over her. It's my fault."

Rolf felt cold. Natalie's situation was bad enough. But Rolf knew Hans had been Rostov's primary target. And there was something Matthews was not telling him. He said carefully, "What about Hans Brenner?"

"Moscow claims they have no idea who Hans Brenner is."

"But he's disappeared, hasn't he?" Rolf stayed calm. "Were you supposed to be watching over Hans, also?"

"Not officially." Matthews studied the crowd.

"What are you going to do about his disappearance?"

"We don't know where he is."

The American didn't look at him, and suddenly Rolf knew. Matthews was using Hans. Matthews had planned this.

Matthews's silence confirmed Rolf's fears. If Hans were also a political prisoner, then Rolf considered it a death sentence. He asked, "And what about Natalie Allred?"

Matthews shook his head.

"She was my friend's fiancée. She's an American citizen."

"Turns out she's only *sort of* American." Matthews sounded apologetic. "I called Rostov to complain, and he sent me proof of her Soviet citizenship. Her birth father was Russian; that's where she was born."

Rolf felt sick inside. "So she's been forcibly repatriated."

Matthews was jostled by someone in the crowd. "Stalin got Churchill and Roosevelt to agree to return all Soviet citizens to Soviet territory, regardless of the refugees' personal wishes. An attempt on our part to extract a Soviet citizen could rupture a delicate relationship between our two nations."

"Major, Viktor Rostov is a dangerous man. You can't be thinking of leaving her there with him."

"We promised Stalin we wouldn't interfere." Matthews's lips pressed together. He stood silently, watching the parade. Dispatch riders of the Royal Navy, Army, and Air Force passed the Saluting Base. King George's salute remained as steady as ever. Suddenly Matthews swore, punching the air and almost contacting the shoulder of a parade-goer in front of him. "I should've gotten her outta Europe right after your trial. Confound that man!"

"Any chance Rostov's misleading us?"

"Rostov's entire existence is a lie!"

"Would he lie about this? Surely he knows we could uncover the deception."

"He doesn't care," Matthews growled. "Not now. Not when he's so far out of our reach."

Rolf studied the older man carefully. "So your position is that he has Hans Brenner with him also."

Matthews grimaced. "I'm not allowed to have a position. Not until . . ." He stopped, sighed, rubbed at his brow, and did not finish.

"Would you mind if I have one? That is, if it doesn't interfere with my current assignment?"

"You're gonna try to get her out?"

"I'd like to. But I have no idea how—at the moment. I'm going to look for a loophole in the Yalta ruling. Or a way to get around Rostov." Rolf hesitated, then looked Matthews squarely in the eye. "Before they died, my parents amassed a business fortune in Chicago. They left it all to me. I want to use it to get Natalie out. Hans too, if he's in danger. Every penny, if necessary."

Matthews threw back his head and laughed. "You're a piece of work!" He sobered. "You realize what diplomacy costs these days? Not to mention international *bribery*."

"Bribery isn't in the budget," Rolf said. "I'm under the impression Lieutenant Rostov won't appreciate a bribery attempt. He wouldn't break Soviet law even to save his own daughter."

Matthews shrugged. "I happen to know Rostov will be just as furious with our interference whether or not we break the law."

"I have to make him want to help us."

"Good luck with that!"

"Then you'll hear my plan? You'll see if it'll work?"

"My dear Charles"—Matthews thumped Rolf's arm—"*when* you have a plan, then by all means, I'll listen to it."

ELEVEN

Regina collected and emptied bedpans into the nearly overflowing collection buckets not yet emptied from the night before. She assisted with an emergency surgery and brought breakfast to each of her patients. One of the soldiers guarding the room of a prominent Party member made an off-color remark about her changing body. She ignored him and thought of the newborn she had held in her arms after assisting with a delivery yesterday. For just a moment she had dreamed it was her own.

Her nausea and constant desire to lean over the washtub had finally subsided. Now she was constantly hungry and never seemed to have enough to eat. Her feet hurt, along with the muscles of her legs and lower torso. Her back ached. Each week brought new pains and new sensations, and soon it would no longer be possible to camouflage her expanding waistline.

With excitement, she thought now of the weekend. Edik was visiting from Kirov and would see her pregnant for the first time. He'd written of his enthusiastic approval, and now they would finally have an entire weekend together to make plans for their future. They would renew a romance that had waited patiently for this reunion, and Regina would forget drudgery and Moscow's loneliness. At least for a weekend she would be happy, with Edik.

She climbed the stairs to begin work on another floor. As two gentlemen descended toward her, she moved to the side to let them past, averting her eyes lest they think her insolent. They did not pass.

Regina looked into their faces and felt something cold creeping up her spine.

One of the men gave her a congenial smile. "Comrade Oryekova?"

She took a deep breath. "Is something wrong?"

"Not at all." His smile deepened. "We need you to come with us."

His smile did not deceive her. She knew who they represented; her papa had been their commanding officer at one time. "Where?"

"You'll be back at work before too long."

"Comrades, my break is not for another hour. I cannot afford to—"

"It's a matter of utmost urgency." The smile was becoming forced.

Regina forgot all about backaches, hunger, and muscle cramps. "What's wrong?"

"It is nothing to worry about." The smile disappeared. "Come with us, please."

Regina accompanied them out of the hospital. They drove to the center of Moscow—to Lubyanka. She saw the familiar structure and her fears were confirmed. She knew what Igor Sushin used to do. She closed her eyes and felt suddenly dizzy as one of the men held open her door.

In 1940 Stalin had ordered that the massive building be expanded. Because of war delays the entire building was still in a state of structural disaster, and she stepped carefully past stone and discarded rubble, under scaffolding and workers, and through the front door.

She followed her escorts up stairs that seemed to stretch into eternity, and into a lavish office overlooking Dzerzhinsky Square. She sat on a lush, comfortable chair near an unused fireplace, rested her hands across her stomach, and looked about the room.

She knew this room; it had been her papa's office before his inexplicable sickness, and she could recall memories from her growing up years visiting him in this room. Over by the far corner had once stood a small table covered with a lace doily. She remembered her papa's brass samovar, teapot, and crystal mugs in their gold-plated cup holders. She remembered sitting there as a child, eating kasha and drinking tea while Igor Sushin worked at his desk. A steel cabinet now stood in the table's place.

She turned as the door opened and a man she knew entered the room. There was nothing to fear from Roman Krajnik; he was a longtime friend of her papa. Ten years her senior and two decades Igor Sushin's junior, he'd worked as an adjutant. Sushin had been instrumental in grooming him to help administer Moscow's branch of the MGB. Who would've thought Krajnik would someday replace him?

A Moscow-born transplant of Ukrainian parentage, Roman Krajnik was fair-skinned and fair-headed, with deceivingly delicate features and a winning smile. His hands had never been immersed in the soil of a collective farm, and his smooth skin had escaped undue exposure to winter's rough touch. He would never have been admitted onto the playing fields of Soviet sports; his grace was more that of a dancer in the Moscow Ballet. Regina knew that Krajnik's parents had once even enrolled him in Moscow's Academy of Fine Arts—until his talents and enthusiasm had been noticed by the Village Soviet and he'd been assigned by the Young Communists League to a more political career.

"My papa would be proud of you. You've distinguished his name with your care of his post. When he returns—"

"You are generous, Regina Igorevna." The man gave her a welcoming smile and held out his arms to her. "I've tried to uphold his trust. Perhaps if he does someday return there will be a place for me at his side."

They exchanged a customary welcoming kiss, and she was grateful for his kind words for her papa. "He'll be forever indebted to you for your loyalty."

"You look famished. Perhaps tea? A few biscuits and jam?"

"Yes, thank you."

He didn't join her as she ate, and she tried not to let the sudden memory of something Igor Sushin had once said spoil her appetite: *one must not eat salt with the man one plans to destroy.*

She shook the implication from her mind. Roman Krajnik was a friend.

"I've been worried about you, Regina." Krajnik was solicitous. "You have so many responsibilities, and yet you still insist on carrying Edik's baby."

"It is no hardship. Edik is proud of me. In November he'll be reassigned to Moscow, and he'll see what a beautiful baby he has."

"Regina . . ."

Regina could hear something in Krajnik's voice. "What is it?"

Krajnik pulled a chair close, sank into it, and placed a gentle hand on Regina's knee. "I feel protective of you, now that Comrade Sushin is unable to be here for you." His face was a study in concern. "For your sake I called you here today—because of the respect I have for your papa, and because I cannot forget watching his little Regina Igorevna grow from a little child, happy with her doll, to a young woman, a proper communist youth who held her red banner high and sang the Anthem of the Young Pioneers! Ah, how you made me glad!"

"Then why is there worry in your eyes?"

Roman Krajnik took her hand. "I wish I didn't have to be the bearer of such news . . ."

"What news? What is it?"

"Your husband—your Edik . . ." He sighed. "He was arrested last week in Kirov."

His words exploded in her head with a violence that frightened her. She stared at Krajnik. For a moment she wondered if she'd heard him properly and she wondered if she should ask him to repeat himself. Then the significance of his words struck as if Lenin's mausoleum had fallen on her. She couldn't think straight but rather felt the numbness in her brain that accompanies a revelation too horrific to comprehend.

"I can see you're distressed. I know it's a difficult surprise for you. I'm sorry." Krajnik leaned toward her, his eyes sympathetic. "I wish I didn't have to be the one to tell you; but the Politburo felt it would come best from me—perhaps with a little less pain—because of my connection to your papa . . ."

She began to tremble, and it felt as if the world had suddenly stopped spinning and then restarted in the opposite direction. *It couldn't be true!* And suddenly, the shock of the revelation was too much to bear. She cried, "Why? *Why?* What has he done? He's a loyal Party member and a hard worker. He would never betray the Party!"

"Regina—"

"My Edik is a model Soviet, Comrade Krajnik!" she continued to plead. "He's a good man and a very important officer. He was transfer-ring to Moscow so that we could be together after the baby comes. He never tries to go to church, and he never speaks with revolutionaries or kulaks. In fact"—here Regina leaned desperately toward the man in front of her—"he's even assisted the Party in identifying revolutionaries and sympathizers! He even denounced his own parents as enemies!" Here Regina broke down and sobbed, and her thin hands flew to cover the shame of her tears. "He—is—a model—Soviet . . ."

"Regina," Roman Krajnik moved to comfort her. "I don't know all the particulars of his arrest—only that it happened five days ago—"

"Where *is* he?" she cried. "Oh, please tell me where he is, so that I might visit him! He couldn't possibly have betrayed the Party! It is all a big mistake."

"I'm sure there's been a mistake," Krajnik soothed.

She felt hope then. "So there will be an investigation? You will order one? You'll discover why this mistake happened?"

Krajnik patted her hand. "If an investigation is warranted, I'll certainly order one."

"Do you promise? Promise me!"

Krajnik's brow furrowed. "Do you doubt my sincerity?"

"No! I do not doubt you'll do all you can—" Regina's eyes widened, and she leaned forward. "You can influence the police! Oh, this is good!"

"Regina, it's not that simple." Krajnik shook his head. "It would be unethical for me to use my position, as head of the MGB . . ." He sighed. "It takes time, investigation, cooperation with the arresting authorities in Kirov. And it takes paperwork. Mountains of paperwork! It may take a few weeks. Or months."

"Months!" Regina could hardly contain herself. "But the baby will be here soon—and I need Edik here with me."

"And in the meantime there are things you can do to keep him safe and help expedite his return."

Suddenly Regina stilled. She studied her hands and thought about Krajnik's words. Finally she looked up and said carefully, "What kinds of things?"

"Eat healthy food, take care of yourself and your baby. Work hard. No matter what your work assignment, work hard! Continue to be a good Soviet—like you know your husband is—and protect the safety of the Soviet Republic. Watch for those who might undermine the Party's goals and the Party's authority."

Regina's insides tied themselves into knots. She knew what would come next.

Krajnik seemed to sense her foreboding. He lifted both hands, palms up, and gave her an apologetic smile. "These are dangerous times. We're surrounded by kulak enemies and traitors. Ever since the war there's been an influx of foreigners who unfortunately are Soviets by birth but whose hearts and minds are corrupted by Western ideals. Who knows which are friend and which are foe?"

Regina felt numb. "You want me to inform on Natalya Ivanovna Karagodina."

"I've always known you were intelligent." He smiled. "Yes. To put it as bluntly as you have, we are interested in the American repatriate Natalya Ivanovna."

Regina closed her eyes, dismayed.

"Regina, it is not as bad as you think. I have the responsibility of deciding who in our city poses a risk. Often that decision has to be made free of encumbering feelings of family, devotion, or friendship. It's a most difficult task—how I wish every woman who denounces her friend, her mother, or her husband could receive the Order of the Red Star for her courage!"

"She is my friend. I'm not comfortable doing what you ask."

"And you'll continue to be her friend. That won't change. In fact, by telling us of any subversive ideas she may have, you'll be showing her a truer, purer friendship!"

"I don't want to harm her."

"My dear Regina, of course you don't," he purred. "Neither do we. Any harm can be minimized if you keep us informed of her opinions, her feelings, and her ideals. Her well-being depends upon swift correction of Western-influenced misdeeds. Don't you agree, Regina Igorevna, that a friend is worth molding into a model citizen and future member of the Party?"

The implication was clear: In order to protect her husband, she was required to betray her friend. But she convinced herself that soon the investigation that Krajnik was promising would be completed and

Edik would be released. And then, Krajnik would no longer require this thing of her.

She could talk to Krajnik without harming Natalya. She would be careful what she revealed about her friend, and maybe, as Krajnik said, it would all be in Natalya's best interest. Besides, Lieutenant Rostov had influence with Krajnik, and Lieutenant Rostov wouldn't let any harm come to Natalya . . .

"I'll do it," she whispered, and instantly she felt like a traitor.

"Good for you." Krajnik rose to his feet. "I knew we could count on you. I'll request that you be brought to my office once a week."

Once a week? Regina was dismayed. "I may find nothing to report."

He smiled at her as a teacher might dote on a student. "It doesn't matter. I'll always be happy to see you—and I'll send any information concerning the status of your husband's imprisonment directly to Doktor Komarov at the hospital. He'll immediately communicate that information to you. I'm positive it will be a restful, positive experience for you and me to spend time together each week. We can talk of your papa. We can discuss your baby's future and your position at the hospital. And we can discuss your friendship with Natalya Ivanovna Karagodina. You'll grow to welcome the respite and the conversation, I'm certain."

"And you will order an investigation into my husband's arrest." Regina wanted to make sure there was no misunderstanding.

"Of course I will."

She felt like dissolving into desperate tears, but she forced herself to say, "*Spaciba bolshoye,* Comrade. Thank you, thank you."

"You take good care of yourself, Regina Igorevna."

"Yes, sir." She hesitated. "Please . . ."

He waited for her to continue, and for a fraction of a moment she thought she saw irritation in his eyes.

"Please, Comrade—tell me where my Edik is."

"Regina, it's not my place to—"

"I must see him! I can't imagine not knowing where he is."

He sighed. "You tell me about Natalya Ivanovna, and I'll find out where he is."

* * *

Regina and Natalie worked together to stabilize an anesthetized accident victim, disinfecting, cleaning, and wrapping until the unfortunate man looked like an Egyptian mummy. Despite the severity of the victim's wounds, Regina could hardly concentrate on the task. Her heart was still in shock at the horrible news Krajnik had given her, and the thought that she'd agreed to betray her American friend in order to protect Edik added to her agony.

She tried to justify it: She knew things like this were expected of all good Party members; why should she be any exception? Besides, if a simple weekly conversation with her papa's friend was all it took to keep her husband safe and warm, what price was that to pay?

"Regina?" Natalie eyed Regina across the unlucky patient. "What's wrong?"

Regina's lips pursed and she shook her head. She fought back tears and felt even worse for her betrayal. She wasn't used to people caring how she felt.

"Regina. Tell me."

Suddenly Regina could no longer control her pain. She dropped the cloth and reached for the nearest chair. "Have you ever . . . felt"—Regina could hardly speak—"like . . . like the breath was being strangled out of you . . . ?"

"Regina, what is it? What's the matter?" Natalie moved to her side.

Regina gasped, heaving dry sobs so quickly that she felt light-headed. "Oh, Natalya!" She sobbed her friend's name and then could not continue for several moments. "He's going to die there! He is going to die!"

"What are you talking about?" Natalie grabbed her shoulders to still her. "Stop this, Regina. You're making yourself sick. He's only a patient—and even though his wounds are severe we have a good chance of—"

"Nyet!" Fresh sobs shook Regina. "My *husband!* My husband has been arrested . . ." She couldn't continue.

Natalie sank to her knees beside her chair, her face revealing her shock at Regina's announcement.

"Edik's been arrested?" She was stunned. "What did he do?"

"I don't know! Oh, he wouldn't tell me!"

"Who wouldn't tell you? Edik wouldn't tell you why he was arrested?"

"No—oh, no!" And then in a torrent of tears she told Natalie about her compulsory visit to MGB headquarters and about Roman Krajnik's announcement. "And he wouldn't even tell me where my Edik is being held!"

Natalie stared at her. "What are you going to do?"

Regina bit her tongue and couldn't answer, fearful that in her agony she would accidentally give away the awful agreement she'd made with Krajnik.

"Lieutenant Rostov will know what to do," Natalie said with conviction. "I'll ask him to find out where your husband is being held. I think . . ." Natalie hesitated, and then lifted her chin. "I know he'll do it—for me."

"No!" Regina imagined Krajnik discovering what Natalya had done. "I will find out." She couldn't meet her friend's gaze. "Somehow."

TWELVE

Regina Igorevna entered the small observation room. She moved forward until she stood inches from the glass window. Her eyes scanned the crowded room beyond the glass, searching for the one individual she knew. The room was filled to overflowing with beds of patients. A few slept peacefully on their own, while others had been strapped down to their beds. Several of the room's residents pushed at the rusty wheels of their chairs, maneuvering awkwardly in the spaces between the beds. Others sat silently at the edges of the room, some staring out the windows and others staring at their hands.

She watched as a nurse prepared an injection for a patient. Another emptied bedpans into a filthy bucket. A nursing student fed a patient who'd been strapped to his bed, forcing thick porridge between his clenched teeth. Most of it oozed down his cheek, across his neck, and onto the mattress.

Regina shuddered. Nurses assigned to Dr. Komarov's psychiatric ward talked little about their experiences, except to express a desire to be reassigned. Regina was exactly the opposite; she wished Dr. Komarov would reconsider his denial of her application and allow her to work for him. Because somewhere in the space beyond the glass lived her papa.

Igor Nikolayevich Sushin had been director of Moscow's branch of the MGB. And then, one day, Roman Krajnik moved behind Igor

Sushin's desk and Sushin moved behind this glass. Regina didn't understand why her intelligent papa had suddenly lost his ability to reason. She hadn't observed the transformation Krajnik claimed to have seen. But thank goodness Krajnik had been there to temporarily take over Sushin's position; Regina was certain the MGB was in good hands with Roman Krajnik—hands that had been trained by Sushin himself.

"You have been neglecting your visits with Comrade Krajnik."

She whirled and saw Dr. Komarov standing at her elbow. His gaze was also fixed on the scene beyond the glass. She felt a return of the discomfort that always overwhelmed her in his presence. She would have more success avoiding him if his permission were not required to see her father.

"Why haven't you been talking to him?"

"Comrade Krajnik?" She couldn't explain the desire to cringe that Komarov's proximity always educed.

"Comrade Krajnik called me. He said you have been neglecting—"

"I can't do it," she blurted, and then she stopped herself. She amended her answer. "I don't have anything to tell."

"My dear Regina." Komarov's voice was anything but pleasant. "It is not just a matter of telling. It is a matter of obedience. Krajnik said to go. Every week. So you go every week."

"Yes, sir." She felt like a small, errant child. She lowered her eyes.

"No need to worry." Komarov took her hand in his and patted it. "You're doing your friend a favor. She will thank you someday. You will see." He glanced again at the window. "Do you see him?"

She retrieved her hand. "No. Is he all right?"

"No improvement, unfortunately."

"Why do I get turned away whenever I try to see him?"

Komarov studied her carefully. "You should let him heal. He needs rest—"

"He needs to get out of this awful place!" she shot back without thinking. She was shocked at what she had just said, and she feared Komarov's retaliation.

But he only moved to a door that opened into the room beyond the glass. "I'll find him for you." He walked into the room.

He caught her attention a few minutes later and pointed in the direction of a far window. Regina entered the room and walked in the direction Komarov pointed.

The smell of ammonia and alcohol, human waste and unwashed flesh, was almost more than she could take. She focused on the purpose of her visit and tried to block out the depressing sights, sounds, and smells around her.

She was upset by how much Igor Sushin had changed since her last visit. He sat with his shoulders drooped forward and his hands moving on the blanket over his lap. His head was turned away from her, but the flesh of his neck and jaw seemed to have aged many years since she'd last seen him. His thinning, colorless hair had been recently combed, and on his lap lay a clean blanket. Regina watched as the man's ancient-looking hands worked at each other, rubbing frail skin back and forth over bony knuckles. His gray eyes focused outside the window.

"Hello, Papa—it's me, Regina."

There was a long moment of nothing, and then his face turned, ever so slowly. She smiled at him, gratified to see a flicker of something behind the watery eyes. If she looked closely, maybe she would catch a glimmer of the old man's former self. She reached to touch the hands, and they stilled in his lap. She said, "I came to see how you're doing today."

Igor Sushin did not respond, but the eyes watched her steadily. His hands remained still under her touch.

"I have sad news, Papa." Regina patted his hand. "Comrade Krajnik told me a month ago that my husband"—her voice caught—"my Edik was arrested. Can you believe it? He was serving the Motherland as a political officer, and they arrested him as if he were an enemy." She took a deep breath. "I know it's all a big mistake, Papa. Lieutenant Rostov found out for me that he's been transferred here to Lubyanka prison—I've tried several times to go see him—but they always tell me he's not allowed to see me. It really hurts, Papa, because I want him to see how well I am—and that his baby is growing . . . and healthy . . ."

She quickly wiped at a tear, not wanting her papa to see her cry. "You could make things right again if you'd get better. Doktor Komarov said there's little hope of that—but I trust you, Papa. You're a strong man and I know you'll come back."

She rubbed the thin, spotted flesh between her hands, feeling the sharp bones underneath the skin. "I wish I knew what happened to you, Papa—one day you're fine and the next you're here. Comrade Krajnik sends his regards, by the way. He's taking care of your post until you can return . . ."

Sushin's gaze wavered slightly, as if he wanted to respond. The hands under hers began again to move, wringing each other.

She hastened to assure him. "It's all right, Papa—Comrade Krajnik has learned a lot from you. He'll take good care of your position until you feel well enough to return." She smiled at him. "He said that he'll look into the arrest of my Edik. He said it's all a big mistake, and that it can be straightened out soon. And Papa . . ." Regina inched closer. "He's given me a chance to help protect my husband from harm: Comrade Krajnik has agreed to try to get him released if I tell him about my friend from America . . ."

The distress in the old man's eyes was discernable now, and the hands would not be placated.

"Papa—what is it?"

He wouldn't take his eyes off her, as if with his look he might relate something of momentous importance. Regina wished he would open his mouth to speak it. But her papa remained silent, and her touch would not soothe the restless hands.

She heard footsteps and turned to see Komarov approaching with two of his orderlies. He told her it was time for her to leave. His attendants immediately removed Sushin, although the man's eyes searched her out one last time before he was whisked away.

THIRTEEN

Natalie had come to expect Viktor's presence at the hospital at least once a week. "Doktor's orders," Dr. Vlasov said with a wink when she questioned the necessity. She had also become accustomed to being the one called to care for him.

On this chilly Friday in October she entered Viktor's room with a steaming bowl of porridge and a pot of tea. She placed both on a small table and muscled the table over to the side of Viktor's bed. He captured her hand in his.

"Lieutenant, no."

"Viktor."

"No, *Viktor.*"

He didn't release her. "I need to know you're all right."

She didn't look at him. "I'm all right."

"Are you eating well?"

"The cook feeds us sometimes." If he was in a good mood.

"Are you warm? The winter will be very cold."

"I'll get by."

"I'll have Regina bring you a pair of *valenki,* good Russian boots. For the snow. And a *shapka-ushanka.* That will protect your head better than that scarf you wear. Do you like rabbits' fur?"

"I can get my own boots and hat."

"I want to help you. I want you to be happy."

Her hand convulsed in his. "Then let me go home."

He released her and she escaped from the room. She forced her eyes to stay dry as she passed the nurses' station, where Olga the head nurse stood, hands on hips, flirting with one of the doctors. She gave Natalie a baleful glare as the American passed. Natalie ignored her and made a beeline for the supply closet.

She slipped inside, closed the door, and leaned against it, struggling with her emotions as she took deep breaths that smelled of mothballs, antiseptic, and mold. Her hand clutched the door handle and her shoulders rubbed against the rough wood. She focused on breathing deeply, evenly. She heard a heavy scuffle in a dark corner and shuddered. Rats in Moscow were as plentiful as cockroaches.

She felt a wave of nausea, but it was difficult to determine if it was because of hunger or disorientation. She found herself thinking of Hans, and suddenly her hunger and the anguish, desperation, and terror of her predicament overwhelmed her, and she stumbled, grabbed for something to hold on to, and fell into a heap against the legs of a supply shelf.

She felt like she was spiraling downward in slow, lazy circles. And strangely enough, the feeling was not uncomfortable. Here she didn't have to communicate with Rostov or strain to see Hans Brenner on every street corner and in every passing face. Here she did not have to fear the future . . .

The door opened and footsteps entered the room. There was a moment of silence, and then a light bulb clicked on. Natalie thought her eyes had been closed. She squeezed them shut now and wished she were dead.

Regina stood in the center of the room. She said nothing at first, and then she crouched next to Natalie. "What are you doing on the floor?"

Natalie struggled against her nausea and pulled herself to her knees. Her voice was barely more than a whisper. "Izvinitye—I'm sorry you found me like this . . ."

"Why are you like this?"

"I came for . . . I—I fell . . ."

Regina whispered, "Have you eaten anything today?"

Natalie shook her head.

"You're weak from hunger. It could happen to anyone."

"But do you see anyone else crawling about the floor like a rodent?" Natalie grasped the edge of a shelf and rose carefully to her feet. Her legs were like rubber and she felt like a fool.

"Sometimes I am so tired, I wish to do the same." Regina put her arm about Natalie's shoulders. "But Olga would tell Dr. Komarov that I am a burden and I would lose my job. She is already complaining that my pregnancy is irresponsible and inconvenient."

"Irresponsible?" Natalie was incredulous.

"Because my husband has been named an enemy of the People—locked away while I continue to insist that I want to be a mother. She claims it makes me slow and stupid. I wouldn't be surprised if Olga demotes me just because of my expanding waistline!"

"I can't imagine why anyone could dislike a baby so."

"It is the way things are. To be pregnant is a sign of weakness and irresponsibility. To actually look forward to a baby is the height of self-ishness. To want another mouth to feed when there is so little for every-one else is almost disloyal." Regina reached for a towel and handed it to Natalie, smiling faintly. "Do you want to know why I think Olga dislikes you so?"

Natalie wiped her face with the towel and sniffed.

Regina leaned close and whispered, "I think she's jealous of your benefactor."

"Viktor?"

"You have a powerful friend, Natalya, and Olga resents that," Regina explained. "She knows it was the lieutenant who got you this position. You have no idea how lucky you are. Many of the nurses would give anything to have Viktor Rostov as a benefactor." Regina's voice softened. "Viktor Rostov is a good man, Natalya. You'd be safe with him. You'd have plenty to eat, a warm bed, and the best assign-ments. You're foolish to think ill of a man like Rostov." Natalie felt Regina's gentle hand on her arm. "You're naïve, Natalya. And you won't survive if you're not willing to do what it takes to protect yourself. No one can help you but *you*." Regina turned to walk away. Then she hesi-tated and turned back toward Natalie. "Olga doesn't hate my baby, as it seems. She only protects herself, as do all Soviet women."

"From what?"

"From the horror of loving a baby too much." Regina turned and walked away.

Stunned at her words, Natalie silently watched her go.

FOURTEEN

Monday, November 4, 1946

At a quarter to six, the four quarter bells of the clock tower played the customary "Westminster Quarters." The chimes reverberated from the confines of the tower, ringing out across the Thames, Charing Cross Road, Buckingham Palace, and out across London, reaching over four miles as the crow flies—farther, because of water's transmission qualities, if the proverbial crow happened to be flying along the river. The bells played their sequence again twenty-five seconds before Big Ben chimed the morning hour, its repaired crack causing a strange *twang* that had become the huge bell's trademark. Sleeping pigeons started, lifted from their perches, and then settled back again.

Four and a half miles to the east a man stood waiting on the bank of the Thames. He heard Big Ben announce six o'clock and used a penlight to check his watch. He walked to his new Jeep CJ civilian All-Terrain Vehicle and slipped behind the wheel.

He pulled away from the river and headed north, and his headlights illuminated the irregular surface of the road as the sounds of Big Ben faded away. He drove past stubble of last year's crops rotting in the fields. He drove his vehicle through Epping Forest, heavy with early-morning frost, until the city lay far behind and the darkness of the forest canopy finally interfered with the sky.

The Jeep slowed, pulled across a bramble-choked path, and then traveled deep into the underbrush. Finally the driver switched off the lights, shut off the engine, and waited.

Satisfied that he was alone, he opened the door and slid from his seat, pulled on a heavy sweater against the chill, and zipped it up to his chin. His breath came in white clouds as he pulled a knitted cap over his hair, folding its hem across his forehead and ears. He donned leather gloves and pulled a pack from the backseat. He slung it across his shoulder, switched on a torch, and began to walk toward a distant, almost imperceptible sound. His feet carried him up an embankment plastered with beechnut and autumn leaves, and there was a strange awkwardness to his step, as if one leg didn't function as well as the other. He slowed in order to move in the most abject silence, one gloved hand on his pack and the other, with his torch, poised to steady himself against the rough terrain, always ready to silence underbrush or rest against a tree trunk. Slowly, steadily, he moved toward the sound.

He saw the fire's glow first, before he saw human shapes, twenty— no, thirty or more—clustered around a dying campfire. He positioned himself in the cold shadow of an oak just out of reach of the fire's warmth. He pulled newfangled night vision goggles from his pack and watched closely, listening to what was being said.

Two figures stood facing the crowd and one raised his hand, his salute immediately mirrored by the others. The man's voice carried across the clearing. *"Heil Hitler!"*

The words received an enthusiastic repeat from the crowd.

The other man spoke. "The conquerors want us to believe that the Reich is dead. The Allies have driven us, captured us, imprisoned us"—at each accusation the assembly rumbled its approval—"tortured us, bullied us." The speaker stepped toward the crowd, and the man hidden in the trees saw the uniform of a Nazi major. "I, myself, was captured, tried, and sentenced by a war tribunal—even though I'd only been following orders."

The crowd was becoming restless, and the speaker fed the crowd on its own frenzy. "We're survivors, my fellow countrymen. Survivors! We are the ones who'll make this dream a reality. We are the ones who'll resurrect the vision of our Führer and bring the Fatherland to the heights of its power!"

"In the name of the Führer!"

"We'll make Germany strong again!"

"In the name of the Führer!"

"We'll annihilate our foe and again raise the flag of our nation!"

"In the name of the Führer!"

The intruder stood still as a statue under the cover of trees, binoculars to his eyes. His attention remained riveted to the speaker, and his hands on the goggles never wavered.

* * *

Rolf finished his speech and separated himself from the crowd. He shook the hand of the meeting's organizer and walked away from the bonfire.

He entered the cover of the trees. He paused, listening for several moments to the awakening sounds of the forest. He heard nothing out of the ordinary. He reached his vehicle, covered his Nazi uniform with a nondescript overcoat, and headed for home. It would do no good for him to be followed, he knew, and he kept his eyes on the rearview mirror.

As the sun rose, he drove toward London. He soon noticed a Jeep following, and he altered course. He negotiated London's increasing morning traffic with the vehicle stubbornly on his tail until a series of maneuvers and one hazardous U-turn brought his car opposite the Jeep. Before he sped away, Rolf saw the face behind the wheel.

The Jeep did not follow. But Rolf felt the prickling of a disturbing memory relating to that face—a memory that played at the edges of his consciousness but refused to come forward and introduce itself. So he was extra careful to make sure he was not followed as he continued his journey home. Finally he pulled his car into the barn behind his cottage and climbed the steps to the house. He walked through a tiny living room, removed his overcoat, threw it over the back of a chair, and walked toward the nearest bedroom.

In the doorway he removed his uniform jacket as his eyes studied the still form on the bed. Seven-year-old Alma lay sprawled with his head where his feet should be, his arms over the edge of the bed, and his comforter in a heap on the wooden floor. Affection for his son swelled in Rolf's chest. He moved to the second bedroom, aware that his love for the person who lay in this room was just as strong as his affection for his son. He approached the bed, leaned to kiss the woman's cheek, and caressed the dark curls that fell about her face and neck.

Her eyes stayed closed but her arms came up to wrap around his neck. "Where have you been?" she whispered, and the warmth of her breath made his heart race. "I've been here all alone . . ."

He sat on the edge of the bed, returning her embrace. "I went for a drive. Out toward Great Monk Wood."

"Epping Forest?" Marie Schulmann finally opened her eyes, and Rolf read understanding in their doe-brown depths. "The rally?"

"That's right."

She studied him and finally nodded. "I see. I'm glad you're safe."

"I'll always come back to you." He kissed her forehead. "And—I won't ever betray you. You understand that, don't you?"

"Come back to me now," she whispered, muffled against his neck.

"I have to go to work." His voice hinted at the injustice of it.

"So all of this is just 'good-bye'?"

"No. I'm not here to tell you good-bye."

"You would leave without telling me good-bye?"

"There already have been too many good-byes." He kissed her deeply. "I'll never tell you good-bye again."

"But you're going to work, Rolf. You've got to say something to me before you leave for work. So what will you say?"

"I'll say, 'I'll see you at seven.'"

"Seven?"

He nodded. "This isn't good-bye. I'll see you in a matter of hours."

"All right."

"What are you doing today?"

She shifted her body upward and leaned against the headboard. "There's no school today, so I'm taking your son to Buckingham Palace at eleven. Then we're going to mail the letter Alma wrote to his aunt Berta in Germany—addressed to the dry cleaning place, of course. Then we'll find the nearest market, buy whatever dinner items we can carry in the basket of our bicycle, and then return home to organize our ridiculously large pantry." She smiled.

"Do you like the house?"

She nodded. "Seems almost criminal, all this luxury, after what we've been through."

He grinned. "Perhaps we can have lice imported from Ravensbrück and barbed wire from Sachsenhausen. Maybe the camp cook would agree to work for us."

She swatted him with a pillow. "I think I can get used to it, Rolf Schulmann."

"Charles. My name is *Charles Goodwin,* remember?"

"I married a man named Rolf Schulmann. Almost six months ago. I distinctly remember his name was Rolf Schulmann. I was at the wedding, remember?"

"Then you're in the wrong bed, madam, because I'm Charles Goodwin." He pulled her close. "Now how am I supposed to get to work on time? If I'm late they'll fire me."

"No they won't. Matthews arranged this job for you and he likes you. Remember what you did for his daughter?"

"You mean, not breaking her husband's legs during the war?" Rolf kissed her neck. "I'll miss you today, Mary Goodwin. You and Alma."

"You mean Charlie, don't you?"

"You and Charlie. I'll miss you both. Don't answer the phone while I'm gone."

"Why do we even have a phone, if I'm not supposed to answer it?"

"Matthews might need to contact me."

"Matthews doesn't need to call here. You've got a phone at your desk, don't you?"

"Matthews isn't going to call me at work."

"Rolf?"

"Yes, Mrs. Goodwin?"

"Do you know I love you?"

"Do you love Charles, too?" Rolf feigned hurt.

"With all my heart. Now go to work."

"I don't want to go to work anymore." He buried his face in her hair, breathing in deeply.

"You'll watch the changing of the guard with us, then?"

"I'd love to. I wish I could. And I love *you*, Marie Schulmann. I'll see you at seven." He finally pulled away and stood.

He could feel her eyes follow him as he moved to the door. He hesitated, his hand on the doorknob, and then he said quietly, "Marie?" He felt a curious lump forming at the base of his throat. "This is going to sound crazy, but I want for you and Alma to do something for me. Right away."

"Of course. What?"

He took a deep breath. "Pack a bag, with shoes, clothing, money, a few food items, a little water—"

Marie rose and moved to him. "What is it, Rolf?"

"And I'll take it to the airport. I'll buy tickets for the two of you. To France. I'll leave them with your luggage. I'll rent a storage box—"

"Rolf." She laid a hand on his chest. "What is it?"

"No more than a feeling." The lump in his throat solidified into a knot. "Would your father mind if . . . ?"

"Of course not. He would welcome us with open arms. All right, Rolf, I'll take care of that today."

Relieved, he pulled her close and kissed her again.

"Still no 'good-bye'?" she teased softly.

"I can't bring myself to say it."

"God bless you, Rolf Schulmann, till you return home to us."

He drove a different route than he'd taken the previous day, the face from the Jeep still fresh in his mind. He thought about Marie as he passed Big Ben and crossed the Thames. He thought about that first meeting in a tiny French café. She had been terrified, he could tell, but she had tried so hard to follow her training. He thought about the night in the mountains when he finally apprehended her, and of the devastating loss of his friend Félix Larouche. It was too painful a memory for him to dwell on too long, and his mind moved to other things: Marie's escape from the Gestapo, her protection of Rolf's son, Alma, and the final, heart-wrenching sight of Marie at Ravensbrück.

Rolf pulled into the parking lot, entered the building through the back door, and took the stairs two at a time to his office. His secretary was not at her desk, but there was a pile of mail for him. He took it and closed himself in his office.

He selected a letter from a dry cleaning establishment. He opened it and read, "The manager has a question about your silk shirts." He folded and pocketed the letter, then tossed the empty envelope back on the pile.

His secretary arrived in the outer office. Aged in her midforties, she'd weathered the war in London and had emerged at the other end dry as a dead cornstalk. She yawned, dropped her purse onto her chair, and wandered into a tiny lounge where she plugged in a hot plate and began to prepare a teakettle.

Rolf reached for his rain jacket and gloves. "Beatrice," he said as he walked toward the outer door with his gloves in his hands, "I'm headed to the cleaner's. I'll need you to dictate a letter for me when I return."

Beatrice raised her hand and waved him to silence. "Leave it to me, Mr. Goodwin, leave it to me."

"Oh, and Beatrice? Tell Ronald I'm taking a few hours off. Turns out there's a family emergency: I've decided I need to watch the changing of the guard with Mary and our son."

FIFTEEN

Rolf walked out of the office, down the stairs, and onto the street. Rain fell in insistent, freezing waves, lightly bouncing off his hat. He walked past Belvedere Road and out toward the Thames. He took a double-decker bus across the river at Westminster Bridge Road and continued past Buckingham Palace. He descended two stops past Hyde Park Corner and entered a park. He began to stroll, turning after forty paces and retracing his steps toward the bus stop.

He paused under the bare branches of a cherry tree next to another pedestrian hunched against the rain.

The man hissed, "No name, understand? No name."

Rolf turned and acknowledged his contact with a nod. His contact was trim, young, and well dressed. He sported the blond beginnings of a goatee. The unobservant may have mistaken him for a recent Cambridge graduate, although he lacked a certain refinement, as if he was only playing dress-up with an older brother's clothes. Rolf wondered if maybe this man might not be a bit of an error in judgment on Matthews's part; something about him made it obvious he was an undercover agent—perhaps he battled an ego that made it difficult to entirely blend in.

The man nodded in the direction of a panhandler shuffling toward the bus stop. "I want t' help 'em," he lamented. "I really do. But who knows what the blokes'll do with it once I give it to 'em? Booze, more'n likely. Booze. What's the world comin' to, I ask ya? What's it comin' to?"

Rolf reached for a low hanging branch. "You have something for me?"

"A message. And a request."

"Which do I want first?"

"The request. Matthews wants you to tone it down a bit."

"Tone it down? Tone what down?"

"The Nazi thing. He says you're gonna get yourself killed. Someone's after ya."

"I know someone's after me. Matthews gave me a specific assignment. What's he doing—dismissing me?"

"Nah. But 'e thinks someone's got your number. Seems the Soviet Union, France, and Scotland Yard's got Nazi hunters out sniffin' for anything stinkin' of Nazi—and they're offering the tsar's gold and the queen's crown jewels for any catch resultin' in a conviction. So unless you've got a death wish, keep away from those Fourth Reich blokes—at least till Matthews gives the 'all's clear.'"

"Tell Matthews I'm close to what he wants. Tell him—"

"Tell 'im yourself! What d'ya think I am? You're gonna get yourself killed, I say—killed!" The man spat toward the filthy gutter. "And that nice family of yours deported."

"I'm almost finished."

The man shrugged. "Suit yourself. It's your 'ide they'll be 'angin' out t' dry, not mine. Besides, what do I care? I'm just the messenger boy." Another spit. "If ya want my advice, though, you're lookin' for—"

"You said you also had a message?" Rolf interrupted.

"That's right, 'cause I'm just a messenger boy, right? Nothin' I say makes a dollop o' difference."

"What's the message?"

"Matthews says to tell ya 'e now 'as a position—whatever that means." The man snapped a twig and chewed thoughtfully on the end of it. "Wanted ya to know your friend—the German bloke—isn't as dead as the Soviets are sayin'. Says they 'ave confirmation 'e's in the USSR."

Rolf felt his spirits soar. Hans was still alive. Hans was living a nightmare, but he was still alive. Rolf forced himself to hide his joy from his cynical contact. "Nemesis got the upper hand after all, I see," Rolf mumbled, and he shook his head. "Tell Matthews I got the message. And I'll watch my back. That should satisfy him."

His contact grunted around the twig and glanced across the park at an arriving bus. "This one's mine." He frowned at Rolf. "Ya don't look German—got that much in your favor. But they catch ya spy'n at the rallies and you're hog slop. Got it? Hog slop. Take care, Goodwin; I'm beginning to like you. I'd hate t' see ya dragged off to Nuremburg—or *worse* . . ." He tossed aside the twig, spit, and walked away. Suddenly he stopped. "Want my advice? Grow out your 'air a bit—get rid o' that military cut. Grow a mustache. Put on a bit o' stones 'round the middle. Right, then, that's everything I got for ya, understand?" He walked away.

For a few seconds Rolf didn't move, although he knew it was dangerous to linger after a meeting. Matthews was still working on Hans's case, which meant Matthews was still behind Rolf's plans.

What plans? Rolf berated himself. The fact was, Natalie and Hans had disappeared in May. It was now November and their good friend Rolf Schulmann had no plan.

Marie had told him about Lieutenant Rostov. She had described in detail Major Matthews's efforts to rescue Hans and Natalie from Rostov while Rolf had been on trial in France. And Matthews himself had described his own twisted relationship with the Russian officer— how Viktor Rostov had once been Matthews's friend—how they had worked together on plans to rebuild a shattered Europe. And then, something had changed.

Lieutenant Rostov received a new assignment from Stalin. He was ordered to capture enemy scientists to assist the Soviets in constructing a nuclear weapon. Before the war Hans Brenner had worked with the nuclear scientist Edwin von Hausen, and so when the Americans rescued von Hausen from Rostov, Rostov had turned his focus on Hans.

So Hans was in the Soviet Union. He probably didn't even know Natalie was gone. If he knew that Natalie was with Rostov in Moscow it would break his heart. Rolf knew what it was like to lose the one you love—and to worry that your loved one was suffering. When the Gestapo had captured Marie . . .

He could not think of it. It was still too painful, even after all this time. And the thought of Marie made him long to be with her, and suddenly the urge to tell Marie the latest news overwhelmed him. She would be at Buckingham Palace with Alma by now. He turned swiftly on his heel and headed back in the direction of the bus stop.

SIXTEEN

Monday, November 11, 1946

It wasn't so bad, the girl thought as another lash burned across her shoulders. She could handle this almost indefinitely if it meant that someday she would be allowed to see her papa again. She stared past dirty strings of blond hair at the slippery mud inches from her face.

"Get up, pig."

Lucya Rostova rose to her knees, her eyes downcast. She dared not look at the guard.

"Fill the bucket, citizen."

Lucya Viktorovna Rostova retrieved her bucket. Stone after stone found its way back into the bucket while the guard watched, his whip coiled and slapping impatiently at his leg. "Drop it again and I'll have you locked in the Hole."

She shuddered, and her work-roughened fingers began to shake.

"Stand up."

She stood, keeping her blue eyes lowered and her willowy frame as straight as the pain would allow. "Move." Her skeletal knees shook as she began to walk. But she didn't complain. She carried a weight that almost equaled her own because the guard's whip said she must. And she had to, because she feared solitary confinement even more than the guard's whip.

She inched forward, slipping on the muddy road as she found a place in the line of women. She didn't look back at the guard with the whip. She kept her eyes on the shoulders in front of her and her bucket steady. She couldn't stand upright with the weight of the bucket at such an awkward angle, but she ignored the sharp warning between her shoulder blades.

She was confident her papa would find her and save her. She *knew* he would. She knew he would never leave her to die in this place. That thought had comforted her more than once over the past few months, and it was almost enough to make her body strong—at least strong enough to carry her bucket from morning to night.

It wasn't so bad. Everything she'd experienced since her arrest she'd survived. It wasn't so bad, because she knew her papa was even now working to find where she had been transferred and have her released. She wasn't an enemy of the People. She wasn't a criminal. She wasn't a traitor to her country. Perhaps these other women were—but *she* wasn't. There'd been a mistake made at Lubyanka; she was *Lucya Viktorovna Rostova*. She was the daughter of Lieutenant Viktor Nikolayevich Rostov, a loyal Party member, an officer in the NKGB, and an ally to Comrade Stalin. Her papa would find a way to rescue her.

She dared not rest her bucket, and so she tried again to push away any thoughts of pain. Instead, she thought about Viktor Rostov. She hoped he would hurry. But until he came for her she would try to be brave. For his sake.

* * *

Rolf Schulmann picked up his letters from his desk. He pulled a single sheet from an envelope and read that his silk shirts were waiting for him at the cleaner's. He retrieved his hat and overcoat, said a few words to Beatrice, and slipped out of the office.

This time he took a bus away from the river, getting off a few minutes later and backtracking three blocks, taking side streets and alleys until he arrived at a dry goods store sixteen blocks from his office. He climbed to the third floor flat and entered without knocking.

The young man who greeted him did not seem surprised at his arrival. Without a word he led Rolf to a back room, where several long tables groaned under the weight of electronic equipment, radios, and typewriters. Half a dozen men and women sat with their backs to

Rolf, hunched over their respective stations and oblivious in their thick headsets. Their fingers flew, typing conversations and adjusting radio dials. There was little in the way of human sounds, only the rattle of typewriter keys and an occasional cough or scrape of a chair.

Rolf's escort walked to the farthest table and touched the shoulder of a scrawny young towhead. The young man practically jumped out of his skin before tearing off his headset and jumping to his feet.

Rolf's companion introduced the boy. "This is Private Harry Devlin. He's our newest recruit, from East Berlin. He's got a jump up on the Soviets, sir—was a radio operator in the Köpenick district until Lieutenant Rostov returned to Moscow. Knows how the Soviets breathe, if you catch my meaning."

"Is he the one Matthews sent to me?"

"Yes, sir."

Rolf addressed the boy. "What is it you have for me, young man?"

Devlin cleared his throat. "Got an intercept from Moscow, sir— has to do with that business with Lieutenant Viktor Rostov."

Rolf nodded. "You speak Russian?"

"Yes, sir." The boy looked pleased.

"And you're Irish?"

"Yes, sir. My father was an Irish diplomat assigned to Moscow. My mother was Russian."

"So, you have dual citizenship?"

"Yes, sir."

"What makes you exempt from the Yalta Conference ruling that forces all Soviet citizens to return home?

The boy grinned. "They'd have to catch me first, sir."

Rolf nodded. "So you escaped East Berlin."

"With Major Matthews's assistance, sir."

"Very well." Rolf was satisfied. "What have you found out for me, Private Devlin?"

SEVENTEEN

Wednesday, November 13, 1946

"Rolf Schulmann!" Major Matthews took Rolf's hand firmly in his own. "How healthy you look! Life in Great Britain has continued to be good for you. And how is the missus? I assume the two of you are safe and doing well?"

"As safe and well as we can be, considering whom I work for." Rolf cracked a grin.

Matthews nodded. "Good, good. How's your little boy?"

"Great. He enjoys the opportunity to go to a *real* school—that's what he calls it—after being tutored for so many years by his aunt Berta and Marie." Rolf saw the question in the major's eyes and he nodded. "His teachers think he's adopted and we're from Chicago."

"As it needs to be. Excellent." Matthews indicated a seat for Rolf. Rolf sat and laid his briefcase across his legs. Matthews took a chair behind his desk, brushed aside a pile of files, and leaned forward, his hands clasped in front of him on the desk's surface.

"I have that action list I promised you," Rolf began, "complete with names, ranks, organization—"

Matthews blinked. "Already?"

Rolf pulled a folder from his briefcase and tossed it onto Matthews's desk. "Their top leaders in Great Britain—including contact information, business addresses, names of wives, girlfriends, children, relatives, housekeepers, and the family dog. Oh, and I've also included a detailed list of Nazi contacts, meeting locations, maps, and tentative plans for future rallies. They're recruiting heavily right now in Ireland, Spain, Portugal, and as far away as Brazil. These names will get you in at their front door."

Matthews stared at the folder in front of him. "You have all of that here?"

"Everything you asked for, sir."

Matthews peered at him. "You have an escape plan for your family— just in case?"

"Yes, sir." Rolf shifted in his chair.

"Good." Matthews thumbed through the documents, paused at several, and then swore softly. "You got Harijs Svikeris for us. How in blazes did you manage Svikeris?"

"A bit of luck, I suppose. He was at the most recent rally—he actually shook my hand." Rolf raised his right hand with a wry grin.

"Svikeris alone is worth the risks of this operation. You know that, don't you?"

"I'm glad, sir."

"Well done, Rolf Schulmann. *Very* well done." Matthews leaned back into his chair. "Now, I know you well enough to know you've got something else on your mind."

Rolf leaned forward. "Natalie Allred."

"Ah, yes." Matthews rubbed his chin, and his eyes searched his desk. "I have an important correspondence here somewhere . . ."

"I have a plan, Major."

Matthews continued searching. "I've received a cable from Washington. I know it's here somewhere . . ."

"Major," Rolf said quietly, "just tell me what's wrong."

Matthews stopped searching. "The Central Intelligence Group has been reorganized. My assignment to the new Office of Special Operations is under review. Basically"—Matthews cleared his throat— "they're trying to determine if their operating budget covers my salary."

Rolf said carefully, "What are you trying to tell me?"

Matthews wouldn't look at him. "I've been told to 'let it go.'"

Rolf eyed him thoughtfully. "Let what go?"

"The Natalie Allred situation. Lieutenant Rostov."

Rolf was incredulous. "They want you to leave her in Moscow?"

"I've been ordered to tell you to cease and desist. Maybe they think our involvement will strain whatever relationship we still have with the Soviets."

Rolf couldn't think how to respond. The two officers studied each other in silence. Finally Matthews said, "I guess too many questions can get people killed."

Rolf flinched. "I can't imagine I've been careless."

"I'm only reminding you of the dangers involved in this line of work. Secrets need to remain secrets or someone inevitably dies. I guess Washington thinks *this* situation should remain a secret."

"And the sacrificial lamb in this case is Natalie Allred?"

Matthews's gaze wavered. "She's a Soviet citizen, Rolf. There's nothing I can do. I can't go after her." He turned his hands palms up, as if in surrender. "I'm not even supposed to talk with you about her."

"Can you talk to me about Lucya?"

"Lucya?" Matthews blinked. "Lieutenant Rostov's daughter? Lucya Rostova?"

Rolf inclined his head.

"Why?"

"Because you sent an agent to find her."

Matthews swore. "Who've you been interrogating behind my back?"

"Don't worry; it's just what I figured you'd do . . . in the eventuality that you needed a bargaining chip with Rostov."

"Why do you want to talk about her?"

"Because I have a strong feeling Hans Brenner and Natalie Allred are in danger."

Matthews hesitated. "What do Hans Brenner and Natalie Allred have to do with the lieutenant's daughter?"

Rolf reached for his briefcase. "Last week that new agent you sent to me intercepted a coded transmission from the Kremlin." He retrieved a file and handed it to Matthews.

Matthews opened it and read silently. He put the paper down and scowled at Rolf. "I don't see the connection."

"Between an order to transfer the daughter of an MGB officer to a transit camp in the east, and the order to move an unnamed nuclear scientist to a classified location?"

"I don't see the connection between the lieutenant's daughter and your friend."

"Maybe you should, Major Matthews—for the safety of your agent searching for Rostov's daughter." Rolf closed his briefcase. "Six months ago my associate Jacques Bellamont was wounded trying to save Natalie Allred from Rostov's men. He contacted you and informed you of the abduction, hoping you would get that information to me. We both know Hans was Rostov's ultimate target, and since Rostov knew Natalie's location, I had to assume Hans Brenner's whereabouts were no secret. You placed him in harm's way in order to get him into the heart of the Soviet nuclear program."

"That's quite an accusation, Schulmann."

Rolf indicated Private Devlin's intercept. "This states that Rostov's daughter is to be *transferred* instead of returned to him—in anticipation of the performance of a certain nuclear scientist on a classified project. This message gave me the answer I needed."

Matthews's brow knit and his fingers drummed the desk in slow, rhythmic unity. "You're treading dangerous ground, my friend; both with the Office of Special Operations and the MGB."

"So is Hans Brenner. So is Natalie Allred. So, unwittingly, is Lucya Rostova."

"All right. All right. Does Rostov suspect Hans's allegiance, do you suppose? Is that why he's holding Natalie hostage?"

"Not a chance." Rolf was vehement. "At least, not as long as Hans behaves. My wife insists Natalie is a personal interest for Rostov. I don't think there's any connection, other than Rostov's possessive desire for Natalie to stay in Moscow." Rolf furrowed his brow. "Although there *is* the possibility that the MGB suspects a connection between the American nurse and the German scientist."

"So to what classified location did they take Hans?"

Rolf shook his head. Private Devlin hadn't been able to intercept any answer to that question. He shifted uncomfortably in his seat. "Your exit strategy for Hans is no use if we don't know where he is, Major Matthews."

Matthews studied his desk and said nothing.

Rolf watched Matthews, then finally broke the silence. "You do plan to get him out, don't you?"

"I did . . ."

There was another uncomfortable silence. Rolf, growing more anxious, persisted. "Past tense?"

Matthews gave no reply.

"You've been ordered to leave *him* there, also?" Rolf felt anger prickle at the base of his throat. "That's a great way to repay Hans for the risk he's taking for you. Abandon him to the sharks and expect him to fend for himself."

"The OSO is not interested in sacrificing field agents," Matthews shot back. "I don't have a choice."

Rolf felt growing anger as a physical thing, crawling up his insides like a giant poisonous insect. He rose to his feet. Matthews slammed his fist into the table and also rose to his feet, his face flushing dark red. "Confound it, Rolf, what do you expect me to do? 'Cease and desist,' the order states. 'Cease and desist'! That means your friend is going to have to go it alone."

"And Natalie is supposed to grow old and die with the man who abducted her?"

Matthews scowled. "That's the law, confound it. That's the *law*. And those are my orders. There's nothing more I can do."

"Major Matthews." Rolf tried to contain his anger. He spoke carefully. "We're both fathers . . ."

"What's that got to do with Hans and Natalie?"

"Would you go after your daughter—if *she* were the one in Moscow instead of Natalie?"

Matthews flinched and dropped his eyes.

"I would do the same, if it were my son. I feel the same way about Hans Brenner and his fiancée as I would about my son, Alma."

"You can't save the world, Rolf Schulmann."

Rolf leaned forward, his face intent. "But I *can* save Natalie Allred. And Hans."

Matthews's anger slowly deflated. He sank back into his chair. "My orders are clear . . ."

"But *I* will go after them. Not you, not the OSO."

"Not if you want to keep your job, you won't. Not if you want the protection of the United States."

"Then prosecute me when they're safely home," Rolf challenged. "Until then, give me use of your agent—the one you sent to find Lucya Rostova. Tell me how to contact him." He took a deep breath. "You also mentioned Rostov had a contact in England; I want that contact's name. And then"—Rolf leaned toward his superior, his pulse pounding in his throat and his jaw set—"I'll meet with Lieutenant Rostov. And I'll appeal to the father that is concealed somewhere behind the Soviet officer's mask."

EIGHTEEN

Saturday, November 16, 1946

The sundry stenches of day-old fish, rotten cabbage, mold, and sewage assailed Rolf's senses. Waves lapped at the wharf and seagulls screamed through a thick fog. The cold, salty sea air was like sandpaper against his face, and thin drifts of snow were already melting into slush in the streets. Over the years ice had worked its way underneath the cobblestones and expanded the soil, pushing the street into precarious hills and valleys.

An occasional street lamp challenged the fog, but even then, the light cut only a few feet into the gloom. Few pedestrians braved the cold this time of night, and those that did hurried on their way with nothing on their minds but a warm destination and a cup of tea.

On the last street before the wharf, concrete steps lead to a basement haberdashery. The porch lamp had long since been extinguished, but through a small window near the door, light from an electric bulb cast a weak glow onto the steps. Rolf descended and knocked on the heavy wooden door. He didn't expect an immediate response—certainly the proprietor took offense at visitors at this late hour. It didn't matter. Rolf was positive the owner was inside—he'd followed him earlier that evening and watched him close up shop.

When his knock produced no results, Rolf tapped on the window glass with his keys. The outcome was as expected: The proprietor opened the door.

"You're going t' break my bloomin' window, gov'nah—so if ya don' mind." Rolf thought he looked like a miniature, wrinkled version of the American comedian Will Rogers. Except that the look in the man's eyes indicated little use for levity.

"Are you Connelly, of Connelly and Associates Fine Menswear and Shoes?"

"Who wants t' know?"

"My name is Goodwin—Charles Goodwin. I'm here about a personal matter."

"We're closed. Come back in the morning."

Rolf inserted his boot between the closing door and its frame. He pushed the door open. "You're open now, Mr. Connelly. I'm here for that suit of gabardine wool—the one made of fine Russian cotton fibers?"

Connelly stared at Rolf, and then he reached for the nearest armchair and lowered himself into it. Above his head a wooden crucifix shuddered on its nail as the cold night air filled the room.

Whoever would've thought, mused Rolf as he studied the shell-shocked form in front of him, *that this unpretentious man would be an agent of the Soviet Union?*

"Ya can't just force your way in 'ere at any bloomin' hour. I've got my rights, I do, and you've got no right bustin' in 'ere." His words carried little conviction, and he seemed on the verge of mental collapse. Rolf had said the right words.

"Tell me about Lieutenant Viktor Rostov."

"Who?"

"I'm going to need you to contact him for me. In a few days I'm going to have a very important message for him."

"I don't 'ave the slightest idea who you're talkin' about."

"Yes you do. You're going to be my link to Rostov."

"Ya work for Scotland Yard?" The man sounded dubious. "Ya sound like a bloomin' American t' me. I'm no traitor. I'm a loyal Brit—"

"Prove it," Rolf said kindly. "I'm in no mood for an arrest. But I know you work for the Soviets. I know about your connection to Rostov. Of course, the Soviets wouldn't trust you with the big, important stuff. But that's not going to make things any easier for you over at the Yard. I'm authorized to tell you that if you help me, you'll be allowed to keep your business"—Rolf's arm swept the small, musty room—"your freedom, and your life."

A long silence ensued. Finally the man asked, "In exchange for what?" He wouldn't look at Rolf.

"Any information the Soviets feed you, you'll pass on to me. When the time comes, help me contact Rostov."

For a long, agonizing moment, the man deliberated. The eyes darted from Rolf to the door, to Rolf, and back again to the door. Rolf could almost hear the mental gears turning as Connelly thought things through.

"Look, Connelly—you really have no choice."

Again the agonizing silence, and Rolf saw the turmoil in the man's eyes. He felt sorry for him.

"They'll kill me if they find out." It was little more than a whimper.

"We'll protect you. You have my word."

"An' what word is that?"

"The word of one Christian man to another."

Again Rolf endured the silence. Once in a while Connelly's eyes flickered, as if a shadow had passed over his thoughts.

"All right." The man's knuckles were white on his lap. "But Rostov returned to Moscow months ago."

"I know that. But you have a way to contact him—in case of emergency."

Connelly swallowed. "It's got t' be a very, very big emergency."

Rolf smiled. "Then when the time comes, let's make it a big one."

NINETEEN

Natalie and Regina typically ate meals together each day in the nurse's station, sharing their bread and whatever else they could scrounge. Natalie had become accustomed to the tedious hours of work, the marathon work weeks, and the lack of a day of rest. But it was hardest on Sundays, when she wished she could take time to at least *reminisce* about attending church and spending leisurely afternoons reading scriptures or visiting friends. Here she didn't dare even mention church, let alone God.

This Sunday, Regina didn't show, and Natalie went looking for her.

She found Regina on the floor of the bathroom, knee-deep in suds, with sleeves rolled above her elbows and her pregnant middle hanging low to the floor, wet with soapy water.

Regina looked up and gave her a tired smile. "Seems this hospital has more need of cleaning staff than nurses."

"Regina!"

"I've been reassigned." Regina leaned back on her knees and wiped at her face with the hand that held the sponge. "Every day from noon to midnight."

"To do this?" Natalie was incredulous. "They've got a dozen people to do this!"

Regina gave her a twisted grin. "Not any that can do it as well as me."

"This isn't right. Not for you or the baby." Natalie turned on her heel. "I'm gonna give Olga a piece of my mind."

"Doktor Komarov assigned me," Regina said quietly. "Not the head nurse."

Natalie stared at her. "He should know better!"

"It's okay, Natalya. Don't worry about it."

"I'm going to talk with him right now."

"Natalya . . . !"

Natalie found the psychiatrist in the corridor near his office. Before he could get to his usual pleasantries, Natalie exploded. "Regina is on the floor in the bathroom, Doktor, and you put her there. Why?"

His welcoming smile faded. "It's for her own good."

"How is kneeling for hours on a concrete floor good for a woman almost nine months pregnant? Besides, she's a nurse! A good one. You shouldn't have done this to her."

Yuri Komarov shrugged. "She *is* a good nurse. A talented one. But she has a stubborn heart and, even worse, a subversive tongue. She must reflect on her crimes and resolve to do better."

"Stubborn? Subversive? Crimes?" Natalie couldn't help herself. "*Crimes?* Her crime is caring about her husband and wishing him safely home! Her crime is wishing her father well again and out of this dismal place."

"Yes, Natalya Ivanovna; those are her crimes." Komarov didn't blink an eye. "As a good Soviet she should denounce her husband as the traitor he is. She should allow me to treat her father without complaining about his condition. She should show her loyalty to the Party and to Comrade Stalin through her—"

"Pardon me, sir, but the *crime* here is yours." Natalie couldn't believe what she was saying. But she couldn't stop. "It's a crime to treat her so! Not only do we need her in the operating wing, but she's due to deliver *at any time.* She shouldn't be down on her knees like a maid, cutting off her circulation, inhaling fumes and endangering her own health and that of her baby."

"I don't expect you to understand." Komarov's words were cold. "You can barely communicate with us, let alone understand the higher purpose of Comrade Stalin's goal. Don't let your personal feelings interfere with your duty to your government."

Natalie felt the blood rush to her face. She had never felt so angry in her whole life. She fancied opening her mouth and saying things about Comrade Stalin that had been stewing on the back burner of her mind ever since she arrived. But she remembered Viktor's warnings and bit her tongue so hard that she tasted blood. She clenched her hands in the folds of her frock, lowered her head, and said nothing.

"The best way you can help her"—the doctor leaned closer—"is to urge her to work hard—as hard as she can—and think about her crimes. This is the first test of her loyalty to the Motherland; can she sacrifice her own feelings for the benefit of the society in which she lives?"

"Does the society require her to destroy herself and her baby?" Natalie said slowly though clenched teeth.

"Yes!" Komarov was emphatic. "If it is for the betterment of our society, then yes! Now please, let's speak of this no more. I have work to do." He turned and left her standing in the hallway.

Dr. Vlasov found her still standing in the hallway a few minutes later. He saw the look on her face, shook his head, and said nothing. Natalie could hardly concentrate as she accompanied him on his rounds, and he didn't try to pull her into conversation as he usually did. She was grateful for that.

She thought about her earlier feelings of despair at the lack of a proper Sabbath day, and she decided that, no matter the consequences, she was going to make this Sunday a Sabbath day that meant something.

When her shift ended she removed her nurse's frock and folded it into her purse. She would wash out the bloodstains that evening and wear it the next day clean and fresh. She didn't want to cause Olga any more anxiety than she already did. She washed her hands and straightened her hair, pulling it back into a very Western ponytail instead of tying it up in her white scarf. This evening's events would be her own little rebellion against a dictator who deprived his citizens of the right to worship as they chose.

She didn't go home. She knew the other tenants of her apartment would notice, and news of her absence would get back to Viktor, but today she didn't care. She gathered a broom, rags, and a bucket of hot soapy water and went to find Regina.

She found her in an empty, half-lit corridor, on the floor as she'd been in the bathroom. Her hands and knees were red and raw, and her face, when she looked up at Natalie, was pale. Natalie fell to her knees and began to scrub. "Go home, Regina."

"I have this hallway and three rooms still to clean," Regina said. "I can't go home. Do you want me to lose my job?"

"Is this job worth keeping?"

Regina threw her arms around Natalie's shoulders and began to cry. "No, it's not. But I have to keep it anyway or Doktor Komarov will kill my papa. I know he will."

"Then let me help you," Natalie said, tightening her embrace.

"Oh, Natalya!" Regina burst into fresh sobs. "Thank you! Thank you!"

Natalie fashioned pads for Regina's knees to protect them from the rough marble floors. She and Regina scrubbed until close to midnight, and then they cheated death by raiding the hospital kitchen. They didn't find much, just a few onions, cold mush, and a container of calves-foot jelly. They found plenty of vodka and shared a good laugh at the idea of a cook walking around the kitchen half anesthetized all day.

At midnight it was too late to go home by way of the streetcar. Natalie did not fancy walking for two hours in the blistering cold and then turning around to come back at six in the morning. So she stayed.

They fell asleep in the middle of a conversation in the nurse's station, Regina curled on her side on top of the table and Natalie on a rickety cot near the door. Regina was still asleep when Natalie pulled her blood-stained smock from her purse, shook it out, and put it on.

She left the light off and slipped quietly out the door. She would deal with Olga's displeasure at her appearance when that time came.

* * *

When Rolf arrived home that evening Marie handed him a brief cable. It read:

Mr. Goodwin, the gift you purchased has been delivered to the address you specified. Thank you for your business.

It was signed, *JM*

James Matthews. The talented young agent Reynolds was in place. Now all Rolf needed was for Viktor Rostov's heart to change. He prayed that it would change quickly.

He was on the next bus to Brighton. He had a certain haberdashery to visit.

TWENTY

Tucked into the green meadows of the Bernese Alps, the tourist community of Interlaken nestles between the lakes of Brienz to the east and Thun to the west. On Hoheweg Street, Interlaken's main thoroughfare, sits the opulent and restful Victoria-Jungfrau hotel, perfectly situated for a tourist to enjoy a vista of the Alps' crown jewel: Jungfrau peak.

Lieutenant Viktor Rostov didn't consider himself a tourist. Although dressed as one, he wasn't here to enjoy the Alps. His reasons for being here were private, and, he hoped, secret.

Viktor placed his gloves carefully on the counter and reached for the pen. He signed "Richard Grant," relinquished his MGB-issued American passport, and accepted his key. He waved off the bellboy, retrieved his own suitcase, and carried it to the stairs.

His room was on the third floor. He climbed slowly, carefully, placing one foot in front of the other as he concentrated on his breathing. His heart had been weakened, Dr. Vlasov informed him, by the stresses of his work. Viktor believed it had more to do with the stress that came from worrying about his daughter. That and the tensions he felt between himself and Natalya Ivanovna. *Rest,* his doctor had ordered. *Rest.*

He placed his luggage inside the door of his room and walked to the lounge. He wasn't going to stay long enough to unpack. In fact, he'd be gone before the hotel dimmed its lights that evening. After he met with his contact, he would take a leisurely and too-expensive dinner in the grand dining room, chat amiably with a few guests, read the newspaper, and then disappear.

In the morning the hotel cleaning staff would find his suitcase, stuffed with worthless rags, sitting by the door in a room vacant for the entire night.

It was too early in the season for the hotel to be at capacity. It was too early in the day for all guests to have arrived. Instead, there were only three other guests besides himself in a lounge designed to accommodate three hundred. He settled into a seat near the roaring fireplace and glanced at the other people. None was his contact. He wasn't expecting him for another three minutes.

The message indicated this meeting was about his daughter, or he would've allocated this charade to an associate. He was getting too old for these spy games. He didn't want to leave Moscow if he didn't have to.

The man sitting across from him turned the page of his magazine. *Saturday Evening Post,* it looked like, although Viktor's eyesight was not what it once had been. Minutes passed and his contact didn't enter the lounge. Rostov's anxiety level began to rise.

It seemed the cleaning staff had forgotten to replace the reading materials. He surveyed the room and noticed several options lying on the seat beside the reader of the *Post,* including his secret favorite, the *New York Times.* He stood and went to retrieve it.

As he reached, his hand froze midair. The *Post* reader had a Colt revolver in his hand, hidden by the magazine, and it was pointed in the general direction of Rostov's midsection.

"I understand you have a bad heart, Lieutenant." The man's voice was deep, pleasant. "I hope your actions in the next few seconds don't make your condition worse."

Rostov straightened slowly, the *Times* forgotten. "How do I know you?"

"From Paris, most likely. Lyon, perhaps. And probably Chamonix."

"The friend of Hans Brenner. You were on trial in Lyon. You dined with Natalya and Mr. Brenner in Paris." The heat rose in Viktor's face. "You're the one who stole my scientist in Chamonix."

"I understand you've evened the score."

"More than adequately."

With his gun Rolf Schulmann indicated the glass doors to the terrace. "A bit more privacy, Lieutenant?"

Viktor hesitated, and Rolf's lips twisted. "Still hoping for the arrival of your contact? I'm sorry to disappoint you, but it was I who summoned you here."

"Impossible."

"For your people in Moscow, perhaps, but not for my friends." The German stood and indicated the patio. "After you."

Viktor turned and walked through the door. He was not yet worried. The man was obviously an associate of Matthews, but that didn't necessarily spell disaster. Viktor had dealt with Matthews's henchmen before. At Rolf's insistence he settled himself into a settee near the edge of the redwood deck, strategically located to allow the greatest enjoyment of the magnificent peaks. Rolf sat across from him, his back to the view.

Viktor grimaced. "I assume you're not here to discuss the Alps or the weather."

"I wish I were. But I have a less pleasant subject in mind: Natalie Allred—"

Viktor's anger flared. "That's not a subject I'll discuss."

"And your daughter."

Viktor stood abruptly. "Another subject I refuse to discuss!"

Rolf brandished the revolver again. Viktor sank into his seat. Rolf said, "Maybe we can come to an agreement, Lieutenant: You stay in your seat and I keep the weapon in my lap, and I'll explain why you should change your mind about discussing these two important subjects." Rolf settled back into his lounge chair, and any onlooker might have thought the men were vacationers interested only in a good chat, a great view, and a relaxing weekend away from the office.

Rolf cleared his throat and began. "I know Natalie's with you in Moscow. I know, also, that she's not happy about that fact."

"How can you be so sure?" Viktor snapped.

"Strange as it may sound, I know her better than you do."

"Impossible."

"I know her character, Lieutenant—her morals, her desires, and her allegiances. Those are things I doubt she would share with you. Besides"— here Rolf's voice softened a decibel—"she's deeply in love with my friend Hans—which of course is difficult for her, since you have Hans hidden somewhere working on a bomb." He watched Rostov carefully.

"I see the difficulty." Rostov's gaze didn't waver. "But I have no idea where your friend is."

"You've tried to convince us of that, Lieutenant," Rolf replied. "And I want to offer our condolences on the imprisonment of your daughter Lucya Viktorovna. I know you love her very much."

"My daughter has nothing to do with this."

"We know she was the reason you pursued Hans Brenner."

"You're hoping I'll divulge something I shouldn't. Say, perhaps, his location?"

Rolf's face showed concern. "We know the conditions of your daughter's imprisonment, Viktor. We know that she wasn't returned to you as promised when you delivered Hans Brenner safely to your superiors."

Viktor hoped Rolf couldn't see his turmoil. He hoped his emotions were adequately in check, or he might give away the despair he felt at that broken promise.

"We know why you need him, Rostov. But your reasons, personal as they are, would shock your Comrade Stalin. Is he aware that you acted in pure self-interest? Certainly the interests of the State trump what you feel for a daughter! And yet, you still continue to hope." Rolf's brow knit. "Why? Why do you continue to hope for your daughter's return, when the interests of the State are the very purpose of your existence? May I hazard a guess, Lieutenant?"

"You've hazarded many things this morning, Rolf Schulmann, so a guess wouldn't be much more of a hazard."

"My guess is you already know, deep down, that Stalin won't keep his promise. Deep down you know your daughter is lost to you."

Viktor swore, long and low, the menace in his voice unmistakable. He then rose to his feet, ignoring Rolf's weapon, and moved to stand at the rail, his back to Rolf.

After a few moments Rolf walked to his side. "I didn't come to offend you or threaten you." He spoke calmly. "I'm here to make you an offer."

"How generous of you."

"I'm prepared to assist you, Lieutenant, in recovering your daughter." Rolf paused. "Major Matthews has discovered where she is."

Rostov whirled to stare at Rolf in a blatant departure from his usual control.

Rolf continued. "We have an agent who can secure her and within twenty-four hours have her out of the Soviet Union. We can do for you what you're too patriotic to do for yourself."

"Patriotic." Rostov spat. "Do I detect a hint of sarcasm in the word?"

"Not at all." Rolf shook his head. "I understand what it means to be loyal to one's country and to be torn between duty and family."

"Where is she?"

"Siberia. Where's Hans Brenner?"

"I know she's in Siberia!" Viktor roared. "*Where* in Siberia—if your intelligence has discovered that much."

"It has."

"And you're going to dangle that information in front of my nose like water in front of a dying man?"

"I have no desire to toy with her safety, Lieutenant. Agree to help me and I'll tell you where she is."

"Tell me where she is and I'll get her out myself!" Viktor's teeth clenched. "And I'll expose whatever spies have given you this intelligence. Then let's see you get *them* out of our Gulags!"

Rolf didn't respond. Calmly he watched the Soviet's agitation. Finally Viktor took a deep breath, steadied himself against the railing, and lowered his head. He stood that way, silently breathing, silently mourning for a daughter suffering. Finally he said, "I don't know where your friend is being held. He was delivered safely to Novosibirsk—one of our factory and laboratory centers. And then, he disappeared." He rubbed his forehead with one large hand. "I would hazard a guess you've never had your child torn away from you, Rolf Schulmann."

Rolf flinched. "I was blessed to have a dear friend protect my son for me. Otherwise you and I would have the same unlucky predicament."

Viktor raised his head. He studied the German carefully. *"Blessed?"* It came out as a soft curse.

"Without God's help and the courage of an American woman, my son would be dead."

"I don't believe in God."

"That's all right, He loves you anyway. Perhaps He is giving you the opportunity to change what you believe."

Viktor wanted to cry out. Instead he whispered, "God loves me? And yet He allows my daughter to suffer hideously, and you won't tell me where she is so I can save her."

"Help me and I'll not only tell you, I will personally help you get her out."

"I don't need your help! Nor do I need the help of a God who allows my daughter to suffer while *your* child goes free." Viktor gripped the railing. "No. Absolutely not. My daughter will be released." Viktor turned on Rolf. "You're wasting your time, Rolf Schulmann. I will not betray my country—as you did yours."

TWENTY-ONE

In the camps they say a thief will take everything you own—the boots from your feet, the coat from your shoulders and the gloves from your fingers—but a thief will not touch your bread. It is considered sacred. In fact, Lucya had heard of inmates sentenced to death by their criminal peers for stealing a quarter-loaf from an old woman.

"Give me your shawl." The woman reached for the coveted object while she stared with glittering eyes at the bread in Lucya's hands. But she only demanded the shawl.

"It's mine. I need it in the gravel pits to stay warm."

"I don't care, little fiend. Give it to me." The woman's hand grabbed the bright red shawl.

Lucya was desperate. "It was a gift—from my papa—my mother's before she died. I couldn't part with it even if I didn't need it to survive."

The thief let out a string of foul curses. Lucya cringed at the sounds and held her shawl tighter.

"Give me the shawl, vermin, or I promise by this time tomorrow you'll no longer need it." The thick evil in her threat was something Lucya had heard many times, but this time she knew the woman meant it. Her fingers loosened. She didn't resist when the woman's claws tore it from her shoulders.

She tried to keep her attention on her bread. She ate it carefully and slowly, pulling bite-size portions from the chunk and rolling them slowly in her trembling fingers. Then she placed the ball in her mouth and savored the taste before chewing. The bread tasted different. Perhaps it was the bitter taste of defeat: *Her mother's shawl . . . Papa's gift!* She fought back tears and it became almost impossible to chew, let alone swallow. But she ate anyway; because if she didn't, she would die.

TWENTY-TWO

Natalie threw her coat across her mattress and flung herself down on top of it. She felt the heat of the kitchen stove and didn't want to close the door, even for the little privacy it would offer. *Let them stare,* she thought; the warmth was worth the gossip.

She heard movement at the door and looked up into Regina's twinkling eyes. It was as if a ray of summer sunshine had just danced through her door.

"It's not fair, you know," Regina mused, "that you can rest so comfortably. I sit and my legs immediately go to sleep. I stand and my stomach pulls my backbone down to my shoes!"

"How much longer?"

Regina grinned. "I'm a week past my date." Her smile brightened further. "I'm positive they'll release Edik any day now."

"Is that what Edik said? Have you finally seen him?"

Regina's sunshine diminished. "No. They still won't let me in. But Comrade Krajnik promised me—" She stopped suddenly, and her brow knit.

"Your father's friend?"

Regina nodded, hesitated, and then renewed her smile and held out something clutched in her hand.

It looked like a dead raccoon. Natalie stared. "What is that?"

"It's a shapka-ushanka, silly! It keeps your head warm."

"Is it from Viktor?"

Regina nodded.

"I don't need it."

"Yes you do."

"No!"

"Listen, idiot, in a Moscow winter, the only people who don't need shapkas are the ones who don't have heads."

Natalie took the cap from Regina's hands, surprised at its weight and awed by the warm softness. It ran through her fingers with the cool softness of real fur.

Regina giggled. "You look like a child with a new puppy—happy to have it, but half afraid it's going to bite you. Put it on, Natalya, and see how warm it is."

"I can't accept it, Regina. Not from him. It's too nice, and I don't want him getting the wrong ideas . . ."

"What wrong ideas might he get?" Regina was genuinely curious. "This is Russia. This is *winter* in Russia. That is a Russian winter cap; it's as practical a gift as a teakettle, so how could accepting it be inappropriate?" Regina's face brightened. "I'm supposed to do something to make you happy tonight." Again Regina was all smiles.

"Viktor said that?"

Regina grabbed Natalie's coat. "You know him—always worried about you."

Natalie frowned. "And so he sent you to see if I'm all right."

"He sees the same thing I see when I look at you." Regina sobered. "You're half dead with grief. You need to lighten up, Natalya. You need to live again. Besides, your gloom could drive a dead man to commit suicide. Now take this coat and let's go. Rostov ordered me to take you to the theater tonight, and if we don't leave this moment, we're going to miss the opening of *Figaro* and Rostov is going to have me labeled an Enemy by morning."

Bitter air assailed the two girls as they left the apartment building. Natalie had to admit Viktor had been kind; the shapka he sent enveloped her head in the warmest embrace she'd ever felt, and when she pulled it low over her ears and pulled the coat tight around her it felt as if she hadn't left the warmth of the stove. It was better, even—she was warm all over instead of on just one side.

She would have to thank him. She didn't like the prospect, but she knew she had to do it. She shook the thought from her mind and followed Regina across the bridge.

Along the bank, once-lustrous grass had frozen into tiny, razor-sharp needles. Trees stood bare and brittle, gray and heartless against the winter night.

"It's getting cold. Should we be out?"

"*Pah,* Amerikanka. Welcome to Russian winter. This is nothing. Wait until your breath freezes in your throat and your lungs bleed. Wait until you have to wear your shapka while you boil water for tea and you don't feel your feet in your boots. Then it's truly winter."

"I've never liked the cold."

"Ah, but winter can be so exciting! Someday I'll take you ice skating on the river and skiing in the mountains . . ."

"Ice skating on the river?"

"Or we can have your lieutenant take us for a drive on it. It doesn't matter."

"Drive? On the river?"

Regina laughed. "It's quite an adventure. It's dangerous and exhilarating all at the same time. It gets your adrenaline pumping and the excitement of it warms straight through you. It's better than coal in the stove for keeping you warm."

Natalie peered at Regina. Only her friend's nose and eyes escaped her wraps. Her eyes twinkled as she spoke and her nose had taken on the appearance of a maraschino cherry. A shawl muffled her mouth like a scarf, muting her words as she spoke. Natalie knew that it was her Russian friend's cheerfulness and buoyancy that had saved her during those first weeks and months. She couldn't help thinking that Regina's friendship was a gift from Heavenly Father to a daughter who might have succumbed to darkness without it. Regina's companionship acted as a gentle reminder that God still cared for her—even in this country that seemed to have forgotten what it meant to care for God.

Like so many other pedestrians, she leaned against the railing and stared down at the dark, sluggish Moskva River. The world seemed muffled by the ice particles masquerading as snowflakes that pricked her face and careened off into the darkness, flickering and then disappearing into the inky depths below.

Regina joined her at the rail. She pulled down the scarf protecting the lower parts of her face and stuck out her tongue to chase snowflakes. "You need to open your mind to the possibilities, Natalya. This is a great place to live—and there will be many people here who will be your friends. You are very fortunate. Lieutenant Rostov has given you more than just a warm apartment and an enviable appointment to the most important hospital in the country. He's given you respectability, and an opportunity to become a productive member of the most advanced society in the world."

Natalie did not respond. She was accustomed to this line of talk and was not interested in debating the point. She glanced upward at the shadows that were the onion domes of the Cathedral of Saint Basil the Blessed, her mind already working forward toward tomorrow's necessary interaction with Rostov. "Regina," Natalie finally said, "I'm not in the mood for theater."

"What?" Regina feigned surprise, and then hurt. "You realize you're threatening my very existence if Rostov finds out."

"Let's not go, and say we did."

"All right. I don't think I'd be able to sit that long, anyway. I'd be up by the second act, dancing in the aisles trying to get the feeling back into my legs. Look—the moon's coming out!"

"In all this snow?"

"Look!" Regina pointed, and Natalie saw the moon's silvery edge break free of the dreary gray. "Enjoy the moon, Natalya—you might not see it again till spring."

Natalie felt her spirits sag at the thought, and she watched as the moon's rays danced across the sleepy river below her feet.

"It's not that bad," Regina murmured. "If the moon comes out completely it's going to be a beautiful night. What's that noise?" Regina hesitated, cocking her head sideways, her breath coming in tiny puffs as she listened. She had to squint to see in the darkness, even though the moon had emerged enough to bring out more details below. It sent shimmers of silver across the water, dancing with the breeze and with the frenzied froth produced by a sudden multitude of winged shadows.

"Look at the geese!" Natalie ran across the bridge to the opposite railing and leaned over the water. "I've never seen so many geese!"

Regina leaned around her protruding belly to see. "They're big enough for you to hitch a ride south—all the way to Africa if you want!"

Such a simple thing, to say something that would make someone think you might want to leave the Soviet Union . . . Natalie's eyes quickly scanned the darkened bridge for eavesdroppers. All she saw were a romantic couple on the other side and a young man wrapped in a thick overcoat and beret, leaning against the railing half a dozen meters away smoking a cigar. He also seemed enthralled by the sight of the geese below.

Regina continued, unconcerned. "They come from north of Leningrad and fly their way south all the way to Southwest Europe or the African coast. Can you believe it? And they stop here overnight— once in a rare while—when they can't gather the strength to make it any farther. They sleep on the river, and it takes them many miles out of the city center before they continue their flight in the morning." She shifted her weight from one foot to another.

"You doing all right, Regina?"

"Can you believe the hospital cook?" Regina shook her head, smiling. "He gave me old bread and yesterday's tea."

"What's wrong, Regina?"

"I've been having cramps since I ate—not too bad; they come and go."

"Let's get you home. Whatever possessed you to come out with me feeling like that?"

"A desire to escape the four walls of my prison? Because I prefer to listen to your quaint accent than the shouts of babushkas fighting over the washbasin."

"Regina—"

"You're good for me, Amerikanka. You remind me there's a great big world out there with good people in it. You give me hope that maybe Stalin is mistaken about the West—"

"Regina . . ." Natalie glanced at the man with the cigar. "Careful . . ."

"Natalya—I think you've done really well for how hard things have been," Regina said. "For your sake, I'm sorry you had to come to Moscow. But for *my* sake, I'm glad you're here." She turned away from the rail. "Do you believe in fate?"

Natalie hesitated. It wasn't fate that brought her here to Moscow; Viktor did that.

"You're here against your will. But I think it was supposed to happen." Regina's hand tightened into a fist. "I—I don't know how to explain it any better. But I just feel that"—she hesitated, an awkward, self-conscious moment, before continuing—"that I needed for you to come." She hastened to add, "I don't know why. I'm sorry—it's a strange thing to say. I shouldn't have brought it up."

"Why?"

"Because it's cruel for me to benefit from your pain."

"No," Natalie clarified, "I mean, why is it a strange thing to say?"

Regina turned and leaned into the railing, studying the geese below. "Papa used to talk about fate." She brushed at a lock of hair that had fallen free from her shapka. "He used to say fate made us who we are— and that fate brought friends together for the benefit of mankind." She gave Natalie a half smile. "Lieutenant Rostov bringing you here wasn't entirely his choice. You know that, don't you? Comrade Stalin decreed it. Rostov was just the means fate used to get you here."

"To me, fate implies no possible decision on my part," Natalie said.

Regina turned fully to look at her. "You believe in providence, then, don't you?"

"You mean divine intervention? Of course."

"Shh!" Regina giggled and made a show of furtive glances to the right and to the left. "You could be drop-kicked all the way to the Arctic Circle for saying that."

Natalie lowered her voice. "I don't consider providence and fate the same thing, Regina; one denotes divine control, which suggests that someone intelligent is looking out for our welfare. The other suggests that things just happen—like a wave on the seashore."

Regina fingered the railing with one gloved hand. "All right. Then perhaps providence brought you here."

"Or maybe God turned His back on me, Regina. I don't know . . . my faith has been shaken, I guess. I joined a church not too long ago, and I guess I built up such a store of dreams . . ."

"What sort of dreams? Were you planning to become a nun?" Regina straightened, and a mischievous light switched on behind her eyes. "I get it! That's why you won't enter Lieutenant Rostov's apartment! You want to become a nun!"

Natalie returned Regina's grin.

"Seriously." Regina sobered. "I think you're here for a reason. And I think you being here is going to affect me somehow." She shrugged. "That's it 'in a nutshell'—as my English teacher used to say."

"I can't accept that."

"And I can't accept that my husband is being held prisoner less than a kilometer from here in Lubyanka—the most notorious prison in the Soviet Union. But that's the unpleasant truth. It's fate—*Oohhh!*" Her unexpected howl ended in a long, low moan. "Natalya," she whimpered, "I think fate says my baby's coming."

Natalie threw an arm about Regina's waist and urged her toward the foot of the bridge. "Not fate, Regina; I think providence has a hand in this one. C'mon. We'll catch the last streetcar to the hospital and—"

"No! Not the streetcar! I can't survive the streetcar right now. Can you imagine me hanging out the back door when the baby decides to make an appearance? *Chort vozmi!* The thought of hanging on for dear life at one end and giving birth at the other is disagreeable. We have to get to Viktor's apartment. Look—it's right there across the river!"

"No!" Natalie panicked, refusing to accept that Regina might be right. "I'll find another way. Didn't you say your father's friend has an office here at the Kremlin?"

"Lubyanka."

"All right. Maybe he's working late . . . and he can drive us to—" She stopped. The look in her friend's eyes reminded her of a young doe cornered by wolves. "Not a good idea?"

"I'm sure he's busy, Natalya. Not even for a baby would I want to interrupt his important work . . ." She closed her eyes. "I won't make you break your oath. We'll take the streetcar."

The enamored couple had wandered away, and Natalie could see the distant figure of the young man who'd been watching the geese. He was headed at a trot across the river. There was no one to call to for assistance.

Suddenly Natalie felt as though she were being quite heartless—this was no time for the evil streetcar. Much as she hated to admit it, Regina was right; they needed to go to Viktor's residence.

Regina had begun to double over, her legs shuffling as she tried to keep her feet under her on the icy bridge. "This—is—not going to work, Natalya—"

"Viktor's apartment, Regina—it's just a few more minutes. You're going to be fine," Natalie said as she steered Regina around to head across the bridge.

"Oh, the pain . . ." Regina gave an involuntary giggle and then clenched her teeth. "You'd think, after a woman had carried a baby for nine months, God would reward her for her trouble by giving her a pain-free childbirth."

"I thought we weren't supposed to mention God."

"So arrest me! You're right: Some things fate can't orchestrate, and I think having a baby's got to be one of those things. *Oohhh* . . ."

"So you believe in God?"

Regina hissed through her teeth, "When—I'm—having—a baby!"

"Fair enough."

"Hurry, Natalya!"

"Regina, you're a nurse. You know this takes time. It feels uncomfortable, but you're going to be all right for a few hours."

"Uncomfortable?" Regina shrieked. "I can't stand this for a few more hours!" Regina clutched at Natalie's coat sleeve. "You get me to Rostov's apartment right now, Natalya Ivanovna, or you'll be delivering my baby in the middle of this street."

"This is ridiculous, Regina." Natalie felt a tiny wave of panic. "You haven't been having contractions for more than a few minutes, and already you're—"

"Maybe it wasn't old bread," Regina moaned. "It's been bothering me all afternoon . . . ever since my break . . . so I just thought . . ."

"All right, hold to me tightly, Regina—look; it's only a few more meters. I hope Viktor's at home . . ."

"He's right there," Regina gasped, and she pointed at a figure approaching them at a jogging run, coat flying out behind and a blanket in his arms. Natalie stared, wondering how Viktor knew they were there, let alone in need of his assistance.

He slid to a stop, breathing a little too hard for the short distance he'd run, and threw the blanket about Regina's shoulders. "I saw you from my apartment," he gasped. "My driver's gone for the car."

Natalie couldn't help challenging him. "And how'd you know to call your driver? How'd he get here so fast?"

"Natalya . . ." Regina moaned, and Rostov swept her into his arms, staggered a bit, and headed for his building.

"He just brought me home," Viktor panted. "I saw you . . ." He couldn't continue.

"Really?" Natalie probed. "And he dropped you off and drove away, and then went to go get the car? Makes perfect sense to me."

"Natalya, this isn't the time . . ." Rostov hefted the weight in his arms. He didn't look at her.

"You were having us followed, weren't you? That driver of yours was standing here on the bridge, smoking his evil-smelling cigar while we stared at the geese. You've been following us!"

"Natalya . . . !" Regina's cry was pitiful to hear, and it was almost lost in the sound of bells ringing on Red Square. "Listen to that!" she sobbed. "They're singing 'Regina's having her baby; Regina's having her baby.'"

"Regina, please don't cry." Natalie hurried along beside Viktor. "I'm so sorry your husband couldn't be here with you."

Regina's tears fell freely. "Welcome to the world of Socialism . . ."

Viktor glanced at Natalie, his eyes anxious. "Is she all right? She's talking nonsense."

"Viktor, where's your driver? I'm starting to get a little worried about her."

"He'll be here soon." Rostov shifted his load more securely in his arms. Natalie could see the strain of his effort on his face, and she was reluctant to admit to herself that her fears also included concern for his heart. She felt awkward, hurrying alongside him in the darkness.

"Viktor? Are you all right?" Her exceptional unease for his welfare almost gagged her.

He was too winded to answer, and so she continued, embarrassed. "I'm glad you're here. I had no right to accuse you as I did." She slowed as a car approached, and the man from the bridge leaped from the driver's seat to open the back door. Rostov lowered Regina into the seat and motioned for Natalie to follow. He slid into the passenger's side of the front seat and rested his head against the dashboard. The driver pulled away from the curb, wheels spinning on the ice.

Except for Regina's moans and an occasional word of comfort and encouragement from Natalie, no one spoke the entire drive to the Kremlin Hospital. When they arrived, Rostov's driver left to find a doctor and Viktor helped Regina from the backseat.

Olga arrived and took brusque control of the situation. She and Viktor hauled Regina to the operating room and laid her down not too gently onto a table. Viktor left to see Dr. Vlasov, and Olga ordered Natalie from the operating room.

"For heaven's sake, Olga!" Natalie protested. "I know how to deliver a baby!"

"You are her friend." For once Olga attempted to be civil. "Be reasonable, Amerikanka; your presence might distress her and make things worse."

"Regina asked me to stay with her—"

"She is not in her right mind at the moment. Come see her in the morning, after it is all over."

Natalie glanced once at Regina, and then back at Olga. She relented. She turned and walked out of the room.

She paced the halls, desperately worried for Regina and her baby. Viktor found her and tried to comfort her as Natalie cried, sobbing until the epaulet on his uniform coat was soaked through.

"Natalya, it's going to be all right," he soothed. "Olga will do what's necessary. And besides, the doctor won't let Regina suffer needlessly."

"Which doctor is it?"

"Vlasov. My doctor. He's a good man."

"He's a cardiologist!" Natalie sniffed. "Does he know how to—"

Viktor just laughed, and pulled her into his arms.

Dr. Vlasov would be careful with Regina. In her stiff, cold way, Olga was a good nurse. Despite her disdain for Regina's situation, Olga would do a good job. Olga was putty in the hands of Dr. Vlasov. She wouldn't try anything that might bring the wrath of that man down upon her head—especially not in the operating room.

"How do you know it's Dr. Vlasov?"

"I asked him. I know you're comfortable with him. I—I want to do anything I can to make you comfortable, Natalya."

His words, spoken so gently against her ear, made her uneasy. She stepped away from him, but he captured her hand.

"Natalya, please, don't leave me. Stay here with me."

"I'm not leaving . . ." She hesitated, pulling her hand from his. "I'm going to stay here—for Regina."

"Let me hold your hand."

"Viktor . . . No." She struggled with her emotions, forcing herself to try to see past the man who had so violently abducted her and destroyed her life to the good man Regina always claimed Viktor was. She couldn't. Her mind refused to forget, refused to accept that she might have been wrong about him all these months—that her feelings might have been clouded by the crimes Viktor had committed against her and Hans.

TWENTY-THREE

Saturday, November 30, 1946

The night passed as slowly as the Moskva River winding lazily through the city on its meandering, meditative path. Natalie couldn't help leaning in at the door to the operating room, which Olga kept locked. She could hear Regina screaming. She could hear, several times, Olga shouting at her to be quiet. She heard Dr. Vlasov calling for a clamp, telling the nurses to hurry.

Something wasn't right. In the early morning hours Regina called out for Natalie, begged Olga to let her in, and then shrieked her husband's name, over and over. Then she fell silent. There was a sharp slap, and then Natalie heard a tiny wail, so faint she might have imagined it.

Twenty minutes later Olga exited the room, her frock drenched in blood, and hurried away.

Natalie slipped into the operating room.

It looked like a battlefield—or at least a battlefield hospital, on one of its busiest days. Regina lay in a sodden, unconscious heap on the table, attended by Dr. Vlasov and a nurse. Another two nurses hovered about a tiny form in a metal bassinet across the room. Natalie hurried to Regina's side.

"She lost a lot of blood." Dr. Vlasov sounded tired. "She hemorrhaged, the baby was transverse, and I finally used the forceps. We've stopped the blood . . ." He leaned against the table and wiped at his eyes with the back of his sleeve.

"Will she make it?"

Vlasov nodded. "Regina won't give up without a fight—and she's still got fight left in her. I wouldn't be surprised if she's on her feet within a few days. There was one other complication . . ."

"What?"

"The placenta didn't expel in one piece. We . . . had to remove the pieces by hand."

Natalie felt sick. She'd seen such a procedure performed on another mother after childbirth. It was a sight that would turn even the most hardy stomach. Many patients couldn't stand the agony and passed out before the procedure was completed. She wondered if that was what had happened to Regina.

She asked, "How can I help?"

"Stay with her. I've patched her up the best I can—it's in the hands of God now."

Natalie stared at him, startled. But he didn't explain his dangerous slip from decorum. He only smiled sadly, shook his head, and turned away.

One of the nurses attending the baby brought the tiny, tightly swaddled bundle for Natalie to see. The nurse slipped the baby into Natalie's arms. "When Regina wakes up have her try to nurse her."

The other nurses left. Natalie held the baby and marveled at her delicate face, porcelain pink on white, a definite dimple in one cheek, and soft eyelashes. Natalie felt like a criminal, stealing from the true mother these precious first moments with her newborn, but the sight of the little gift from heaven made her long even more to be reunited with Hans. She kissed the baby's forehead and thought about the man who'd captured her heart. *He's not dead,* she told herself whenever despair clouded her hopes. *Rostov has surely deceived me again, and this time I won't believe it. I'm tired of believing him. It's time to believe in myself—and in Hans's love.* Natalie held the quiet bundle close to her and thought about Hans. *He'll know I'm here. Somehow he'll know, and he will find a way to save me.*

"Her name—is Ina." The feeble voice barely carried past the birthing table.

Natalie turned, and Regina gave her a weak smile. Natalie leaned toward her and transferred the baby into her arms.

Regina held the infant close. "Edik will approve of her." It was almost an entreaty.

"Of course he will. She's a beautiful baby. I'm so happy for you."

"And then he'll be released and we'll be together as a family . . ." Regina's smile deepened. "And someday you'll be reunited with this man you love so much—this German who you insist is still alive."

Natalie couldn't answer without revealing the anguish that suddenly tore at her heart.

"And then you'll record your marriage here in Moscow—"

"Regina—" Natalie began.

But Regina continued, ". . . and you and I will raise our children together, work together, and continue to be close friends for the rest of our lives."

"I hope we can be friends longer than that." Natalie touched Regina's arm. "I hope we can be friends for eternity."

"Sometimes life in the Soviet Union seems like an eternity—especially for a woman here against her will. I'm sorry, Natalya; I didn't mean—"

"No, eternity is a beautiful thing. It's more than just this life—it's also the life we'll have after we die."

Regina studied her, curiosity evident in her tired face. "The only thing I know is that when we die, our bodies are buried under the steppe—and the foxes and polecats are the only ones who remember where they are. What do you mean, life after we die?"

It wasn't something she would have done, except that she was the only nurse still remaining in the room with Regina. Natalie was surprised that the words flowed easily, explaining her beliefs about eternal life and eternal marriage, and her deeply preserved hopes that someday she and Hans Brenner would be able to marry for that eternity.

Regina was fascinated. She whispered question after question, cuddling her baby and nursing her as she and Natalie conversed. "But what about my Inuchka?" She lengthened her baby's name with a term of endearment, a common practice among mothers in Moscow. "Will she be allowed to marry someday for eternity?"

That broke Natalie's heart. Ina would be raised under the dark shadow of a repressive, godless flag and would probably never hear about the gospel, or eternal marriage, or a Savior.

"I want my Ina to someday be married in a temple—for this eternity." Regina pulled her infant close and kissed the tiny eyes, now closed in sleep. "Oh, Natalya—I never dreamed I could feel such love for another human being! I would do anything so that my Inuchka could have such a wonderful gift." And then she sighed, as if she, too, understood the dreadful reality of her situation.

The hour spent talking to Regina about things repressed for so long was liberating—like stepping out of a dark closet into daylight. That was how Natalie had felt, ever since she'd come to the Soviet Union— like she'd been locked in a dark closet. Now, for just a few moments, she could breathe again—and even though it hurt to breathe because she knew that soon breath would again be denied her, she reveled in it for the few moments that she could.

TWENTY-FOUR

When the bells of the basilica heralded morning's arrival, geese from the Moskva River took startled flight, flapping in panicked disarray until clear of the churning water. Then they organized themselves into their v-shaped pattern, fighting a stiff breeze that pummeled their ascent. This flock was one of the last to leave the lake country north of Leningrad, and they would have a grueling battle with winter before they reached Africa.

As the morning sun broke through the dismal cloud cover, the flock continued to fly. They passed over suburban gardens owned by the residents of the city, over struggling collective farms and poverty-stricken villages. As the day wore on, the lead position was relinquished to other geese. Each took his turn breaking the wind for his comrades, and in this way the flock was able to fly more than three hundred kilometers before finding a place to rest.

In the morning they again took flight. They passed over birch forests, white with snow and morning's frost. As the sun began its afternoon journey, they finally descended over a meadow and landed on a lake in the middle of a dense coniferous forest.

"Look at those birds!" A Gulag camp laborer took imaginary aim at the magnificent flock of geese coming to rest nearby. "I could eat one by myself, I tell ya, and net a dozen more for bribing the guards."

"Think they'd let you go, do ya?" His companion chewed on a stick as if on a coveted cigar. "When the last nail's pounded?" He sneered.

"This here's a secret installation we're constructing, and not a one of us is ever going to see a patch of sky other than this one right here." He indicated with his dirty finger the fading light overhead. "The only living souls that's going to leave this forest is them birds. So get back to work before the whole lot of us gets shot!"

The workers continued to squabble while fifty meters to the south two more individuals studied the lake and the geese.

"You've been here from the beginning, Comrade Brenner, and you can see for yourself the great strides we're making—as an installation, as a comradeship of scientists, and as a nation! You must be proud, my friend, to be a part of such a great undertaking."

"An honor indeed." Hans Brenner stepped over a fallen log and followed his guide to the shore. Formerly a Nazi lieutenant, Hans was currently just an unlucky German scientist who'd been abducted and relocated to the Soviet Union. He'd already passed through the most trying times—in Novosibirsk he was so lonely and discouraged that he'd almost ceased to function. But when he finally understood that his continued existence depended upon his cooperation, he'd forced himself to heal.

He didn't look like a German now, dressed as he was in the baggy tunic and breeches, warm winter cap called an ushanka, heavy boots, and coat of a Russian peasant. After months of captivity he spoke Russian almost like a native and had managed to hide his unhappiness from everyone. But he'd never been able to deceive himself.

He missed Natalie. He missed Rolf, and Marie, and German food, and Germany . . . but mostly he missed Natalie. He heard someone say once, that absence from someone you love makes you love them more. It was true. He loved Natalie with a passion and a longing that consumed him, gnawing at his innards like a ravenous rat. All he could think about outside the laboratory was Natalie. And inside the laboratory it was getting more and more difficult to keep his mind on what he needed to do, day after day, in order to keep from getting shot . . .

The last time he'd touched her was the day she'd agreed to marry him. And that was the day he'd been abducted by Rostov, who said Natalie was no longer Hans's concern. Hans was certain Rostov had Natalie with him in Moscow. And as soon as Hans discovered how to escape this secret installation, he would find his way to Moscow—he'd heard rumors that it was a mere four hundred kilometers away—search out Viktor Rostov, and destroy him.

Hans's companion was enthusiastic about this little stroll into the woods—but then, Andre Sakharov was enthusiastic about anything that pertained to the perfection of a nuclear weapon.

Andre Sakharov was the closest thing Hans had found to a feeling human being—and a friend—since the moment he was tossed head-first into the Soviet Union. He remembered the first day he saw Andre, when Andre had walked up to him at the hospital in Novosibirsk.

"What's wrong with you?" Andre had asked in German.

"Bullet."

"You've got a bullet wound in your chest?" The scientist eyed Hans's bandaged torso.

"My entire torso is one big wound," Hans lamented.

Andre gave him a sad smile. "Probably your entire pride, too. Be glad you're still alive; Comrade Rostov wants the Americans to think you're dead."

Or at least Rostov wanted *one* person to think it; Rostov probably hadn't wasted any time before telling Natalie that Hans was deceased. Someday Rostov would pay for his crimes. Hans would live for that day.

In the meantime, Hans and Andre Sakharov began to work together at the laboratory in Novosibirsk. And then, one night, Hans had been dragged from his bed by anonymous brutes, trussed like a sacrificial goat, blindfolded, and bundled by truck to this secret location.

Andre Sakharov had been transferred also—as head of the new facility and supervisor of a project that would finally bring the Soviet nuclear program to the forefront of the arms race. It was he who'd influenced the powers that be to have Hans brought along for the ride.

"And see, here, Brenner"—Andre always pronounced *Brenner* with a twist of the tongue that made Hans smile—"the new laboratory facility will overlook this lake." Sakharov's arm swept the shimmering lake, its flocks of geese resting for the evening, and the dense woods beyond.

"And before too many more days have passed, there'll be a great fence erected to keep all intruders out." *More likely a fence to keep me in,* Hans thought. "This city is as secret as America's Los Alamos, you know."

"America's what?"

"See what I mean? Even a prominent German nuclear scientist hasn't heard of Los Alamos. And the Americans will never hear about *Arzamas-16*. Even if they ever do hear about the ancient monastery town of Sarov, they'll never imagine it could be a secret nuclear test site. Never in a lifetime of years will they discover that we were able to steal their secrets, their scientists, and ultimately their bomb!"

Their bomb. What did their bomb matter? His bomb had fallen the night he parted company with his bride-to-be. Of course he'd known he would end up here; the abduction had been agreed upon between Hans and Matthews. He'd made a deal with Major James Matthews; Soviet nuclear secrets in exchange for papers to go to America. But the escape, the gunshot wounds to the chest and shoulder, the weeks of rehabilitation . . . all consequences of Hans trying to change his mind at the last minute—because his worry for Natalie's safety when he realized she was in danger trumped any secret deal with Matthews.

He'd heard that God didn't like people killing each other. He barely considered Lieutenant Rostov human, though, so it would be difficult to restrain himself. But even though he wouldn't end Rostov's miserable life, he felt justified in beating Rostov to within a few inches of it. Then, if Natalie were still alive—Hans had to swallow against bile rising in his throat at the idea of how she might have been treated—he would take her and they would flee. Somehow, Natalie and Hans would escape this country, get married in that temple in America, and then settle down to have a family and live a quiet, safe, and peaceful life together.

Andre was talking to him. Hans forced himself to listen, pushing to the back of his mind two very pleasurable thoughts: first, his hands locked about Rostov's neck, and then his arms wrapped about Natalie Allred.

". . . your significant experience with the American language. I would like for you to read from our newest batch of American intelligence—something about it is a little unusual. We have reason to believe our sources have been compromised."

"What makes you think a little bit of English experience makes me the expert you need?"

"We don't have a lot of options right now," Andre replied. "Besides, Comrade Asimova recommended your assistance on this one."

Rima Asimova? Was she spying on the Americans? Hans thought of the fresh-faced college graduate who'd come to live with her scientist father at the compound soon after Hans arrived. She supposedly worked in communications, but she hung around Hans so much that Hans wondered if she was beginning to have a thing for him. She never seemed to do much besides follow him around and ask a lot of inane questions. Hans hated it when she flirted and batted her eyes at him. Even though she was one of the prettier faces around the place, he felt a queasy sort of unease whenever she got too close.

So she was more than just the spoiled daughter of a nuclear scientist who insisted on her own office; she was somehow an integral part of the program. He never would've guessed.

There were many things he never would've guessed: that the gentle Andre Sakharov had been the ruthless man who ordered political prisoners used for the construction of Arzamas-16; that these prisoners would be worked to death's door and then summarily shot to protect the secret of the Soviet Union's newest nuclear research facility; that he would ever be trusted enough to see intelligence obtained from the Americans; and that he, a seasoned Nazi officer and wilderness expert, would still be trapped here in this prison after so long.

He had to get out. He had to escape before those fences went up. He'd seen and meticulously copied the drawings for them: They were to surround the entire monastery and compound, built with two deadly rows of razor-sharp barbed wire, guard towers, and guarded gates. He would have to think of something soon.

Tonight he would take advantage of this opportunity to view secret intelligence documents that might give him more fuel for the fire he was stoking for Major Matthews. Then he would escape, somehow, and he would save Natalie.

Andre checked his watch—a German model, Hans observed. "Comrade Asimova is waiting for you in the control room. I'll apologize to her for the delay—but this has been such a beautiful evening. Don't you agree?"

Hans liked Andre. He liked his tenacity, and he liked his courage in the face of fellow scientists' paranoid mistrust. But he wouldn't miss the man when he found a way to escape this place. That was one thing he'd discovered in this life—it was easy to like someone and leave them—it was all a matter of necessity in order to preserve the relationships that really mattered. And Natalie Allred was worth preserving.

It could be a trap; he would have to watch himself closely tonight. His work was always under scrutiny and he was always under guard. He couldn't even go to the bathroom without an escort. Even now, soldiers watched them from fifty paces behind, Shpagin submachine guns at the ready.

He would see what the intelligence reports said; then he would take that intelligence, the information he had gathered about this secret facility, and his coat—and he would find a way to disappear.

Somehow he would escape and save Natalie. He *knew* he would, because several years before, Rolf Schulmann had told him Heavenly Father answers prayers.

TWENTY-FIVE

Andre Sakharov delivered him to the communications building, and Hans was surprised to see several fellow scientists and military personnel waiting for him in Rima's office. There was a somber mood in the room, as if at a funeral. *My funeral,* Hans thought, *if I make even one mistake.*

Rima Asimova didn't look happy. That was a bad sign. She stepped forward and announced, "Comrade Brenner. We intercepted a message that has us all confused. We thought you might help us understand its significance." She indicated the desk. The others watched, cheerful as pallbearers, as he took a seat.

Hans tried to ignore the general malaise. Something was wrong—this *was* a trap; he was sure of it now. But he could still survive if he knew exactly how they were trying to trap him.

"So, Rima—looks like you've been promoted." He tried to sound confident past the lump in his throat.

Rima ignored his comment and placed a paper in front of him. "This came through regular channels from Moscow. Perhaps they made a mistake with the English—although we don't see how they could have. We're concerned that there seems to be a message within a message, as if our normal channels have been compromised."

Hans looked at the document. It read:

> *Oppenheimer, as per our conversation, we are required to categorize our results in the form provided by HQ. This*

*should be no problem. Your laboratory results are impressive.
The possibilities of a hydrogen-based system are terrifying,
but not to be dismissed. Please comment . . .*

It was dull reading. Nothing in the document made any impression on Hans, other than the obvious conclusion that this was nothing more than a communiqué between nuclear colleagues. There was nothing that the Soviets didn't already know. Hans wondered again what all the somber fuss was about. And then he reached the third paragraph:

*Your news about the accident was distressing. Please accept
the white roses as a token of our sympathy. Your brother's
condition I'm sure will improve soon. His friend is still
missing, and we are still trying to recover her . . .*

His gaze didn't waver, but his hand hidden under the table clenched his knee. He finished reading and glanced up at Rima Asimova. He spoke carefully. "I'm not sure what I'm supposed to find. I'm just a scientist. What do you expect me to see?"

Rima tapped a slender finger on the paper. "I think there's a message hidden in this third paragraph—the one that talks about the accident and the roses. What accident do you think it means?"

"How am I supposed to know?" Hans raised his hands, palms upward. "I don't even know who sent this communication—let alone who this *Oppenheimer* is." He kept his breathing steady. "I'm assuming this is from a scientist in America? At this Los Alamos that Comrade Sakharov talks about?"

"Oppenheimer may not know who sent it, either," Rima said. "Hans, tell these men about white roses."

Hans wasn't expecting this. Viktor Rostov had once given one to Natalie in a bouquet, and it wasn't an innocent gesture of friendship. "White roses?" he asked innocently. He kept his voice light.

"Hans, these men"—Rima indicated the pallbearers arranged behind her—"have concluded that this message was meant for you."

Hans was beginning to conclude the same thing. "For me?" he scoffed. "A secret communiqué sent across the wires to a scientist in Los Alamos?"

"Yes. A *German* scientist in Los Alamos."

"One I do not know," Hans clarified. "I didn't even know there was such a place until Comrade Sakharov—"

"We know you don't have a brother." Rima cut him off. "But according to our sources in Berlin, your German friend, the one who kidnapped Professor Edwin von Hausen from us, considers himself a brother to you. We think the accident mentioned refers to your abduction by Lieutenant Viktor Rostov, an officer with the MGB. The friend mentioned is Natalya Ivanovna Karagodina—a nurse Rostov repatriated to the Soviet Union."

For all these months Hans's anger at Lieutenant Rostov had been tempered by his desperate hopes that he was wrong, that Natalie was actually safe at home in America. The shock at having his suspicions confirmed was almost more than he could take. He struggled to keep his emotions hidden from his interrogator.

His efforts failed.

"You recognize the name," Rima said. "I can see it in your eyes that you're surprised we know about her. We know she was the nurse of your friend Rolf Schulmann while he was convalescing in Berlin. This message"—she indicated the paper in front of him—"was sent by someone to inform you that she is in Moscow with Comrade Rostov. That bothers you." Rima's eyes flashed. "She must've meant something to you."

Now Rima's eyes bored into his. "And there's also reference to a possible rescue . . ."

Hans snapped back at her. "That's as farfetched a notion as the idea that Germans eat bratwurst and beer with every meal." Hans's palms were beginning to sweat. "You could've read that nonsense into any message you intercepted."

"Yes," Rima smiled, "but the source of this message was Brighton, England."

Hans's voice rose. "I've never been to Brighton! I've never been to *England,* for that matter—let alone know anyone who lives there."

"Tell us about white roses, Hans."

He threw up his hands. "Rostov likes white roses. Correction; his *deceased wife* liked white roses. From the way you're acting, you'd think she was the only one in the Soviet Union to like white roses."

"Who knew about her love for white roses, besides Comrade Rostov?"

Hans shrugged. "I would think lots of people."

"Did Natalya?"

"After what he's done to her? Of course."

"Rolf Schulmann? Your 'brother'?"

His pulse pounded. "How would I know?"

"And Major James Matthews, of American intelligence—Rostov's friend during the war?" Rima continued. "Rostov has an agent in Brighton, England—according to our source within the MGB—and he had access to channels and frequencies we would most likely intercept—along with the times these messages might be intercepted. Since you've disappeared off the radar, Rostov might be working with American intelligence to contact you."

Hans rolled his eyes. "Kind of a long shot, don't you think?"

"So is the invention of a nuclear weapon. Wars are lost for not paying attention to the 'long shots,' Comrade."

Hans countered. "What makes you think Rostov would send me a message? He's a loyal Soviet—I know that for a painful fact. Besides, he has no reason to—"

"We believe Major James Matthews sent it," Rima interrupted. "Utilizing Rostov's agent in Brighton. Our next challenge is to find out if Rostov instructed his agent to assist the Americans. Matthews and Comrade Rostov were once friends, you know."

Hans's throat felt dry. He didn't think for a minute that Lieutenant Rostov had anything to do with this message. But he was certain that this 'long shot,' as he'd dismissed it, was meant for him. Rolf had sent it. Dear, kind, resourceful Rolf Schulmann, working for American intelligence. Somehow Rolf was devising a plan to get Hans and Natalie out.

But Rolf didn't know where Hans was. So Rolf had shot a figurative arrow into the sky, with, knowing Rolf, a desperate prayer in his heart. And the arrow had reached its zenith, fallen, and then had miraculously found its mark. There was no other way Rolf could've made contact with a man who'd been abducted, shot, transported halfway around the world, and then moved to a location that officially didn't exist.

"All we need is proof that Rostov has been interacting with American intelligence, and then we'll know."

The fact that they suspected Viktor Rostov was disconcerting. If they arrested Rostov, they would arrest Natalie, and she would be interrogated, tortured, forced to divulge her engagement to a Nazi officer . . . Hans could hardly breathe at the thought. He had to leave here immediately.

"I'm disappointed in you," Rima said with mock regret. "You had such a bright future here . . . And then you go and do this . . ." She sighed. "And all the time you were here in the Soviet Union with an agenda, and possibly even an escape plan! Hans Brenner, we're placing you under arrest."

Hans smirked. "Taking our job a bit seriously, aren't we? Since when have you had the authority to arrest me?"

"Since I was assigned by the MGB to keep an eye on you. Hans, darling"—her sarcasm was getting on his nerves—"how you've disappointed me!"

Hans exploded. "I had nothing to do with this message, and I don't appreciate that you would attribute it to me. What's my crime?"

"Espionage would be our first guess," Rima said. "Conspiracy to defraud the Soviet Union would follow close behind. Don't bother thinking of creative ways to escape, Hans Brenner—remember we're in the middle of nowhere, it's rather cold outside, and you're going to be executed in the morning anyway."

"Rima"—Hans panicked—"I had nothing to do with this!"

"You should never, ever, have made a deal with the Americans." She walked to the door.

"Take care," Hans growled. "Comrade Sakharov needs me. Execute me and your carcass may be the one next to mine in the morgue."

"I'll take that chance." Rima blew him a condescending kiss and left the room.

TWENTY-SIX

It was past sunset when Hans heard the gunshots echoing from over in the vicinity of the lake, where the military housed its slave labor and where Andre Sakharov had described his future laboratory to Hans.

His guards left their posts. Hans did not wait to find out why but attacked the heavy door to his cell. He pushed his metal cot into the door. It crashed into the solid wood, and Hans tried it again. Finally the door gave way, leaving nothing more than a few splinters hanging from its heavy iron hinges. Hans sprinted through the opening.

He borrowed heavy boots, coat, and a furry ushanka from the guards' station. He grabbed a rifle and ran out into the night. He checked the chamber of his weapon as he ran. Four bullets. It would have to do. Nobody gave him a second glance.

"Prisoner riot," a guard shouted at Hans, fooled by the uniform. "They've murdered several guards and escaped into the forest. Administration is calling in troops from Moscow—trained dogs, I hear."

Hans reached the low-roofed laboratory and strode down the hall. He grabbed a flashlight, screwdriver, matches, and a bottle of vodka from a supply cabinet, flung open the door to his office, turned on the flashlight, and then hesitated, taking in the damage revealed by the steady beam.

His office had been entirely dismantled, with filing cabinets opened and papers flung about the room, a trash can overturned, his desk destroyed, and the mattress of his narrow cot sliced to shreds. He ignored the mess, waded across the room, and bent next to his cot. Holding the torch in his mouth he used both hands to lift the steel frame. He bent low to the floor and trained the flashlight's beam up into the hollow leg. He reached one finger up inside. The documents he'd hidden were gone.

He sat back on his haunches, thinking. Outside, army transports rumbled in the direction of the camp. He still heard sporadic gunshots from near the lake. He left his office and trotted across the complex toward the communications building. He slipped inside and found Rima Asimova in her office, staring out the window in the direction of the uproar. He closed the door and she turned. She emitted a strange little squeal.

He ignored her and began to dismantle her desk, pulling out drawers, searching through each before tossing it aside.

She began to inch around him, heading for the door.

Hans spoke without glancing at her. "Don't even try it."

She whimpered. "What do you want with me?"

"Not a thing." He discovered a wad of rubles hidden in the second drawer—more than any Soviet citizen should have in his possession.

"That's mine. Put it back."

Hans pocketed the money.

"What are you doing? Let me out or I'll—I'll scream."

"Be my guest." Hans picked up the desk, flipped it completely over, and let it crash to the floor. He hacked at the wood veneer with the screwdriver, peeling chunks off as he searched for any hiding place. She watched him through her eyelashes while he demolished the desk. Finally he turned to look at her. "Where are they?"

"Where are what?"

"The papers you stole from my room."

"I have no idea what you're talking about." She feigned indignation. "I did no such thing!"

"Rima, you have about three seconds. Then I'm going to burn this building to the ground, using your desk as kindling."

"Hans," she whined, "you're frightening me."

"Tell me where they are."

"Nyet!"

Hans broke the neck of the vodka bottle against a corner of the overturned desk, spilling potent alcohol across the wood. He proceeded to empty the entire contents over the desk and across the floor while Rima Asimova wrung her hands. He produced a match and looked expectantly at the woman.

Rima was no hero. She pulled the papers in question from her coat pocket and held them out at arm's length. She whined, "You would sell our secrets? You would betray your fellow scientists and destroy all that they've worked for? You . . . would betray . . . *me?*" She sniffed and made a show of struggling to hold back tears.

Hans glanced through the papers. "There's one missing, Rima; there was a list of all the scientists at this facility. Where is it?"

Rima lifted her chin. "I would never betray my comrades by giving it back to you!"

Hans struck the match. He held the flame over the pile of alcohol-soaked wood. Rima promptly pulled the list from her pocket and passed it over. Hans glanced at it once and then stuffed it and the other papers into the inside pocket of his coat. He shook out the spent match, produced another and showed it to Rima. "Where's the key to this room?"

She handed it to him.

"Where's the backup key?"

"In a drawer in the front office."

"And the extra key you made for yourself?"

She blinked. "Underneath the cushion of that couch."

"Get it for me."

She retrieved the key, real tears moistening her eyelids. He left the office, closed the door and locked it from the outside, leaving Rima standing inside next to the shattered desk. He visited the front office and located the third key, left the building, and then tossed all three keys into the snow. He kept the flashlight, screwdriver, matches and rifle.

Near the forest he stumbled over a body. He leaned, felt for a pulse, and found none. He trained his flashlight's beam onto the man's face. It was a prison guard. Hans transferred the dead man's documents to his own pocket, returned to his feet, and began to run.

TWENTY-SEVEN

Tuesday, December 3, 1946

The telephone rang as Marie buttoned Alma's coat for school. She ignored it.

"Have all your books?"

Alma nodded and said, "Miz Adams says I have to recite the multiplication tables today."

"You'll do fine. Remember, you said them for Papa last night?"

Alma nodded. The telephone rang again, and again she ignored it.

She pressed his cap down and lowered the ear flaps, snapping the strap beneath his chin. She retrieved her bicycle, straddled the seat, and lifted Alma to the handlebars. He balanced against her chest while she pedaled out onto the main road. He squealed with delight when they coasted down a gentle slope and flew around the corner onto another street. Marie laughed with her son, reveling in his glee.

At his school, Alma hopped from the bike and retrieved his books. He skipped toward the door of the school. Watching him go, she suddenly she had a strange, choking desire to hold him in her arms.

"Charlie!" she said, and she was grateful she'd remembered to use his alias. She swallowed hard, battling moisture in her eyes. "Sweetheart—"

"What is it, Mami?"

She dropped her bicycle and took him in her arms. "I love you. You know that, don't you?"

He nodded against her neck.

"I love you so much, my sweet boy."

"Mami, Miz Adams will scold me if I'm late for class." He looked at her and his brow furrowed. She smiled at him and smoothed a lock of hair curling around an ear flap. Finally she let him go. He skipped away, his books on their strap bouncing against the steps as he mingled with his peers.

She picked up her bicycle and pedaled home.

She'd just removed her coat when the telephone rang again.

As Rolf had instructed her, Marie ignored it and went on with her morning chores. She ironed Rolf's shirts and hung them in the closet. She couldn't help moving them to one side and sliding aside the secret panel at the back of the closet. She studied the contents of the small space for several seconds before her hand reached out and touched the Nazi major's uniform. Dark memories made her shudder, and she quickly closed the panel and rearranged his shirts. Some memories were best not revisited.

In the living room the telephone rang again. This time it didn't stop for several minutes, and Marie tried to ignore the sound by burying herself in preparations for dinner. The telephone fell silent, but it was several minutes before her ears stopped ringing.

She trimmed and prepared a roast, and when the telephone again began to ring, the knife slipped, slicing her hand. Trembling, she cupped her hand and hurried across the kitchen to the sink. She ran warm water over the cut and tried to block out the insistent ringing in the other room. She wrapped a kitchen towel around it, pressed tightly against the flow, and walked toward the living room. Just as she reached the telephone, the ringing stopped.

She returned to the kitchen and searched through the cupboard for a bandage, her nerves on edge as the telephone began to ring again. After five rings it stopped, quieted, and rang again. Again and again.

Marie marched into the living room and pulled the cord from the wall. She felt suddenly dizzy, and sank into Rolf's armchair. She leaned toward her knees and focused on breathing evenly. She wondered if it was caused by loss of blood or fear of who was at the other end of the line.

And then she saw Alma's lunchbox sitting near the door. She bandaged her palm with cellulose tape and grabbed her coat.

She hurried to fetch her bike from the barn. She pedaled as fast as her legs would allow back to Alma's school, ditched her bike, and took the steps to the door two at a time.

The administrative office secretary studied her disheveled hair and flushed cheeks. "Has the nurse called you? Is Charlie sick?"

"No."

"Is it a family emergency?"

"He forgot his lunch . . ." Marie hesitated. Somehow it was more than that. But how does one explain a gut feeling?

"You can leave it here. I'll see that he gets it."

Somehow that didn't make things better. "I—I think I need to take him home."

"Miz Goodwin—" The woman took on a conciliatory tone. "I know you're a new mother—and your adopted son has emotional needs after losing his German parents in the war—but you understand, don't you, that regular attendance is important to your son's transition?"

She was grateful Major Matthews had forged adoption documents to explain Alma's German accent. "I understand. Please, will you direct me to his classroom?"

The woman sighed. "He's on the playground at the moment. If you would like to wait . . ."

Marie ran out the door and down the steps. She circled the building, following sounds of children at play. She saw Alma's teacher and approached her. "Mrs. Adams . . ."

Alma's teacher smiled at her. "Charlie forget his lunch again?"

"Well, yes." Marie's eyes searched the playground. "Where is he?"

Mrs. Adams pointed toward the swings.

Alma wasn't there, nor could Marie see him anywhere about. Her heart pounding, she began to circle the playground, dissecting each group of enthusiastic youngsters for a brown-haired boy with dimples and deep blue eyes.

She crossed the sports field and searched as far as her eyes could see, taking in the panorama of the school buildings, the playground . . .

She saw another, older group of children playing around back of the school, kicking a football or crouching together to converse.

And then she saw two figures standing apart from the children; one was a small boy, and the other was a man crouched in front of him.

She felt suddenly lightheaded. She ran across the grass and down a flight of cracked concrete steps until she reached the duo. She gasped, "What are you doing with my son?"

For what seemed an eternity the man crouched in front of Alma did not answer. He didn't even look at her, as if he didn't consider her sudden presence worth the courtesy of acknowledgement. She grabbed Alma's arm and pulled him away from the man as if from a poisonous snake. "Get away from my son! What do you think you're doing?"

Finally he rose to face her, and she had the nasty impression he reminded her of someone. It wasn't a physical resemblance to anyone she knew, but rather, an emotional one: His eyes, when they locked with hers, carried in their hard depths an evil that she remembered. Even though he was physically different—tall, sinewy, and strong— deep in the recesses of those dark eyes this man reminded her of the wiry Gestapo captain who'd almost captured her outside a small German village in the Rhône-Alps. She shuddered, a shudder so violent that the man noticed, and he smirked.

"Marie Schulmann?" His use of her real name shook her.

"Get away from my boy."

"I don't want to hurt the boy—I just want to chat with your husband."

Clutching at Alma, she turned and fled. The man did not follow.

TWENTY-EIGHT

Lucya Rostova hadn't felt warm since before she could remember. She was cold, from her head beneath its rags to the worn soles of her boots. The cold penetrated her skin and took up permanent residence in her bones.

Her cheekbones protruded, stretched taught against skin red and raw from the constant cold. Her blue eyes squinted against the bitter wind and her jaw clenched, lips pressed together in an effort to keep the razor-sharp cold out of her throat.

She barely glanced at the panorama of suffering before her—she'd seen it all before. She'd witnessed this scene so many times that its tragedy ceased to affect her. A woman cried bitterly, and Lucya turned away. She wasn't calloused or unfeeling—she knew the woman was a newcomer and therefore more prone to emotion. Most likely she had a husband somewhere, perhaps in another camp, who was also suffering. Perhaps she had children who'd been relocated to a children's home. Children she might not see ever again.

It was no use feeling sorry for these women. But sometimes she couldn't help it; the sorrow and suffering around her broke her heart.

She filled her bucket, preparing herself for the excruciating weight. She balanced as best she could and straightened. Her feet shuffled as she made her way toward the Depository, where trucks sat with engines idling at the base of a shallow cliff. She followed the muddy boots of the woman in front of her, up the gradual incline to the point directly above the trucks. She heaved the bucket into her arms and poured the contents into the bed of the truck. The rocks clattered violently against the wood surface of the almost empty truck, the sound reverberating through her head and jarring her skull.

Now the bucket was light, at least for a few minutes.

Fill, heft, shuffle, climb, lift, pour, and then return to fill again. She felt pain in her hip that became a dull throb and then a debilitating, angry monster, gnawing at her ligaments and fighting her every step. She tried to ignore the pain. Fill, heft, shuffle, climb, lift, pour . . .

She saw a group of officers walking near the trucks, and she lowered her head and hoped she wouldn't merit their attention. And then she slipped on the muddy path and fell, her chin striking the bucket as it slammed into the ground. Her rocks spilled in the mud. Quickly she rolled to her knees and began to refill her bucket, not daring to glance at the group of officers. She heard laughter, and then heavy steps coming her way. She cringed, her shoulder muscles tightening in anticipation of a blow.

But none fell. Instead, a young officer knelt at her side and reached for a stone. He dropped it in her bucket and reached for another. Lucya glanced upward, surprised.

His eyes met hers. She felt a small shiver of recognition course through her veins, as if she'd dreamed of eyes such as these. They were blue and kind, with tiny laugh lines at their corners that intrigued the lonely girl. His blond hair curled about the rim of his ushanka and his face was as handsome as any boy she'd ever known. He seemed like a Soviet version of a golden Greek god from one of her papa's books, who'd leapt straight from an ancient mythology text to help her fill her bucket. And the sight of him so close took her breath away.

"Are you all right?" he asked.

She chewed at her lip, fearful.

"Can you speak?"

She dropped her eyes. "I'm not supposed to talk to you."

"I see." He nodded, then reached for more stones. "I'm new here. I don't know all the rules—"

"Sasha!" called one of his laughing comrades. "What do you think you're doing?"

The young officer glanced over Lucya's shoulder, his clear eyes flashing a hint of annoyance. He returned his gaze to Lucya. "I'm sorry you fell." He cleared his throat. "Listen . . . I—"

"Leave the wretch alone, Sasha!"

For just a moment Lucya's eyes again locked with his, and she thought she caught a glimmer of a smile in their depths. For just a moment she felt a gentleness in his presence that warmed through her ragged coat and thin dress, penetrating to her bones and almost negating the effects of the cold. Then he stood and walked away, wiping his hands on his pants. He didn't look back.

TWENTY-NINE

She accepted her evening bread with reverence. She cradled it close to her chest as she trudged toward the women's huts with her bucket. She walked through mud and slime and even worse, yet her mind was on more pleasant matters and she didn't care.

She still felt the warmth of blue eyes that had kindness in their depths, like an entire circle of stoves stoked with precious wood just for her comfort. Her evening's path took her of necessity past fences separating the men's huts from those of the women, and tonight the inevitable hoots and crude invitations did nothing to lower her spirits. How could mere insults matter, when there existed eyes such as those?

She passed the stables, where horses utilized by the road crews were guarded for the night. Prisoners were not allowed to care for the steeds; there was too much opportunity for escape. Several guards commented as she walked past. She did not even hear them.

But she did hear the words spoken from the doorway: "You work too hard, citizen."

She stopped, turned, and, in the dim light of the stable's electric lamp, saw an intriguing sight: Next to the stall door stood a kitchen table, set with an incongruous white linen tablecloth. In the center of the table rested a shiny copper samovar, like a steaming sentinel, surrounded by plates of food and cups for tea. Next to the table sat the young officer who'd helped her when she fell; the same officer whose kind blue eyes had made her thoughts so pleasant.

He gestured for her to come closer. She swallowed hard. Her feet wouldn't move.

"Tea, citizen? To go with your supper?" He indicated the precious bread in her hands.

She dared not accept. She'd been told not to fraternize with the guards so many times that it was part of her nature. To do so could mean time spent in the Hole.

And yet, this was an officer—and what he'd asked her to do could be considered a command. If she didn't obey she could be severely beaten. What was she to do? She remained frozen in place.

He rose to his feet. "Are you afraid?" He walked toward her and suddenly she *was* afraid. But the tone of his voice was not unkind. "I've been watching you, citizen. I worry that you're working too hard."

She lowered her eyes and whispered, "Work in the Soviet Union is a matter of honor and glory."

He laughed. "You read that somewhere! I can't imagine you feel that way after sixteen hours in the mud."

"It's written above the gate to the women's huts. It must be true."

Again he laughed, and the sound cheered her. "My name is Aleksandr Ivanovich Lazerev. My friends call me Sasha." He repeated his invitation: "Come, citizen—drink tea at my table."

She went. It was as if part of her suddenly separated from her body and watched, astonished, as she brazenly disobeyed rules carved into her very soul.

Aleksandr held a chair for her, as if for a lady instead of a political prisoner. She sat while the part of her that had distanced itself looked on in horror. He retrieved the teapot from off the top of the samovar and poured steaming liquid into a cup. He grasped the metal handle around the cup and placed it in front of her. Then he seated himself and poured his own tea.

She couldn't believe this was happening. Even though she'd already broken a bucketful of rules and regulations, she watched in detached awe as her hand reached for the tea.

"Do you ever miss home?" the officer asked. "You have a family, I imagine. A papa? Mama? Brothers?"

"I—have a papa."

"Where does he serve the Leader?"

"Moscow," she whispered, and lowered her head. "At least, he's supposed to be there . . ."

"*Supposed* to be there? What, have you not heard from him?"

She dared not look at him, keeping her gaze on her cup. "He doesn't write. Or I don't receive his letters."

"If he loves you he would write. Do you think he loves you?"

Her hands hugged the warm cup, her head lowered so that the steam from the liquid warmed her chin. She swallowed. "I'm a political prisoner and an enemy of the People. It is dangerous to love an enemy of the People."

"He's a good Party member, then?"

"The best." She did not meet his gaze. "The Motherland means everything to him."

"Everything? You think he's chosen his country over his love for you. Is that what you believe?"

She glanced at him then and hoped her eyes didn't betray her fear.

"You think he's denounced you?" Aleksandr persisted. "Because you're here in the camps?"

She'd considered that. "I have been convicted, sir, and I would hope he wouldn't associate himself with me. It's too . . . too . . ."

He must have sensed her fear. "Don't worry, young citizen." His voice was so gentle it hurt. "I want to be your friend."

Suddenly she couldn't stop trembling. This was a high-ranking young officer she was talking to—he professed to be her friend while secretly he might be planning to betray her to the commandant. She straightened. "Sir, I don't mean to be ungrateful—for your kindness, and for the tea—but I shouldn't be talking to you like this." She glanced quickly at the other guards caring for the horses. "It's not proper . . ." Carefully she set down her cup and began to rise.

"Wait a minute." He caught her elbow, sending shivers all the way up her arm. "Let me show you something." He called to one of the guards. "Dmitri! What have you done with my Orlovs? Bring them here." He smiled at her. "Wait till you see them. I found them at a farm near Moscow—paid a hefty sum for the three of them. Had a harness made out of Ural leather on my way out here. The sleigh should be finished soon—and then I'll be spending a good portion of my time working with them—at the commandant's request, of course . . ."

She had no idea what he was talking about. But she didn't have the courage to ask. Besides, the more Aleksandr Ivanovich talked the longer she could stay here with him—it wouldn't be proper for her to leave before she was invited to do so—and she wasn't sure she wanted to be invited to leave—at least, not yet . . . Suddenly the idea of a night in the Hole because she spoke to an officer was not so dreadful.

"They'll need to be acclimatized to the harness, you know—bit of a tough job getting all three working together. But that's why I'm here . . ." Suddenly Aleksandr stopped, saw the look on her face, and chuckled. "You don't have any idea what I'm talking about, do you?"

"No, sir." She felt color rising in her cheeks.

"There—three Orlov Trotters!" He pointed over Lucya's shoulder, and she turned to see what he pointed at. She stood abruptly, and tea splashed against her frayed sleeve. While she'd been paying attention to Aleksandr's banter, Dmitri and two of his comrades had approached from the other direction, bringing with them the three most beautiful horses she'd ever seen. Surrounded already by horses and their care-givers she had completely disregarded three more sets of hooves, and now she was standing less than two meters from the snow-white hides. Instinctively her hand moved, as if to stroke a silky mane.

"Go ahead." Aleksandr took one of the bridles from its guide. "She loves to be rubbed—especially here." He indicated a spot between the horse's ears. Aleksandr guided the horse's head closer to Lucya, and she reached and touched the sleek hide. The mare watched her with doe-brown eyes, as if she might be capable of dissecting Lucya's mood.

"What—is her name?"

Aleksandr shrugged. "What do you suggest?"

She stared at him. "I can't name your horses!"

"Actually, they belong to the commandant—a gift from my papa in Moscow." Aleksandr caressed the mare's head, scratching between her ears with his long fingers. "I just think of them as mine. What would you name this one?"

She hesitated. She would never have presumed to name the com-mandant's prize horses. But the beautiful white mane, light gray hide that was almost as white as snow, and expressive eyes inspired her, and she whispered *"Snegurichka."*

"Little Snow Maiden," Aleksandr murmured, his eyebrows arched in surprise. He indicated the other two horses. "Then this stallion would be . . . Grandpapa Frost . . . and this steed would be . . . *Yolochka.*" The third horse tossed its distinctive black mane, as if objecting to the title.

"Yolochka?" She studied the third animal, trying to understand what it was about the horse that had inspired Aleksandr to name it Little Fir Tree.

Aleksandr gave her a lopsided grin. "I told you I wasn't good at names."

"I like it."

"Someday I'll take you for a ride in my troika. Ever been in a troika before?" He seemed enthusiastic about the idea. "You helped name them; you will help me train them."

She was bewildered. Why would he do that? She was nothing more than a slave, and he, one of the slave masters . . .

Suddenly he reached and touched her hand, the rough skin of his finger startling her into retreat. "Don't be so afraid, little one." His words were no more than a whisper. "Please understand, I'm your friend."

"I—I must go." She stepped away from the table and the three horses.

"Lucya . . ."

She was shocked to hear him use her given name. It was disconcerting enough that he knew who she was, but for him to speak to her in such an intimate way was downright distressing. "Thank you . . . for the . . ."

She turned and ran before she finished.

THIRTY

She saw the face of Aleksandr Ivanovich everywhere she went. She remembered his unexpected touch at the most inopportune moments. But thinking about him seemed to give her the stamina to endure almost anything. And she was grateful to him for that.

He was waiting for her in front of the stables Friday morning. "I brought you these from the warehouse."

She hesitated, and then she turned to see what he held in his hands. It was a pair of women's heavy winter gloves, in thick, dark brown, fur-lined leather with peasant's brightly colored designs embroidered on the back of the hand and the wrist. Lucya stared but did not have the courage to accept them when he offered them.

"Take them, Lucya." His smile made her heart do somersaults against her ribs. "They'll keep your pretty hands from becoming cal-loused like mine."

She gave him a faint smile in return but did not move to take the gift. "The foreman will punish me if he thinks I took those from the warehouse."

"He'll do no such thing. I'll keep you safe."

Her cheeks burned. She lifted her chin, but in her embarrassment she couldn't make herself look at him. She knew he would be angry, but she said it anyway. "Sir, I don't want to become your camp wife."

He hesitated, clearly surprised at her words. She felt her face begin-ning to redden and she prepared herself for unkind words.

But he didn't mock her. Instead, he only shook his head. "I'm not asking anything of you. I told you, I'll protect you—from everyone, including myself."

And when he said it, her eyes finally lifted. She looked at him and knew that he was telling the truth and that somehow he would keep his promise. "Thank you," she whispered, and accepted his offering.

"I'll try to get you a warm coat, also—to replace that rag you're wearing."

She gave him a last look and fled to the safety of the women's hut.

* * *

Lucya's fortunes began to change. That evening the men across the fence left her alone. It was as if someone had stitched a sign to her back stating that she was the express favorite of an officer, and that if they valued their lives they would treat her with respect—or better yet, not treat her at all. Lucya knew that the distinction of being under an officer's protection wouldn't lessen her workload, nor would it win her a crumb more than her usual allotment of bread. But word spreads fast in the camps, and the attention she received in her hut made her realize she'd become somewhat of a celebrity, as women went out of their way to ask her how they could net their own lieutenant—or at least a shift foreman.

As she filled her bucket the next morning she was summoned by the disciplinary officer and ordered to come with him. Her workmates threw each other significant glances; she was obviously headed for the solitary confinement of the Hole. Whispers flew, and the foreman had to threaten to withhold rations for the evening meal to get everyone working again.

Lucya picked up her bucket and walked toward the officer.

"Leave your bucket."

She panicked. If she set it down it would disappear. When she returned she would have no way of filling her quota and she would be beaten. She hesitated, unsure.

"Don't worry. You won't be punished." That promise from a disciplinary officer was akin to a signed contract. She set the bucket down and followed the man.

She wondered why he had summoned her, and the fact that he was the officer in charge of discipline made her knees weak. Had they found out about the gloves? She felt her chest constrict at the thought. How was she going to explain them?

She walked as quickly as she could, but she was weak from anxiety combined with lack of food, and by the time they reached the administration building she was hardly able to put one foot in front of the other. But at least she did not have to carry that bucket . . .

He led her through the doorway, down an empty corridor, and into the officer's mess. She could feel her heart pounding against her ribs and out through her skin, and even though Aleksandr's promise that he would protect her was enough to take the edge off her terror, she still feared the unknown.

Sometimes a life changes with the seasons, as a body ages and abilities ebb. Sometimes a life can be changed in an instant, when a tree falls the wrong direction or a mine shaft collapses. And sometimes, a life has already shifted direction, and the difference is only discovered through a series of rapid-fire events that take one's breath away. That was how Lucya felt now, as a woman entered from the far end of the mess who was instantly familiar to Lucya. The shawl she held in her hands was the one stolen from Lucya not so long ago. Lucya's pulse quickened.

The guard prodded the thief, and the woman gave back Lucya's shawl. Lucya ignored the promise of retribution in those hateful eyes and pulled the filthy shawl close to her heart. "Thank you," she whispered, as much to the woman in front of her as to the disciplinary officer. "Thank you."

Still numb with shock, Lucya was escorted by the officer out of the building. But they didn't return to the quarry. Instead, he led her toward a cluster of newly constructed huts, with prisoners still painting eaves and hanging doors. He ushered her inside a finished hut, where instead of fifty bunks packed in rows less than two feet apart there were only twelve bunks huddled about a large wood stove at the center of the room. Thick wool blankets and cotton pillows lay over each, and a row of lockers stood against the far wall. No foul stench of overflowing bathroom buckets regaled her nostrils, and the sweet smell of new timber was as fragrant as any perfume she'd ever smelled.

"You have a new work assignment." Her escort left her there, standing in the middle of a new bunkhouse with her beloved shawl cradled in her arms, two warm stoves, twelve empty beds, and a multitude of unanswered questions.

* * *

She became more courageous and shuffled closer to the stove until her hands no longer needed her gloves and her toes began to thaw, and she even dared sit on the edge of one of the bunks nearest the fire, until night fell and the stove cooled. She waited, huddled there as if suspended between two chapters of her life, unsure what tomorrow would bring and afraid to go back. The disciplinary officer had told her to wait. He'd told her she was to receive a new work assignment. And she dared not move from this room until she was told what to do next.

She heard a sound then, one that she hadn't heard in a very long time. Could it be laughter? Even the tramp of prisoners' boots approaching through the snow sounded almost like dancing. She stood quickly, fearful of being caught on another's bunk, as the door opened and eleven women entered the barracks. Lucya was curious. They didn't seem like prisoners in a work camp; they wore clean clothes, they had combed and styled hair, their eyes sparkled with health. They looked as if they'd just entered the shopping district instead of a prisoner's hut.

One of the women approached. She smiled at Lucya and said, "My name is Anya Somova. I'm the foreman for the women's administrative group. They told us you were coming."

Lucya hesitated. "I—"

Anya patted her arm. "Come with me. I'll get a uniform for you, and blankets and sheets. Tomorrow you'll take a bath."

A bath. She hadn't had the luxury of a bath since arriving at Vtoraya Rechka. She didn't know how to respond, and she stumbled over the question that had been plaguing her for most of that solitary afternoon. "Will they still keep my bucket for me? If I lose it they will be angry . . ."

Anya laughed, but without menace. "Forget your bucket—you have a new work assignment now, here, with us." Her arm swept the room, taking in the women going about their nightly routines. "And we don't need buckets."

Lucya felt relief wash over her in such a violent flood that it brought tears to her eyes. She wiped at them furiously, hoping Anya hadn't noticed.

Anya motioned for Lucya to follow her, and they walked through the bunks, past two women stoking the wood stove with firewood, past an occupied bathroom with a privacy door, and into a storage room at the back. "You'll need a blanket"—Anya eyed Lucya critically—"perhaps *two,* until we can get meat on those bones, and a good coat. I see your gloves are adequate. Good. That means your hands will be healthy and can work fast."

"What will my hands be doing?"

"We mend soldiers' uniforms and sew new ones for the officers. Can you sew?"

"I sewed my own wedding dress."

"Good. Are you married, then?"

"No."

Anya's eyes flickered, as if she understood the chasm that can separate the making of one's wedding dress from the actual use of it. "Many of the women here are young, like you. Many had hopes of marriage crushed by this war. Many more are mothers with infants in the camp nursery. They're allowed to visit and nurse their children every four hours instead of every five, like the women in the road gangs. Are you from the road?"

"The quarry."

"That would explain the bucket." Anya loaded Lucya's arms with blankets, a pillow, a cotton sheet with only a few patches, underwear, two dresses, and a coat. "Administration likes us to look our best, so wash your hair once a week and take care of your clothes. Many of us are camp wives, you know. Are you a camp wife?"

"I have a friend . . ."

"Ah, yes. He's an officer?"

"An officer at the stables."

"How fortunate for you."

Lucya wanted to explain. She wanted to tell Anya that Aleksandr was not like those other officers, that he was gentle and kind, and that he never asked anything of her that she would be embarrassed to give. But she held her tongue. Even though Anya was one of the kindest women Lucya had ever met in the camps, she didn't think Anya would understand.

"You will sleep here." Anya indicated a bed. "You have an upper bunk. Are you strong enough to climb?"

"I think so."

"Good. If you have any problem I can move things around a bit. Dinner is in an hour. Unfortunately, that's one thing the same for us as for those at the quarry." Anya's lips twisted. "But your health may improve with the lighter work load. Many improve when transferred here. Consider yourself lucky. Did your officer get you this assignment?"

The idea had occurred to Lucya. "I think so . . ."

"Good. Make sure you thank him." She patted Lucya's arm and walked away.

That night the wood in the stove crackled and shifted, and women around her snored contentedly. She didn't have to share her bunk with any other prisoners, and the narrow mattress seemed as big as a wedding bed. She felt comfortable for the first time in months. She couldn't keep tears from falling, even though she hated staining her beautiful pillow. "Thank you, Aleksandr," she whispered toward the ceiling. "Thank you, thank you . . ." She drifted into the most comfortable sleep she could remember. Maybe, just maybe, because of a young officer's kindness, she would survive until her papa came for her.

THIRTY-ONE

Sunday, December 8, 1946

Lucya woke to find sunlight painting the curtains on the windows. She looked around her. Every bed was still filled. She sat, uncertain, and wondered what she was supposed to do.

Never had she seen the morning sun through the windows of a sleeping hut. Always by this hour she was at the quarry, hefting her bucket and dodging the guard's lash. She wondered if all of her new friends would be punished for this unprecedented sleep-in. Oh, how she dreaded solitary confinement!

The woman across from her stretched, yawned, and curled into a fetal position beneath her blanket. She opened her eyes and found Lucya watching her.

She answered Lucya's unspoken query. "Administration gives us one day off in ten. Go back to sleep." The woman closed her eyes again.

It took a moment to sink in. A day off? From work? She'd never heard of such a thing. A day off to do what?

It seemed most of the women already had plans to sleep most of the day. Morning bread enticed them temporarily from the warmth of their mattresses, and they shuffled outside in coats and valenki boots, hair sleep-ruffled, to gather their portion. Then they carried it back to their bunks, where sleep overtook them again, sometimes with the bread still cradled in their arms. It was a day like Lucya had never known. Not even as a free citizen had she ever known a day free of all responsibility.

Well, not *all* responsibility—after several extra hours of sleep, the women washed their dresses and themselves, cleaned the hut, and ventured into the bitter cold to chop wood for the two stoves.

And Aleksandr came to see Lucya. As she carried wood toward the hut she saw him standing there, stunningly handsome in his officer's uniform and ushanka complete with official insignia. But even his presence couldn't outshine what he had brought with him: three prancing white horses—Snegurichka, Grandpapa Frost, and Yolochka. And the three horses were hitched to a gleaming new sled.

The sight was breathtaking. The women accompanying Lucya stopped and stared. One dropped her armload of wood. All three turned their stare finally on Lucya.

"Are you free, then, for the rest of the afternoon?" Aleksandr's voice was the icing on the cake, and Lucya felt an unexpected shiver of pleasure run up her spine.

"I—" Lucya swallowed, a lump in her throat making words almost impossible. "I have to carry this wood . . ."

"Are you *crazy?*" hissed one of her comrades. "Give me the wood and get out of here!"

She relinquished her load. It felt like a dream. A very, very good dream . . .

She took his proffered hand, and he hoisted her into the sled.

"What will the commandant say?" she asked in a trembling voice.

"These are his horses—remember?"

She couldn't shake her anxiety, cultivated through months of conditioning. "Do you have permission to use them?"

He laughed, and the good-natured sound wrapped itself around her heart and drew her to him. She looked at him with shining eyes, and he returned her gaze. "Where to, young maiden?"

To Moscow. To my Papa. To the train station. Away from here.

"Where are we allowed to go?"

"Wherever we want—as long as I have you back by dark."

Daylight in Vladivostok was precious, and nightfall couldn't be more than three hours away. But she was grateful for those three hours. "That sounds beautiful."

"Ever ridden in a troika before?"

She shook her head. "I've seen them, though—they're always in the New Year's parade at the Kremlin. Comrade Stalin's first-in-command rode in one."

"Why not Comrade Stalin?"

She smiled. "He doesn't show his face much. Do you know what the women call him?"

"What?"

"The Mustache." Suddenly she clapped her hands over her mouth. She couldn't believe what she had just said to a man in uniform. "Please—I don't want to get in trouble—"

Aleksandr laughed. "The officers call him that also—behind the commandant's back."

She smiled at him. "Thank you—for everything you've done for me."

"It was easy. They were looking for another girl. I thought of you."

She shifted uneasily, and her hands clenched in her lap. "I—I don't want to accept it, if it means . . ."

He turned to look at her. "Don't think that of me, Lucya. You're my friend. I helped a friend. That's all. I expect nothing in return."

"The women think—"

"Then let them think!" He shook the reins emphatically. "It doesn't matter to *us* what they think, does it?"

"No," she said as she looked down at her hands.

"To me, it only matters what *you* think."

She nodded and felt the peaceful feelings of moments before flood her soul. It amazed her that a man would treat her with such respect—especially in such an evil place. It was a miracle that she'd met him, and she had to admit that it was because of him that she was still alive.

Her mother had been one who prayed to God—in secret, of course—never when Papa was around. But Lucya had seen her praying—even as she milked the goat. Perhaps it was because of her mother's example that Lucya had faith that her papa would come and get her. Because in her darkest hours, in the most desperate moments, Lucya herself had whispered an awkward, secret prayer or two: *God, please send Papa to rescue me. Please bring my papa . . .*

God hadn't sent her papa—not yet. But he'd sent a handsome young officer with a kind heart and gentle eyes. And Aleksandr had reached out his hand and protected her from harm. God had answered her prayers in a strange way. But she wouldn't complain. In fact, she felt peaceful about everything, here in this old-fashioned troika, with Aleksandr Lazerev struggling with the reins.

"They're not used to pulling as a threesome," he tried to explain.

"And you're not used to driving them as a threesome."

He grinned at her. "Are you having a good time?"

"Yes."

"Are you warm?"

She giggled. "No."

"Someday I'll also find a way to make you warm again."

"My new accommodations come very close to fulfilling that promise."

"I'm glad."

She was flying, and even with razor-sharp wind slicing at her face she felt a thrill that she hadn't felt since before her arrest. She watched as the forests gave way to frozen grassland and finally to crisp, gray ice. Aleksandr reigned in the three horses.

"It's the sea of Japan," Aleksandr explained. "On the opposite shore are the islands of Honshu and Hokkaido, and then Kyushu, and about three hundred smaller islands that belong to the recently conquered empire of Japan."

"I've never seen the sea before," Lucya murmured. "I've never seen anything greater than the Ob."

"Someday I want to take you across that sea."

"Oh no." She laughed. "Someday my papa will come for me, and I'll go the *opposite* direction—back to Moscow."

Aleksandr said nothing, only studied the uneven ice near the shore, his face thoughtful.

She watched him closely, marveling at his maturity and strength. She marveled at how easy it was to like him. And yet, her regard for him was still tempered by the fear of his position. She took a deep breath. "There's more to you than you've told me. Can't you tell me about you? About your family?"

But he shook his head. "Not now, Lucya. There will be a time for that, but it's not now." He glanced at the sun, now low on the horizon. "We have to go back."

"And we can't talk as we go?"

He turned to look at her, and his eyes studied her carefully, deeply. Then he leaned toward her, hesitating for just a moment as his breath warmed her face, and then he moved away. "Someday I'll tell you about my family, and all about myself. I promise you that."

THIRTY-TWO

Hans Brenner hitched a ride to Gorky in a collective farm truck. It was out of his way, but he planned to take the train west to Moscow. He used his stolen documents and money to purchase a train ticket, and then he waited for the train to arrive. He wrapped the uniform coat tightly about him and slouched on a bench on the train platform. He tried to look as sullen as possible to discourage any friendly banter that might reveal the truth.

The truth was that he was scared. He didn't like the feeling. He'd acquired a heavy dose of humility since his capture, he realized, and he whispered an awkward prayer in his heart. Over and over: *God, please get me out of here. Help me find Natalie. Help me break every bone in Rostov's body . . .*

"I know you're from the factory."

Hans started, turned, and glanced at the person who'd taken the space next to him. The youth was barely over the threshold of maturity, and even with a heavy winter coat was slender as a beanstalk. He had his hands shoved deep into his pockets and his collar turned up against the cold. One eye watched Hans with steady determination, while the other floated as if it could not decide what to focus on.

Hans shrugged. "That's a safe bet, friend, seeing Gorky has lots of factories."

"You work at the *Autozavod*—at the Ford factory."

"Do I?" Hans felt a creeping annoyance—like one might feel toward a yapping puppy. "What do you want, Comrade?"

"You're not Soviet. You're American."

"However did you guess?"

"You speak Russian like one. Americans speak with a distinct accent, no matter how they try to hide it."

"And how do you know so much?" Strange, Hans mused, to be thought of as an American. "You're a professor of linguistics at the university? Or, maybe you teach Russian to Americans at the factory?"

"Very funny." The boy rubbed one dirty glove across his nose. "There are many of you Americans here to build the motorcars. We've spoken with many Americans over the months—the Mustache entices you to come from America, and then he works you like lab rats while he sits up nights in his Kremlin tower and plans how to crush America. And if you breathe wrong you're threatened with arrest and deportation to Siberia. Power—it's all about power. Don't think I don't know. My parents were arrested and sentenced to three lifetimes in Kolyma. Believe me, I know." The young man glanced once over Hans's shoulder, scratched his neck under the collar of his coat, and hunched down even lower on the bench.

"And why are you telling me this?"

"Because I'm a reasonable man, and I've been watching you. You seem a decent fellow—younger than most of the Americans here. I want to give you a choice."

"A choice? How nice."

The youth nodded. "Either you do as I tell you or the Mustache gets you."

Hans chuckled. "I'll take my chances with 'the Mustache.'"

"Fair enough. 'Cause you've got an MGB policeman on your tail."

"Really." Hans was mildly amused at the youth's cloak-and-dagger approach.

"He'll kill you if you set foot on that train."

"No he won't. I have a passport."

"Do you, now?" The boy raised an eyebrow.

"And a signed permit from the People's Commissariat of Internal Affairs."

The young man fingered a button on his coat. "So does everyone."

"Everyone?" Hans wished the youth would find someone else to annoy.

"Every American who boards the train from this platform, trying to escape to Moscow."

For a moment Hans didn't know what to say.

The youth indicated Hans's breast pocket. "You've stolen factory secrets and escaped with a pilfered uniform. You have all the proper documents and you're not worried about the MGB tail. You're tired of the rigors of slave labor in the Soviet Union and you're ready to head home to your girl. That's your story. Did I leave anything out?"

"I admit, you have me at a disadvantage." Hans tried to ignore the sudden, strange lump at the base of his throat. "I don't even know your name, and you seem to know everything about me."

"Everything except your name." The youth held out one grubby, gloveless hand. "I'm Arseni. First name only, that's the deal."

"Hans." He barely touched the hand. "And I'm not American."

"You're German?" Arseni nodded as if a great mystery had been explained. Then he revised his earlier story: "You're one of those captured German scientists; they've suspected your loyalty for some time now. You're dissatisfied and you've become sloppy. They decided to dangle the bait and see if you'd grab for it. Sorry, my friend, you've proved their suspicions correct. Now, when you enter the train, that agent standing near the wood stove is going to follow you and shoot you in the back. He'll take your bags and make it look like a robbery. I guarantee if you take this train, you're never going to leave Gorky." Arseni cleared his throat. "That is, unless you do exactly as I say."

"This has happened before?"

"*Da.* Of course. I've sat and watched as brainless old scientists escaping from the laboratories around Novosibirsk pull the same stunt over and over. They've tried, failed, and all been caught in the same net."

"Novosibirsk?" Hans sniffed. "Your family is from there?"

"I told you, half-wit; my family's in Kolyma."

"You only said your parents were sent there."

"My babushka lives in Novosibirsk."

"You're a long way from your grandma, my friend. What are you doing so far from your family?"

"Maybe I've got a *new* family now," the boy said with a sneer.

"You mean, you're part of a gang? Maybe it's *your* man waiting to shoot me in the back."

"Take that chance if you want to." Arseni shrugged.

Hans was irritated, disappointed, and afraid, but he was also convinced. If what Arseni said was true then he dared not get on the train—at least not with the documents he was carrying. At Arzamas-16 they would've noticed the dead guard was missing his documents almost immediately. And Rima, that good little Soviet, would've taken care of the rest. Best case scenario, he would end up somewhere north of the Arctic Circle with a coal pick in one hand and a number sewn to his sleeve.

However, the fighter in him was not about to surrender. "All right, Arseni; what do I need to do?"

"First of all, don't get on that train."

"I think I've figured that out."

"Second, you're gonna hand me all your documents—there, the ones in your coat pocket."

"My passport?"

Arseni nodded. "And the nuclear secrets you're carrying."

"I'll die first."

"That can be arranged."

"Besides, if the MGB suspects me, you can't think they'd trust me with any *real* secrets." Hans thought bitterly of how he'd let Matthews down. Silently he said good-bye to the promised travel papers to America.

"Oh, they're real, all right," Arseni countered. "You may be a political prisoner, but you're no idiot. Your jailors figured you'd be intelligent enough to tell the difference. They gambled their agents wouldn't let you take them past Gorky."

"What do *you* want with them?"

"Maybe I'm a loyal Party member." Arseni smirked. "Maybe I plan to turn them in for a medal and a pat on the back from Stalin."

"You wouldn't risk the MGB thinking you'd read them."

"Maybe I can't read."

"And maybe you're not carrying any identification, either, which explains why you want mine."

"I'm carrying papers." Arseni sounded hurt. "The new, improved sort, of course."

"You mean forged."

"Whatever works, my friend."

"And your thief comrades back you on this, or is this a one-man job?"

Hans might have imagined the hesitation. Arseni's voice lowered. "You wouldn't ask that if you knew who was standing behind you."

"If I turn and look you'll attack. I may be a dumb German but I'm a smart political prisoner. You said it yourself." Hans shifted his body to look fully at the youth. "And the fact is, Arseni, you're acting alone, and I could jump you right now and easily subdue you—you're such a slight, malnourished thing—then turn you over for questioning to that MGB man you pointed out to me." Hans smiled. "Maybe they'll give *me* that substantial reward you mentioned."

Arseni's annoying smile didn't waver. "I can see we're going to get along quite well."

"Thanks. But I've decided I have a train to catch. I hear it coming." Hans moved to stand up. "Now that you've warned me to watch my back I'll be all right."

Arseni captured Hans's sleeve. "Do you want them to kill you?"

"You're such a young, inexperienced thief, Arseni. How many Germans have you managed to convince to turn over their stolen secrets?"

Now the hesitation was unmistakable. Arseni was aggravated. He reached inside his coat, and lightning-quick Hans captured his bony wrist. "Remove your hand slowly, Comrade, and bring the knife with you. That's it. You don't know who you're dealing with here. I'm not just any old German scientist." Arseni attempted to twist free and Hans intensified his grip to bone-crushing force. "I'm a desperate, *dangerous* old German scientist who's been on the run for a long time. I'm cold, tired, hungry, and cranky as a hibernating bear. So give me the knife."

Hans saw a flash of anxiety in the youth's eyes, and suddenly Hans felt sorry for him. He wondered what it would be like to be one of the many petty thieves growing up on the Soviet Union's filthy streets, struggling for survival while trying to elude the police. Firmly Hans twisted the knife from his grip. "You're a member of a criminal gang and you have to support your 'family' or they'll expel you."

Arseni flashed him a look of disdain, but Hans could see the growing despair behind the look. "Everything I said is true. They *do* suspect you! You *will* die if—"

"I believe you, Arseni. Don't worry." Hans pocketed the knife, but he didn't release the bony wrist. "You're a brave boy—irritating, perhaps, but brave."

Arseni spat, "I'm not a boy," and tried to twist free.

"I'm sure you're not, after all you've been through. What happened to the rest of your family? Why come all this way from Novosibirsk?"

"None of your business."

"I agree. But you need to steal to survive, don't you? That's why you need my passport—to sell for ration coupons?"

Arseni straightened. "I *alter* them—and sell them to people the City Soviet won't allow to travel."

"You're probably very good at it."

"The best. Let go of me."

Something inside Hans wanted to help the boy who'd probably just saved Hans's skin. "All right, Arseni." Hans let go of his wrist. If Arseni ran, it was none of his concern. "But I'm going to keep the secrets I stole from the laboratory."

"You'll never get anywhere with them."

"Yes I will. You're going to help me elude that policeman over there, and then I'll pay you to alter my passport. Then you're going to help me jump the next train for Moscow."

"No way I'm gonna do all that."

"Yes you are. I'll pay you. I'll pay you whatever you want."

"You can't afford what I want."

Hans smiled. "Do you think I'd steal only nuclear secrets? Give me a little credit, Arseni—as one thief to another."

Arseni's face softened for a brief moment. "Maybe you're smarter than I thought."

"Richer, too—if you can modify ration documents as well as you claim to be able to modify passports."

Arseni's face broke into a boyish grin. "I'm the best at that, too."

"Then your fortune's made. That is, if you agree to help me."

From the distance a long, piercing whistle cut the cold night air. Arseni nodded. "You've got yourself a deal, German. Follow me."

"We've got a tail—remember?"

"Not if you don't get on that train. You're not the man they want if you don't get on that train."

Hans followed Arseni. They left the platform and walked through the vaulted station, out the entrance, and across an almost vacant, frozen city square. The policeman followed them onto the square.

"I didn't get on the train," Hans grumbled, "and he's still following me."

"What did you steal from them?" Arseni swore. "Get on that car." He ran with Hans toward a streetcar stop, the vehicle in question just beginning to pull away. Both made a flying grab for the handle leading up to the rear door. Hans made contact while Arseni's hand slipped and he tumbled away. Hans let go and leaped off the car. He wasn't about to leave the poor boy to a grisly fate.

"You *are* a half-wit!" Arseni scrambled to his feet. "You're gonna get us both killed."

"I changed my mind." Hans strode back toward the train station. "I'm getting on that train for Moscow—"

"What about the new passport?"

"And you're catching a train going the other direction."

"Not in a thousand years."

Hans indicated the determined MGB policeman. "Does this man know you?"

"I'm not *that* dim-witted, German."

"All right." Hans walked right up to the approaching officer and decked him with a powerful left hook. The man did a dramatic back somersault and sprawled onto the cobblestones. Hans quickly relieved him of his gun, his identity documents, his ushanka, and his coat. "Give the man your coat, Arseni," he ordered, "or he'll freeze to death."

He tossed the pilfered uniform at the boy. "And then you're going back to Novosibirsk."

"You can't make me." Arseni donned the heavy coat and hat.

Hans pocketed the policeman's identification papers. He tossed the ones he'd borrowed from the dead guard to Arseni. "As soon as his headache wears off he's gonna be looking for you." Hans unrolled a thick wad of currency and ration coupons, donated by the patriotic Rima. "Half of this is yours if you go back to your babushka in Novosibirsk."

Arseni licked his lips. "Why pay me to go home?"

"Because you need the money. And your grandma needs you." Hans hesitated. "And because you saved my life tonight."

"What if I don't want to leave?"

"Yes you do. I saw it in your eyes. You hate it here."

"Nobody tells me what to do, German."

Hans tossed him the money. "And that's why you're going home. You're fed up with taking orders from the thieves-in-law. You're going to take care of your grandma with that money. And if you know what's good for you, you won't stray more than a couple of kilometers from the ones you love ever again. Got it?"

Arseni nodded, speechless. He actually looked relieved.

"Give me your address in Novosibirsk," Hans said. "Who knows? Maybe I'll have need of your talents someday." He doubted it, but the compliment had the desired effect on the boy. "And if I ever need you in Novosibirsk," Hans concluded, "I'll come find you."

THIRTY-THREE

Monday, December 9, 1946

Regina found that mothers with small babies seemed to be given special consideration on the crowded streetcars. The conductor seemed to wait a few extra seconds for her to board. Helping hands always pulled her and the baby inside the car, and someone always offered her his seat.

On December 9, it was because of the latter selfless act that Regina failed to recognize the car idling near the hospital stop. She might've stayed on the streetcar and ridden past had she known who was waiting for her.

As it was, she stepped from the streetcar into the arms of the MGB.

Roman Krajnik glanced once at her baby before ushering her to his car. "You've missed several of our weekly visits. I came to help you remember."

She'd been avoiding him. "I always have so much to do at the hospital . . ." She ducked to avoid the roof of the car. "I'm very sorry."

"My time is important, Regina. You should respect that."

She held her baby close. "I know. I'm sorry. It was impossible—"

Krajnik slammed her door, cutting her off midsentence. He moved around the car and slid into the seat next to the driver. "These visits are non-negotiable, Regina—they're imperative both to the safety of your friend Natalya Ivanovna and to that of your husband."

They drove in silence for several minutes. As they passed the Kremlin the sun escaped its prison of heavy clouds for a brief, blissful moment, the newly fallen snow reflecting the light like glittering diamonds. Ina whimpered in her sleep, and Regina pulled her up against her shoulder and leaned her cheek into the baby's warmth. She focused on the gentle, rhythmic expansion of the tiny chest and the sweet smell of her baby's warm breath, and for just a moment it didn't matter that she was being driven against her will to the place she had grown to hate. The only thing that mattered was cradled in her arms, and she would do whatever it took to protect her.

Except that her husband also needed her, and for his sake alone she would again betray Natalya Ivanovna.

Igor Sushin's office no longer produced any good memories. The air hung heavy with her dread, and she realized she was clinging to her baby as if to a security blanket.

"How is your baby?" Krajnik asked. It was as solicitous as a remark on the weather.

"Healthy."

"Is she eating well?"

What a strange question. "She seems satisfied."

"Are you able to continue your daily responsibilities?"

"I carry her with me. She hasn't been a problem."

Krajnik's brow knit. "You carry her with you? What are your responsibilities?"

"I clean the floors."

"And how do you carry the baby while you clean floors?"

"Natalya Ivanovna fashioned a baby sling. I wear it while I work."

He did not seem pleased by the American's creativity. "And how is your friend, Natalya Ivanovna?"

"Healthy. She works hard."

"Does she still confide in you?"

"Yes. She trusts me." Regina realized too late that her words bordered on cynical.

Krajnik seemed not to notice. "She's lucky to have such a friend as you."

Regina's breath felt tight in her chest.

"What have you and she discussed recently?"

"Eternal families."

Krajnik blinked. "*Eternal* families?"

Regina nodded. "A man and a woman can be married in a temple and then they can be together forever."

Roman Krajnik seemed taken aback. "Excuse me?"

Regina forced a smile. "Natalya said that if we're worthy we can be married for eternity."

"Worthy of what?"

"Worthy of this eternal marriage." Regina hesitated. "It's complicated."

Krajnik grimaced. "Is she forcing religion on you?"

"No. I asked, she explained. That's all."

"She explained what? About temples? About this eternal marriage? About God?"

"Yes. She plans to be married someday for eternity."

Krajnik smirked. "And what does Comrade Rostov think of that? What does he think of this—this 'eternity'?"

Regina laughed. "I don't think he knows she's engaged. She was engaged when she was forcibly brought to Moscow."

"It is what's best for her."

"Yes." Regina sobered.

Krajnik studied her carefully. "So, she's previously engaged." Krajnik's lips twisted. He continued, more to himself than to her, "Poor professor."

"If Comrade Rostov knew of their engagement I'm sure he would honor their promise to each other."

"Would he, now?" The smile deepened. "Then he's a better man than I thought."

"He's a better man than any of us thought, Comrade." Something told her she was walking a fine line between agreement and insolence. She swallowed hard and fumbled for a way to remedy her error. "It's sad, isn't it, about his daughter?"

Krajnik ignored her attempt. "And who is the intended?"

"For Rostov's daughter?"

"For Natalya Ivanovna." Krajnik scowled. "Don't play games."

Regina shrugged. "She didn't say. She only mentioned that she agreed to marry him on the same evening that she was abducted. She was

devastated—but I believe she's hopeful to one day see her fiancé again."
Regina could see no harm in relaying her friend's hope to this man.

"I see. Natalya is a beautiful woman. Her fiancé is a lucky man."
Krajnik's lips twisted again. "And I do feel sorry for our good friend
Comrade Rostov." He glanced at the door as a maid entered. He asked
Regina, "Are you hungry?"

"Yes, thank you." She allowed herself then to focus on the rum-
blings in her midsection.

Roman Krajnik gave orders to the maid, and after she left he said,
"She will also bring milk for your baby."

"Thank you. But I'll feed her myself later."

"It's understandable that you'd prefer to nurse the infant." Krajnik
nodded. "But don't you agree that it's a good idea to prepare your baby
for any unforeseen separations?"

Regina sat, stunned, and tried to contemplate the implications of
such a question. She stammered, "I—I do not see how a separation
could happen, Comrade. Even Doktor Komarov insists that a baby's
proper development depends upon—"

"Regina." Suddenly Krajnik was all solicitude. "Don't worry about
such things. Of course a baby is better off with its mother. But it's
always good to prepare ourselves for unanticipated events. Certainly
you wouldn't want your baby unable to accept nourishment if, for
example, your work schedule required longer hours." He brightened.
"And I have it on good authority that Doktor Komarov is reconsidering
your request to return to Olga's nursing staff."

Regina's heart skipped a beat. If she had a chance to return it would
almost be worth the need to teach Ina to accept another source of
nutrition. She felt a surge of hope, followed by a moment of panic at
the thought of long hours away from her baby.

Then the oddity of having such a conversation with this man who'd
replaced her papa as head of the MGB hit her. Why would he concern
himself with such a maternal subject? Was that why she was here? To
talk about her relationship with her child? She was under the impression that Natalya was the subject of Krajnik's interest.

Krajnik continued. "And the baby will be better off with time away
from its mother, don't you think? A baby needs to acclimatize itself to

its environment—and be cared for by a variety of different caregivers, so it won't always be dependent upon the affections of a mother."

His words rubbed like coarse sand against her skin. Regina rose to her feet. "I have to go to work—the hospital floors are filthy, and I wouldn't want to miss my opportunity to clean them." She felt Ina begin to stir. "You're correct—my baby's development is of utmost importance to me. I'll certainly discuss options with a doctor—this afternoon, if possible! Please—"

"Where did she meet him?" Krajnik cut her off.

"Pardon me?"

"Natalya Ivanovna. Where did she meet her intended?"

Regina stared at the man in front of her, and then sank back into her seat. "Berlin, I think—but they were in Paris when they agreed to marry."

"Is he a Soviet citizen?"

Regina fidgeted in her seat. Then she lied. "I assumed so."

"Why would you make that assumption?"

"Because she said he was Comrade Rostov's student at the university before the war . . ."

Krajnik leaned forward. He studied Regina, and the sudden light in his eyes did a strange little dance that bothered her. He seemed to contemplate her words on a silent, secret level. He murmured, "At which university, I wonder?"

"Excuse me?"

"Comrade Rostov was a guest professor at Berlin University before the war . . ."

Something very much like a faint warning tugged at Regina's consciousness, but she couldn't understand the reason for it. Why should this news be considered anything out of the ordinary? Certainly there was nothing extraordinary about the statements she'd made to Comrade Krajnik. What did it matter whom Natalya chose to love?

"What was the fiancé's name?"

"She calls him 'Hans.' That's all I know."

"It isn't a Russian name . . ."

She knew that. She felt suddenly defensive of her friend. "Neither is 'Krajnik.' Doesn't your family hail from the Ukraine?"

Now a muscle near his left cheekbone twitched, and he eyed her coldly. His fingers drummed the desk's surface. She knew she'd gone too far.

What was his interest? That the American's fiancé was perhaps not Russian? What did it matter? Soviet officers came home with foreign engagements all the time, and their petitions for documents for their intendeds flooded the offices of the Politburo. If Natalya had proof that her man was alive, then what did it matter her fiancé's nationality? Certainly a good marriage would make her a happier and more productive Soviet citizen. Who knows? Perhaps someday she would also join the Party and enjoy the multitudes of benefits accompanying the marriage of socialism and government. Perhaps there was still hope that the woman who was the closest friend Regina had ever had might someday be happy.

Krajnik pushed himself to his feet, and for just a second his expression frightened her. Then he forced a smile. "You're right, Regina Igorevna, you must return immediately to the hospital. The Party appreciates all you do to help us." Krajnik reached to caress her baby's cheek, and for some inexplicable reason, Regina had the urge to snatch Ina away. Krajnik said, "It's always good to see you. *Proshaitye.*"

The word meant this was a permanent good-bye. She was no longer to meet with him. Even though a discontinuance of these conversations had been her desire, the prospect terrified her. She began to fear for her husband's safety.

On the drive to the hospital Ina woke. She became frantic in Regina's arms, as if she could sense what Regina felt, that something was not right. Had Regina said anything that implicated her American friend? Had mention of Natalya's intended somehow fueled Krajnik's interest? Certainly not! There was nothing wrong with being engaged! And what if Hans were not a Soviet citizen? If he loved Natalya, he would become one. It was as simple as that.

Ina was fussing and pulling at her blanket. Regina took advantage of the driver's preoccupation with the traffic to nurse her baby.

Krajnik had been pleased about something Regina said, and that bothered her. She felt a strong urge to warn her friend.

But Natalya was not at the hospital when Regina arrived. She carried Ina down the halls to the psychiatric ward and begged the nurse to let her in. She was surprised when the woman acquiesced.

She found Igor Sushin on a cot at the very back of the ward. His eyes were closed and his flesh cold as the ice on the windowpane.

Dr. Komarov had warned her this moment would come. But the loss was still so great that she slumped with her baby to the floor, her hand on her father's chest and her head close to his. Her tears fell on the wrinkled sheets tucked about his lifeless frame. Ina whimpered as her mother cried.

Finally Regina wiped her eyes. "I miss you, Papa." She held the stiff white fingers and caressed the skin stretched over bones that seemed ready to crumble if pressed too hard. "I wish we could've had a chance to know each other better. You would've liked Edik—he's been good for me. And look, Papa—we have a baby girl." Regina held up her bundle as if he could still see. "I wanted to show her to you." Regina pulled Ina again into her arms. "She has your eyes—and I named her after Mama."

How she wished he could have helped her. He would've known what to do. He would've known how to get Edik out of prison and how to protect Natalya. And Igor Sushin would've known how to deal with Krajnik. As head of Moscow's section of the MGB Sushin had been a powerful man. He'd had the authority to make Comrade Krajnik do what Sushin wanted. He could have recommended Edik's release. The Politburo always paid attention to what her papa recommended.

"Oh, Papa," she whispered. "Comrade Krajnik would have listened to you. He would've had to step down if you'd healed." She leaned closer to the still form. "I think Comrade Krajnik means to harm my husband, Papa. What am I to do to keep him safe? And . . . Oh! Papa, what if he means to let him die?

"I can't save him—and I can't run away—I have no place to go. Ina would starve if I lose my position at the hospital. And besides, even if I *did* have a place to go . . ."

She straightened, as if a new and horrible thought had just occurred to her. "Krajnik would find out—and he might take Ina away from me!" They would put Ina in a *detskidom* and change her name. Regina would be sent to Siberia—and she'd never see her baby again! "I can't imagine spending my life wondering if she's all right. She is my baby, Papa! He has no right to take her!"

Regina had run out of things to say. She wiped at her tears. "If only you could have helped me, Papa . . ."

She kissed his still cheek and rose to her feet. "*Dasvidanya*, Papa," she murmured. "I have to leave now. I have to find a way to save my family . . ." She gave him one last look and then walked away.

Dr. Komarov and two nurses she did not know met her in the main corridor. "Regina Igorevna . . ." Komarov began.

"Papa's dead," Regina accused.

"He died this morning," Komarov replied. Did Regina imagine the coldness in his voice? "I have something to discuss with you. Give your baby to the nurse and come with me."

Regina took a step backward. Without a single word to confirm her fears, she knew something was dreadfully wrong. "I'm late for my duty assignment, Doktor. I—I should be going to work . . ."

"With your baby?"

"It's not a problem."

"Give her to the nurse, Regina. At your break she will be returned to you."

Regina shook her head. "No."

A nurse reached for the infant and Regina pulled her away. The nurse took a step closer and tried again.

"Regina," Komarov commanded, "give it to the nurse."

Suddenly Regina was frantic. She twisted away, but Komarov captured her and the nurse peeled the baby from her arms. Ina started to cry and Regina struggled to free herself. "Give me back my baby!" Her voice rose until it didn't sound like her own. The nurse ignored her and walked away, carrying the hysterical infant. Regina saw one tiny fist flailing, and then the nurse and her Inuchka were gone.

She turned on Komarov, her face dark with anger and panic. "Tell me what's happening. Why did you take away my baby?"

"Regina, everything is all right." Komarov tried to comfort her with an arm about her shoulders but she shook it off. He soothed, "I will

discuss with you the possibilities presented to me by Comrade Krajnik—
about your return to the nursing staff. Come to my office . . ."

"Comrade Krajnik called you?"

"Of course. Right after you left his office. He was worried about
your health."

"My health was fine until you took my baby."

"Patience, Regina. It will be returned at your break, I promise."

Krajnik had called him. Her stomach tied itself into knots. "Izvinitye,
Doktor—it's just that I'm upset about the violent way you separated
us."

"A difficult thing for all of us, Regina."

She swallowed. "You'll give her back on my break?"

"Yes, yes; for a small visit—and to nurse. And then she'll wait in the
nursery for you to finish your assignment for the day . . ."

She straightened. "That is *not* what you promised. You said you
would *return* her to me at my break. She needs to stay with me!" Regina
could no longer contain her fear and despair, and she sobbed, "How
can you understand what it means to have my child torn away from
me? Can't you see that it terrified Inuchka as well? She needs me—right
now!" She pressed a hand to her mouth. "You had no right to take her
from me!"

Komarov soothed, "You're right. Perhaps I made a mistake. I'm
sorry."

Slowly she looked up at him. He truly looked dismayed. "I will talk
to the head nurse in childcare. I'll explain the situation."

"I'll come with you."

Komarov shook his head. "Rest for a few minutes, Regina Igorevna.
I will bring her back to you. Are you hungry?"

Regina hesitated.

Komarov indicated the second nurse. "Will you go with Sonya
Yurovna for a cup of tea while I speak with the head nurse in childcare?"

"Thank you," she managed, and she realized she was feeling a little
weak.

The nurse led her down the hall and through an office to a little
room with one tiny window high above Regina's head. A comfortable

armchair and a small end table comprised the room's furnishings, along with several books, a lamp, and a narrow cot with fresh linens. "Wait here," the nurse said. "I'll be back with your tea."

The nurse returned within five minutes, carrying a tray with a steaming tea kettle, tiny slices of black bread, and a bowl of beet soup. "The doctor should be here soon with your baby. Eat what you can while you wait."

"Thank you."

The nurse smiled at her, left the room, and closed the door.

Regina sipped the tea, ate the bread and soup, and waited. She looked through the window and could only see the tops of several trees and the flash of a tile roof. She watched the door, as if doing so would make it open faster. She sat on the cot and waited.

Finally she stood before the door, staring at the door handle. It had been over an hour. Certainly that was enough time for Dr. Komarov to walk down the hall to the nursery, speak to the head nurse, and retrieve her baby for her. She tried the handle. It didn't open.

Incredulous, she stared at the handle. She tried it again, and it only turned a centimeter before it caught. The door was locked.

First she knocked politely. It was, after all, a mistake. Then she used the flat of her hand to pound on the door. "Help!" she yelled. "Hello! Hello?"

No one answered.

Again she began to panic, her thoughts on Ina. The thought of her baby in danger made her chest tingle strangely. She had to get the attention of the nurse who'd brought her the tea. Somehow the smiling nurse had accidentally locked the door when she left, and maybe Dr. Komarov didn't even know where she'd been taken—and he would think . . . Her panic rose to dangerous levels. He would think she'd changed her mind about wanting her baby!

"Help! Oh, please help me!" She pounded with both hands now, and she screamed the words over and over. "Please, please let me out!"

No answer.

Outside the tiny window a storm was gathering. She needed to get her baby home before the snow fell . . .

She rattled the door handle. Finally she searched the room for something—anything—that would help her with the door. She took a metal spoon from her tray and inserted its slender stem through the crack between door and handle. She jiggled the knob and used the spoon's stem to explore the space between the handle and the door.

She persisted, because she had no alternative, and finally the door clicked open.

For a moment she stood with the bent spoon clutched in her hand, staring at the lock as if she couldn't believe what she'd just done. Then she dropped the spoon on the floor, opened the door, and walked away from her prison.

Dr. Komarov was not in his office and she clenched her teeth in frustration. She walked down the corridor, and no hospital personnel stared at her or seemed to think it odd that she was there. They didn't seem to care that Regina Igorevna had just escaped from her locked room and was overcome with motherly justice.

Regina walked into the nursery, saw the nurse who had taken her baby, and grabbed her. "Where is my baby?"

The woman let out a frightened squeak. "Your baby?"

"Ina Petrovna, the baby you stole from my arms in the corridor." Enraged, Regina grabbed her by the throat.

The woman gasped. "Not here. Not here . . ." and Regina loosened her hold so the woman could explain herself.

"Where is she then?"

"I don't know. I really don't know!"

Regina shook her. "You're *lying* to me!" She released her and began to search the nursery. She rushed through room after room filled with infants, packed three and four to a metal crib. She didn't find Ina. She began to dry heave, and the pain in her chest and stomach wouldn't go away. The nurse she'd throttled tried to apologize, but the effort was pathetic. Regina lunged at her and the woman screamed.

"Where have you taken my baby?"

"I brought her here! Only here! Believe me—I don't know where she went. Doktor Komarov came and he gave her to someone I don't know . . ."

Dr. Komarov. He had her locked in that room and then he gave away her baby. Regina's strength failed her and she crumpled into a heap at the nurse's feet. Her baby. Her Inuchka. Gone . . .

She allowed the nurse to help her to her feet, and she stood, wavering as she tried to regain her balance.

"I'm sorry, Comrade," the woman whispered to her.

Regina shook her off. She walked through the glass doors, through the hospital, and out into the falling snow. Then she began to run, slipping and sliding past the curious hospital guards and through the gate, down the road, and to the streetcar stop. She was half frozen when the car arrived, and sympathetic passengers saw her distress and pulled her inside. Someone threw a blanket around her shoulders and supported her as the car moved.

Ina was gone. Dr. Komarov had taken her baby.

She left the car and arrived at Natalya's apartment complex. She stumbled up the stairs, pounded on the door, and fell through it when it opened. She found Natalya in her tiny room, and between sobs Regina gasped out her story, whispering it in Natalya's ear in the hope that none of the other residents would hear. Natalya's arms came up around the other girl and she held her close as she listened, incredulous, to everything Regina had to say.

THIRTY-FOUR

The desk plate informed him that the secretary's name was Beatrice. Percy Andrews removed his hat and donned his most charming smile. "And when may I see him, Beatrice?

She wasn't charmed. "You'll just have to come back. Make an appointment next time."

"Is Mr. Goodwin in his office right now?" Andrews glanced at the closed door behind her.

Beatrice shook her head.

He glanced at a picture on her desk of a young skirt and her groom. "What a lovely bride. Is that you?"

"Flattery doesn't work on me, mister." Somewhere a teakettle began to sing and she rose to her feet.

"When do you expect him, if you don't mind me asking?"

"He had a pressing engagement in the south. He's not expected back until tomorrow morning."

He cleared his throat. "Actually I live south of London. I could meet him if you tell me where he—"

"He only meets new clients in his office." Beatrice walked away to find the teakettle.

Andrews turned his attention to her desk. He was reaching to open a drawer when he noticed the mail on the edge of her desk. He sifted quickly through it and was gratified to find a bill addressed to Charles Goodwin, Attorney at Law.

He glanced in the direction the secretary had gone and then picked up the letter.

The envelope had a return address for a dry-cleaning establishment nearby. It matched an address suspected by Scotland Yard. He slipped the letter into his coat pocket and left the office without waiting to say good-bye.

* * *

"Mami!"

She knew that scream. She'd heard it once before, when a Gestapo captain had terrified Alma in war-torn Germany. She dropped her dishrag and ran toward the sound.

Alma stood in the doorway of his bedroom, his face as white as a sheet. It didn't take Marie more than a split second to see the reason why.

At the doorway stood a familiar figure, one whose presence in the school yard had shocked her with its emotional resemblance to that same Gestapo captain. He showed her a gun. "Move, mum, against this wall. I can't have you attempting another escape with the boy."

It had been bad enough in the school yard, to see someone cross the boundaries of decorum with her boy. It was inexcusable here. She straightened, ignored the gun in his hand, and walked across the room to take Alma into her arms.

The man was annoyed. "All right, then, so that's the way it's gonna be."

"I am this boy's mother."

"Stand against the wall."

She moved to the wall, next to the grandfather clock. She pressed her shoulder against its comforting pulse and pulled Alma close to her side. "My husband will be back by five."

"Great, Miz Schulmann. Then we'll just sit here and keep each other company until he shows up in three minutes."

"My name is Mary Goodwin. My husband is Charles Goodwin. You have the wrong house."

"You mean your hubby's been *masquerading* as Charles Goodwin, attorney and model American-turned-British citizen. But *I* know what he really is." The man wagged his finger at her. "I've got him all figured out."

"Well, then. You know where he works."

"Yeah, I know where he works."

"Then meet him there. You're terrifying my son."

"I prefer the low-key approach," the man drawled. "Take his boy and his woman and make him come to you. Besides, he's not at his office."

"Actually, you're scared," Marie countered. "You know he works near enough to Scotland Yard that you'd be apprehended before you could disappear with him."

"Now don't you give me no lip. Your husband's the criminal, ma'am—not me. I'm a bona fide government employee, and I'm here on government business."

"Really. In that case, give me your business card and I'll send my husband to your office."

"Now don't you patronize me, woman. My job is to apprehend Nazi scum that's illegally taking advantage of the Queen's good will. Your husband's one o' the worst."

She lowered her voice and tried to reason with him. "Look—I don't mean to insult you. There's got to be a way to work this out without violence. My husband hasn't hurt you personally, and certainly there's no need to threaten his family."

It backfired. The man went ballistic. "Your husband robbed me of everything, woman. Everything! He arrested me when my plane went down in France!" The gun waved dangerously as he warmed to his grief. "My leg, my girl, my life . . . See this?" He pointed with the gun barrel at his leg. "Sure, I've learned to use it again, but it's nothing like it would've been had your Nazi husband let me go home. As far as I'm concerned, your husband's gonna rot, mum, and you and his Nazi spawn are gonna pay for the way he ruined my life."

Close by her side, Alma clutched at her hand, and although the boy was silent and unbelievably brave, she could feel in the frantic strength of his fingers a hint of the fear in his soul. She was devastated that he had to hear such evil spoken about his beloved papa, and in her heart she prayed for deliverance from this predicament. She said, "He'll be home soon. Let us go."

He seemed not to hear her. "Did you know there's a bounty on your husband's head the size of Great Britain? I'm a full-fledged Nazi hunter,

Miz Schulmann. Nazi hunting's the way to make your fortune, and luckily as soon as the war ended and I made it home, I saw the writing on the wall. I hooked up with MI6 and got myself a bit of specialized training, along with a 'Wanted' list of fugitive Nazis a mile long and a wad o' expense money. And then one day I'm going through this list in more detail, and I see a name that rings a bell. It rings that bell mighty loud, understand, because it's the name I remember from France: Major *Rolf Schulmann!* Tried and found not guilty by the French and Americans. But the British were smart—the British place this guy on their *most wanted* list for crimes against OSE agents parachuted into France."

"*I'm* one of those agents," she said calmly.

He stared at her. "Eh? You're a British agent—and then you *married* the monster?" He chuckled. "Then you deserve what's coming to you. You realize your husband's been plotting the return of the Reich while you sleep? He's got blood on him, make no mistake. He's going straight to prison, and *I'm* gonna be the one to put him there."

Marie didn't respond. At her side, Alma trembled and clutched at her skirt. Andrews leaned toward him. "Bet you didn't know that about your papa, did you, you little nipper?" The man taunted the boy. "Now you've seen what he's really like."

"It's on the dresser in the bedroom."

He blinked. "What is?"

"The letter." She thought quickly, improvising as she spoke. "It came this morning. He doesn't know I've read it. He knows you're on his trail, and he sent a letter to his American Nazi friends hoping to be granted asylum. Someone answered . . ."

The man grinned. "Doesn't matter where he goes, mum. I've got the authorization to go wherever I need to go—do whatever it takes. Take off your shoes."

"What?"

"I said take off your shoes." He waved his gun at her. "Do it now."

Marie slipped off her shoes, then she crouched and loosened the laces of Alma's boots. She whispered in German, "You're doing fine, Alma. We must be brave."

He swallowed, nodded, and clutched at her. She wished she could take him in her arms and tell him everything would be all right.

"Now hand them to me."

She held out the shoes. Andrews pulled them from her grasp and pointed with them. "Where's your purse?"

"Does MI6 know you're robbing me?"

"Whatever it takes, Miz Schulmann. Hand over the purse."

"It's on the fireplace mantel."

"Your house keys. Give them to me. And your passport."

"They're in the purse. You have my purse, remember?"

He chuckled and wagged a finger at her. She pulled the keys from her pocket and handed them over.

"Empty your pockets. Give me everything you've got in them."

"I only have a couple of farthings, and a bus token or two."

"Give them here."

"What are you trying to do?"

"I figure you're smart enough not to run barefoot for help this time o' year. Now stand by the door like a good mum while I get that letter."

She moved with Alma and stood in front of the door.

"It's snowing, mum—try escaping and you'll be hobbling on stumps after the doctor's finished with you." He moved into the bedroom. She could hear him demolishing the room in his search for the fictitious letter. In her bare feet Marie slipped out the front door. She hoisted Alma into her arms and ran for the barn and her bicycle. Halfway there she slid to a stop, ignoring her burning feet, and turned back toward the house. She skirted around the corner and ran toward a Jeep parked a few hundred meters down the road.

The intruder had left his key in the ignition and the engine running.

She could hardly feel her feet. She hustled Alma into the seat, climbed in next to him and drove away. She told Alma to crouch down on the floorboards in an attempt to keep him warm. She clenched her chattering teeth, hunched her shoulders against the cold, and drove straight to London's new Heathrow Airport, fully opened to civilian air travel in May.

She fumbled with the combination for long-term rental locker number thirty-seven, located in the modular building that served as a passenger terminal. And then she and Alma retrieved their bags, donned new shoes and coats, took their tickets, and headed for the counter.

They were on a flight for Paris within six hours.

* * *

Andrews never found any letter. He didn't let it faze him, but the theft of his prize Jeep practically burst every blood vessel in his body. He commandeered a bicycle he found in the barn behind the Nazi's cottage.

He also found a can of petrol. He took out his anger on the property of the Nazi fugitive who had ruined his life, burning the barn to the ground, followed by the cottage.

He pedaled into London, cursing and sliding the entire way. He ditched the bicycle and "borrowed" a Ford sedan from the parking lot of an upscale hotel, the keys left in its ignition by the valet. He returned to his own flat, opened his closet, and donned his old RAF pilot's uniform, smoothing wrinkles with his hands as he checked his reflection in the mirror.

He drove across the Thames and sauntered into the cleaning establishment located on Westminster Bridge Road, the one whose address he had filched from Schulmann's office. He showed his credentials and asked to speak with the manager. He complained that Charles Goodwin had sent him a message requesting an aerial pickup from down south, but had neglected to provide an address.

"Beatrice sent me. His secretary, remember? Said you could help me out of a pickle. If I'm not there in two hours, I'm fired."

He left with the address in his hand.

THIRTY-FIVE

The pounding on the door seemed to come from his head; a throbbing headache had settled there that refused to go away.

Viktor Rostov opened his eyes and stared at the ceiling, and then he heard it again. Someone was pounding at the door with an intensity that brought his feet to the cold floorboards. The neighbors would hear and wonder about his night visitors. He moved quickly across the room and flung open the door.

Natalya Ivanovna stood on the threshold, hair disheveled and eyes wild. She had valenki on her feet and a coat thrown over her nightdress, but nothing to warm her hands or her head. She trembled like a rabbit that had temporarily escaped the jaws of a mountain lion. "Viktor," she pleaded, "I need your help."

Viktor saw a flicker of light beneath the door across the hall and knew the neighbors had noticed the commotion. He placed his arm around her shoulders. "Come inside. You must sit down or you'll certainly fall down."

"No!" She resisted the pressure of his arm. "I can't come in. But I need to talk to you, Viktor—there's been a horrible mistake!"

"There must be, or you wouldn't have set foot near my door." Rostov knew there was bitterness in the words, but he couldn't help it. "How am I to offer you tea with you standing and shivering on my doorstep? Besides," Rostov said as he glanced at the door to the nearest neighbor's apartment, "there are some things better discussed in a place more private than the hall. Come inside, Natalya, out of the cold. Look! You didn't even remember to wear your shapka!"

"Viktor, isn't there someplace we could talk? Someplace else? I can't go into your apartment—I *won't!*" She was on the verge of tears.

He relented. "All right. Wait there—I'll be only a minute."

He pulled on winter boots, then gathered his coat and an extra ushanka and brought it back to the girl shivering in the hallway. Gently he brushed the hair from her cheeks and placed the ushanka over her head, pulling the ear flaps down. The hat settled until her round blue eyes were barely free of the fur, looking up at him with a mixture of fear and gratitude. "I admire your determination to stay out of my home, Natalya, even in a moment of obvious distress. But I'll never understand it."

"Viktor, please, let's hurry."

He led the way down the steps and into the harsh night, and they walked side by side away from the scrutiny of the neighbors.

Natalie wasted no time. "He took Regina's baby!"

"What are you talking about?"

"Dr. Komarov. The doctor said it was for—for her own good." Natalie gulped bitter cold air. "He made terrible accusations, Viktor—about her husband being an enemy of the People and about Regina sympathizing with his revolutionary ideals, and . . ." She was starting to hyperventilate, and she turned on him, her swollen red hands clutched at his arm. "Viktor, you have influence! People listen to you. He would tell you where the baby is if you asked him!"

Rostov felt the tightness growing in his chest, and he warmed her freezing hands with his gloves. "Natalya, what do you expect me to do about it? What made you come all this way on a freezing cold night to tell me this? Certainly, it's a terrible thing—"

"You have to help! Please, I haven't asked you for much since you brought me here. But you said you'd be here for me if I needed anything. Viktor, I—I need you now. Please help me now." She lowered her head and her shoulders began to shake.

Suddenly it was more than he could take. He took her in his arms. He felt again the horror and disbelief he'd experienced when he first learned of his daughter's arrest and exile. That day a portion of his soul had died. And until now he'd imagined that pain unique to him alone. But the woman in his arms, the one he loved and could not have, was experiencing that pain right now.

"The baby isn't even yours," he said softly, trying to understand.

Natalie did not look up at him. "This baby . . ." Natalie hesitated. "It's hard to explain. But for some reason this baby means everything to me. We have to get her back, Viktor—we have to get her back!"

Viktor Rostov stared down at her, and his heart beat frantically in his chest. With all his soul he longed to help this woman who meant so much to him. But something caused him to hesitate.

She persisted. "I know you can find her. I *know* you can!"

Of course he could. He should be ecstatic right now. He should take advantage of her desperate need and make a few demands of his own. He would help her, but only on condition that she step over the threshold and into his home. She'd been cruel all these months, rejecting him with a brutal frankness that he'd never been able to forget or forgive. Besides, if he helped her find Regina's daughter, Rostov's own daughter would be placed in even greater danger, and Viktor's own life would suddenly be worthless.

Everything he had worked his entire life for would be destroyed. He would lose his position at the university, his standing as an MGB officer, his home, his friends, his Party membership. He would be stripped of his military rank and military honors. He would be labeled an enemy of the People, and he would be hunted and arrested. If by some miracle his life was spared, he would become a prisoner like his daughter, and sent to one of the hundreds of camps to work for the remainder of his days—for that is how long his life would last; only a matter of days. The hard punishment labor of the Gulags would bring his heart to the very brink of destruction.

It was not worth it. Natalie talked of the baby meaning everything to her, and that is what Lucya meant to Viktor. *Everything.* It wasn't right for Regina to have her daughter and Viktor to lose his.

It wasn't right. He closed his eyes. "I will not help you," he said. And yet, how it broke his heart to refuse Natalya!

The declaration seemed to be more than she could take. She didn't say anything for several moments, and when she finally did speak he could barely hear her words. "Is it because I wouldn't come to you?"

"Yes. But it is more than that."

"Your daughter."

"I will not make her existence any more precarious. Not even to help my—" He stopped suddenly, shocked at what he'd almost revealed to her. "Not even to help you. I cannot throw away what precious life I have remaining, when I might still be able to find a way to help Lucya. I am only *one* man, Natalya—and one man can only do so much."

She whispered, "Viktor . . ." and then said nothing more.

Viktor accompanied her home and then returned through the blistering cold. Tiny razors sliced at his cheekbones and he pulled the flaps of his coat up about his neck, overlapping the earflaps of his ushanka.

The look in her eyes as he bade her good night at her door would haunt him forever. He didn't know how to describe how it hurt him— to see her sorrow, and disappointment—as if before his refusal she'd finally begun to forgive him. But what was he to do? The Politburo was becoming more and more suspicious of him—as if his loyalties to the Kremlin were in question! The thought was absurd! What would they find suspicious about repatriating a woman who was by all rights a Soviet citizen?

Could they have discovered the way the German named Rolf Schulmann tricked him? Could the secret police think he'd met deliberately with an agent of American intelligence? Could they possibly think *him* a traitor to the Motherland? Viktor's step quickened.

Another bundled form approached the Moskva bridge as he crossed. "Good night, Comrade," the man greeted Viktor.

"Good night."

The man continued past. Besides the polite words exchanged, there was no other attempt at civility.

They watched every step he took—Viktor was certain of that. But he knew there was nothing he could do about it. If he turned now, he would see the man who had just passed him leaning against the bridge railing, contemplating the lights of the Kremlin. And then when he resumed his walk, the man would follow. That was the way it worked.

He thought about Regina's baby and imagined his former pupil holding the tiny infant in her arms. It was unfortunate; Regina would've been a good mother.

Suddenly Regina's face became that of his deceased Alyona in his mind, and the baby in her arms became his daughter. Rostov's step faltered. He tried to erase the image but it continued unbidden. In his thoughts his wife approached him and offered him the baby. Reluctantly he took it, tried not to look down into the tiny girl's eyes but was unable to resist. He saw the trust there, and the love of daughter for father, and it melted his heart.

If it had been *his* baby taken away, he would've been frantic with grief and desperate for her return.

Cursing under his breath, he shook off the disturbing image. The People had decided Regina was an unfit mother. Who was he to disagree?

Just as the People had decreed that Viktor was unfit to be Lucya's papa.

The thought shook him to the core. Was that why they hadn't yet kept their promise? Always they said, "Be patient, Comrade Rostov, these things take time . . ."

How much longer must he be patient? Until Lucya's back breaks and her spirit shrivels and dies? Must he wait until her heart ceases to beat and her breath turns to ice in her lungs?

Or must he wait until he himself passes away? He had to accept the fact that his own heart might not beat much longer. And then who would care for his daughter? Who would be left in this world to love her, to protect her and fight for her? He'd spent his entire life serving the People. Was this how the People repaid him?

He should be shocked at the thought—he was thinking *Western* thoughts—selfish, self-serving thoughts about what *he* needed. What *he* wanted. What *he* deserved.

It was good the MGB couldn't read his thoughts. They could track him on a cold winter night, but they couldn't read his thoughts. It was comforting to know that at least his thoughts were still his own.

And as he approached home his thoughts became more dangerous still; thoughts so dreadful he feared the man following him might be able to sense them. Thoughts that began to shape a new chapter in his life, and possibly a new one for his daughter and for the American nurse Viktor loved as well. He wanted to keep Lucya safe. He felt the same way about Natalya, even though he realized that the way she looked at him might never change. His own existence was precarious—he was not treated by his peers with the same respect as before. That was why they followed him. That was why they didn't keep their promise and return his daughter to him.

All his adult life he'd wanted one thing: to be a model Soviet citizen and serve his country. He loved his country! But the other loves of his life were now in danger, and he knew that this time he would have to sacrifice something.

Even in his sorrow, he knew the decision he had to make. If he helped Natalya and Regina, he would be labeled a traitor. And if he was arrested for treason, his Lucya would die.

On the other hand, if he didn't help find Regina's baby, he could still lose everything. What assurances did he have that Lucya would ever be returned to him? It had been over six months since he had delivered the German scientist Hans Brenner to the Soviet Union. And yet, for all these months Viktor had believed in their promises.

Stalin should know by now, that no matter how strong a branch, if you bend it too far it will break.

Rostov turned on his heel and strode toward the man following him. For just a moment the man fumbled with his coat pocket, searching for a cigar and trying to look indifferent. Rostov walked right up to him.

"Tell Comrade Krajnik I've made up my mind." And then he turned and continued down the street toward home.

THIRTY-SIX

In the early morning hours of December 10, Percy Andrews watched as the Nazi criminal Schulmann descended into the shadows of the basement haberdashery. Andrews had staked it out earlier and was pleased with himself for his foresight. Scotland Yard had been of some assistance to him—flying him down here to Brighton and alerting the local authorities of Andrews's need for assistance in the arrest. But most of the hard work had been done by Andrews himself.

He brushed off his irritation at the memory of the Schulmann woman's escape. At least she wouldn't be hanging around to warn her husband. He was getting to like this cloak-and-dagger business. Netting Krauts for cash sure beat bombing Krauts for revenge. So much more satisfying to see the looks on their faces when he cuffed them. He'd found his calling in life, and there were more than enough bloodsucking Nazis still on the loose to make him comfortable for the rest of his life.

"Just you give me the nod, gov'nah." The heavyset copper next to him watched the steps where Rolf had disappeared.

Brighton was a good place to catch fish. And Andrews was about to catch himself a big Nazi fish. He would remember this day for the rest of his life. No other capture would have such personal satisfaction for him. *Gotcha, you bloodsucking Kraut . . .*

Rolf emerged from the basement. He paused to glance up and down the street, and suddenly Andrews had a thought. *What is the Nazi up to? Who does he meet with in that basement?*

He was a mite disappointed that so much work would net him only one Nazi fish. Schulmann might be an *important* Nazi fish—to Andrews, at least—but Schulmann was still only one.

Rolf Schulmann began to walk away. Andrews watched him with great curiosity.

"Sir?" The copper fingered his truncheon, his gaze alternating between Andrews and the retreating figure.

"Let me think."

"Eh?"

"Something dodgy's going on here." Andrews eyed the haberdashery across the street. Something big, maybe. Andrews wanted to be a part of it.

"Excuse me, sir—?"

One fish. Or could he capture more? All in one big, profitable net.

Andrews pointed across the street. "I think we have another target in there—and I want to pay him a visit. I don't want to net Schulmann alone."

"Right you are, gov'nah. I'll send one of my men after Schulmann."

THIRTY-SEVEN

Aleksandr took Lucya out for another drive. He'd harnessed Yolochka in the middle; the stallion was the born leader, pulling forward and preventing Snegurichka and Grandpapa Frost from trotting off in opposite directions. Their manes and tails took to the air as they tossed their heads and stamped their feet.

Lucya loved the quiet *swoosh* of the sled's skis and the rhythmic, muffled *th-th-thump* of the horse's hooves in the new snow. It gave her a thrill to speed through a frozen forest with Aleksandr beside her and three powerful steeds to the fore. She turned and looked at Aleksandr, tilting her head sideways as she contemplated her companion's red nose, chapped lips, and frosted eyelashes. His jaw, strong and square, sported the beginnings of a beard. Every other inch of his head was hidden beneath a sheepskin ushanka, and she thought he was the most ruggedly handsome man she'd ever met. Shyly she asked, "How did you get permission to bring me out here today?"

He grinned at her, and she was amazed at his perfect teeth. She had never seen a man with such healthy teeth. "My father is a Politburo official, and he expects the commandant to take good care of me." His smile deepened. She liked his smile. "Remember I told you these horses were a gift?"

Lucya nodded. "A bribe?"

He chuckled. "The commandant was transferred here to Vtoraya Rechka as a punishment for accepting bribes. Didn't cure him, though. He accepts bribes from prisoners—for preferential treatment, better food, things like that. My father knew the commandant's shady history and took advantage of it. I found this matched team at a stud farm outside Moscow and my father purchased it for the commandant." He grinned at her. "It's my father's way of making sure his son gets special privileges. So far it's worked out nicely, don't you think?"

"It's very nice." She smiled up at him.

"And of course, since I was raised around horses, I was the perfect choice to train the team. I found a leatherworker and had him make a troika harness. I promised the commandant that I would train the horses to pull a sled—all three horses, just like in the days of the troika. That's why I'm allowed to take them away from the camp—so that I can train them. And I'm allowed to bring you, because the commandant thinks you are my camp wife. He winks at me and looks the other way."

Lucya blushed, her cheeks staining a deep red that crept all the way from her freckled nose to her ears.

Aleksandr squeezed her hand. "Don't worry—you're safe with me. The deception was necessary in order to receive preferential treatment for you, also. You mean a lot to me, Lucya, and I wish for you to be healthy and safe."

Her blush heated her face so that she almost didn't need her mother's shawl across her mouth. "And you don't require things of me—things that would make me uncomfortable . . ." She could hardly speak for her embarrassment.

He leaned his head close to hers. "And I never will, Lucya. I want to protect you." He kissed the freckles of her nose, and she giggled.

THIRTY-EIGHT

Wednesday, December 11, 1946

They met at the Victoria-Jungfrau hotel in Interlaken, the same as before. Rolf found Viktor Rostov by the rail, looking out over the panorama of the Alps. He waited for the Soviet officer to speak.

Rostov's bowed shoulders, closed eyes, and lowered head made him seem a man finally broken. "I accept your offer, if it's still available. I—need your help."

"I never withdrew it."

"Natalya won't be able to leave to the south; too many checkpoints, too many safeguards—Stalin doesn't plan for any of his citizens to slip through his fingers."

"I understand."

"I'll get documents for her." Viktor gave Rolf a faint smile. "I have a contact—a man who prefers to remain anonymous—who'll prepare them. As for Hans, it will be difficult to get him out of Novosibirsk—"

"Hans Brenner has already left Novosibirsk," Rolf declared. "If we find him, he'll need the services of your anonymous friend as well."

Viktor turned and studied Rolf, and there was a hint of moisture in his eyes. "And now, Major Schulmann, about my daughter . . ."

Rolf nodded. "She is in a transit camp—Vtoraya Rechka—near Vladivostok. She is to be transferred to Kolyma at the beginning of the year."

Viktor's gloved hand slipped on the rail, spilling clumps of snow into the depths below. His eyes registered shock so profound that Rolf wondered if the man's heart would survive. "Kolyma . . ." It was almost a whisper, breathed through clenched teeth. "Vtoraya Rechka . . ." He shook his head, slowly and wordlessly, and his sight was far past the Bernese Alps. *"Kolyma znachit smert!* Kolyma means death!*"*

He beat the rail with his fist. "In the dead of winter she'll be transported across the Okhotsk Sea to Magadan by way of a special Kolyma fleet . . ." He took a deep breath. "They are death ships! A man can barely survive the passage, let alone a woman—and my daughter! She won't survive the journey. And the women who *do* survive—" Here Rostov shuddered. "I can't describe what awaits them in the holds of those ships! Ah, Comrade, I would give my life to free her! I would do anything to spare her from Kolyma's death fleet!

"And then, if by some lack of fortune she survives . . ." Viktor's voice caught, "Do you know what they call Kolyma? *The land of white death!* If it doesn't reach sixty below it's considered a warm day. Do you know what happens to a body in that sort of weather? Your breath rattles in your lungs like sprockets in a tin can. And if you survive the backbreaking labor of the gold mines, your skin becomes weather-beaten leather, indiscernible as human flesh, and your hands—your *hands* . . . !" Here Rostov stared at his own gloved hands as if at those of a monster, and he let out a sob, so uncharacteristic of the solid, purposeful, and ruthless man Rolf knew that it shook him.

Viktor did not continue, and Rolf shifted his feet, uncomfortable in the silence but unwilling to break it. He let the man grieve for several moments before he said softly, "We'll get her out."

Rostov straightened, turned, and curled a fist in Rolf's face. "And if I hadn't caved in to your demands, you would've let her die in that evil place. *Chort-vozmee!* If I were any sort of man I would wrap these hands about your throat and squeeze the life out of you for letting my daughter suffer a day longer than she must. If you'd told me when we first met, I might've found a way to rescue her by now!"

Rolf responded calmly, "And if you'd agreed to my conditions when we first met, we could've helped you." He ignored the threatening fist. "And Natalie Allred and Hans Brenner would even now be safely married."

Again Rostov shuddered, and then he turned away. He seemed to Rolf to be carrying the weight of the entire Soviet Union on his back, and it was several moments before he turned again to face Rolf. "There is . . . another complication."

"This entire situation is fraught with complications, Lieutenant," Rolf replied. "Do you refer to another one? One that I don't know about already?"

Viktor met Rolf's gaze. "Natalya Ivanovna is my wife."

Thunderstruck, Rolf took a step backward. The wave of horror that engulfed him almost choked the breath from his body.

His wife . . .

Rolf stared at the Soviet officer as if he'd just confessed to murder. "For the first time in my life, Lieutenant Rostov, I hope what you've just told me is a lie."

Viktor Rostov did not rescind his statement. Instead, his hands clenched the rail as if he would break it in two. And then, as if a dam had burst, spilling countless gallons of water into the chasm below, Rolf's questions came. And like the violent tumbling and churning of the waves over the rocks they spilled out in a torrent that did not assign significance. He found his mounting anger at this man difficult to keep under control. *Natalie was Viktor Rostov's wife?*

"When did this happen?"

"The moment we stepped off the train in Moscow."

"I can't imagine she gave her consent."

"No."

"Did you tell her Hans Brenner was dead?"

"Yes." Rostov hesitated. "I'm not proud of the fact."

"*Why* did you marry her?"

Rostov folded his arms. "To save her life. The MGB sent an assassin to meet us at the station; she would've been slaughtered in an alley if I hadn't made the decision."

"What decision? To marry her?" A glimmer of reason began to flicker through the dark anger that Rolf was experiencing. He'd heard of the Cossack murders. He'd heard of Soviet citizens who spent the war in Nazi concentration camps, only to be immediately transported to Soviet labor camps upon repatriation. He'd heard of families torn apart and Soviet soldiers executed for the unspeakable crime of working as forced labor for the Germans.

"They would not harm the wife of an MGB officer," Rostov explained. "I told them we were already married. They produced the documents we were required to sign in order for our marriage to be legal and binding in the Soviet Union. I—forced her to sign the documents against her will."

Rolf felt the anger that had been building subside, but the sorrow he felt for both Natalie and Hans wouldn't go away. "How does Natalie feel about it?"

Viktor walked away from Rolf and sank onto the edge of a chair. He said, "She doesn't know we're married."

"*What?*" Incredulous, Rolf moved away from the rail. "She doesn't know? How can she *not* know she's married to you?"

"I haven't told her." Rostov lifted his hands palms upward, as if in defeat. "You must understand, Rolf Schulmann, that I—I love her dearly. I didn't want her harmed." He paused. "On the other hand, I could see how much my announcement of her fiancé's death hurt her. I couldn't hurt her more by telling her I'd forced her to marry me."

"But you said you forced her to sign—"

"Yes," Rostov interrupted. "I forced her to sign the marriage document—in Russian. I did not tell her what it said. I only hoped . . . that one day, when she didn't hate me anymore . . ."

Rolf stared at the man sitting in front if him and felt a strange empathy for a man whose entire life had been one of misery and duty. And in spite of that he had emerged as a man with a shred of decency about him. "Then, you did not . . ." Rolf couldn't force the words from his mouth, and yet, he knew he had to know.

Rostov spared him the embarrassment of continuing. "I found a room for her—far away from me. And she, of her own accord, has never set foot inside my home."

The sudden rush of relief Rolf experienced brought tears to his eyes. "Thank you, Viktor Rostov. I cannot adequately express to you my gratitude . . ."

Viktor stood suddenly, as if Rolf's show of appreciation was more than he wanted to hear. "I'll honor my agreement because I know you'll honor yours, Rolf Schulmann. I know I'm as much to blame as you in this matter—maybe even more so. I will help you because I want my daughter to be free—I want her free from prison and free of the chains that encircle the beautiful country I love. I'll help you to deliver Hans and . . . my wife . . . to freedom." He took a deep breath. "And you will help my daughter escape to America. When Lucya is safely across the ocean"—Rostov paused, and Rolf could hear the anguish in his words— "I will free Natalya from bonds I hope she never discovers were hers."

Rolf nodded. "Your daughter will be escorted to America." He hesitated, then asked, "Will she be living there with her father?"

There was a long silence, followed by words spoken with a heartache Rolf couldn't describe. "Her father will stay in the Soviet Union."

"She will be disappointed."

Lieutenant Rostov moved toward a table, brushed it clean of snow, found a chair, and sat heavily, a sigh escaping his lips as if he'd aged twenty years in the past twenty minutes.

Rolf joined him, glancing at a group of tourists that had arrived to take in the view from the terrace. "We'll need to know the route of the shipment to the north."

"The border is heavily guarded, but there's a nondescript bay west of Leningrad."

The tourists did not challenge the cold for long, and as they escaped to the warmth of the lounge, Rolf said, "Viktor, I am intrigued by the Russian word *troika*. It has several meanings, doesn't it?"

"Several." Viktor's brow furrowed. "I'm surprised you're interested in Russian vocabulary at a time like this."

"A sleigh? Drawn by three horses?"

"A thing of Russia's past, used now only for festivities, parades, special events . . ."

"There's another meaning, isn't there?"

"Yes."

"A group of three, bound by one common purpose," Rolf murmured, and his fingers drummed the table thoughtfully. "Such as the rescue of your daughter."

Viktor gave Rolf a faint smile. "I guess this could be a common purpose. But who are the three?"

"You," Rolf answered, "because without your assistance this rescue would never happen. Hans Brenner, because he has an important part still to play in this plan, and God, because He is the one Who's ultimately going to make everything—"

"Leave God out of it," Rostov interrupted. "I prefer to put *your* name there—you're the one who had the courage to approach me with this ridiculous idea."

"If you want to keep this troika entirely earthbound, that's fine. But I don't believe we have a chance of success without God's help."

"I've told you, Rolf Schulmann—I don't believe in God."

"And as I told you, Lieutenant, your lack of belief in Him does not mean He doesn't believe in you. I believe He has special miracles reserved just for you, Viktor—and when the time comes, if you're willing to *ask* for them, He'll give them to you." Rolf smiled. "Who knows? After all that we can do—after all of our meticulous preparation, planning, and hard work—maybe asking God to intervene is going to be the only way to save your daughter's life."

* * *

Hate had kept Percy Andrews alive during his imprisonment—blinding, burning hatred for Rolf Schulmann and for the German race in general. He had been a pilot, but spent much of the war as an invalid prisoner of war in a Nazi concentration camp. He owed it all to Major Schulmann, with his evil, Nazi face and vicious plot to beguile Andrews into a relationship of trust. In France, Schulmann spoke to him, man to man, and Andrews began to trust him. And then, when Andrews was convinced Schulmann was empathetic to his plight, the Nazi Kraut sentenced him to rot in a concentration camp in Germany.

Andrews was forced to sit out the remainder of the war. Because of Schulmann, Andrews missed D-day, the victorious crossing of the Rhine, the storming of the Eagle's Nest, V-E Day, and even his own dad's funeral. His leg became infected in that camp and he spent several months in horrible camp hospitals, surrounded by stinking, dying prisoners and corpses. All because of that Nazi scumbag.

And then, to add insult to injury, this same Nazi pig was acquitted by a tribunal in France and Andrews's sweetheart abandoned him for an ace pilot with a uniform full of medals and two healthy legs. Again, Rolf Schulmann was to blame. Andrews would never forgive Rolf Schulmann.

And now here Andrews was in Switzerland, with a glass of bubbly in his hands and the Nazi fugitive Rolf Schulmann sitting twenty meters away, talking to the man who could only be Viktor Rostov, the notorious spy that tailor in Brighton insisted was intimately connected to the Soviet government.

It was all so simple, really. Simple, and beautiful. Rolf Schulmann had been masquerading as Charles Goodwin in England while he danced the old one-two with Fourth Reich blokes hiding in England. But it turned out Schulmann was double-dealing with the Soviets. Oh, how MI6 would drool all over this bit of information!

He watched the two men through the glass doors of the lounge. They seemed lost in their conversation with each other—it was an emotional one, Andrews noticed with glee, and realized that their concentration made it even more likely they wouldn't notice Andrews's associate, even now creeping around the hotel, expertly preparing a surprise for the two men that would alter their lives forever—just as Rolf Schulmann had so cruelly altered Andrews's.

And then, as a group of intrepid tourists headed out to the terrace to take in the view, Andrews had a brilliant idea. He leapt to his feet and tacked himself to the tail-end of the group, and he stationed himself as close to the table as possible while he admired the Alps with his new associates.

And he listened.

THIRTY-NINE

Thursday, December 12, 1946

Natalie ached for Regina. The woman's joyful spirit had died three days ago when her baby was taken from her, and Natalie's spirit mourned along with her. She'd tried, as best she could, to comfort Regina, but Regina had withdrawn further and further inside her despair until all that scrubbed the hospital floors was a broken, empty shell.

"Comrade," snapped a voice, "will you keep us waiting all night?" Natalie was so lost in her melancholy that she hadn't noticed the street-car arrive.

She watched the first flickers of sunrise and rode in silence, managed not to miss her stop, and walked the remaining five blocks to her apartment complex. She passed by the swing sets, through the frozen grass, and up the stone steps to her third-story apartment. She ignored the early-morning queue at the door to the bathroom, passed the busy stove, and entered her small room, closing the door behind her. Then she collapsed, still wrapped in her coat and with her valenki on her feet.

She heard the whine of brakes outside but was too tired to care. She closed her eyes and would have remained motionless where she sat, had not the resident from the next room announced to the entire apartment that a government "black crow" had just pulled up outside.

Startled, Natalie sprang to her feet and then chided herself for being so nervous. The dreaded MGB had been to her complex in the past, in their distinctive black vans, wearing their usual black suits and ties, overcoats, and ushankas with official insignia. But never to her building—at least, never in the months since she'd lived there.

She told herself to relax. There was no reason they would come for her. She'd done nothing to make them notice her. She was careful—always careful—to keep her opinions to herself and do her work without complaining. Every individual in her building would be having similar thoughts at that moment.

All bickering at the kitchen stove had ceased. A teapot that dared whistle for attention was hurriedly silenced. Did they think mere silence would save them? She couldn't help the nervous dread that tightened about her chest. Somebody's life was going to change tonight. What was it Regina once said? *Olga will feed you black crow if she ever catches you breaking the rules . . .*

Surely Natalie hadn't done anything worthy of denunciation. She tried to calm her breathing.

Heavy footsteps climbed the stairs and paused at her floor. Natalie clenched her hands together and forced herself to think about the five other communal apartments on her floor. Surely the MGB would go to one of those. Perhaps it was the apartment next door. She'd heard that the father of one of the families in that apartment often met with dissidents.

She leapt to her feet and paced near the window. *Shame on you, Natalie,* wishing *such suffering on another human being!* Was she becoming so calloused that she would rate her own well-being more significant than that of others? How dare she pronounce such an awful judgment and sentence on someone she'd never even met! How could she have fallen so low as to wish evil on anyone, just to save herself?

She saw the van below the window, long, low, and black. It epitomized the evil that Stalin had imposed on this people and the fear that was in everyone's heart—*Will the black crow come for me tonight? For my son? My daughter? My husband?*

She heard a knock at the door and her stomach squeezed into a painful knot. It couldn't be for her. She turned away from the window. She heard the door open and voices in the hall, as her roommates showed the police down the hall, through the kitchen . . .

This couldn't be happening. Viktor had promised to protect her. She'd followed his instructions to the letter, keeping her thoughts, feelings, and religious ideas to herself. She'd worked, and starved, and frozen—all for the Soviet ideal.

She had her defense on her lips and an umbrella in her hand, brandished like a sword. She had no memory of picking it up. She didn't have to wait very long—a matter of seconds, really—but it was sufficient time to go over, in detail, everything she'd said and done since she set foot on Soviet soil.

And then, as the footsteps stopped at her door, she wondered if they were here because she'd asked Viktor to help her recover Regina's baby.

Would Viktor denounce her? Would he take out his vengeance on her in this way?

Four men pushed into the tiny confines of her room. How many did they think it would take to restrain a woman? Her roommates watched from the kitchen as she was disarmed, subdued, hooded, and hauled like a common criminal out the door, all in a matter of a few seconds. Her protests fell on deaf ears, and it wasn't until she was securely locked in the filthy back of the van that she realized she'd been defending her innocence in English. In her fear and panic, all pretence at speaking Russian disappeared.

Even a short journey can seem interminable in an enclosed, terrifying space, and so she had no idea how long they drove, nor the direction of her forced journey. Her own breath came in ragged, terrified gasps, the sound loud under the hood. She forced herself to listen, wishing for some sound—any sound—that would help indicate where they were going. She wished she could tuck her hands under her armpits to keep them from freezing, and she shivered in the dark confines of her prison.

She heard the hollow sound of the van's tires crossing a bridge, and then later, the rumble of cobblestones as they drove through a square. And then the engine died and rough hands pulled her from the van. She was dragged down a short flight of stairs and down an invisible corridor that echoed with the sounds of their heavy boots. Then the sounds became muffled as a door was shut and locked, with a sound that reminded her of a Fourth of July firecracker.

Whoooosh . . . pop!

She was left alone.

FORTY

It was a strange, exhilarating experience to step off a plane in France and not have to dodge bullets or run for cover. Rolf Schulmann paused on the tarmac to take a deep breath, savoring the cold, damp sweetness of Paris air in peacetime.

He walked toward the terminal with his suitcase. He figured he had about twenty-four hours before he was arrested. He might have been exonerated of war crimes at his trial earlier that year, but he knew that anti-Nazi sentiment still ran high in France, and there were many who were not pleased with the tribunal's verdict. He wouldn't put it past a French Communist or two to cash in on any reward offered for his return to France. It would be a lifetime before France forgot the part Rolf had played in their suffering and he was allowed to safely walk the streets of Lyon, Belley, or Izieu.

He showed his American-issued passport at the customs counter.

"What is your reason for visiting France, Mr. Goodwin?"

"My father-in-law lives here in Paris."

"And how long will you be staying?"

"Not long."

He retrieved his passport and crossed the terminal to look at a billboard posted with upcoming flights.

"Aimée says Marie is back in France."

It was good to hear French spoken again—and even better to hear it spoken by an old friend. Rolf turned to see Jacques Bellamont lounging nearby. He still looked the same as during the war, Rolf mused—

dark complexion, rough-healed scars, and the look of a mountain lion hunting his prey. Jacques gave him a welcoming grin.

Rolf returned his smile. "Things got a bit rough in London. How are things for you?"

"I let Soviet criminals kidnap my wife's cousin. Nothing important."

Of course he would see it as his fault. "Glad you're still alive, Jacques."

"So I'm your sidekick on this, I take it? Mind telling me what's going on with Natalie Allred? Aimée's been worried."

"Remind me to fill you in," Rolf said. "You ready?"

"Not going to visit your wife first?"

Rolf shook his head. "If I did, I'd have to tell her good-bye. I promised her I'd never do that again."

"Then let's go."

FORTY-ONE

Viktor Rostov returned to Moscow late in the evening on December 12. He took an unobtrusive commercial flight through the Ukrainian Soviet Socialist Republic, his senses unusually heightened to the possibility of detection. He stopped by his office at the Kremlin and made one phone call. Then he returned to his apartment.

He closed the door and pulled off his ushanka and gloves. He was tired and emotionally drained, and his hand fumbled as he hung his coat onto its hook. He found the chain for the light and turned it on. Finally he turned around.

Hans Brenner stood in the center of the room, his clothes filthy and a rifle held ready in his hands.

Viktor froze. He felt his mouth go dry and a strange, otherworldly emptiness—as if he'd suddenly realized he was experiencing the last few moments of his life.

But when Hans didn't shoot him immediately Viktor felt his courage beginning to return. Still, when he spoke it was around a tongue as thick and dry as an overcooked sausage. "What are you doing here?"

Hans stepped forward, raised the rifle, and struck Rostov directly in the face. The room turned onto its head and darkness exploded behind his eyes. Viktor went down.

He had the most peaceful dream, in which he and Natalya were reunited with his daughter Lucya. Hans Brenner was also there . . .

That was not a peaceful thought. Viktor opened his eyes. He struggled to a sitting position and cradled his head in his hands. "Where have you been?" he groaned. "You disappeared from Novosibirsk, and when I asked about you the Kremlin denied you ever existed."

"Such a short memory your government has," Hans lamented, and he helped Rostov to his feet. "I've been a prisoner in a city that doesn't exist. Maybe you should've asked your government if they plan to send all kidnapped scientists who don't exist to cities that don't exist. Seems convenient to me." He assisted his victim to the couch. "So you've been asking about me?" And then more to himself, "No wonder they were looking for me in Gorky."

"Are you going to kill me?"

"Should I?"

"What do you want with me?"

"I want Natalie. She's not here. What have you done with her?"

"She's never been here, Hans." With a low moan Viktor lowered himself onto the couch, his face ashen. Blood was beginning to cake across one eyebrow where the rifle had connected with his head, and the eyelid beneath had begun to swell shut.

Hans stared at him. "What do you mean, 'She's never been here'? She's here in Moscow, isn't she?"

"She's never entered my apartment. She refused to do so, and I've honored her wishes."

Hans thought about that for several seconds, and Rostov could see the growing relief in his eyes. When Hans finally spoke, his voice had softened somewhat. "All right then, where is she?"

"You don't want to know."

"Yes I do."

"At this moment?" Rostov leaned against the back of the couch, slowly shaking his head against the pain. "In a cold, dark cell at MGB headquarters, approximately one kilometer from here."

Rostov could see that his words shook Hans. The German's rifle came within inches of Rostov's face.

"She was arrested this morning," Rostov tried to explain. "I wasn't here. But it might interest you to know—"

"The only thing that interests me, Professor, is how you plan to get her out."

"There's nothing more I can do for her, Hans."

Hans lunged for the man, and with his weight and the stock of his rifle he pressed Rostov into the back of the couch. Rostov struggled for air. Suddenly Hans seemed to reconsider, and he backed away. "Now you listen to me, Rostov. I came here to take Natalie home with me and that's what I'm gonna do. I . . ." He struggled to continue, past some internal conflict that was making the words he wanted to say difficult. "I need your help."

Viktor stared at Hans. He'd expected threats, emotional explosions, and probably more violence. But he hadn't expected humility. It crumbled Rostov's defenses. "It might interest you to know, Hans, that I've just returned from Switzerland. That's why I wasn't here to protect her."

"I don't care where you went. I only want—"

"I was there with an agent from American intelligence."

Now it was Hans who was momentarily speechless. His face displayed an assortment of surprise, shock, and hope. "You're working with the Americans," he finally murmured, and then he scowled. "To accomplish what?"

"The extraction of one American woman, one German scientist, and one daughter of a traitor Soviet agent from the USSR."

"Interesting." Hans nodded solemnly. He was still dubious. "Are you saying American intelligence is willing to find your daughter in exchange merely for our return to the West?"

"No. But Rolf Schulmann is."

Hans was silent. He leaned forward in his chair, and Rostov noticed the sudden emotion in his eyes. Finally he said, "Rolf Schulmann works for Major James Matthews. I know you're aware of that."

"Of course. But this is his own project. And Rolf and I need *your* help."

"You—you need *my* help?"

"That's right."

"You realize how long it'll take me to forgive you?"

Rostov nodded. "And probably longer to *trust* me—although trust is an important element of this plan." He gave Hans a faint smile. "So I prefer you work on the trust issue immediately. Right now I need your trust more than your forgiveness."

"Fair enough."

Viktor rose on shaky legs. His head exploded from the altitude change and he almost found himself back on the couch. "We have much to do, Hans Brenner. If I believed in God I'd say your arrival was practically providential, although my head has a different opinion at the moment." Rostov rubbed at his swollen scalp.

"You can thank Rima for my providential arrival."

"Who?"

Hans waved off the question. "You told me you couldn't help Natalie. If you can't get her out of MGB headquarters, how do you expect to get her out of the Soviet Union?"

"No," Rostov clarified, "I didn't say I couldn't help her—I said I couldn't do anything *else* to help her."

"All right, what's the difference?"

Rostov gave Hans a tight smile devoid of any humor. He picked up his coat and ushanka, gloves and a scarf. He tossed them all at Hans. "Come with me, Hans Brenner; it's going to be a long night."

Hans abandoned his own filthy coat and accepted the official winter outerwear of an MGB officer. His voice dripped cynicism. "Whatever happened to 'loyalty to the Motherland'?"

Rostov reached for a second coat. "It seems I'm not a good Soviet after all, Hans Brenner," he mourned. "For I'm beginning to doubt my loyalty to a country that forgets her promises." He turned to face Hans. "I'm ready to do whatever it takes to save my daughter's life, even if that means my demise."

"All right." Hans shrugged Rostov's coat onto his shoulders and held out a conciliatory hand. "You have my assistance, sir, as long as you'll help me get Natalie out."

Rostov took the proffered hand. "Your friend Rolf Schulmann makes this possible." He smiled. "I understand you and Rolf have made quite a career of saving each others' skins. Have you ever heard of a troika, Hans Brenner?"

"Of course. A sleigh pulled by three horses." Hans chuckled. "Usually pictured with a romantic couple along for the ride and all three horses perfectly matched and very spirited."

"It has other meanings . . ."

"Like what?"

"Three people bound by one common purpose." Rostov clapped Hans on the shoulder. "Rolf Schulmann is right: We're a troika, bound by one common goal."

FORTY-TWO

Friday, December 13, 1946

Percy Andrews arrived at the Soviet Embassy at Carlton Gardens at ten o'clock in the morning, dressed in a tweed business jacket and striped tie. He'd paid the shoeshine boy on Kensington Avenue sixpence to oil his shoes, and he wore new leather gloves and a bowler hat.

He passed the Soviet guards, showed his British military ID at the door, and waited while his name was noted in the visitors' log. He entered the impressive stone mansion and approached the desk to request an immediate audience with the Soviet Ambassador on a matter of national security. He hinted to the middle-aged, balding receptionist that the purpose of his visit was very important and very, very secret. The receptionist seemed noticeably impressed.

The receptionist picked up the telephone and spoke to someone in Russian. He hung up, glanced at a large mirror on the wall, and then smiled at Andrews. His accent was thick. "Please return this afternoon, Mr. Andrews, at one o'clock."

An inconvenience, nothing more. Andrews touched his hat and left the building.

That afternoon he returned, sixpence poorer but with his shoes again oiled to a high shine. After he cut a deal with the Soviets, sixpence would be nothing.

A young woman with a pretty smile and nice legs had replaced the bald receptionist. She showed him to a private office with a comfortable sofa, several stuffed armchairs, and a polished marble coffee table with London and Moscow newspapers spread enticingly across its surface. On one side of the room a large window overlooked Kensington Palace Gardens, which Andrews considered one of the better views of London. On the other side, a large gilded mirror hung above a carved cherrywood table, with a bouquet of silk roses set in a Czechoslovakian lead crystal vase.

The woman took his coat, hat, gloves, and briefcase. She made it out the door before Andrews leaped after her, informing her that he wanted to keep his briefcase. The young secretary blushed, obviously embarrassed at her blunder, and handed it back to him. She left with his other items and returned with a large silver tray. She set it on the coffee table and offered him tea. She left the entire pot for him, along with a tempting array of liverwurst sandwiches and sugar biscuits. Andrews wondered if even the Queen of England could boast such a spread.

Andrews drank his tea, ate several small sandwiches, straightened his tie, and glanced at the briefcase next to him on the floor. He passed the time reviewing what he planned to say to the Soviet Ambassador when he entered the room. Andrews would rise to his feet—not too hastily, he reminded himself, and greet the ambassador as one might an equal. If he appeared too eager he might be taken for a fool, or a simpleton, and his ability to negotiate compensation would be hampered.

He rehearsed every possible scenario: what the ambassador was sure to say, how Andrews would cleverly respond, how he would stand, how he would laugh derisively at the first offer of payment presented by the ambassador. By two o'clock he was confident he would make a favorable impression.

At two thirty he began to fidget, straightening his lapel, checking his teeth for bread crumbs in his distorted reflection on the teapot. Andrews was certain the ambassador would want what Andrews had to sell. He practiced again how he would negotiate the deal, using the teapot as a stand-in for the overjoyed and grateful Soviet ambassador.

At three o'clock he was quite worried. He crossed his legs, and then he recrossed them in the other direction. The teapot was empty and its contents had gone directly to his bladder. Sandwiches and tea mixed with anxiety created an uncomfortable brew in his gut. He stood and began to pace the room.

He made faces in the gilded mirror. He walked across the room and leaned dejectedly against the windowsill. He watched London's frenzied traffic below, took in the bomb-ravaged skyline and the new buildings already beginning to brighten London's future horizon. His enthusiasm had vanished, and he slumped back into his chair.

He picked at the last of the sandwiches and biscuits and tried to pour one last drop from the teakettle, simply trying to stay busy to calm his nerves. One drop was all he managed.

The door opened, with a sound so foreign to the last few hours of stillness that he jumped wildly. His teacup clattered off its saucer and tumbled to the Persian rug at his feet. Shaken, he fell to his knees, retrieved it, and placed it carefully on the edge of the coffee table. Then he scrambled to his feet, wiped his dirty palms on his trousers, and faced the Soviet ambassador.

He was a short man, thick at the waist, with a luminescent jolliness about him that reminded Andrews of a child's drawing of Saint Nick—minus the beard, of course. The ambassador was clean-shaven and well-dressed, with every seam, every fold, and every crease impeccable.

He offered his hand. "My name is Fedor Gusev, Soviet ambassador to London."

"Percy Andrews." Andrews shook the ambassador's hand.

"I apologize about the delay, Mr. Andrews. It's just that there is so much I must do—and I cannot find the time for it all!"

"Yes, well—"

Both men sat down, facing each other.

"You have something to tell me, Mr. Andrews?"

"Yes, Comrade." Andrews fumbled for his briefcase. "Actually, I also have something to give you."

Gusev watched Andrews pick up the briefcase. "And I assume you'll want to be compensated?"

This was going to be easy. Obviously this Soviet was a man of the world—he understood how things worked. Andrews smiled. He searched his memory for the sum he'd decided upon during his long wait.

Gusev didn't give him a chance to say it. "You look like an intelligent person, Mr. Andrews. Certainly the information you have for us is of the utmost importance. The Soviet Union needs people like you. If I like what I see, I will offer you two thousand pounds."

"T-two thousand . . ." Andrews swallowed. *Two thousand pounds!* It was a princely sum—more than Andrews had meant to negotiate.

"Yes." Gusev confirmed. "Payable upon receipt of the information—and the item—you have with you."

"You mean . . ." Andrews swallowed. "You're gonna give me two thousand pounds, tonight?"

"That is correct. That is, if you can convince me that the information you bring is as important as you claim." The ambassador checked his gold watch.

Andrews scrambled to open the briefcase. Gusev waved him away. "First tell me something, Mr. Andrews; tell me something that will convince me of the importance of your merchandise. Then I will see what you have to show me."

Percy cleared his throat. "I heard something about—about a shipment . . ."

"Where were you when you heard this?"

"Interlaken, sir."

"A shipment? What sort of shipment? Hurry please; I have an appointment in five minutes."

Andrews wrung his hands. "It wasn't clear, sir—it was a shipment of something important . . ."

The ambassador sighed. "A shipment to where?"

"Near Leningrad, sir—the man said it would arrive at a small bay west of Leningrad."

"What man?"

"That is what I'm trying to show you, Comrade." Again Andrews fumbled at the latch.

Again Gusev stopped him. "What man, Mr. Andrews?"

"Mr. Viktor Rostov. Two men, actually—Mr. Rostov and the Nazi fugitive Rolf Schulmann." Andrews frowned at the briefcase. He studied the latch closely. "You understand I expect full payment tonight—"

"Of course, of course."

The process of opening the briefcase seemed more difficult than usual; the latches didn't open quite right and the lock seemed to have developed a minute amount of rust. But finally it snapped open and Andrews reached inside.

The briefcase was empty.

Bewildered, he pulled it onto his lap and opened it all the way. His hands pawed at the interior, as if conjuring up the ability to pull out of thin air the large white envelope he'd placed there so carefully that morning. "Blimey! It's not here!"

"Mr. Andrews . . ." The ambassador gave an exasperated sigh.

"No! It was blooming here! I swear!" In his shock, his carefully groomed accent dissolved into blubbering street slang. "Some bloodsucking thief's up and . . ." Andrews's defense trailed off as his mind combed through the events of the last twenty-four hours. He'd kept it in hand the entire time he was away from his flat. He'd kept it in his lap while the shoeshine urchin shined his shoes. He'd never once let it out of his sight. Except . . .

"The receptionist!" He rose to his feet. "The blooming skirt! She swiped it! She pulled a switcharoo when she took it with my coat . . ." He stopped for breath, realizing as he did so that the secretary had actually been out of his sight for less than two seconds. Could she possibly be that cunning . . . ?

"How dare you!" The Soviet ambassador also rose to his feet, all civility a thing of the past. "Mr. Andrews, my staff is entirely above reproach. We are not thieves, as you insinuate. Most likely you left your bit of merchandise at home. If so, then you've carelessly left sensitive Soviet secrets available for any petty thief to discover. I should have you arrested for placing our Soviet nation in danger! I'm disappointed in you, Mr. Andrews—I expected that someone of your caliber would be more careful." He turned to go.

"But sir . . ." Andrews took a panicked step toward his retreating back. Fedor Gusev ignored him. The door slammed behind the ambassador. Andrews swore, picked up the briefcase, and threw it against the wall.

A few minutes later Andrews left the Soviet Embassy locked between two burly guards. He tried to explain his conspiracy theory to them, but they didn't pay him any heed.

The pretty young receptionist at the front desk had been replaced by the middle-aged, balding one from that morning, who didn't give Andrews even the courtesy of a farewell glance.

FORTY-THREE

Beneath the hood, Natalie's breath gradually turned toxic. It didn't help that she was already frightened, but the dizziness that accompanied lack of oxygen made it hard to stay upright. She felt with her boots, trying to find a chair, or a cot, or a table—somewhere where she might sit down and lower her head. She was afraid she might collapse and hit her head against the hard floor. She worked at her bonds, tentatively at first, then with greater determination, twisting her wrists and arms to the point of utmost agony before surrendering again to her condition. She raised her chin, straining to see downward past the bottom of the hood. Where was she? Was she really alone?

She knew significant time had passed, but she had no idea how long. She only knew that her breath was slowly killing her, her legs were ready to give way, and she was experiencing a new dimension of fear. She sank to her knees, leaned forward and rested her head against the cold concrete.

She heard muffled footsteps and she struggled again to her feet. The lock released, the heavy door opened, and two sets of boots resumed walking. The door closed again. *Swoooosh . . . pop!* She was locked in a room with two anonymous people. She heard a series of soft scuffles, then both sets of boots suddenly went silent. Had they removed their boots in order to keep her guessing their location? Her skin crawled at the thought that they could be two inches from her and she wouldn't know it.

She summoned her courage. "Please . . . What have I done wrong?"

A deep voice spoke next to her ear. She practically jumped out of her skin. "What is your name?"

She swallowed. "Natalya Ivanovna Karagodina."

A pause, then he repeated, "What is your name?"

She hesitated. Had she said it wrong? "Karagodina Natalya Ivanovna."

"What is your name?"

She realized the voice was vaguely familiar. She carefully repeated the foreign name Rostov said was hers, and tried to recall where she had heard that voice before.

There was a long silence, and then to her left, a second voice asked, "What were you doing in Germany?"

Her heart raced. She hadn't expected this. *Germany?* What did Germany have to do with anything?

He seemed to want to keep her guessing. "Why did you lie to us, Natalya Ivanovna?"

"*What?*"

And then, just inches from her face, the first voice asked, "Are you spying for the Americans?"

She was shocked. "No!"

"What is your relationship with the Nazi Hans Brenner?"

She gasped, choked, and couldn't think how to respond. *Hans?* She felt as if her knees would buckle. It was as if her past, present, and dreams had been gathered by this semi-familiar, floating voice demanding answers. "I—I—" Her dizziness increased. "Please, Comrade, I—I can't breathe . . . M-may I sit down?"

For a long moment there was no response, and then wood scraped against stone and something hard pressed against the back of her knees. She sat, and the questions continued.

"Are you spying for the Germans?"

"No!"

Again, from near her shoulder, "Explain your relationship with Hans Brenner."

"He—he is . . . was . . ." Suddenly her tongue would not move and she felt as if a vice had tightened about her skull, squeezing until she had to stop talking. She could not finish her response.

"He was what, Natalya Ivanovna?"

She opened her mouth to respond, *He was my fiancé.* But the invisible vise again closed about her head, and she couldn't form the words. Her tongue felt like lead and the words would not leave her mouth.

After an excruciating pause, the same series of questions began again. And as before, when she attempted to explain her relationship to Hans the words would not leave her mouth. It was as if an unseen vise squeezed her and smothered the answer right out of her brain. She'd never in her life felt anything like it, and in the confines and darkness of her hood, it was frightening.

She heard the door to her prison swing open, and for several moments, silence followed. She next heard the low murmur of voices, and then she was seized by both arms and forced to her feet.

She stood where she was and listened to her tormentors pull their boots back on, and then one set of boots approached. "Walk, citizen." An iron grip on her arm forced compliance. She was dragged through a series of spaces that she could only describe by the sound of her escort's footsteps and the feel through the soles of her boots. Stone, then more stone, then uneven stone steps, then wood that seemed to crackle with every step, and then a smooth, hard surface.

Her escort stopped walking. He untied her wrists and removed her hood.

She blinked in the sudden light. She was in a Spartan, concrete room, facing a long table where sat two men and Dr. Yuri Komarov. She gulped in air and tried to get her eyes to work properly. She squinted at the two seated men. Both wore the uniforms of the MGB; one was unfamiliar to her, but the other was Ivan Volkov, the man who had dragged her away from Viktor in the Leningrad Train Station in Moscow.

He smiled at her, and she wished for the return of her hood.

"Comrade Karagodina." Dr. Komarov approached her, all solicitude. "As representatives of the Ministry for State Security, it is our duty to make sure that our citizens are well cared for. Are you feeling all right?"

She dared not admit otherwise. "Yes."

"Have you been treated with respect by our comrades?"

Her lips trembled, and she could hardly answer. "Yes, sir."

"Good." He gave her a stiff smile. "Then we will proceed." He walked to the table and sat down with the other two men.

The man she did not know cleared his throat. "Citizen Karagodina, we are here to discuss delicate matters of State security. Doktor Komarov is familiar to you. Have you met Comrade Ivan Volkov?"

Wordlessly, she nodded.

"Comrade Volkov represents the enforcement branch of the MGB. He supervises interrogation procedures and punishment for my Ministry. He attended your earlier examination and has informed me of your reluctance to discuss certain issues related to your past."

Volkov had been one of the disembodied voices questioning her. She felt as if a venomous snake had just slid across her body.

"My name is Roman Krajnik," the man continued. "I am Director of the Moscow branch of the Ministry for State Security. I have received direct authority from Comrade Abakumov, head of the Soviet MGB, to act in *all* matters that affect State security for my region. Do you understand what that means?"

She didn't have any idea how to respond.

Krajnik explained, "That means the citizens of Moscow breathe because I've given them permission to do so." He smiled at her. He held up a piece of paper, dangling it in front of her face. His bulgy finger jabbed at the bottom of the page. "Is that your signature, citizen?"

Karagodina Natalya Ivanovna. She recognized the paper in Krajnik's hand; it was one of the two documents from the train station—the one Rostov had filled with his handwriting and then forced her to sign. She hadn't been able to read Russian back then, and so had no idea what she'd signed. Rostov had refused to tell her. Now she squinted at it, inclining her head slightly in an attempt to make out Viktor's handwriting. She felt a finger of dread inching up her spine. *What had she signed?*

"Yes." She swallowed. "That is my signature."

Krajnik stood and walked around the table. He read for the whole room to hear. "I, Karagodina Natalya Ivanovna, pledge that I have not collaborated in any way with the Enemies of the Soviet Union. I have not worked in partnership with the Nazis, shown friendship toward opponents of the Soviet Union, nor done anything that would in any way jeopardize the safety and security of the Motherland. I am a loyal Soviet citizen. I will always defend and honor Comrade Stalin and the Communist Party. Signed, Karagodina Natalya Ivanovna. May 17, 1946."

Shocked, Natalie stared at the paper dangling from Krajnik's hand.

Roman Krajnik approached. "In signing this document you lied to the Soviet Union. We have it on good authority that you had a friend, a Nazi officer named Hans Brenner, and that at one time you planned to marry him. Is that true?"

She realized now what Rostov had done for her: Signing the document he had prepared had both saved and condemned her—saved her life at the train station and condemned her to never speak Hans's name again. And Natalie felt again the eerie pressure in her skull that prohibited her from answering the question. A simple nod of the head would've sufficed, but she couldn't even achieve that. She felt that she was perhaps receiving a significant warning from the Spirit that something disastrous would happen if she confirmed her relationship with Hans. Even after the horrific nightmare of the past few hours—the past few months— could Heavenly Father actually be watching over her? She began to tremble, but she forced herself to stand tall and said, "I will not answer that question."

Krajnik shrugged. "Very well. We will proceed without your participation." He returned to his seat at the table. "Karagodina Natalya Ivanovna, you have been found guilty by the People of fraud, espionage, and treason. You've committed grievous offences against the Soviet Union. You've placed the Motherland in serious danger, in a deliberate attempt to weaken us in the eyes of our enemies to the west."

Natalie was speechless. She felt cold as death, and she couldn't believe what she was hearing. Treason? Fraud? Espionage? Never, ever, had she considered she would be accused of such crimes! Her hands hung limp at her sides, and she couldn't make her brain function and think this through.

And then she began to worry about the ramifications of such accusations. *What would they do to her? What would they do to Viktor for protecting her?*

Krajnik continued, and he spoke to her now as if she were a child who had severely displeased a father. "I was upset, Natalya, when I found out that you'd signed an obviously false statement, with the intent to prolong your life and in order to penetrate our defenses." His voice assumed a measure of concern. "You've been lucky this morning." He indicated Volkov, who had not once taken his eyes off Natalie. "My associate here was of the opinion that you should be punished immediately for your crimes; he asked you certain questions which, if you had implicated yourself, would have meant a swift execution as you stood. I gave Comrade Volkov permission to immediately carry through with your execution if the situation warranted."

Natalie felt as if the entire building was falling on her, stone after stone after stone. *Execution?* Because she hadn't struggled against the Spirit's forceful promptings she was miraculously still alive, but from the severity of Krajnik's words she knew her sentence would still be harsh.

He tossed the infamous document onto the table as he continued. "But we are reasonable men, Natalya. You have not confessed to any crime and we are not going to execute you. However, neither can we release you so that you can carry on with your traitorous plans."

Roman Krajnik frowned at her, shaking his head. "I'm disappointed in you, Natalya Ivanovna. I gave you a chance. I accepted Comrade Rostov's assurances of your goodwill—and have ended up being deceived. By the powers that have been allotted me by Comrade Abakumov of the MGB, I now sentence you to twenty years hard labor in Siberia. Details of your punishment will be decided at a later date."

"No! Sir, there's been a grave mistake!"

She was not given the opportunity to explain the error. Her guards pulled her from the room, rushed her at breakneck speed down the corridor, released her hands, and pitched her into a cell.

Whoosh . . . pop!

She slumped to the cold floor. She found herself whispering, over and over, until it sounded like babbling, "Why, Heavenly Father . . . Why?"

She had no tears to cry. In fact, what Natalie had just experienced felt so bizarre that the thought of crying was almost ridiculous. She was incapable of keeping track of time. She waited in her cell for what seemed like hours, until finally she heard the lock scrape open and a young, freckle-faced guard stood in the doorway. He managed a wolfish grin, revealing several gold teeth.

"Your dinner, citizen." He tossed a piece of bread at her and it broke in two on the stone floor. She didn't move to retrieve it.

The boy hesitated. He stood resting on one foot, watching her. After a few seconds he asked, "Amerikanka?"

She wished he would go away. She didn't want to chat with anyone right now—especially not a freckle-faced youth masquerading as a brute. But she heard something in his voice, something that made her wonder if he was sincerely trying to be nice to her.

She raised her head, studied him for a moment, and nodded.

He leaned out the door and glanced down the corridor, first one way and then the other. Then he turned to her, his mouth spread in an awkward grin. "I'm the night guard. Almost everyone else is gone for the evening. Will you speak English with me?" He hesitated. "For a few minutes?"

Her jaw dropped. What a strange request at a moment like this. But she agreed, and they talked for quite a while. The boy's name was Vyeta, and he and his parents had been transplanted from a small collective farm village in the Urals. His mother was an actress with the Moscow Theater and his father worked as a guard at the Kremlin. When Vyeta finished his studies, he applied to join the MGB police force. He warmed to his subject, his English atrocious and his enthusiasm making the words all but unintelligible.

Vyeta seemed to lose track of time. He spoke of hunting with his father, and asked what youth his age did in America. He wanted to see New York someday.

Vyeta cut off his speech midsentence, as if suddenly remembering his duty. He nodded at her, backed out of the cell, and closed the heavy iron door.

Swooooosh . . .

Vyeta's footsteps faded away down the corridor.

Had her mind deceived her? Had the young guard actually forgotten to lock her cell door completely? What had he said? That he was the only one on duty that night? No; he'd said he was *almost* the only one, that almost everyone else had gone home for the night.

What should she do? Natalie glanced about the cell as if looking for an answer in the cold stone walls. If she sat here, remaining caged when she knew the cage door was open, she could forfeit any possible chance of escape. On the other hand, it could be a trap, set for her by a sly youth who had just feigned interest in Americans in order to trick her. Could Volkov still be trying to find an excuse to execute her?

But what if it was a miraculous answer to her prayers?

She struggled to her feet, took a deep breath, and opened the door.

Her feet in their felted wool valenki made very little noise as they flew down the corridor, past the room of her trial, up a flight of steps and out a side door. Vyeta's freckled face was nowhere to be seen. She pulled her coat tightly about her, gasping at the cold air that exploded into her lungs as she stepped into Dzerzhinsky Square.

She began the longest walk of her life. She skirted Red Square, walked past the vacant streetcar stop, across the bridge, and away from the Moskva River. She passed a clock tower on an old church now used to house the offices of the District Soviet. Faintly she heard a clock inside strike eleven times. She knew that at this hour of the night she would have to make the entire escape on her own two feet, and in this weather it would be difficult. She wondered how long she had before Krajnik discovered her absence. She wondered what they would do to Vyeta for losing her. She wondered if she would freeze before she reached safety. And she wondered where she could go that could possibly be safe.

The only place she could think of was the Spaso House. And even there, she had little hope of finding a listening ear in General Smith. Her only hope was that he could help her contact Viktor and that he would not report her—at least for a few hours—to the authorities.

It was a dangerous decision, fraught with a hundred things that could go wrong. But in the end, she turned her feet toward the Ambassador's residence.

Now that she had a destination in mind, another question demanded an answer: Who told Roman Krajnik about Hans Brenner? She couldn't imagine Viktor would be the culprit—for the explicit reason that he was the one who wrote that document.

And then Natalie remembered her conversation with Regina, the morning after Ina was born. Poor Regina! She'd been so interested in the subject of eternal marriage, and so sad that something like that was not even in the realm of possibility for herself and her family. She was trying so hard to reunite her family. And now Ina had been taken from her . . .

Natalie's step faltered. Could Regina have been recruited to inform on Natalie? Hadn't she said that she was doing all in her power to protect her imprisoned husband? Could she have made an agreement with Roman Krajnik? Was Krajnik the friend of her father's that Regina had once mentioned?

The thought made Natalie physically ill. Regina was her friend. Regina would never do such a thing—would she? Certainly a friendship was sacred—even in the Soviet Union. Others might inform on their neighbors and comrades, but not her friend Regina.

But what did it matter to the State, if brother denounced brother, son denounced father, husband denounced wife? *Oh, Regina!*

Regina was a *stookatch*. An informer. It was more than Natalie could take. She leaned forward and broke into a stumbling run.

In Regina's defense, though, it might have been an accident. Could Regina have told Krajnik about Hans Brenner without knowing it was damaging to Natalie—just because she was required to report anything and everything to the MGB?

She could hardly breathe. Each breath froze like icicles and clung painfully to her throat. Her muscles ached, and her boots did little to protect her feet. She had never felt this lonely in her life. Another few blocks and she would be there. She was glad she had decided not to go home; the police could be at Natalie's apartment waiting for her. And even if they weren't, her fellow tenants would turn her in as soon as she reached the door. They would fear for their own freedom.

She slowed to a shuffle, willing her tired feet forward and onward through the heavy drifts, across a stark, empty square. She saw the pillars of the Spaso House, and even though her emotions still reeled every time she thought of her first visit here, she was suddenly grateful for the sight. Her gaze rose automatically to the flagpole.

Then her feet hesitated. The windows were dark, but she could make out the outlines of two shadows standing on the balcony near the empty pole. She couldn't make out details—only that both seemed taller than

Krajnik, not quite as slender as Volkov, and not as bulky as Komarov. And they were leaning over the railing and watching the square below.

She retreated toward a cold, desolate playground slightly to the east of the house. Both shadows moved, disappearing from the balcony.

Moments later they threw open the door and pursued her. Oh, how her legs burned as she ran, and she couldn't keep her feet under her in the deep drifts. Her arms flailed wildly in her effort to maintain her balance. She knew they had several advantages over her—strength, height, and the fact that they had not been walking through the bitter cold for hours. She could hear the muffled thump of their boots as they chased after her, gaining on her as if she were standing still.

"Natalie! *Natalie Allred!*"

At first her mind refused to accept the reality behind the voice; it was Hans Brenner's voice, but Rostov insisted Hans Brenner was dead. In spite of what she'd told herself all these months, this voice seemed too good to be true. Yet the voice called her by her American name. And when she stopped and turned, the man had Hans Brenner's face.

She couldn't move. She couldn't breathe. It was impossible! Her legs became as stiff as the stone of the Spaso House and she stared at the man who approached. He didn't slow down but swept over her as an eagle pounces on its prey, capturing her in his arms and crushing her to him, pulling her up off of her feet and into a place of safety so fierce and beautiful she was unable to do more than gasp out his name.

"Natalie," he whispered back, with an agony that broke her heart. "I—I can't . . . I can't . . ." He kissed her, and then he couldn't stop kissing her to explain what it was he couldn't do. She didn't mind. What were broken, unfinished sentences when the man she loved had returned impossibly from the dead? She had no words to describe the way her heart fluttered and leapt, over and over, dancing against her ribcage and her entire soul. She could only think, again and again, the name of the man she'd thought lost to her for eternity. *Hans . . . Hans . . .*

It didn't matter that Viktor was there too. Besides, he'd turned away and retreated to stand beside a frozen swing set, his back to them and his gloves jammed deep into his pockets. But it seemed strange to her that he would be here, with the man he claimed to have killed. Oh, how she detested Viktor for his lies!

"Natalie, you have no idea how I worried . . . but you're alive and safe . . ."

She still couldn't find a way to respond, and she reached and held his face in both her hands, the rough stubble of a new beard prickling her cold flesh. She touched his ears, cold and real, removed his ushanka and ran her fingers through hair that had grown long. She blinked back her tears and saw Hans struggling to do the same. Her fingers touched old scars—lifelong reminders of her dislike for the man standing nearby. "He told me you were dead, Hans," she accused through her tears. "He told me his guard killed you."

"I know. I'm sorry. I thought about you every day. Every *hour*, Natalie. I didn't know what happened to you."

Now that she had someone to hear her suffering, she couldn't stop. "His men took me from Aimée's apartment! That night we said good-bye . . ."

She felt Hans nod. He buried his face in her neck. "You can't imagine how I felt, Natalie, when I found out what Rostov had done to you."

"Hans, where have you been?"

"In a gilded cage. I've been a well-fed laboratory rat in a politically nonexistent laboratory." He chuckled, even though the sound held unresolved suffering. "I wonder which is better—a Berlin gutter rat or a Soviet lab rat. I'll have to think about that one."

"Hans, quit referring to yourself as a rat." She laughed through her tears. "I love you so much!"

"If you've had enough of Moscow, would you like to come with me to America and get married?"

She began to sob into his coat. Viktor Rostov glanced once at her and then again contemplated the playground. Finally, his voice as cold as the ice-encased swing set, he said, "We need to go."

"Hans," Natalie whispered, "what is *he* doing here?"

"Lieutenant Rostov has something to tell you."

"You're forcing him to apologize?" She didn't think she could stand the awkwardness of such a scene.

"No. What he's done to you goes beyond an apology. He's here to help you. Isn't that right, Professor?"

"We must go now." Rostov's words were clipped. "Someone's bound to recognize us, and then we'll all be in danger."

"Will the ambassador allow us to—"

"Stay?" Viktor finished for her. He snorted. "And risk his reputation with Comrade Stalin? Not likely."

Viktor Rostov drove them to an apartment complex several kilometers from the Kremlin Hospital. He pushed open the heavy steel entrance and they climbed the steps with Natalie clinging to Hans, as if afraid that she might lose him again.

Natalie hesitated at the threshold. "Where are we?"

"Doktor Vlasov's appartment." Viktor opened the door with a key and walked inside.

The memory of Dr. Vlasov's kindness made Natalie reluctant to place him in danger. "They'll destroy him, Viktor, if they find out that he helped—"

"He's not here, Natalya," Viktor snapped. "I sent him away and told him not to come back for a few days. Then he can claim he didn't know."

"But you have his keys . . ."

"He keeps them in his desk at the hospital." Rostov faced her. He seemed awkward, angry, and unsure of himself—completely different from the man she'd known over the past months. And even though he had wounded her, she couldn't help but feel a little anxious for him. He cleared his throat. "What did the MGB do to you, Natalya?"

"They've sentenced me to twenty years hard labor."

He didn't seem surprised. "The document you signed. I'm sorry— it was a chance I had to take." He turned away.

She said gently, "They might—might accuse you . . . "

"They already suspect me." His voice was resigned. "It doesn't matter."

"They might think we worked together . . ." She took a deep breath. "What was the second document, Viktor?"

He didn't answer. He carefully removed his gloves, ushanka, and coat.

Suddenly, Viktor's strange silence made the contents of that second document terribly important to her. "Krajnik didn't mention the second document I signed. What was it, Viktor? What did you force me to sign?"

Viktor tossed his coat over the arm of a chair. "It's not important."

"It is to *me*, Viktor. It has my signature on it—right next to yours."

"Do you want to hear what I have to say?" he growled. "Or do you want to keep interrogating me?" He wouldn't look at her. He added simply, "I've found Regina Igorevna's baby. I'm going to help you get her back."

FORTY-FOUR

Saturday, December 14, 1946

As the sun finally disappeared on the evening of the fourteenth of December, there was nothing but snow and gray skies as far as the eye could see. During winter in Moscow, the eye sometimes couldn't see very far.

Fortunately Natalie was not here to admire the scenery. Besides, what scenery might have once been admired now lay hidden under layers of snow, ice, and neglect. At this detskidom, this orphanage for babies and children up to age five, the garden lay fallow and the once-majestic granite walls remained concealed behind layers of Moscow grime. No one had the time or resources to care for the walls and gardens of an orphanage.

When she entered the home she understood why. The nurses would have more urgent matters; they would be hard pressed to keep the dozens of children in their care fed, washed, and changed. Natalie viewed row after row of beds, each inhabited by at least one child—sometimes two—and the overpowering smell made her wonder if perhaps the washed and changed part of the equation might often be set aside.

She accompanied the head nurse, Galya Valinovna, on a tour of the facilities.

"And this, Comrade, is the room for infants and toddlers."

Natalie had heard the sound, like so many crying seagulls, from several rooms away. She stood in a room as big as her high school cafeteria back home in America. Rostov had advised her that this building had once housed Arbat Quarter administration, and that it had been deemed structurally deficient. Therefore it had been vacated by government staff and renovated to fit the more modest needs of a growing population of parentless children. The chronic sadness of the babies reverberated off the frost-covered walls and up to the thick beams of the ceiling at least twenty feet above Natalie's head.

It was a room impossible to heat. Natalie held her clipboard with hands that would not stay warm, and she could see her breath as she asked, "How many cribs?"

Galya smiled. "We have one hundred and twenty cribs in this room."

In the dim light Natalie could make out several tiny heads wobbling above the edges of their cribs, and tiny hands grasped the cold steel railings. Babies stared into space or cried miserably and reached toward passing nurses. It was a dismal, heart-wrenching sight, and she had to force herself to stay calm. She was disturbed by this apparent neglect and she hoped her masquerade would not be discovered because of a trembling hand or an angry word.

"And how many children, Comrade Valinovna?"

"A little over three hundred."

One hundred and twenty cribs. Three hundred children! She was repulsed by the overcrowded conditions, the cold, the smell of soiled diapers, and the desperate sounds of neglect. The nurse in her cringed at the Soviet efficiency that would fit so many rows of cribs in one room that there was barely room to walk between them. And the woman in her cried out, anguished that she couldn't reach for the nearest baby and cuddle away his despair. She had the irrational wish to have the time and means to save all of them—or, at least, hold each one until the tears ceased . . .

"Impressive." Natalie made a note on her clipboard. "And where are the newborns?"

"Infants under the age of six months are over here"—Galya swept one hand to her left—"babies from six to twelve months over here"—again the woman pointed—"and twelve months to two years are in the center." Galya pointed to the cribs with the bobbing, crying heads in the middle of the room. Natalie made a mental note of the fifteen or so cribs in a drafty corner, each spread with a stained sheet and filled with miniature forms. Most of the infants lay tightly bundled, arms and legs wrapped in cocoons up to their chins. These babies, at least, seemed content, but several had worked their way out of their wrappings and now flailed their arms and legs about in the bitter cold, inconsolable in their grief.

"How many infants age newborn to six months?" She raised her pen and let it hover over her clipboard.

"Does the Ministry of Health need the ages of the children?" the nurse fretted. "I would have to check our records, Comrade Serova— but you must understand, our population is forever in a state of flux."

Natalie nodded. "I understand. I believe I can convince administration that it's not feasible to know the exact ages of the children. How many staff members are at your disposal?"

Here the head nurse was confident in her answer. "Eight nurses, and a kitchen staff of three; once a week we have two maids scrub floors; we have two laundry engineers, two administrative assistants, and myself."

Natalie made a note on the clipboard. Only eight nurses! No wonder they could stifle motherly instincts and ignore tiny outstretched arms as they walked through a room.

She asked a few more questions. Galya explained the babies' daily schedules, emphasizing the speed and efficiency with which the nurses had been trained to administer the babies' gruel. Infants received a bottle twice daily and were fed a thin mixture of boiled oats and goat's milk in the interim. One nurse was assigned to care for the sixty-three infants in the infants' section. In fact, she was there now, propping bottles on rolled towels next to the tiny heads.

Natalie could hardly stand it. She wanted to run to the infant section and search for tiny Ina, grab her from amidst all this suffering, and flee from this awful room. But she clenched the clipboard, her knuckles white as she restrained herself. A mistake could cost Regina her baby.

"And why are most of these children here? Surely they're not all orphans."

Galya shook her head. "Only a small percentage. But we prepare ourselves for the probability that most of the children of kulak criminals will not be reunited with their parents any time soon. And, to be honest"—Galya gave a little half shrug—"most of them will never see their parents again, even after the parents are released."

"I see." Natalie's heart cried along with the babies in the room. She glanced at her watch, and Galya caught the motion.

The head nurse cleared her throat. "I don't want to weary you, Comrade Serova . . ."

"Not at all. May I have a look at the babies?"

Galya led the way. Natalie's eyes darted from one crib to another, visually examining each infant, and silently praying that Ina would be obvious to her. She had the horrible thought that she might not recognize Regina's baby; after all, Ina wasn't *her* baby—and so she prayed hard, studying each tiny face as she discussed with Galya diapers and socks, warm blankets and woolen caps. She studied each miniature feature as she negotiated the medical supplies Galya required. She searched each face, looking for dimples, and eyes that shone like blue sapphires, while at the same time praising the head nurse for her organization and leadership. And then she saw Ina.

Regina's baby lay awake, still in the blanket her mother always wrapped her in, her porcelain skin white as the snow that surrounded the detskidom, her once-bright eyes dull, and her body limp. She didn't wave her hands or kick her feet, and Natalie could hardly contain the bile that rose in her throat. Ina's health was not good.

"And this one?" She could hardly keep her voice steady, let alone impersonal as it needed to be. "What's the problem with her?"

Galya looked into the crib and shrugged. "It's hard to say. Perhaps she's not eating well. Maybe she refuses her bottle or has a fever. We lose many at this young age."

They were interrupted by the sound of heavy footsteps approaching the nursery at a determined pace. Natalie dropped the clipboard and swept Regina's baby into her arms, and then turned with Galya to face the looming threat. She felt her heart skip a beat at the sight of two MGB policemen, and she clutched the baby protectively to her. Galya greeted the two men but they swept her aside. "Karagodina Natalya Ivanovna?" The younger of the two men stepped forward.

He'd used her name. Her cover was blown; Natalie could not look in Galya's direction.

"You are under arrest for impersonating an officer of the Soviet Ministry of Health, and for attempting to abduct a baby owned by the State. Hand over the baby and come with us."

She did as she was told. Her hands trembled as she presented the precious bundle to the indignant Galya. Galya shifted the baby to one arm and shoved Natalie as hard as she could. "Imbecile!" She spat. "You would have me lose my job?" Suddenly her eyes grew wide. "You're that American—the friend of this baby's birth mother! I was warned—that you might try to steal the baby. *Ey ty Durak!*" She swore and pushed Natalie again before returning Ina to her crib.

Natalie certainly felt like a fool as she stood silently and was handcuffed. The older policeman reached a hand into the crib to play with the baby. "Is this the child of Regina Igorevna?"

"Yes, Comrade." Galya's chest heaved and she threw an accusing finger in Natalie's direction. "This horrible woman would destroy everything I've worked for my entire life. Her masquerade has made me look like a fool, and I want her punished!"

"She will be." The older officer bent and retrieved the clipboard from the floor. He studied what Natalie had written. "What information was she requesting from you?"

"It's all there. Supplies, numbers of staff, children under my care . . ."

"Did she ask you questions about the baby Ina Petrovna?"

"Yes sir. She asked what was wrong with it. I thought her special interest in the babies was odd . . ." Galya glared one more time at Natalie.

"What is your name, Comrade?"

"Galya Valinovna. I am the director of this detskidom. I've been the director for twenty-five years—"

"You could help us, Comrade Valinovna, by accompanying us to the station to make a statement. Did you know that this woman has already been convicted of serious crimes?"

Galya's face went white. "Of course I will come with you."

"And we'll bring the baby along." The older policeman said, reaching to pick up Ina. "We'll need to show the authorities evidence of the woman's attempted theft."

"Of course. I'll get my coat."

"And a few things for the baby of course, Comrade—blankets, milk, a few diapers . . ."

"Right away."

While the older policeman held the baby and waited for Galya, the other escorted Natalie to the waiting Black Crow. It was a desperate, depressing feeling to be once again facing a ride in the back of the horrible MGB van.

"Watch your step, citizen."

"Please," she implored, "take off these cuffs."

"Not until you're inside." The policeman was polite, but firm. "You must be inside before I'll remove the cuffs."

She relented, allowing him to help her into the back of the dreaded vehicle, among boxes, bags, and more boxes. He climbed up behind her and unlocked the cuffs. Then he turned her around, pulled her into his arms and kissed her.

"You're trembling, Natalie."

She clung to Hans's uniform jacket, provided by Viktor. "It brings back too many awful memories. And I was so afraid that horrible woman would find out . . ." His embrace soothed her until her trembling subsided. And then she giggled.

"What could possibly be funny, Natalie?"

"It's a little unnerving, that's all."

"What is?"

She reached and warmed his ears with her hands. "To be kissed by a man who looks like my fiancé and smells like Viktor Rostov."

Hans chuckled. "Don't let him hear you say that. He might feel really, really bad."

"And he doesn't really smell as bad as he *could*, you know . . ." Natalie tried awkwardly to explain. "It's just that these hairy winter coats never get washed, and after a while they start to smell like the person who wears them. I meant no disrespect to Viktor. He is, after all, very conscientious and clean . . ."

"Natalie . . ."

"What?"

"Stop talking."

They had to part company when Viktor Rostov and Galya appeared from the children's home. Galya was carrying the baby, and Viktor had a bag of supplies over one shoulder. Hans kissed Natalie one last time and backed out of the vehicle. "I'm sorry, citizen—I'm going to have to lock you in."

"Please, just please hurry, Hans. I don't know how long I can stand it back here," Natalie said quietly.

He lowered his voice and whispered, "Did you know that I love you?"

"Don't you ever leave me again, Hans Brenner."

They drove away from the children's home, a dozen kilometers down the road and around many corners. They pulled up next to Viktor Rostov's automobile, hidden in a backstreet alleyway, and Viktor and Hans exited the prison van. Viktor pulled several bags from the seat of his car and tossed them into the front of the van next to Galya.

"What are you doing?" she demanded. "Where are we?"

"Do you know how to drive?"

"What?" Her eyes widened. "Drive?"

"Can you drive this van?"

"Why would I need to drive a police van? I'm the director of the children's home."

"Because we're going to leave you here with this van," Rostov explained. "If you know how to drive, then you can get back to the children's home." Rostov shrugged. "If you don't, then you can wait until they find you in the morning."

"I'll freeze to death!" she shrieked.

"No you won't."

"Yes I will! You're not the police. Who are you? It's going to freeze tonight!"

"I'm an MGB officer. These bags hold medical supplies from the Kremlin Hospital for your nurses. There are blankets in the back of this van that are my donation to your orphanage. Consider them either a gift or a bribe. You decide."

"A bribe for what?" Galya's eyes were round saucers of panic, and she clutched the baby to her as if to squeeze the answers out of her.

"You'd better hand me the baby."

"No! What do you want with her?"

"To save her from you. Give her to me."

Whimpering, Galya did as she was told. Rostov took the baby and turned to go.

"Where are you taking her?" Galya shrieked. Then she noticed that Hans had freed Natalie and was standing with her near Rostov's car. "What is that horrible woman doing over there? Why did you let her out?"

She continued to shriek while Hans helped Natalie into the car and Rostov handed her the baby. Rostov returned and tossed the van keys onto the seat next to the head nurse. "Drive south; you should get there eventually." He walked away.

"Where are you going? Come back here. Come back here!"

* * *

Regina woke to the touch of someone's hand on her arm. She sat up, frightened, but then she recognized Natalie.

"Regina. Come with me."

Regina was too bewildered to argue. She slipped her feet into valenki, accepted her coat from Natalie's hands, and followed the American out the door.

Regina stuffed her gloveless hands into her pockets and walked with Natalie across the customary apartment playground and around the corner of the building. A figure separated itself from the darkness and approached them, holding a soft bundle in his arms.

"I didn't want to wake anyone," Natalie explained and took the bundle from the stranger's arms. She handed Regina her baby.

Regina began to sob, clutching Ina to her heart. She collapsed to her knees and rocked back and forth. "Thank you, thank you . . ."

Natalie knelt next to her. "It was Viktor, Regina. He found her for you."

"I thought . . . that I'd never see her again . . ."

"I know."

"Please tell him . . . I don't know how to tell him . . ."

"I think he understands. Come with us, Regina. Rostov knows someone who can alter our passports and get us permission to travel."

Leave Moscow? The thought was frightening to Regina. "But where would I go?" Regina looked up at her. "My husband is here." She blinked back tears. "My *life* is here!"

"But the MGB will soon know we've taken your baby. They'll come for you. They'll take your baby again."

Regina stood, awkwardly, and shifted the bundle in her arms. "I can't leave my husband."

"Regina . . ."

"No, Natalya. I will not do it." How could she explain to this American that her family meant everything to her? Natalya was not married; how could she understand the love of a wife for her husband— even if that husband was an enemy of the People? "I *cannot* do it!"

Natalie looked worried, but she said, "All right. Today we'll be at Dr. Vlasov's apartment . . . if you change your mind . . ."

Regina glanced at her, curious, but said nothing. She turned to study the man with Natalie.

"Regina," Natalie smiled, "I want you to meet—"

"Hans?" Regina gasped. She stared at the silent stranger. "This is *your* Hans?"

Natalie nodded, and Regina hugged her. "Oh, I'm so happy for you!" She made an awkward attempt to shake Hans's hand, and then shooed them both away. "Go! Get out of Moscow and be happy with your Hans." Her eyes shone with tears. "And then I promise you'll understand what makes a woman brave danger to keep her family together."

"Regina, what will you do?"

"Go. Don't worry about me." Regina felt a sick emptiness settle over her as she thought that she would never see her good friend again. But she said, "I will think of something to keep my Inuchka safe. Go!"

FORTY-FIVE

Yuri Komarov tried to ignore the insistent pounding on his apartment door. He rolled his bulk away from the sound and pulled the comforter over his head. It wasn't until he felt the cold hand on his neck that he sprang to his feet. Ivan Volkov stepped back and stood quietly, watching him.

Dr. Komarov swore. "How did you get in here?"

"Krajnik wants you." The intruder reached and switched on the overhead bulb.

"What is it?" Komarov snapped. "I understand the need to sacrifice all for the Motherland, but surely a man's sleep is still his own?"

Ivan Volkov didn't answer. He wandered into Komarov's kitchen and commandeered a bottle of Vodka from a cabinet. He downed half of its contents and then tossed the bottle into the sink. He grabbed an apple from the kitchen table. He walked back into Komarov's bedroom, holding the fruit in his hand. He removed his knife from his belt and sliced it cleanly in two, then took a huge bite.

Komarov eyed the slender blade and couldn't help an involuntary shudder. He reached for his tunic, slipped it over his nightshirt, and tied it about his ample middle. "What is Comrade Krajnik doing up in the middle of the night?"

"Waiting for you." Volkov's tongue worked about his gums for a few moments, and then he raised his knife and began to pick his teeth.

"Do you have to do that here?" Komarov eyed the knife and its owner. "It makes me shudder, you know, to think where it's been."

Volkov looked amused. His raven eyes studied Komarov as if dissecting carrion. He continued to pick his teeth.

Roman Krajnik met Komarov and Volkov at Lubyanka. In his office the MGB officer pulled out a chair for the perturbed doctor, and Komarov sank into it with a groan. He tossed his ushanka onto Krajnik's desk. "Did you have to send *him* to collect me?" Komarov jerked a thumb in Volkov's direction. "Do you realize how disconcerting it is to awake to find a murderer next to one's bed?

"He's harmless, Doktor."

"He's an *assassin*!"

"He's harmless to friends of the People. Vodka, Comrade?"

"Ah, yes, 'the People.'" Komarov grimaced and took the proffered glass. "But why did you send him? So that he could wave his weapon in my face?"

"If Volkov really wanted to wave his weapon in your face"—Krajnik folded his arms—"you wouldn't live long enough to care. Now, we must focus on important business."

"*What* business? What business could be so important at two in the morning? Explain, please, Comrade."

Roman Krajnik took a seat across from him. "I propose, Comrades, that we—the three of us in this room—form an official tribunal, for the specific purpose of bringing to trial and to swift judgment the following individuals—"

"A moment, Comrade." Komarov set down his vodka. "Are you suggesting that we form an operational *troika*? A secret governing body? But those were only authorized by Comrade Stalin before the war." He stared at the officer. "Operational troikas were abolished by the Politburo in 1938. Take care, Krajnik; Comrade Stalin obviously felt that their purpose had been fulfilled."

"And what was their purpose?"

"To bring to justice dissidents and traitors to the Motherland." Komarov's mouth pressed into a thin line.

"To *swift* justice," Volkov said softly, studying the tip of his blade.

Komarov turned and stared at Volkov as if the man had suddenly decided to stand on his head. "Stalin knows what he's doing," Komarov insisted, again glancing uncomfortably at Volkov. "If he decrees—"

"Yes. Comrade Stalin knows what he's doing," Krajnik broke in. "I've never questioned that fact. However, *I* am in charge of the safety and security of the citizens in my city. I've been given control of the Moscow MGB in order to see that this directive is carried out. And if I were to choose two trusted colleagues—two patriotic, *discreet* friends— and form a top-secret unit, it would be considered a legitimate part of my job description. I have been given complete discretion in—"

"And whom, may I ask, would we be processing?"

"Citizens Viktor Rostov, Natalya Ivanovna Karagodina, and Regina Igorevna, and the German scientist Hans Brenner."

The room was deathly still. Komarov contemplated that information. Finally he rubbed his chin. "A sad thing, when a person turns against his country."

"And betrays the very system that feeds and clothes him," Krajnik agreed. "Now regarding Regina Igorevna . . . Yes, I once considered her father my friend. What a sad task we have—to destroy his daughter as we did her father . . ."

Komarov pushed back his chair. He hesitated. "Have we found them?"

"Volkov's men are looking as we speak. It won't be long."

"When would we begin the proceedings?"

"These are exceptional circumstances. We must begin immediately—this morning. We must try all these individuals right now, in absentia—so that as soon as they are found, Comrade Volkov will carry out their sentences."

Volkov fingered the knife in his belt. Calmly he met Komarov's shocked stare. Komarov gaped at Volkov, and then at Krajnik. "So what you're saying, then, is that the sentence will be death."

"There is reason for it." Krajnik shrugged. "Natalya Ivanovna has escaped. But there is more—much more! Natalya Ivanovna's German fiancé, a scientist by the name of Hans Brenner, has escaped with sensitive nuclear documents from one of our secret laboratory sites—we can safely assume his infatuation with the woman isn't the only thing that brought him here! And do you know who helped him escape? None other than our comrade Viktor Rostov. He sent a secret message meant to confuse us; he sent it through an elaborate channel of accomplices in Europe and America until it finally was intercepted, as Rostov knew it would be, by our talented intelligence services. The message was actually for the German scientist Hans Brenner, instructing him to gather Soviet atomic secrets, escape from a nuclear laboratory where he was working, and meet Rostov here in Moscow. Volkov himself saw the fugitive German enter Rostov's building! How much more proof do we need of his treason?

"And Regina Igorevna has betrayed her country, spoken against the People, and accepted the assistance of Rostov, Natalya, and Hans Brenner in recovering her infant daughter, when you, Doktor, deemed it dangerous for the child to be raised by this woman. What more evidence do we need of their treason?

"But still, the worst I haven't yet told you." Krajnik picked up a large envelope. He handed it to Komarov. "We received this just a few hours ago. Ambassador Gusev considered it of significant importance to have it flown in right away. Open it, Doktor, and look at what's inside."

Komarov pulled several photographs from the envelope and shuffled through them, uncomprehending at first, and then, as he studied each picture, his face began to darken, his teeth clenched, and he began to shake his head. "Lieutenant Rostov."

Krajnik concurred. "Photographs of our fine, upstanding comrade, intelligence expert, war hero, and professor, Viktor Rostov. But they don't only depict Lieutenant Rostov. No! They portray a meeting between Rostov and this other man"—he pointed at a photo—"in Switzerland. And do you know who that man is? My intelligence source tells me he's a Nazi major named Rolf Schulmann—a notorious, treacherous intelligence officer who, during the war, effectively undermined the efforts of Allied agents in France. After the war he disappeared—like so many other coward Nazis that still infest our planet. But he was discovered by a bounty hunter named Andrews—and Ambassador Gusev has relieved Andrews of them."

"So our good friend Comrade Rostov has betrayed us all." Krajnik had won Komarov's full attention.

Krajnik nodded. "And not only has Citizen Rostov brought into the Motherland an American spy and a German scientist who has stolen nuclear secrets, Citizen Rostov has undermined *your* authority, Komarov. He interrogated your head nurse, Olga Popova, and forced her to tell him the location of Regina Igorevna's baby. He bribed a guard to gain Natalya Ivanovna's freedom, and together they abducted a baby that is legally owned by the State. And now, he has conspired with the enemy—most likely in revenge for his daughter's imprisonment. And so, my fellow Soviets, these are the reasons we must sit now, as a special troika, in judgment of these four treacherous individuals. This is a case of espionage, treason, and betrayal by all four members of this dangerous crime ring, punishable by immediate death."

FORTY-SIX

Viktor returned to Dr. Vlasov's apartment at four in the morning, his face flushed and his usual calm control a thing of the past. "Get your things together." His breathing was labored. "I have our papers; we must leave on this morning's train for Leningrad."

Alarmed, Natalie said, "You need to rest, Viktor, or your heart—"

"My heart is fine." He brushed her off. "We have to leave now—"

He was interrupted by a soft knock on the door. It shook Rostov. He glanced at Hans. "Dr. Vlasov promised us three days . . ."

"The neighbors," Natalie whispered. "They've begun to suspect something. Maybe they called the police."

Hans shook his head. "The MGB would break down the door. This one doesn't want to be heard."

Rostov opened the door. Regina darted inside, her face flushed as if she'd been running ever since she left her apartment. Her eyes were wet, and she held Ina bundled in several blankets and carried a heavy bag over one arm.

"Regina!" Natalie cried. "You've changed your mind. I'm so glad you're coming with us."

Regina shook her head, blinking hard. In her arms Ina whimpered softly, and Regina's arms about her child were a death grip.

Viktor said, "I have papers for you and the baby as well."

Regina didn't respond, still fighting unexplained tears.

"You must come," Rostov urged. "You know Komarov will take her away again."

"Regina," Natalie pleaded, and Regina turned and met her gaze. The look in her eyes would haunt Natalie forever.

"I'm not going."

"Regina, it's going to be all right," Natalie soothed. "No one will know who you are. See?" Natalie held a paper in front of the mother. "Your name has been changed to *Sonya Danilovna* . . ." Still Regina didn't respond, and Natalie's voice trailed to uncertain silence. "Regina?" she whispered, fearful of the silent, haunting struggle in her dear friend's eyes.

"My husband will die if I go." It was said simply, as if it were common knowledge that husbands of fugitives were put to death.

Viktor spoke again, and although time was not on their side, the gentleness in his voice touched Natalie like she never imagined it could. "Regina, it's a terrible decision you have to make. And yes, you're right; your husband—if he's still alive—will suffer if you choose to escape with your baby." He hesitated, and then he continued quietly. "But your baby will die if you don't."

It was an impossible task to decide between a husband and a baby, and Natalie could see how it aged Regina, this decision that tore her soul in two and sent the pieces in opposite directions. Regina's fun-loving, happy face had taken on the appearance of abject misery, like one of the multitudes of war widows whose youth and vitality had been buried alongside the body of her husband, or of a babushka whose body has shriveled through decades of sorrow and suffering.

Regina looked first at Rostov, and then at Hans and Natalie. Her eyes were swimming with tears but her voice carried resolve. "I'm not going."

Rostov frowned. "You know your daughter will be taken from you again. And you could be—"

"I know what will happen to me," Regina whispered. She turned her face to Natalie, who was taken aback by the courage in her gaze. She brushed at a tear. "I've already decided. For my husband's sake I will stay here." And then Regina lifted her chin, raised the sleeping bundle, and held it out toward Natalie. "I came to give you my baby, Natalya Ivanovna. She is yours. Yours and Hans's. I want you to raise her as your own daughter."

Natalie was stunned. Never would she have ever expected or imagined Regina would do this. She didn't take the baby. She couldn't. She couldn't get her arms to function and they lay useless at her sides. "No, Regina!" she gasped. "Bring your baby to America and raise her—"

"And have her papa executed because I made that choice?" Regina cried, and the sound was pitiful to hear. "How would I tell my daughter, my Inuchka, when she is older, that the choice I made killed her papa? How could I live with myself knowing that I might have been able to save Edik if I'd made a different choice?"

"Regina, you can't give up your baby! It will hurt too much! You can't do it!"

"Don't talk to me of hurt, Natalya Ivanovna!" Regina's voice rose until it broke. "How could I possibly *not* hurt? This decision hurts more than any I've ever made! I'm choosing whether to cut out my heart or my soul, and oh, how it hurts! I can hardly speak for the pain of it, and yet the decision must be made!" Regina gasped, choked, and struggled to find her composure to continue. "Do you remember when you spoke to me of eternal families—of the eternal family you will have with Hans someday? Oh, how I want my baby to be part of an eternal family! I want her to be cared for in a family that is safe, and free—and can be forever. *I* can't give her that gift. Never in a thousand years can I give her that gift!"

Regina continued, and the words were heart-wrenching. "And yet, by giving her to you I *am* giving her that gift! It's the greatest gift I can give her. It is the *only* gift I can give her! I love her too much not to give that to her, and in the process, I give my husband a chance to live. Oh, please don't turn my child away!" Regina pushed the baby toward Natalie with even greater urgency. "Please take her and love her with all the love I can't give her!"

Natalie began to cry. Hans stepped forward and silently took the baby from Regina. He placed the infant in Natalie's arms. He wrapped his own arms around Natalie's sobbing shoulders and pulled Regina into his embrace as well. "We will care for her, Regina Igorevna, and her life with us will be our gift to you. Don't worry—she'll be much loved, and she will be happy."

Regina's arms, as if suddenly searching for the warmth of the baby lost, wrapped themselves tightly around her torso, and she began to cry uncontrollably. "I won't worry about her, because of your kindness. But I . . ." She could hardly continue. "I will never forget her . . ."

"Regina," Natalie whispered, but the woman gathered her coat about her shoulders, pulled away from Hans, and fled from the apartment.

FORTY-SEVEN

They did not take Rostov's car the entire distance to Moscow's Leningrad Station at Komsomol Square. Instead they walked the remaining few hundred meters, taking a back way until they arrived at the square. Rostov had told them to assume Krajnik would have men looking for them.

Rostov stopped and set down his luggage before they reached the entrance to the station.

"What is it, Viktor?" Natalie asked. "What's the matter?"

"Have you ever had a feeling"—Rostov hesitated, as if trying to formulate his words—"that the path you were about to take might be the wrong one? And the feeling persists, no matter what you do, perplexing you to the point that you can hardly turn around without it shouting at you 'Don't do this! Do this instead!'"

Hans asked, "Rostov, what is it?"

"I don't think we should go through Leningrad."

"Viktor—" Natalie began.

"I know, I know—we're here, the train is leaving soon, we have our passports." Rostov's grip tightened on his satchel, and when he turned to look at Natalie the agony in his expression shocked her. "But I have the most overwhelming feeling . . . that if I don't go to Vladivostok, my daughter will not make it . . ."

Natalie placed a hand on his arm. It was a voluntary gesture she'd never before made. "Rolf's people will get Lucya out. He'll keep his promise. You'll see your daughter in England in one month—"

"I can't. I must go to Vladivostok. Something tells me I must go there."

"Rolf will get her out, Viktor."

Rostov shook his head. "No. I—I feel if I don't meet her in Vladivostok, I'll never see her again." Rostov turned, determination and desperation a curious mixture that deepened the lines on his face. "I've never felt such certainty about anything, Natalya Ivanovna. If I don't go to my daughter right now, she won't make it out of Siberia alive."

For a moment no one spoke. The loudspeaker chose that moment to announce the boarding call for their train, and the sound echoed through the square. Natalie felt the desperate panic of having to make a life-changing decision with insufficient time to think it through properly. She glanced at Hans and saw the same turmoil in his eyes.

Ina awoke and shifted in Natalie's arms. Natalie held Hans's gaze and felt again the shock of his love for her, and as the train whistle shrilled, and Rostov paced, Hans and Natalie touched hands. She took a deep breath, her eyes wavered ever so slightly, and then she nodded, answering his unspoken question.

Hans turned to Rostov. "We're coming with you."

"No, Hans, take Natalya and the baby to Leningrad. Get them on that boat and get them out of here."

"We both agree, Rostov—this feeling of yours shouldn't be ignored. There's some reason we're not supposed to go through Leningrad. We need to go with you to Vladivostok."

"*I'm* supposed to go to Vladivostok," Rostov snapped. "*You're* supposed to get out of the Soviet Union. It's part of my agreement—"

"I understand. But the feelings you have right now may be for all of us. Maybe God is sending you a warning—"

"I don't know this God!" Rostov turned on him. "I only know what I feel."

"But He knows you, Rostov, and He may be protecting you and your daughter from harm. He may be protecting Natalie and me also. And He may be giving you a chance right now to accept His assistance."

"Don't speak of this right now." Rostov gave Hans a warning scowl. "It would only take one passerby with a listening ear . . ." He lifted his suitcase and reached for Natalya's arm. He ushered the three of them away from the train station. "I'll be grateful for your continued assistance, Natalya, although I think your decision to come with me is foolish. Come, we'll get these travel permits altered by my associate."

* * *

Ivan Volkov pushed his shoulders away from the wall. He watched dispassionately as the train pulled away from the station, headed to Leningrad. He was disappointed; the fugitives had not tried to board.

Volkov knew Krajnik's intelligence was sound; the ambassador to Great Britain discovered that Rostov was going to smuggle the American girl and her German lover out of the country by way of a tiny fishing port west of Leningrad. Krajnik's men reported to Volkov that the group left Vlasov's apartment not long after midnight, taking the Oryekova baby with them.

But they'd never arrived at Leningrad Station.

The next passenger train to Leningrad wouldn't leave Moscow for at least another twenty-four hours. Would Rostov and his companions be able to stay hidden that long?

Volkov was no idiot, no matter what the shrink Komarov thought him. Sweden was the obvious choice if one was determined to escape— and had the money to charter a boat from a fishing port near Leningrad. But if they were not headed to Leningrad on this train, then where were they going?

Rostov was too intelligent to attempt an escape to the south. The only other options for Rostov lay to the north or to the east. The north would be watched very closely, beginning tomorrow. And only an imbecile would think he could elude the MGB for the entire nine thousand three hundred kilometer journey to the east.

Volkov knew Rostov was no imbecile. Rostov would take the train to Leningrad tomorrow.

* * *

Komarov accompanied Volkov to the train station the following day. They took different sections of the track, lounging with their policemen and watching the confusion that accompanies the boarding of a train.

Rostov and his fellow conspirators did not appear, and the train for Leningrad slid out of the station without Volkov making any arrests.

Komarov began to pace. He smoked cigar after cigar as he strolled down the center of the platform. He approached the ticket counter and took out his frustrations on the young ticket-taker.

He left the kiosk and made an angry beeline for Volkov. Volkov saw the look in the doctor's eyes and curled his fingers carefully around the hilt of his knife.

"You imbecile!" Komarov screamed at him as he approached, and passengers up and down the platform turned their heads. "You forgot about his daughter!"

Volkov did not like the way Komarov addressed him. "I didn't forget about his daughter. Rostov doesn't know where she is. Why should she be important right now?"

"Because, you sniveling carrion, the train bound for Vladivostok pulled out of Yaroslavl Station five minutes ago. Perhaps Rostov knows where she is after all."

FORTY-EIGHT

Wednesday, December 18, 1946

For the fishmongers of Tokyo, Japan, life begins before three in the morning at Tsukiji market. Labeled the largest fish market in the world, Tsukiji houses more varieties of fish and tons of seafood per cubic meter than any other location on earth. While the rest of the world sleeps, frozen tuna from as far away as Finland is bought and sold. Auctioneers crow a dialect fellow Japanese cannot possibly hope to understand, while designated buyers poke and prod the frozen tuna—sometimes weighing in the hundreds of kilos, and all frozen solid as the icebergs of the arctic.

The sights are dazzling and the smells are enough to drive a landlubber insane. Surrounded by fresh fish, squid, jellyfish, and octopuses of every shape and size, Jacques Bellamont held his nose and informed Rolf Schulmann that insanity was looming.

"I don't care if it's fresh. It's still the most repugnant smell ever to penetrate the earth's atmosphere." He grimaced. "How long, pray tell, are we imprisoned here?"

"Imprisoned?" Rolf grinned at his friend. "Only long enough for us to find a fisherman hungry enough to rent us his boat."

"You mean, 'idiot enough,' don't you? We're foreigners, remember, and we're not getting the nicest welcome as it is." Jacques jerked his thumb at the crowd of shoppers, and Rolf had to admit that they were drawing quite a bit of attention.

"We'll make this as quick as possible—I promise."

"Great. What are we looking for, exactly?"

"Squid."

"Squid?"

"From the Sea of Japan. And then, if we're lucky, a person with whom we can negotiate."

"I found it. I found squid. Is this a squid?"

"Octopus."

"What makes you such an authority?"

"I promise, Jacques; that's an octopus. A small one, but an octopus just the same."

"Don't tell me someone eats this."

Rolf glanced at the crowd. It was apparent there was a certain curiosity swelling in the ranks at the sight of two Westerners invading their space. "I wouldn't be surprised if the number of foreigners at these venues grows," he mused, "now that the Allies have won the war. There's going to have to be some kind of understanding reached—and I wouldn't be surprised if it ruffles a few feathers for a while . . ."

"Rolf?"

"What?"

"Is that squid?"

Rolf looked where Jacques pointed. He followed Jacques across a slippery aisle, through a mountain of butchered fish parts, and to a small corner stall. Planks formed coarse troughs, and these had been filled with ice. On the ice, arms and tentacles undulated and swelled, garnished with row after row of suckers. In the center of this cephalopodic display rose an entire specimen of this sea creature; muscle-bound arms and tentacles twisted about the gigantic head. It had a sharp beak, staring eyes, and a soft, muscular form. It looked alive—almost intelligent—sitting regally displayed for all to see.

Jacques eyed the creature suspiciously while Rolf approached the stall's owner.

"Excuse me, please . . ." He bowed respectfully to excuse his interruption and spoke the unfamiliar, memorized Japanese words. The owner of the stall returned the traditional greeting. His eyes, lost in creases of advancing years, plenty of toil, and experience, studied Rolf without the same distrust of foreigners shown by others at Tsukiji. Rolf wet his lips and continued, struggling to form the Japanese words he'd learned for the occasion. "My associate and I are searching for—"

The man raised one wrinkled hand, pointed it at Rolf, and said in broken English, "You—wait."

Rolf was taken aback. He straightened, staring at the man. But the stall owner turned away to address the needs of another customer. Rolf was left wondering what to do. Had he just been dismissed?

Jacques sidled up behind him. "Won't give you the time of day, eh? I say we take his king squid and bludgeon him with it." He watched as the ancient fishmonger reached one frail arm to gather a customer's order. "On second thought," Jacques murmured, "maybe all it'll take is one of these slimy tentacles . . ."

Rolf turned away and couldn't help the disappointment that welled inside of him. They had only a few days to find a boat, and the way things were going, it was going to be more of a challenge finding someone to help them than he'd imagined.

"You—wait!"

The English words were strangely out of place called out over the cacophony of the market. The fishmonger pointed definitively in Rolf's direction. The man nodded, unsmiling, at Rolf, and then turned back to his customers.

Rolf and Jacques waited. They found half-rotten wood crates, turned them on their ends, and sat next to the stall. Jacques picked at a squid's tentacle, playing with the clammy suckers and mumbling to himself about smells, seafood, and strange customs.

Rolf observed as the fishmonger worked, amazed at the strength and stamina of a man obviously decades past his prime. He also wondered at the English words, spoken with great fervor and very little experience, commanding them to wait. Wait for what?

The afternoon sun warmed the stalls and intensified the smells. Jacques, valiant as always, kept his opinions mostly to himself, letting out an occasional expletive that would have fried calamari—especially when the stall next door dumped a basket of fish guts, blood, and slimy water onto the stones. They slithered like snakes in every direction, ending ultimately on Jacques's boots and trousers.

Rolf began to doubt their decision to wait. If this man had no answers for them they were fast losing the opportunity to find someone else. They didn't have time to do this again tomorrow. He silently whispered a prayer, wondering what to do. *Wait,* came the quiet answer. *You—wait.*

Eventually the old fishmonger sold all of his squid. Rolf and Jacques helped him drain the crude wooden trays and clean his stall. He rolled thick canvas over his display tables, removed his apron, and folded it carefully. He retrieved the broom from Jacques and a scrub brush from Rolf. "*Chotto matte, kudasai*—Please, wait." The fishmonger bowed an apology and shuffled a few steps away to store them in a miniature wooden shed.

"What is he doing?" Jacques wondered.

"I think he has what we need—or we have something even more important that he needs . . ."

"What could we have that he needs?" Jacques demanded.

"I don't know. I just have a feeling . . ."

Jacques swore. "We're running out of time. Care to explain how your feelings are going to get us where we need to go?"

Before Rolf could respond, their wrinkled host returned carrying a book. "My name Mitsui." He pointed at Rolf. "*You.* Read. English." Rolf could see that the man's English vocabulary was waning. "Buddha said—you read."

Rolf glanced at the book and caught his breath. The man was holding an English Book of Mormon. It was an older edition, different from the one Rolf had carried during the years of the war, and in remarkably good shape for its age. "How did you get this, Mitsui-san?"

Mitsui struggled to explain, his lips forming the strange sounds and the gestures of his wrinkled hands attempting to fill the gap between speech and comprehension.

Before the war Mitsui had lived in Hawaii. He married a young woman there, and she began to read the book to him. She read all the way to the section entitled Moroni before she became ill and passed away.

Mitsui returned to Japan, taking the book with him. He tried to read, but his eyesight was poor and his English was worse. Throughout the war he prayed for Buddha to help him find someone to read the remainder of the book to him. And then this morning, five years after the bombing of Pearl Harbor, Buddha finally answered his prayer; Mitsui knew Rolf was the one who would read to him.

Rolf felt an overwhelming gratitude that he could be the one to answer this old man's prayer, and as he accepted the book from Mitsui, he realized that reading to the old fishmonger could create a relationship of trust that would help them find the help they sought. He opened the book to Moroni and began to read.

He read slowly, stopping often to help Mitsui understand. He read and explained for several hours, while Jacques explored the marketplace. The Frenchman had no desire to listen to the words Rolf read. Finally Jacques found a bench nearby, curled his body onto its surface, wrapped his coat about his lanky frame, and fell asleep.

As the sun began its evening descent Rolf read the last verse. He closed the book and looked up at Mitsui. The man's eyes were damp, and he looked thoughtful. Mitsui's hand rested on Rolf's shoulder. "You good man," the fishmonger said. "You need help?"

Rolf nodded. "I need a boat."

"Why?"

"To help a friend."

"Where friend?"

"Across the sea of Japan."

"You save friend." Mitsui understood. He rose carefully to his feet. Rolf returned the book to him and Mitsui bowed low. *"Domo arigato, Rolf-san. Domo arigato gozaimasu."* He thanked Rolf with the formal gratitude of one who feels he owes his life for a kindness.

Rolf and Jacques followed the man through the Tsukiji market toward the docks. All the earlier fish market activity seemed to have shifted this direction, and sailors of all ages, colors, and ethnicities bent and lifted, packed and pulled, yelled and cursed. It seemed foreign ships regularly frequented the greatest fish market in the world, plying their wares and auctioning off their livelihoods on a daily basis. Rolf and Jacques were not as alone in this foreign land as they'd imagined.

If this man couldn't help them, here were a plethora of choices to try next, Rolf thought.

"Come."

They descended stone steps to the wharf, made slippery with new fallen snow. As the sun disappeared, flaming torches flickered among strings of electric light bulbs, causing shadows to dance against the sides of the boats. Shark carcasses the size of small cars lay stacked in rows as deep as a man's waist, while octopi no bigger than an infant's fist lay in ice-filled crates. And they passed mountain after mountain of tuna corpses, headless and slimy, packed tight in dirty snow and stacked along the edge of the dock. Fishermen called to each other as they unloaded their catches, and the smell of the sea and its offerings assailed the nostrils with an intensity that bordered on nauseating. "I know," Mitsui said, and pointed. "This way. Man . . . warrior . . ." He eyed Jacques, his expression discerning. "Like you. He help."

"A warrior with a boat, I hope," Jacques mumbled, and followed Mitsui.

"No," Mitsui corrected. "Fisherman with boat. Knows warrior."

Rolf watched as Mitsui bowed his respect to the owner of a squid boat. The two spoke at length, and Mitsui nodded often in Rolf's and Jacques's direction. The man turned and studied them, his dark eyes unreadable. Finally he nodded, bowed once more to the old man, and returned to his ship.

Mitsui turned to Rolf and Jacques. "Ayato-san take you to warrior. Warrior help you. You wait with him. Long trip—several days. He take you to island—Okushiri. Very cold. He warrior—and smuggler. You like."

"What does he smuggle?" Jacques smirked. "Squid?"

FORTY-NINE

Friday, December 20, 1946

Natalie felt the hand on her arm and awoke to see Hans leaning close.

"What time is it?" She mumbled, trying to clear the sleep-fog from her brain.

"Almost midnight." His breath escaped in tiny clouds and he spoke in a whisper so as not to be heard through the thin partitions between compartments. "We're at Novosibirsk. Viktor has gone to see about our tickets. I have to see a friend—about internal passports for Vladivostok."

The train panted and shuddered as if recovering from extreme exertion. She glanced out the frosted window at the narrow platform, filled with bundled passengers, luggage, and children. Baggage strewed the platform as far as she could see, as if some giant hand had taken it all and thrown everything back haphazardly across its surface. The chill Siberian night air, even in the train compartment, was near unbearable.

Everything felt surreal. She looked at Hans. In the half-light from the platform lights his face seemed strange. She whispered back, "The passports Viktor provided in Moscow—?"

Hans shook his head. "They only give us passage to Novosibirsk. From here, we're required to reapply."

Natalie sat up, suddenly wide awake. "But Hans, we *can't* reapply. Viktor said they'd be looking for us by now, and the illegal way we're traveling, with Regina's baby . . ."

"I know." Hans's voice soothed her. "That's why I have to see a friend. My acquaintance may not be the most savory—but he's promised to help me if I ever need him. We'll be all right."

"Let me come with you."

He shook his head. "Tonight Ina would not survive the cold."

"And a train platform is any better?" Natalie felt the fear a child might feel at being abandoned in a strange place by its parent. "And she needs milk, Hans. Where are we going to find milk? We have to buy milk for Ina."

"At this time of night?" Hans reached for Natalie's suitcase. "Come with me, Natalie. I know a place where you can wait."

"She needs milk, Hans."

"I know," he said. "Come with me."

He opened the compartment door and ushered her into the narrow corridor. They left the train at the first exit and navigated their way through the waiting passengers and piles of luggage, across the platform, and up a flight of stairs. Ina awoke and began to whimper against Natalie's chest.

The ceiling of the vast marble hall they entered echoed with the sounds of humanity. The waiting area teemed with passengers, and the smell of unwashed flesh made Natalie cringe. She wondered if some of these poor souls had been here for days. Many seemed to have set up camp in the hall, with blankets hung for privacy and luggage strewn in haphazard abandon. Men sat on bags, evil-smelling cigars jutting from whiskered faces as they chatted with other passengers. A woman knitted stockings as she leaned against a satchel, and another lay prone, her mouth hanging open as she slept. Breath escaped in little puffs of white. The hall was bitter cold.

"Hans, this is as bad as the train platform. How am I supposed to keep her warm?"

"There's a place reserved for mothers with small children. I think you should wait there for us."

"Really?" She was dubious. Since when had the Soviet Union been concerned with the comfort of women and small children?

She saw the door, then, with its sign: Room for Mother and Child. "How did you know, Hans?"

"Rostov sent me to this city. I lived here for a while . . ."

Ina began to cry. "All right," Natalie agreed. "I'll wait in there. But please—*please* don't be too long. Hans, I'm worried . . ."

He wrapped his arms around both Natalie and Ina, pulled them close, and kissed Natalie. She imagined she felt a hint of his warmth through all the layers of coats, blankets, and baby, and she wished he would never have to release her. "Hurry back, all right?" she whispered.

"I promise." Hans reached and pulled a loose edge of the blanket around the baby and murmured, "We'll be back long before the train leaves. You'll be all right here?"

"I'll be all right. What are you going to do?"

"I'm going to find a military automobile and steal it." Hans leaned over the soft bundle and kissed her again, and his eyes searched hers. "Natalie . . ." He hesitated, and she could see a flicker of something in his eyes as he searched for the right words to say. "She did the right thing."

"I could never have given up my own baby. Never."

Hans nodded. "And yet, she *did,* Natalie. Because she loved Ina too much to let her suffer anymore."

Natalie dropped her eyes and could not respond. She turned and walked through the door. A woman behind a desk handed her a form. She filled it out, produced her forged documents, and the woman accepted them without any question. *Thank you, Viktor.*

She was led into a room with little white cribs, bright pictures on the walls, and a woodstove in the corner. Heat radiated throughout the room, thawing her numb fingers and toes. A woman wearing a nurse's uniform produced a voluminous quilt, which she wrapped about Ina and pointed toward a rocking chair near the stove. "You can nurse your infant there."

Natalie hastened to explain. "I can't nurse her."

The woman nodded. "I understand. That happens when there is not enough nourishment for the mother. I will bring something for her."

Relieved, Natalie sank into the nearest chair. The nurse brought back a bottle filled with frozen milk, a pot of water, and instructions for

Natalie to warm the bottle on the surface of the stove. She left Natalie and returned to her duties.

Gratefully, Natalie watched the milk begin to settle in the bottle, and she soothed the increasingly fussy baby in her arms until the ice disappeared and drops on her wrist indicated the bottle's temperature was right.

Ina took it, and gradually her eyes drooped, lulled by both nourishment and warmth into sleep. Natalie propped the bottle against Ina's wraps, leaned her head against the back of the chair, and rested her own eyes.

She was afraid to sleep; her eyelids continued to droop and then fly open. In a daze she stared unseeing at the white ceiling and its incongruous crystal chandelier. She did not want to miss Hans's arrival when he finished talking with his contact, and she did not like to be alone. Even though she was warmer than she had been in months, and the tiny baby in her arms had had her fill of nourishment and finally slept peacefully, Natalie felt nervous, agitated, and afraid. Something was wrong—something that transcended her fear of being alone and her fear for Hans's safety.

She tried to alleviate her fears by thinking about her future with Hans; they would leave the Soviet Union, say good-bye finally to Rostov, and take Regina's baby far away to America. Ina would be sealed to them in the temple in Salt Lake, and . . .

The thought of Regina made her empty stomach twist itself into knots. Even though Regina wanted it this way, Natalie felt like she was robbing her best friend of her most precious possession.

But Regina had done it to protect the baby. And she was right; Ina would have been taken again. She would have been taken, and then she would have disappeared as quickly as Komarov could orchestrate her disappearance, so that Viktor could not possibly intervene this time. Regina had lost everything: her father, her husband, and now her baby daughter. Natalie ached for her, and knew that nothing she could do could repair this injustice.

The only thing Natalie could do now to help Regina was protect her baby.

Natalie stared up at the ceiling. She would do it. She would do for Ina what Ina's mother knew she could never do for her daughter:

Natalie and Hans would rescue Ina from the evil that was present in the Soviet Union—and then they would seal her to them and make her a part of their eternal family.

* * *

Hans recalled a thing or two from his months on the streets of Berlin. He slipped behind the wheel of a police automobile parked behind the sleeping station and utilized his screwdriver to access the inner workings of the starter. Then he tried to hotwire the motor. When nothing happened he peeled open the hood, saw ice on the engine block, and began to search the vicinity for dry wood. He found split logs piled near the station's back door, selected two from the center of the pile that were relatively dry, returned to the car, struck a match, and finally got a steady blaze. He held the wood steady, just close enough to the engine to melt the ice.

He finally coaxed the vehicle to life, and then he drove to the address given him by a young thief in Gorky.

He knocked on the unassuming cabin door, and as he waited for an answer to his knock he danced against the cold, his hands tucked into his armpits and his feet constantly moving. Anyone caught unprotected in this cold would freeze instantly, he mused, and he realized if Arseni did not let him in soon he would fall into the category of the unprotected.

Arseni did not let him freeze. He cracked a smile as soon as he recognized the German on his doorstep. Soon Hans was huddled next to a stove, his hands outstretched to its friendly warmth, and Arseni was enticing him with a glass of vodka.

"It'll warm your insides, friend. Drink it."

"I don't drink vodka."

"Strange, you German."

"I promised God I wouldn't drink liquor."

"Your God must never have visited Siberia, if he would prohibit you from drinking vodka."

"Oh, I think He's been here once or twice."

"Well he's obviously not here now." Arseni snorted. "Drink it. He won't see you drink vodka during this blizzard."

"No thanks."

Arseni drank it himself. "What are you doing here, German? Don't you know the MGB will shoot you on sight after what you did? Didn't you steal something rather important from them?"

"Yes, Arseni, I'm as bad as you are."

Arseni laughed. "Don't tell me it was to visit *me* that you came to Novosibirsk."

"No. But the fact that you live so close to the train station happens to be convenient. *Very* convenient, in fact. We need your help."

"Who is 'we'?"

"Natalie and myself. And one other."

Arseni straightened, delighted. "You brought your girl? Here? What for, may I ask? To watch you get shot? Ah, I know—you brought her to show me. You want my approval of her. Is she pretty, then?"

The fire was warm and comforting, but there was something nagging at Hans. He couldn't decipher the feeling, so he discarded it. "I didn't bring her to see you." Hans grinned, and felt his lower lip crack. "We need internal passports for Vladivostok, and I knew I could count on you . . ."

"Absolutely. I am honored you thought of me."

"I need them this morning. Before the train leaves for Sverdlovsk." The troublesome feelings would not go away.

Arseni stared at him. "In this blizzard?" His hand swept toward the window. "Impossible! How do you expect me to finish everything in time—for two people?"

"Three."

"A third? Who else is with you, Hans?"

"An MGB agent who—"

"MGB!" Arseni sprang to his feet. "Are you out of your mind? You brought an MGB agent here? And you wish me to share my talents with him, is that it?"

"He is—a friend." Hans had to force out that word. He was not certain he could ever see Rostov as a friend. "And he is no longer working for Stalin."

Arseni relaxed, slightly. "It is still risky, my friend." He ran long fingers through his hair. "It is my life on the line, and that of my comrades-in-crime . . ." He gave Hans a faint smile. "You have not divulged my secret, have you?"

"Of course not." *Natalie . . .* The feeling was becoming more intelligible. "The man has no idea about you. Besides, he did the same for us, in order to get my fiancée and the baby out of Moscow."

"A baby? How fast you work. So there are four of you?"

"It is the baby of my fiancée's coworker. At the mother's request Natalie and I are taking the baby out of the country."

"You will need documents showing the baby as your child. You will not get a baby past the authorities without proper documents for the baby, also. And I cannot get four sets of documents in one night—even without the snowstorm."

"It is a matter of life or death. We must be on tonight's train."

Arseni studied him, and Hans could see his jaw muscles working. "I am not a miracle worker—like this cold-sober God you talk about. How do you expect me to convince my comrades that this is enough of an emergency to make them leave their warm beds—to help a crazy German, his fiancée, a baby, and the MGB?"

"Because Natalie is innocent of any wrongdoing." Suddenly he could not keep his mind off her. The feeling that something—something to do with Natalie—was wrong persisted. He wanted very much to be back at the freezing train station instead of next to this warm stove.

"I'm sure she is." Arseni turned toward his bed.

"Because the documents I stole may help the Americans know what Stalin's nuclear scientists are planning."

Arseni yawned.

There had to be a way to get through to the young man. "Because the MGB agent with us has a daughter on her way to Kolyma."

Arseni studied Hans carefully. "You are a clever fox, Hans Brenner. You remember what I said to you before you left Gorky."

"He's going to Vladivostok to attempt to rescue her." Hans tried to concentrate on the strange feeling that pestered him.

"You're lying. You fabricated that story to get me to help you."

"It's true. Her name is Lucya Viktorovna Rostova, she's seventeen, and she's in a transit camp near Vladivostok. She is scheduled to board the Kolyma fleet soon."

"How can I know you are telling the truth?"

"I could bring her MGB father here to prove it to you."

Arseni gave a low, menacing laugh. "You wouldn't dare."

Hans barely heard him. The feeling was so strong now that his conversation with the thief seemed a million kilometers away. *What is it, God? What is it you are trying to tell me about Natalie?*

Suddenly he sprang to his feet and reached for his outerwear. He threw on his coat and ushanka and strode for the door while he donned his gloves.

Arseni stared after him. "What's the matter, German? There's no need to get so angry about a glass of vodka . . ."

"Natalie's in danger."

"Why didn't you say so in the first place?" Arseni reached for his own coat. "I will assist you."

"No, Arseni." Hans pulled open the door, letting in an icy squall so vicious that it momentarily took his breath away. "Go for the documents."

"I will help you first."

Hans shook his head. "The best way you can help me—"

"I will come with you to the train station, Hans, and then I will see about the documents. That is the way it will be. Besides"—Arseni grinned—"thanks to you, I now have an automobile."

FIFTY

Saturday, December 21, 1946

Natalie lost her struggle. She succumbed to the warmth of the stove and fell asleep. She dreamed about Hans, and her mother in America . . . and introducing Hans to her mother in America . . .

She opened her eyes. The wall clock said she had slept for more than an hour. Ina was asleep with the half-finished bottle still between her lips. Where was Hans?

Several more mothers joined her next to the stove, nursing fussy infants or peeling moist diapers off wrinkled bottoms. A baby wailed and Ina stirred, stretched, and began to eat again.

It was hard to imagine, here, in this far-away nightmare, the possibility of a celestial marriage with Hans. But she would not let that objective be lost in the uncertainty and danger that still faced them. They would make it to America. And then they would be married for eternity, as Rolf and Marie had been.

She heard the nurse talking, and then a masculine reply. For only a second she thought it was Hans. No, it did not sound like Hans. Viktor? It did not sound like him either. But her senses were suddenly on high alert. She leaned forward to see past the stove, and her eyes met those of Roman Krajnik.

Half a world away from Moscow, Krajnik had found them. He strode across the room, past the tiny white cribs and the wood stove; he grabbed her arm and wrenched her out of the rocking chair. Natalie clung to the baby and the half-empty bottle shattered on the tile floor.

"Where is Rostov?" He shook her and Ina began to cry. "Where is he?" There was murder in his eyes, and the fear in Natalie's chest was so tight she could not respond.

Again he shook her, and the nurse at the door turned away. There was nothing she could do; Krajnik was an officer of the MGB, and one did not protest the actions of the MGB.

"Where is Lieutenant Rostov?" The mothers near the stove stared in horror. Several babies joined Ina in her tears.

"I don't know." The words did not sound like her own. Krajnik struck her, and his grip on her arm was all that saved her from falling to the floor. Ina's cries turned to shrieks.

Krajnik glared down at the baby in her arms, and for one horrible second he looked like he might hurt her. But he turned his attention back to Natalie. "I could execute you right here, Natalya Ivanovna. For abduction. Theft of State property—"

"State property?" Suddenly she found her voice. "You mean Regina's baby?"

Again he struck her, and the room spun. "Citizen Oryekova has lost the right to be the mother of this baby. It is to be held in a children's home until the age of adoption. Where is Citizen Rostov?"

Citizen Rostov. *Citizen* Oryekova. As soon as comrades became nothing more than citizens, that meant they had become enemies of the People. Viktor and Regina had both lost everything: their coveted Party membership, their children, their good names, and their freedom. Natalie's heart went out to them both, and she was surprised that her sympathy for Viktor was just as poignant as her sorrow for Regina's plight.

"I don't know." She flinched, cowering protectively over Ina's form as Krajnik moved to strike her again. But he seemed to think better of it. He dragged her away from the stove, through the maze of cribs, and past the nurse. Natalie glanced at her and the woman's eyes met hers. Both women silently shared a sorrow that they could not combat, and Natalie saw the conflict in the woman's eyes before Krajnik pulled Natalie from the room.

He marched her through the front door of the mother and children's wing, through the smelly waiting room with its marble walls, thick potent smoke, and waiting passengers, down the stairs, and across the narrow train platform toward a waiting train.

Natalie panicked. "No! Comrade Krajnik, no. Please, no!" And she struggled, violently, against the vise around her arm. She might as well have tried to stop one of the trains. She was hauled aboard and forced down the corridor, past curious passengers on hard wooden benches, and into a private compartment. Krajnik's luggage awaited him in the center of the floor, and he shoved her past the bags until she fell against the seat. She protected Ina from the fall with her shoulder and arm, and Krajnik sneered.

"Why try, Natalya? She'll probably be dead before we reach Moscow."

His diabolical words chilled her. She tried to reason with him. "I must not go back. Please, Comrade Krajnik, please no . . ."

He ignored her. He stepped out of the compartment and Natalie saw another familiar figure waiting there for him. Ivan Volkov's eyes raked her with the same snake-like fascination that she remembered from their first terrifying encounter at the train station and then again inside Lubyanka. As it had then, when he locked eyes with her now his look made her skin crawl.

He wore the same black overcoat, black tunic, and leather gloves, and he had his hair slicked back and covered with a fur-lined cap set at an arrogant angle. He carried his wicked, slender blade hooked through his belt for all to see, as if his vocation were a source of pride. She withered inside at the sight of him.

Krajnik spoke with his policeman in a low voice, and the man nodded, smiled at Natalie, and folded his arms. He leaned against the wall across from the compartment, as if he planned to stay. Krajnik turned again to face her. "Stay here, Natalya, while I wait for Rostov. I cannot imagine either the lieutenant or your German would abandon you at the train station. They'll both be back to get you, and I will be there waiting for them." He produced a pistol and checked the chamber. "Hans Brenner, I fear, will walk into a bullet when he returns to the mothers' room to retrieve you." He closed the door and locked it. She heard his footsteps fading down the corridor.

No. *No!* Hans would return for her, and Krajnik would kill him. She had to warn Hans. Holding Ina close, Natalie struggled past the luggage and swept up the privacy shade on the door. Volkov was no longer there. She rattled the door handle. She turned and threw her shoulder against it, over and over, until her shoulder could no longer stand the pain. Ina began to wail again.

Natalie moved to the window and searched the platform outside. She saw Krajnik's assassin lounging on a bench down the way, watching the entrance and picking his teeth with his blade. His presence and the evil-looking blade had cleared the platform of commuters in his general vicinity. She remembered the drama at Moscow's Leningrad station six months before, and she wondered if Volkov was intent on finishing the job he had begun that night.

She had to warn Hans—and she had to get Ina away from here. She had no idea what she was going to do if she managed to free herself from this compartment or this train—her documents were in a desk drawer in the mother and children's room, and her warm gloves, her supplies for Ina, and her coat were still near the stove. Krajnik or Volkov would capture her if she went back there to try to retrieve them. And yet, without proper documents, what hotel in Novosibirsk would dare accommodate her? On the other hand, how could she sleep outside in this deadly cold with an infant and no way to keep warm? It was impossible. Natalie could not attempt it. They would both die.

But Krajnik's words still haunted her, and she realized Ina would die if she did not try.

Natalie laid the still-crying Ina on the bench, tucked the quilt she had not had a chance to return to the nurse securely about the tiny body, and turned to contemplate the pile of luggage.

She threw open Krajnik's suitcase. She removed a leather belt, several businessmen's silk ties, and two crisp-starched white shirts. She ripped a shirt in two.

She slid the compartment door's privacy shade completely down and closed the curtain. Then she wrapped the strips of shirt around and around the door handle and the metal leg of one of the benches that was bolted to the floor of the train. Next she ran the silk ties back and forth between the facing seats and through the sturdy oak armrests six inches away from the door. If Volkov deciphered the riddle of the door restraint he would have this new obstacle to delay his advance. She took the leather belt and wrapped it around the steel of the outside window frame where the frame had separated slightly from the wall of the train and had never been repaired. The cold made her fingers clumsy, and she watched Volkov as she worked.

She left the belt hanging while she searched one more time through the MGB officer's suitcase. She took several pairs of his dark wool socks, a thick overcoat, a small folding knife, a pair of fur-lined gloves, and money. She pocketed the socks, gloves, and money, unfolded the overcoat, and studied it carefully. With the knife she sawed at the back seam of the coat, finally separating the lower hem and cutting halfway up the back of the coat.

She glanced out the window at Volkov and then slipped her arms into the sleeves with the coat in front of her instead of behind, and secured the large buttons awkwardly behind her neck and upper back. She wrapped the makeshift tails about her waist and knotted them together behind her back so that the remainder of the coat hung in front of her like an awkward, twisted balloon. She folded and pocketed the knife, glanced out the window, and saw Volkov boarding the train.

Natalie reached and kicked at the exterior window with the heel of her boot, striking it over and over with as much force as she could muster. The tough glass finally cracked, and then shattered, spilling crystal shards onto the platform below. Behind her she heard rapid footsteps in the narrow hallway, and then a low exclamation from her captor as he encountered the closed interior window and curtain separating him from the compartment. Then she heard a key turn in the lock and she glanced at the door in time to see the latch move until it met the restraints of Krajnik's shirt.

"Natalya." Volkov's voice was barely controlled. "Open the door."

Natalie did not respond. She probably should have, she realized, to win herself a few precious seconds. But her heart was pounding so hard in her chest that she doubted she would have been able to produce more than a terrified squeak. Besides, Volkov would have already guessed her intent and would not waste any time.

With trembling hands Natalie lifted the baby. She fumbled Ina's tiny body into her sling fashioned from Krajnik's overcoat. She adjusted the crying baby until she lay firmly against her stomach and chest. She rechecked the knot behind her waist. And then with one arm supporting the bundle she slipped one leg through the widened opening and tried not to think about the impossible distance between her body and the platform below.

Suddenly the interior window exploded, and Volkov's sturdy hand entered the room and tore the curtains from their rods. Then for just a moment his eyes met hers. Natalie did not wait for him to comment on her precarious positioning, her body halfway in and halfway out of the train. Nor did she wait to see what he would do with the tangles of starched fabric holding the door handle closed. She slid from the window and fell to the length of her arms, hanging from the straps of Krajnik's leather belt and hoping that the extra length of the belt would bring her shoes to within a few feet of the ground. Ina, pressed against her chest, continued to cry, and Natalie was grateful that her weight was not smothering the baby.

She was still trying to collect her courage to let go, when she heard the compartment door explode inward on destroyed hinges and collide with the silk ties. Volkov flung the shattered door aside, barreled across the remaining space between himself and the exterior window and lunged halfway out, grabbing for Natalie's arms.

She let go of the belt and fell away from the train.

By the time she righted herself Volkov was no longer at the window. She turned and ran.

Her escape from the train occurred in the most profound silence, with Volkov not saying a word and nothing but the panicked beating of Natalie's heart to break the stillness inside her head. She did not hear the exclamations from the hordes of passengers waiting to board the train as they watched her run, probably wondering what had possessed the woman to launch herself from a window with a screaming baby strapped to her torso.

Natalie headed for the mother and children's room. She saw Roman Krajnik waiting at the top of the stairs. He shouted at her and began to descend.

She turned and ran across the platform. She had no idea how far her desperate dash would take her from the nightmare behind. But she knew that she could not sit passively by while Regina's baby was destroyed.

She did not imagine for an instant that if she eluded her pursuers her troubles would be over—Hans's life was still in danger, Krajnik meant to arrest Viktor, and Volkov was about to capture her. She had no place to escape the cold, and Ina was frantic with terror. Instead, she ran for the sole, instinctive purpose of outrunning her pursuers, with the panicked hope that somehow, she would be able to find a way to warn Hans and save the baby.

She did not look behind her. She leapt from the narrow platform, landing awkwardly and twisting her ankle. She set out limping across the tracks, her boots slipping in the deep snow and her breath coming in short, frantic bursts. It hurt to run. It hurt to breathe, and her chest felt like it would explode.

She left the tracks and cut across a field. Ina stopped crying, and Natalie shifted her precious bundle so that the baby would not smother. Ina's eyes, wide and fearful, met hers for the briefest of moments, and then Natalie heard shots fired.

She ducked and ran, cradling Ina in the coat in front of her and praying that Krajnik's bullets would not find their mark in the blizzard. She heard him yell something at her from the train's platform.

Her feet slipped often and her face was growing numb. *Please, Heavenly Father, please help us . . . please warn Hans . . .*

Krajnik's gun stayed silent. Perhaps Krajnik realized the dire predicament she was in, out in the deadly Siberian elements with a tiny baby and insufficient warmth. Besides, Viktor Rostov was his main focus, not a fugitive American woman and a newborn baby. A Siberian blizzard was a cruel, heartless place to die. Krajnik did not need to go after her. Krajnik would leave her to Siberia.

She crouched in the bushes, her breath wet with blood from lungs that could not function in the cold. She stole a glance at Ina and gave a strangled sob. The baby's eyes were closed, and with the desperate pounding of Natalie's heart she could not feel any movement of the baby's chest against her own. She could not tell if the baby was asleep or dead. "Please, Heavenly Father . . ." she whispered, and tried desperately to shelter her tiny charge from the cold.

And as if Mother Nature were taunting her, snow continued to fall. Heavy ice particles clung to her exposed head and neck, and she pulled the socks from her pocket and stretched them so that they would fit across the baby's tiny scalp. She left only the tip of Ina's nose exposed and pulled the quilt up across her tiny mouth. Ina did not move.

She pulled on Krajnik's gloves and huddled in the bushes. She squinted into the white darkness, searching for something—anything—to crawl under to get out of the storm. She could see nothing.

Oh, Father, how I need You now! She was not even sure the words had left her lips, numb as they were. It no longer hurt to breathe, and she could not feel her legs under her skirt.

"What a fitting place," said a voice above her, "to finish what I began."

She looked up. Ivan Volkov's face leered above her, but she saw only the shadow of the blade held in his hand. He raised the blade, and then suddenly Ivan Volkov disappeared.

She did not have the energy to wonder how he had vanished so suddenly. His blade dropped mere centimeters from her body, the tip buried deep in the snow and the handle perpendicular to the ground, waving back and forth as if strummed by some invisible hand.

She could no longer feel her arms about the motionless bundle, and her eyelids felt heavy. She did not respond when a hand shook her shoulder, nor could she stand up when someone tried to lift her to her feet. She whispered, "Please help me . . . I have a baby . . ." but she could not move. She didn't want to move. She preferred to stay right here, with strange, ethereal warmth seeping into her bones . . .

FIFTY-ONE

It was past three in the morning before Viktor returned to the train station. He'd promised Hans he would hurry, and it had been more than three hours. He felt slow panic simmering as he made a beeline for the stairs. He took them two at a time until he reached the enormous marble waiting room on the second floor. He strode toward the mother and children's room and was violently knocked to the floor by a porter laden with bags.

Rostov struggled to his feet. The porter made an awkward attempt to assist him, and Viktor's first inclination was to deck the young man in return. But he took a deep breath instead, struggling to calm his nerves. He had a long way to go before he could curb his temper, he realized, and he accepted the porter's apology. He was turning to go when the porter touched his arm, leaned close, and whispered, "Your sister isn't here. I was sent to warn you; you're walking into a trap."

"My *sister?*" Viktor was shocked. For a moment he thought he imagined the words. He looked at the porter, a young, scruffy, and dreadfully lanky Siberian specimen with a lazy eye and an eager face.

The young man nodded, and he gestured for Viktor to follow.

Viktor followed the porter as if following his luggage to a waiting train. They fought their way through a crush of people on the narrow platform, struggling to stay in sight of each other as two shuddering trains began to fill. One of them was the train they needed to Sverdlovsk. They wouldn't be on it.

"This way, please." The boy-porter was enjoying his masquerade, and Viktor couldn't help but ask a few questions. "What is my sister's name?"

"Natalya Ivanovna." The young man seemed unruffled by Viktor's distrust, as if he'd been expecting a grilling.

"Who was with her?"

"A tiny baby. And her husband." The porter abandoned his luggage props at the edge of the platform.

"Her husband?"

"Yes, Comrade—your friend—the one who told me you needed help."

"How did you know—?"

"I do not know all the answers." The young porter rolled his eyes. "I'll take you to her. She is resting. She almost froze to death tonight—she and the baby."

Viktor's knees went weak. He'd left Natalya safe with Hans and now this young stranger was taking him out of the train station and toward a waiting car, and telling him that he had almost lost Natalya. How had this happened?

They drove through unfamiliar streets, frozen, empty, and harsh. Snow continued to fall until they arrived at a cottage. Viktor couldn't help the pounding of his heart against his ribs as he contemplated what he would discover upon entering the home. The porter noticed his trepidation. "It's all right. You'll see."

Natalie lay asleep in a bed, covered with mountains of blankets, and Hans Brenner sat at her side. An older woman huddled near a stove and Viktor caught a glimpse of a tiny, naked leg. The woman held Ina in her arms, the miniature body frail and white. The woman was carefully, methodically massaging Ina's tiny limbs. Ina's whimpering cry broke Viktor's heart.

Hans spoke. "Krajnik's here. He's watching the train station. He took Natalie from the mothers' room and she escaped. I found her in a field—"

The porter cut in, "With one MGB man about to dissect her with his knife."

"Arseni!"

"You should've seen what Hans did to—"

"*Malchi,* Arseni! Enough!"

Did Viktor hear a catch in Hans's throat? Viktor moved to Natalie's side, and the love he felt for her rose inside him, almost choking off his air supply. He glanced at Hans. "How'd she happen to be in the middle of a field?"

"She jumped out the window of the train they put her on." Hans tucked a blanket under Natalie's chin. "Krajnik shot at her, and Arseni and I circled around through the field and intercepted her there. Krajnik's assassin had already found her. It was . . . almost too late."

Viktor's tongue suddenly felt thick, unmanageable. He'd almost lost her. He'd almost lost the woman he'd protected all these months. Now he had to find a way to thank Hans, and the words would not come. He couldn't bring himself to say them. Instead, Viktor turned away.

Under the mountain of quilts Natalie stirred, moaned, and finally opened her eyes. She finally focused on Hans. She whispered his name and he leaned close to hear her words. "How is Ina?"

"Arseni's grandmother is helping her."

"Will she be all right?"

Hans hesitated. "We still don't know . . ."

From the stove came a sharp retort. "Now don't you go worrying the girl! Your baby's going to be fine. I know what to do for her."

Natalie looked relieved. She clutched Hans's sleeve and whispered, "Krajnik is here. He came for Viktor, and he plans to kill you."

"I know."

Natalie asked, "Hans, did you get the documents?"

Hans glanced at Arseni. The youth busied himself removing his wraps. "My contact couldn't have them for me until morning. He tried, but . . ." Hans shrugged.

Natalie's hand slipped from beneath the blankets and captured his. "We need to wait—for Ina to recover."

"That's what we'll do." He squeezed her hand. He looked up at Rostov. "I know you're worried about Lucya . . ."

Rostov nodded. "But it's the way it should be. Besides," Rostov pulled papers from his coat pocket and tossed them on the table. "With Krajnik here, these tickets are now useless. He knows now that I'm going after my daughter. He will watch the trains. I'll have to find another way for us to get to Vladivostok."

The woman holding Ina spoke. "The only other way is by airplane—and I can promise there's no pilot crazy enough to fly in this weather.

And after this snowstorm it will take pockets as deep as Lake Baikal to make a pilot crazy enough to fly."

Both Hans and Natalie spoke at once. "I have money . . ." They stared at each other.

Hans explained, "I took it from the laboratory."

"I borrowed it from Krajnik's suitcase." Natalie tried to smile.

Rostov laughed and slapped Hans on the back. "After the storm is over I will find us a pilot crazy enough to fly us to Vladivostok."

FIFTY-TWO

After several long days in a fishing vessel Jacques decided the market hadn't been so bad. He spent almost every waking hour leaning over the side of the rail. "It's not the waves," he insisted to Rolf. "It's the smell."

They docked at a small inlet just off the Okushiri Island's runway. Not far from where Ayato cast anchor they reached the home of their smuggler. Jacques felt confident that he should be the one to reason with him.

"You're certain he speaks French?" Rolf asked with a grin.

"He's a smuggler. He'll know a few languages. Why wouldn't French be one of them?"

They were met at the door by a young man with a Samurai sword strapped across his back. Rolf and Jacques dutifully removed their footwear at the entrance and slipped their feet into slippers. They followed their sword-wielding guide into the back of the home. The man they sought was seated behind a desk.

Rolf saw no chairs. He and Jacques lowered themselves to their knees. Jacques began, *"Parlez-vous—?"*

The man interrupted in French. "I speak seven different languages and thirteen dialects." He looked down at Jacques with contempt. "It is necessary in my line of work."

"We were told we could count on you." Jacques tossed an open folder onto the desk. It took several seconds for the man to reach for it, as if hinting that nothing thrown at him was worthy of his time.

He was a curious combination of Asian and Slavic, with black hair and eyes the color of a sea churned dark and cold. He must have been in his late thirties, his features muscle-bound and slightly threatening. His long torso suggested more than average height, and a scar under his chin ran crosswise to the width of his jaw. He wore several rings on each hand, great big jewels set in gold. He had a heavy gold chain about his neck and a cigar positioned in the corner of his mouth. He did not look pleased to see them.

"What *are* you, exactly?" Jacques's voice held suspicion.

"I'm an Okushiri citizen."

Jacques rolled his eyes. "I mean, what is your line of work?"

The man sneered back at him, exposing perfect teeth. "I'm a businessman." His eyes raked the Frenchman and his German companion from head to toe. "You in the export business?"

"That's right." Jacques didn't blink an eye.

The cigar moved, bouncing as the scarred jaw chewed. "Got someone on the inside?"

"Of course."

"Someone I know?"

Jacques swore. "Why would I tell you?"

The man's gaze flickered. He chewed his cigar and studied Jacques. Finally he seemed to relax a notch. "The name's Yakimoto," he said, and he gave them a cursory bow, utilizing only his head. He finally opened the folder and dropped his eyes to the photographs. He spread them on the table in front of him and gave each a thorough inspection. "What's so special about this cargo?"

"If you're paid, what does it matter?"

"It matters to me. It's my boat."

Jacques indicated pictures of Hans and Natalie. "They're associates of my friend here," he jerked a thumb at Rolf. "They've been prisoners since they were abducted from the streets of Paris."

Yakimoto studied the picture of Hans. "German?"

Jacques shrugged.

The man wasn't entirely convinced. "A Nazi?"

"Formerly." Jacques displayed his irritation wonderfully. "Does that matter?"

Yakimoto ignored the question. "And her?" His dirty thumb smudged the white nurse's uniform. "American?"

"Soviet."

"Liar. She's wearing an American army uniform."

"Doesn't change who she is."

"Undercover?"

"No. My sister."

The man snorted. "And this pretty thing?" The captain's eyes lingered on the girl in the mutilated photograph. "She your sister too?"

"The daughter of a Soviet diplomat to Japan."

Yakimoto sneered. "There are no Soviet diplomats to Japan."

"She's the reason we need you."

Yakimoto leaned back in his chair, Lucya's photograph still in his hand. "Political prisoner?"

"A *very wealthy* political prisoner."

"There are no wealthy Soviets these days. And you can't trust the ones that are."

"There are plenty of wealthy Soviets. But they're all on their way to Kolyma, like this girl."

Yakimoto nodded. He understood. "She single?"

Jacques shrugged.

Yakimoto tossed the picture back onto the table. "I can't help you. I don't help prisoners from the camps, and I certainly don't help the Americans." His glance at Rolf, kneeling silently next to Jacques, held malice.

"We're not asking you to help us rescue her from the camps." Jacques said. "Just from Vladivostok. We've got somebody—"

"Absolutely not." Yakimoto folded his arms.

Rolf stood, the fear he felt for Hans's safety and that of his friends a tight knot in his chest. "We pay well, Yakimoto, if that's what is worrying you."

"You're an American agent."

Rolf shook his head and pointed at the picture of Hans. "This is personal. That man saved my life, and I intend to do the same for him."

"I said no. And I don't trust the Americans."

"I'm not an American."

Yakimoto glanced at his bodyguard.

Jacques scrambled to his feet. "We won't trouble you further. Thank you for your time."

Yakimoto spat, "Save it for the Japanese," and threw the folder at Jacques. He glared at Rolf. "Prove you're not American."

"I was a German officer in the war."

"Prove it."

Rolf shook his head. "There's nothing I can say that would prove my claim. If I told you I was stationed in France and that I arrested and imprisoned American agents, you would think it a lie. If I showed you an Iron Cross, you'd think I stole it off of a corpse. Short of producing a picture of me shaking Hitler's hand, I can't think of any way to prove it."

Yakimoto did not seem happy, but he finally said, "Fair enough. If you're not American I'll help you. For a price, of course."

"Of course." Rolf stood his ground. "We'll accept your help on one condition."

Rolf's words had an instant effect on the smuggler. Rolf saw the temperature climbing Yakimoto's neck toward his cheekbones. Obviously Yakimoto didn't like conditions being placed upon his generosity.

"What condition?" It came out like a threat.

Rolf took a deep breath, ignored the strangled warning coming from Jacques's throat, and said, "That we charter the entire boat—not just one or two cabins."

"Why?" Now the threat in Yakimoto's voice was deadly.

"Three reasons," Rolf began, and he felt Jacques's hand on his arm.

"Yes?" Yakimoto's eyes darted toward his swordsman.

"Because we want complete control of where you dock—and when. And because we don't want to be seen by any of your usual contacts in Vladivostok."

Yakimoto's face had darkened to a disagreeable shade of purple. "You said there were three reasons, *gaijin*. What's the third?"

Rolf didn't hesitate. "Because I don't agree with the type of trafficking you're involved in. Those women have families and homes. Send them home to their families."

Yakimoto laughed, the sound ugly mixed with his anger. "Purchase them from me and I'll send them wherever you please. Otherwise keep out of my business and I'll keep out of yours. Understood?"

Rolf glared at him. "Yakimoto-san, I'll charter the entire boat. Minus the normal cargo. That's the only deal I'll make."

"There's no deal then!" Yakimoto lunged to his feet. "Get out of my presence, gaijin, or I'll cut your throat! How dare you attempt to regulate my affairs! Your morals are yours alone, and I won't have you pushing them on me or my business. Is that clear?"

Without a word Rolf turned his back on the smuggler and walked away. Jacques followed.

They collected their shoes and walked out into the night. Snow turned to slush as it fell, clinging to everything it touched. The snowfall and the dark, empty street seemed surreal to Rolf.

They walked toward the docks, through a rough-and-tumble assemblage of buildings, down a moldy alleyway, and up a flight of moss-blanketed stone steps. They walked down a quiet street, past stone walls bursting with moss and mold, and bamboo and persimmon trees peeking from hidden gardens, their branches stark against coverings of wet snow. Icicles dripped from red tile roofs toward cobblestones below, and about it all was an aura of silence that was almost like entering a shrine.

"Now what?" Frustrated, Rolf turned to Jacques.

"Patience, friend—it's not over yet." Jacques's chin jerked slightly, indicating that someone was following them.

Rolf did not turn. "Ayato's boat is twenty minutes' walk from here. We'll have to outrun—"

"Run and you'll never see your friends again," Jacques hissed. "I can promise you that. Now turn around."

Rolf and Jacques turned. Yakimoto stood in the darkening street with his bodyguard by his side. He folded his arms and studied them, his face impassive. He repeated his motto: "I don't work for the Americans."

"I'm not an American," Rolf reaffirmed.

Yakimoto's eyes bored holes in his. "No one has ever defied me before—and lived to see the morning sky. I'll compromise with you, gaijin—but only because I appreciate your courage. I'll let you take out the boat—entirely empty. I'll let you drop anchor where you will. I'll let you keep your own schedule. However, I will fill the boat for the return journey. Agreed?"

"Fill it with what?" Rolf demanded.

"Don't try my patience, gaijin."

"It is a simple enough question, Yakimoto-san. Fill it with what?"

"Political prisoners," Yakimoto snapped, exasperated. "From the camps. They're worth a fortune to me—the rich ones, of course."

"Of course." Rolf extended his hand.

Yakimoto stared at it, and then took it in a strong, vigorous handshake. "About that wealthy daughter of the Soviet diplomat to Japan—"

"She's not really wealthy," Rolf said. "Neither is she a Soviet diplomat's daughter."

"I know that." Yakimoto smiled for the first time. "But she'd better be single."

FIFTY-THREE

Monday, December 23, 1946

Rough hands pulled Lucya from her bed before the sun rose above the horizon, and she was dragged across the snow to the administration building. Her captors dumped her in a shivering heap on the floor of the commandant's office, and it was several moments before she dared look up at the second man in the room.

She was certain that she'd seen the man before. He was someone her papa knew, someone who worked for the Kremlin in some capacity. She knew it. But what was he doing here, in this camp near Vladivostok, on the other side of the world from Moscow?

Suddenly her heart skipped a beat, and she felt a surge of joy. Her papa had sent him to bring her home! She couldn't imagine any other reason for his presence here. Her papa had remembered her and had found a way to pardon her.

"Is this her?"

The commandant pulled at the remains of a cigar. "I thought you said you knew her in Moscow."

"Of course. But she's changed so much . . ."

The man's words stung, and Lucya tried hard not to let her hurt show. Had she changed as much as that? Was she so different that this man—what was his name?—who was a friend of her papa, couldn't recognize her?

"That's her. Make no mistake."

"Well, then." The man didn't even look at her, and Lucya felt again the shame of being no more important than a piece of meat in a butcher shop. "I'll have to take your word for it. Has she been any trouble?"

"No more than the next prisoner."

"She needs to be put in solitary."

His words, so unexpected in her hope, sliced like a dagger.

"Well, we don't just put anyone in solitary, Comrade. Not even for someone of your persuasion. Understand? I'm a man of principle, and she has to be guilty of some misdeed before—"

"It's not a moral issue, Commander. It's no more than a matter of hiding her for a few weeks."

"Hiding her?"

"From possible—complications. She might attempt to escape, or she might be the focus of a rescue attempt . . ."

"Escape?" The commandant guffawed. "No one escapes in this weather. Even the stupid ones are too smart to try. They know they'll freeze before they reach Vladivostok. And the only way out is by train or boat—"

"What is her sentence?"

"Kolyma. She's one of the politicals bound for the mines."

"When does the next Kolyma ship arrive?"

"A week, if all goes well. The *Dzhurma* is scheduled to arrive around the thirtieth."

Kolyma? Could Lucya have imagined it? Was that what the commandant said? It couldn't be true. He was mistaken. She was supposed to stay here with Aleksandr and wait for her papa. Her papa was going to arrive any day now and rescue her from the horrors of this frozen wasteland.

"A little late in the season, don't you think?"

The commandant shrugged. "It may have to winter on the ice."

"And what about the prisoners aboard ship?"

The commandant didn't answer, only chewed the stub of his cigar. The man said, "Make sure she's on it."

"Of course, Comrade. But in the meantime, there's no reason for the Hole."

"Convict her of petty theft and throw her in solitary until the *Dzhurma* arrives. The solution's that simple." The man tossed a purse on the desk.

The commandant shrugged. "Prisoners steal all the time, and then they always claim innocence. Don't worry yourself about it." He reached for the purse. "You are correct; better she be confined as a punishment for thievery."

"How long can she survive in there?"

"Her body? Three weeks. Her mind?" The purse disappeared into a desk drawer. "Three days."

FIFTY-FOUR

Wednesday, December 25, 1946

As late afternoon approached at the navy base in Vladivostok, the commissary specialist looked up from his desk to see an MGB officer standing in front of him. The man looked like he'd traveled a long way without eating or sleeping. He looked almost ready to collapse into an official heap on the tile.

But he was a ranking officer. The specialist leaped to his feet and saluted him, almost upsetting his chair in the process. "How may I help you, Comrade?"

The officer produced his identification documents and laid them on the desk. "My name is Comrade Zabrovsky—assistant director of the Moscow branch of the MGB. My subordinate and I have just arrived from Moscow with a very important prisoner—a woman convicted of treason. Our orders are to escort her personally to Vtoraya Rechka as soon as possible. I need a State vehicle for the evening."

"You're in luck. The *director* of the Moscow branch of the MGB is also here on business. Would you like me to contact him and inform him of your arrival?"

The man seemed perturbed at the news. "Nyet." He shook his head adamantly. "There's no reason to bother Comrade Krajnik. I have the assistance I need. I just need the auto."

The commissary specialist consulted his list. "We have one still available in the navy fleet, sir. I will call them and have them bring the vehicle around. Will you be needing a driver?"

"I prefer to have my subordinate drive."

"As you wish."

"I appreciate it. I will wait at the refectory with my prisoner."

The specialist picked up the receiver on his desk. His eyes followed the officer as he left the building and descended the stairs, and he thought he saw him stumble as he took the last step. It must've been a long and arduous journey. He decided he would inform the visiting MGB director of his associate's arrival anyway—just as a courtesy.

* * *

Lucya had experienced different levels of nightmares in her life. Some nightmares whispered in and out of her dreams and plagued her only while she slept. Often all that remained when she awoke were vague feelings of unease—a certainty that what she had experienced while she slept had been a nightmare. Other times, the nightmare remained in her mind when she awoke, terrifying her with its implications and imprinting itself forever on her memory. And then there was the new category of nightmare, recently discovered, where the nightmare continued without pause when she opened her eyes. That was what she was experiencing now.

She no longer slept. But the nightmare continued. Howls of prisoners as unlucky as she echoed through the vast stone corridors and she felt the cold steel of the door frame against her cheek. She tried to block it out, the darkness that penetrated her soul, but it was impossible. The cold was something she could deal with—they had left her her mother's shawl. But the fear that she was powerless to clear her mind of the darkness was more than she could take.

Her door opened, and Aleksandr stood there. At first she didn't recognize him, as her mind struggled to make sense of a sudden beacon of light in the midst of darkness. But his smile brought it all back, and as she struggled to rise to greet him, he moved forward and took her in his arms.

"Don't worry, my sweet Lucya. I'll carry you." And he did. He stood with her in his arms amidst the squalor and darkness of a living nightmare that, with Aleksandr here, was already beginning to fade.

He carried her through the steel door and down the corridor, up the stone steps, through the guard shack, where the guard on duty did not give them more than a cursory glance. He carried her outside into the cold that burned her skin and hurt her eyes, and lifted her into the waiting sled behind the three prancing horses. He climbed up beside her and pulled a sheepskin over both of them, pushed warm gloves onto her hands, and wrapped a comforter about her shoulders and tucked it under her legs.

"You came for me . . ."

"Just rest, Lucya. It'll be all right."

"I'm so tired . . ."

"I know."

He picked up the reins, and the horses lunged against the harness. She lay against his shoulder and watched him as he drove, and she was again happy. He hadn't forgotten her. It didn't matter, at that moment, that she worried that she was too weak to live until her papa came for her. Aleksandr had found a way to deliver her from the torment that was consuming her, and that was all that mattered.

"Lucya, did you know we saw each other once," Aleksandr murmured, "when you were just a girl?"

Her eyes widened as she looked up at him. She didn't know what to say. The revelation was surprising to her, and she struggled to find a memory from her childhood that would include the stunning blue eyes of a young Soviet officer.

"It was during the war, in '41. You came with your father—you, and your brother and your beautiful mother—to a function at the Kremlin. It was Stalin's birthday celebration, and your father was one of many invited. I'd been recently assigned as a military attaché to the NKVD, assigned to serve with your father. Lieutenant Rostov requested that I attend the celebration . . ." Aleksandr paused, and once again he glanced down at her. "And I saw you there." He smiled at her. "I looked over, and I saw you standing there by your mother's side. You were thirteen years old—fourteen, maybe—and you were so beautiful . . ."

"Ohh!" Her eyes widened and her jaw fell slack. "You were that officer who . . ." Suddenly she giggled. "You *blushed!* You were staring at me—and when I looked over and saw you . . . you blushed!" The memory of that evening warmed through her soul like the welcome sunshine of spring. She saw the color she remembered from that long-ago moment creep again toward his cheekbones, and her heart soared. "You—remembered me . . . !"

He nodded. "And when I learned that you were in danger . . ." He stopped, and his arm encircled her shoulders. He seemed to battle with his emotions, and he struggled to continue. "You asked me once about my childhood. Now I want to tell you: I was a child in America—in Texas, where I rode horses and roped cattle with my papa. After my mother died, Papa took a job with Ford to make cars. We came to the USSR to help Ford establish a factory near Gorky. I was only eleven when my father died in the factory, and I was arrested for no reason in '33. I was sent here to Vtoraya Rechka. Three years later I escaped. I stowed away on a vessel that took me to Japan, where I eventually worked my way across the world back home to America. When I was sixteen I lied about my age and joined the military, and soon I convinced the army that my Russian background was essential to the war effort. I was trained as a spy, and in 1940 I was sent to infiltrate the NKVD—"

But she didn't care about all that. One thing shone through all the confusing names, dates, and circumstances. "You're—an *American?*" Her voice wavered as the news sank in.

Aleksandr gave her a compassionate smile. "And in America, today is a special holiday, where people give each other presents." He kissed her forehead. "I want to give *you* a present, Lucya: My real name is Alex Reynolds, and I work for the government of America. I came here to find you."

Her voice was barely over a whisper. "You came here to find me? You came back to the Soviet Union—to find *me?*"

He nodded, and his eyes shone. The emotion there was so genuine, so loving, that she couldn't keep back her tears. "Alex . . . Rey-nolds . . ." Her lips formed the beautiful sounds, and her eyes sparkled with wonder. "Why would you do that, Alex Rey-nolds?"

"Two reasons, my darling Lucya," he explained. "First, I think I've loved you from the moment we saw each other at that celebration. I *knew* you were in my future; I just didn't know yet how I was going to make it work." He kissed her cheek, his breath a warm, gentle counterpoint to the freezing air.

She didn't know how to respond. His revelations were so wonderful, and yet she was still trying to understand and accept them.

"The other reason," Aleksandr continued, "is because your father wants me to rescue you."

Her eyes went wide. She struggled to sit up straight. "My papa?" The thought sent such joy cascading through her wounded soul that she forgot to breathe. "Ohhh! That *is* a wonderful gift!"

He nodded. "Recently he agreed to assist the Americans in exchange for getting you out of Siberia—and the Americans had me find you."

Her brow furrowed. "I can't believe it. Papa—helping the Americans? He would never betray Comrade Stalin. Never! He loves his country and he loves me—and he wouldn't endanger either his country or me by helping Westerners . . ."

"Lucya, he's done neither. He hasn't endangered his country. He's only agreed to help two good people return home in exchange for me rescuing you!" He squeezed her frail shoulders. "I know how much your father loves your country. And I know how much he loves you. In fact, your father is probably one of the most patriotic Russians ever to set foot on Russian soil. And I wouldn't doubt he knows his sacrifice is similar to a death sentence. He's doing it for you, dear Lucya. So that you can live, and grow up with the freedom you deserve. So that you can someday return to this great land and help it become the powerful, beautiful country your father knows it can be."

"He—he would sacrifice his citizenship for me?"

Alex nodded. "That and much more. He would sacrifice his *life* for your welfare."

Those words rang true. She'd always known her papa loved her. She'd always known he would find a way to save her. She'd never imagined that he would find such a magnificent way of doing it—with a man who captured her heart so lovingly . . .

And now, with the arm of this kind officer—no, the arm of this *American cowboy*—around her and the message of her papa's sacrifice in her ears and her heart, she felt a peace flooding through her that enveloped her as the warmest of shawls on a cold winter night, and she knew that everything would be all right.

"Will I see my papa?"

"I don't know. I assume I'm the one to escort you away."

"And you'll do so in this troika?" she teased.

He chuckled and pulled her closer. "If it were humanly possible. Oh, what fond memories we share! But we'll carry only our memories with us this time, little Lucya—a ship waits for us off the coast to the east."

She shivered against him, the cold inescapable even with his arms tightly around her and the furs from the sled tucked across her knees. But she shivered also from pure joy—at her papa's sacrifice and because of the kindness of this man.

Suddenly an awful thought interrupted her peace. Alex would leave her. He would get her out of the Soviet Union and then he would abandon her, returning to his work and forgetting her. The tears blurred her vision. "Alex . . ."

He leaned close to hear her whispers.

"You have only pretended to love me—for the sake of getting close to me."

He didn't feign surprise. He didn't protest violently. He let her cry. And then he asked her a simple question. "Lucya, will you marry me?"

She wiped at her tears with a dirty corner of her sleeve. She sniffed, rubbing at her nose and pushing a wisp of hair back behind one ear. She looked up at him and saw a lopsided grin that melted her heart. She took a deep breath, straightened in his arms, and forced herself to return a portion of his smile. "You may not like me once you see what's really under all this dirt."

He laughed, gathered her into his arms, and crushed her to him, and for several minutes the bewildered horses had to find their own way. "I'll take you, dear sweet Lucya, dirt and all—that is, if you'll have *me* after I've misled you for so long."

"If I recall, sir, you've also protected my honor on a number of occasions—and never asked me to compromise myself in payment."

"My mother raised me to be a gentleman, ma'am," he drawled. "How would you like to live in Texas?"

Texas! Her eyes grew wide. To her it seemed that the word denoted a land as massive as the entirety of Siberia, and she had a wild, glorious image of her Alex in a cowboy hat, driving a troika across vast frozen ice fields of Texas. And they would have two entire rooms to themselves—

and use of a kitchen—in a community apartment in the city during the bitter winters. And in the summers they would go to their tiny *dacha* and raise beets and cabbages. She would like that. And her papa would live nearby . . . and teach at the university . . .

"What are you smiling about?"

She didn't know how to describe the peaceful scene to him, so she only snuggled in closer and smiled up into his eyes. "I think I would love to live with you in Texas, my Alex. Yes, I think I would like to marry you."

He seemed satisfied. He gave her shoulder a squeeze, gentle this time, as if suddenly concerned she might crumble in his arms.

"When we are married, will we ride together like this? In a troika?"

Alex threw back his head and laughed, a sound so musical, so genuinely happy, that Lucya couldn't help joining him. "My sweet Lucya." He grinned. "Do you know what today is?"

She did not. Her days were usually a never-ending series of undesirable events, and she'd given up trying to remember their delineation on a Russian Orthodox calendar.

"Today is December twenty-fifth, nineteen hundred and forty-six." He smiled at her joyfully.

She studied him, wondering if he would explain his enthusiasm for that particular date.

"This is the day Grandpapa Frost arrives in Texas, driving his troika with his snow maiden at his side!"

Her eyes grew wide. "Grandpapa Frost visits Texas?"

"His name is a little different . . ."

Oh, this was good! "And he drives a troika?"

"It's similar . . ."

"And do the children receive gifts from him—placed under the tree?"

Alex nodded.

"I think I am going to like Texas!" Lucya clapped her gloves together joyfully and then settled into the warmth of Alex's arm.

And that is how they stayed, together in each others' arms, until the camp faded behind them and up ahead was only a short ride to the open sea, and freedom . . .

Lucya heard the motor's rumble and did not turn to look. Perhaps if she ignored it, and kept her face buried in Alex's shoulder, the beautiful dream would continue. Alex would not be executed for helping a prisoner escape, and she would not be thrown back into that nightmare of the Hole that had encompassed her every waking moment. Perhaps she would get to see her papa again, someday, and she would not die.

The black automobile drove alongside the sled, and the driver motioned for them to stop. Alex ignored him. Lucya saw the face behind the wheel, and she recognized the man who'd bribed the commandant to throw her into solitary confinement. He met her gaze, and the look in his eyes sent the chill sea air deep into her lungs, penetrating deep into her soul. Finally she remembered his name: It was Roman Krajnik, the man who'd known her papa in Moscow. She was certain now that it had been Krajnik who had ordered her removal to the camps.

Krajnik sounded the horn, loud, incessant, and the three horses began to panic. Snegurichka leaped to the left, tossing her white main and showing the whites of her eyes. Grandpapa Frost pulled back on the harness, high stepping as he fought against Yolochka's determined attempts to escape. Alex tightened his hold on the reins. "Lucya, hold onto me with all your might. Can you do that?"

She nodded, too frightened to speak, and he removed his arm from around her to attend to the horses. He pulled out a whip, and for the first time Lucya saw him strike the beautiful animals. The team swerved off the road at his command, ploughed dizzyingly through a snowdrift, and came leaping out in a farmer's field, lumpy with snow. The horses didn't care for this new arrangement, and they fought the reigns and Alex for several moments. Meanwhile the car slowed to a stop behind them and Roman Krajnik emerged.

"Lucya Rostova," Krajnik called out, "I'll shoot you unless you stop."

Lucya clung all the tighter to Alex's arm and threw a fearful glance over her shoulder. Alex regained control of the horses and now began shouting at them, urging them to greater speed. Again Krajnik's voice drifted across the snow, this time as thin as a reed: "There's no way you'll escape me. Your father's a traitor. His felony makes your freedom forfeit. Your companion is driving you into even greater trouble than you already are. Come back here . . . !"

Lucya heard a gunshot. She cried out as the bullet tore a piece from the edge of the sled. Alex hunched forward, his entire being intent on making the horses obey, and Lucya exclaimed, "Oh, Alex, it's no use! He'll capture us and you'll be murdered for helping me. Take me back! Take me back!"

"Lucya." He turned to her and grinned, although she could see the worry in his eyes. "We're going to make it. Just you watch. He can't follow us, and he doesn't know about the ship."

The next shot ripped through Alex's arm, and he groaned, toppled forward, and almost lost the reins. Lucya screamed.

"Alex, there's a lot of blood!"

"Will you help me, Lucya?" Alex gasped. "Will you hold the reins for a moment?"

Mute with fear, she nodded and released his arm in order to grab the reins. Alex opened his coat, tore a strip from his tunic, and used his teeth and his good hand to tie a tourniquet above the wound. He pulled it tight and reached again for the reins. "It's not so bad," he said with a tight smile, and Lucya recounted the multitudes of times she'd said the same thing—just to keep from losing her mind.

She returned his smile. "No, Alex, it isn't so bad."

"See? Look back there." Alex grimaced against the pain. "He has to find another route. He knows he isn't the best shot."

"And now where will we go?"

"To the ship, of course. He won't be able to follow us where I'm taking you."

"And what if he reaches the ship first?"

For a moment Alex didn't respond, and then he leaned to take the reins and kissed her. "Lucya, you've had to worry about everything for a long time—your father, yourself, your future . . . Now it's my turn. Close your eyes, lean your head against my shoulder." He grimaced. "No, maybe you shouldn't do that—and let me worry about everything for a while."

"And what will I do, while you worry for the both of us?"

He smiled. "Think of names for our children."

"How many will we have?"

"A dozen or so." He laughed, and the sound ended in a hiss of pain. He clenched his teeth and continued. "And they'll all look exactly like their mother . . ." He couldn't continue.

"Alex, don't talk anymore, all right?"

"Talking takes my mind off the pain. Sort of."

"All right, then tell me how we're going to get out of this nightmare. What ship is waiting for us?"

"A friend of your father commandeered a fishing vessel from Japan."

"A friend of my papa?" She was pleased. "Will my papa be there?"

"I don't think so." Alex shook his head. "But they haven't told me much—just that it was time to get you out, and where to meet the ship."

"Oh, Alex, are you going to be all right?"

"I've been through worse than this."

She could see the Sea of Japan, now, filling the horizon and her vision. She leaned forward and gasped. "I don't see a ship."

"It's there."

"How do you know? Doesn't the sea ice over near shore?" She swallowed against rising panic. "How will this fishing vessel make it close to shore, Alex? What are we going to do if the boat doesn't arrive?"

Alex didn't answer, and Lucya felt sorry for him. Here he was, gallantly trying to save her, only to have his plans thwarted by a man with a gun. And if the boat he'd been promised didn't arrive, they were trapped against the sea. For several moments Alex drove in silence, his face thoughtful. He held his wounded arm close to his body as he drove with the other.

The horses were beginning to tire, their once-magnificent manes caked with mud and ice. Their sides heaved with the effort of pulling through the frozen field, and their breath came in frustrated, rapid grunts. They would not last much longer. Suddenly Lucya pointed, almost losing her balance in her excitement. "I see it! At least, I see a boat! There! See? On the horizon . . ." Her excitement trailed away, as they both realized it wasn't coming any closer.

"I knew they'd make it," Alex mumbled. "But the ice must be out about two miles. The ship can't come any closer." His hand on the reins tightened into a fist. "We're going to have to go out and meet them."

"Over the ice?" She'd heard of that being done; youngsters recklessly racing their sleds over ice that could reach thicknesses of ten meters in the dead of winter. But this was still relatively early in the season. "It's risky, Alex—the ice may not yet be thick enough. And all the way to the boat?"

"We may have to walk partway," he admitted.

She nodded and once again clutched at his arm. Alex flinched.

"Lucya," he grimaced, "I know you're frightened. But when I lived with my father in the American village outside the Ford factory, my friends and I did it all the time. We drove our sleds out onto the Ob as early as December. I think we'll make it."

"All right." She smiled at him. "I trust you, Alex Rey-nolds."

FIFTY-FIVE

Viktor drove Hans, Natalie, and Ina to the rendezvous coordinates.

"I see it," Natalie said, pointing. "The boat's at least a couple of miles out. Are they coming any closer?"

"My eyesight's not what it used to be," Viktor murmured, and he drove the car to the water's edge.

Hans and Viktor got out of the car and walked onto the ice. Natalie watched from the car, trying to soothe an increasingly fussy Ina and wondering which of the men would be first to disappear through the ice. It was not a contest she enjoyed.

Viktor shielded his eyes with one hand as he gazed out over the water. He said something to Hans, and then both men returned to the car.

Viktor gunned the engine and drove out onto the ice.

Natalie clutched Ina and tried not to think about what swirled beneath them. She reminded herself of what Regina had said to her once, what felt like a lifetime ago, about driving on the ice. Hans reached and took her hand in his, and that was almost enough to make her feel better.

They drove halfway to the boat and then Viktor coasted to a stop. "Better not go any farther," he said quietly and exited the car.

Hans followed and pulled the luggage from the car. He opened the door for Natalie and helped her to her feet, then slung Ina's bag over his shoulder and picked up two suitcases. Natalie stood very still, feeling off balance on the slippery surface. The ice was punctuated by razor-sharp chunks, some sharp enough to cut through the soles of her shoes. A brisk wind blew across the surface of the ice, lifting clouds of fine snow into Natalie's eyes, nose, and mouth. She held Ina close, bury-ing the lower half of her face in the bundle of blankets as she followed Hans toward the boat. Viktor lagged behind, looking first in the direc-tion of the boat and then back toward shore. *Wondering if his daughter has arrived yet*, she thought.

Then she saw two figures from the boat running toward them across the ice. They faded in and out of the swirling clouds of snow, and Natalie squinted to try to see them. Suddenly Hans gave a yell and dropped one suitcase to wave at the approaching men.

"Rolf!" Natalie was thrilled to hear pure joy in his voice. "Over here!"

Within moments the two friends were reunited. Hans and Rolf exchanged an energetic, back-slapping hug, and then Rolf pulled Natalie and baby Ina into his arms. "You have no idea how good it is to see you, Natalie," he said joyfully, and he gave her a mighty kiss on her cheek.

Jacques was a bit more awkward about the reunion, and Natalie wondered if he felt guilty about losing her in Paris. She gave Ina to Hans, walked over to the crusty guerrilla fighter, and threw her arms about his neck. "Thank you for coming to get us, Jacques Bellamont."

He grunted. "Shouldn't have lost you in the first place," he said, and he wrapped her into a hefty bear hug. She saw him brush impa-tiently at a tear.

She pretended not to notice. "I thought they killed you when they came for me. The man who abducted me said he had."

"No such luck." Jacques grinned.

Viktor stood apart from the rest of the group, watching the reunion with a tolerance that bordered on impatience. He glanced back at the faraway shore, checked his watch, and then turned to Rolf. "Have you seen her?"

Soberly Rolf shook his head.

Without another word Rostov strode off across the ice, heading back in the direction of his car. Natalie saw him go, and suddenly she was running after him, calling his name. He stopped and turned, and there was forcefulness to the movement that made her also stop in her tracks. They stood facing each other in the swirling snow.

She couldn't think what to say to him, and suddenly she felt foolish for her impulsiveness. "Viktor, I—" She swallowed.

He strode toward her and pulled her into his arms. One hand found the back of her neck and he pulled her face close to his, pressing her cheek against his and breathing softly, evenly against the side of her face. He did not say a word.

She stood there, stunned, and her brain refused to tell her what to do.

After a few moments he released her and walked away.

* * *

Viktor Rostov stood in front of the desk and addressed the camp commandant. "I'm here to discuss the transfer of one of your prisoners; a woman by the name of Lucya Viktorovna Rostova."

"Rostova?" The commandant didn't offer him a seat. "What's she to you?"

"She's a prisoner here, isn't she?"

"For the moment. What do you want with her?"

"When is she leaving for Kolyma?"

"I never said she was. How'd you know that?"

Rostov took a deep breath. He handed the man his forged documents. "I'm here from Moscow to see about her transfer. Her father has signed a confession and—"

"The second one in a week!" the commandant suddenly exclaimed, and rose to his feet. "Never known a prisoner to be so popular with the comrades in Moscow."

"Excuse me?"

"The head of Moscow's MGB was here two days ago. Said Rostova's father might be coming for her."

The news shook Viktor. He wet his lips and thought quickly. "And that's why I must get her out of here right now. Before her father finds her. Where is she?"

"Out for a drive."

Rostov's jaw dropped. "A *drive?*"

"That's right," the commandant said. "With her boyfriend. He's the officer in charge of the stables. And when she gets back, she's going back in the Hole where she belongs."

"A *drive?*" Rostov was still incredulous.

"Yep. Can you imagine hitching three Orlovs to a sleigh in this weather? Idiot."

Rostov cleared his throat. "Where did they go?"

The commandant waved in the general direction of east.

"Who is this officer?"

The commandant shrugged. "The son of some influential Party member. He always gets what he wants. He's a mama's boy."

Rostov turned and strode from the room, much to the surprise and consternation of the camp commandant.

FIFTY-SIX

Snegurochka, Grandpapa Frost, and Yolochka fought against their restraints as they reached the edge of the ice. They knew what lay beneath their feet and they did not trust it. Alex had to seize the whip and crack it loudly over their heads until they finally relented and danced out onto the ice.

Alex urged the horses to a run. Finally they began to work together, stretching their legs in a synchronized gallop that made the sleigh fly across the rough ice. The horses' hooves pounded, thudding against the slippery surface and stirring up snow flurries wherever they struck. Ahead of them, the ship did not seem to be getting any closer. Lucya's dirty fingernails dug into her protector's arm and she couldn't keep from turning to watch for Krajnik's car.

She heard the sound of a motor before she saw the car, and then she blinked, rubbed at her eyes, and squinted through the snow. "Alex—look! There are *two* cars! One is almost here and the other is still on the shore. Alex!"

"The one closest doesn't look like Krajnik's." Alex glanced a second time, just to be sure.

The ice groaned beneath them, and Lucya turned to meet Alex's gaze. "How much farther do we have to go?"

"Another mile."

"Alex, the ice . . ."

"It'll hold a little longer."

"Alex, the first car's gaining on us . . . !"

"They're gonna have to ditch their vehicle in another few minutes, Lucya. Watch; we'll make it to the ship before they do."

"You're sure?"

He hesitated. "To be honest, no. I don't know if we're going to be able to go much farther . . ."

Behind them, the car slowed, inched to a stop, and killed its engine. The doors opened and a figure rose from the driver's seat. And then as Lucya watched, the figure began to run toward the sled.

For one long moment she couldn't breathe while the past and present, the future and the impossible, all blended in one violent emotion that took her breath away. She opened her mouth and her lips released one long, desperate sound. "Ooohhh!"

"What is it?"

She jumped to her feet, the sheepskin sliding to the floorboards and her arms lifting high above her head. She waved with such enthusiasm that any witness might have found it hard to believe that she'd been imprisoned and tortured, beaten and abused, frozen and starved almost constantly for more than eight months. She waved her emaciated arms and gasped, "Papa! Papa! Let me out, Alex! Oh, stop the sleigh! Stop the sleigh!" She began to clamber over the side of the sled before Alex had time to respond, and she had to hang on for dear life until he had the horses under control. The sleigh glided to a stop, and Lucya tumbled over the side onto the ice. "Papa! Papa!" She could hardly see him for the happy tears, and she slipped dangerously back and forth as she began to run to meet him.

"Papa! My dear Papa! I knew you'd come for me! I knew you'd come!"

* * *

Viktor saw her running toward him and he threw a worried glance across his shoulder. The other car was gaining, he saw, and as he watched, the vehicle altered course, headed straight for his daughter, and accelerated.

His heart began its deadly dance. No matter how he ran, he knew he was not going to reach Lucya in time. He shouted at her, hoping she would hear above the accelerating engine of the other car. "Lucya! Get—back—in the sleigh!" But deep down he knew that a return to the sleigh would not save her.

The car continued to pick up speed, its wheels whining, spinning on the rough ice as it zeroed in on Rostov's daughter. Viktor caught a glimpse of Krajnik inside, his hands gripping the wheel and his face close to the windshield. For just a second his murderous eyes locked with Viktor's, in a triumph so complete that Viktor was stunned.

As he closed in on the girl, Krajnik's mouth opened in a silent howl of victory, and when the car cut Viktor off from his daughter, she finally turned to run.

The ice shuddered beneath Viktor's feet. There was a hollow boom, followed by a series of ear-splitting crackles that made his blood run cold. He screamed his daughter's name but was surprised when only a whisper escaped his lips. He had no time to think; only to watch as the unthinkable unfolded in front of him.

In less time than it took for Viktor to repeat his daughter's name, the ice gave way and the speeding automobile and Roman Krajnik broke through and were gone. And then, her feet buckling beneath her, Lucya was lifted upward and thrown forward by the violent thrust of a house-sized chunk of ice. Her feet slipped out from under her and her body slammed into the ice, slid forward, and followed Krajnik's car into the swirling, inky depths.

He didn't have time to feel the shock of losing his daughter when she was no more than a stone's throw away. Instead, his body lunged forward and he threw himself headfirst into the angry, churning water.

What breath there had been was sucked from his lungs and a thousand icy knives stabbed every inch of his flesh. He imagined a leering Krajnik at the giving end of every single one of them, and he thrashed about wildly as the unimaginable cold seeped instantly into his brain.

There was not a single ray of light—neither from the ice nor from the sky above. He couldn't tell which direction was up, and his arms and legs were fast losing their ability to move. He fought panic, worse than any fear he'd ever felt in his life. He felt his chest constrict violently, burn with a searing, terrifying heat, and then go numb. His arms and legs quickly lost the strength to move, and he could do nothing but drift helplessly with the swirling current.

He closed his eyes, and then opened them again. It was no use; he could see nothing. In fact, within a few seconds his face was so numb that he couldn't even feel if his eyes were open. His head ceased to throb and his burning lungs ceased to burn. He felt strange warmth beginning to creep over his torso, spreading from his lungs to his heart and all the way to his fingertips. He experienced a moment of complete peace.

Was this the way he would die? He'd thought his heart would someday claim him. But if this was what it was like, it wasn't really so bad . . .

Except that his daughter didn't deserve to die like this. Viktor forced his sluggish brain to recount something Rolf Schulmann said to him once—words that, in this sleepy, peaceful moment were struggling for his attention.

He has special miracles reserved just for you, Viktor—and when the time comes, if you are willing to ask for them, He will give them to you. Who knows? After all that we can do . . . maybe asking God to intervene is the only way to save your daughter's life.

Then Viktor Rostov did something he'd never done before. He prayed. He sent his dying thoughts up to the God of Hans Brenner, the God of Natalya Ivanovna, and the God of Rolf Schulmann, and he asked Him to spare Lucya's life.

Something soft brushed against his limp hand, and he closed his fingers impossibly around it. He did not try to look at what he had captured; instead, he began to shake the strips of rubber that used to be his legs. For what seemed like a torturous length of time he continued to battle with his legs, until his head pressed against the underside of something hard.

He was under the ice. He almost gave up right there. But his body suddenly moved sideways, his head scraping and bumping against the bottom of the ice until he broke free and found himself staring at a fist holding the collar of his shirt.

Hans Brenner and another man lay over the edge of the ice, their bodies angled away from each other and their shoulders hanging out over the water. Hans Brenner's hand tightened on the shoulder of Viktor's coat, and he scrambled to his knees and pulled Viktor bodily from the Sea of Japan. He hauled him halfway onto the ice and then saw what Viktor held locked in his hand. He reached down again and captured the wrist of Viktor's daughter and pulled her limp body entirely clear of the hole. The other man immediately shed his coat and wrapped her in it, pulled her away from the water, and enfolded her in his arms. He held her close while Natalie ran toward them with several blankets in her arms.

She wrapped one around Lucya and then slid onto her stomach next to Hans. Her voice sounded miles away. "Please get him out, Hans—please, please save him!"

"I'll need your help, Natalie." Hans was shivering now. "I—I can't do it . . . by myself . . ."

Natalie reached for his arm and together they dragged Viktor Rostov onto the ice and away from the edge. They rolled him onto his back and Natalie threw a blanket over his still form.

Viktor's gaze turned to Natalie. He did not feel his lips move. "Natalya Ivanovna . . . You—have—been—my joy . . ."

He saw then, in her eyes, the esteem that he wished he could have seen in Moscow, and she leaned close and kissed his cheek. "You did it, Viktor." She touched the deadly gray skin of his face. "You saved your daughter's life." Her face stayed close to his, and he wished he could feel her touch.

But he could feel something else—something that enveloped his numb flesh with a sensation not unlike warmth, and even though he couldn't understand the sensation, he was grateful for it and wished it could surround him always. Natalie smiled at him and whispered so that only he could hear, "I *forgive* you, Viktor. And I love you for what you've done to make things right."

He did not try to answer. It was enough that she had forgiven him.

He looked and found his daughter, her pale face serene as she rested against the shoulder of the young man that to Viktor's foggy senses seemed vaguely familiar. Viktor watched as her eyelids fluttered open and she glanced up first at her protector and then across at Viktor.

Their eyes met and her blue lips formed one word: "P-Papa . . ."

He had saved her. He'd finally listened to his heart and had been granted a miracle by a God that hadn't abandoned him in his darkest hour. And now Lucya would be safe with these people, who believed in God and in miracles that can make hands touch in the dark immensity of an icy sea. She would be safe because of this God of miracles.

I love you, my precious Lucya. I love you with all my heart.

Viktor's eyes closed and he went to sleep.

FIFTY-SEVEN

Lieutenant Viktor Rostov was laid in the captain's cabin of the *Fujiyama*. Lucya took up residence there and kept almost constant vigil over the body of her beloved papa.

Snow began to fall as the boat pulled free of the ice. Natalie pulled Ina's blankets close about the baby and settled into a seat below deck. Hans folded her into his arms and together they watched through the porthole the amazing white nothingness of a snowstorm at sea.

She must have slept, warm against Hans's side, because Ina's wail brought her head up. Ina had kicked her legs and arms free, and Natalie spent several minutes soothing her back to sleep.

She was rewrapping Ina when she caught a tiny flash of white through a tear in one of the blankets. She leaned closer, and then caught her breath. "Hans, look."

Hans leaned close. Natalie separated the threads more and worked a piece of paper from the cotton lining. She opened a letter written in English, with each word crafted in Regina's meticulous, beautiful hand. She read it out loud to Hans:

> *To my precious Ina,*
>
> *I write this letter with the hope that you will someday have an opportunity to read it. I know your parents—the ones who are raising you: Your papa is courageous and brave. Your mother is kind and gentle, and was a good friend to me. I love your mother with the love of one sister for*

another. And because I love her so much it was natural to think of her when I finally realized I had to give you away.

Please don't fault me for this. It is because of my love for you that I gave you to her. I have no doubt that by the time you read this, I will be dead. But I will go to my grave happy, because by giving you to my sister, I gave you life.

Natalie couldn't continue. Hans took the letter gently from her hand. He read for her,

Your mother spoke once of eternity. If it's true, this eternal life, then I will still be watching over you as you grow to womanhood. Think of me when you go to school in America and fulfill your dreams. Think of me when you marry the one you love for eternity. Think of me when you hold your first daughter in your arms. Think that I also held you, for many hours, and my love for you was so deep that I could not allow you to suffer anymore.

Think of me, my sweet Ina, and live.

Regina

Natalie cried in huge, gasping sobs, and the sound broke Hans's heart. "Hans, I can't bear it. Oh, I can't bear this!"

He held her close and they cried together, and as the boat carried them away from captivity, they talked of Regina, and Ina, and of the future.

And they planned together a life Regina would have wanted for her daughter.

FIFTY-EIGHT

Major James Matthews met them at the harbor on the south end of Japan's Okushiri Island. From the island's eight-hundred-meter runway they flew with Viktor's body to Pearl Harbor, where his body was prepared for burial. And then, at Lucya's insistence, he was transported to Amarillo, Texas.

A military convoy took Lucya and her father, Alex Reynolds and Major Matthews, Hans, Natalie, Ina, Rolf, Marie, and Alma seventy miles from Amarillo to the ranch owned by Alex Reynolds's grandparents. And there, on December 31, 1946, Viktor Rostov was buried, as his daughter directed, in what Lucya considered the vast frozen ice fields of Texas.

Because the Soviet Union had been an ally of the United States and Viktor had once been Matthews's friend, Matthews pulled a few strings and arranged a funeral for Lieutenant Rostov—complete with unobtrusive military honors. A lone trumpet softly crooned "Taps." An American flag and a Soviet flag were draped side-by-side over his coffin, and before the coffin was lowered into the grave, Marines folded both flags and presented them to Lucya. "On behalf of two grateful allies . . ."

Lucya clung to Alex as her father was lowered into his grave. She watched silently, her hand locked about the arm of her fiancé's coat, while Texas soil and Texas snow covered her father's coffin.

Rolf said a brief, meaningful prayer to dedicate the grave. Then Hans and Major Matthews set the headstone—at Lucya's request it was a smooth black marble marker in the austere tradition of the Soviet Union.

The modest crowd began to disperse, and as the wind swept waves through miles of prairie snow, Lucya Rostova approached the grave.

She knelt in the snow. For several moments she didn't speak, but contemplated her father's grave. Then she whispered, "I know you'll miss home, Papa, so I brought you something." She pulled a misshapen object wrapped in a frayed bit of cloth from her skirt pocket. She loosened twine from around the cloth, opened it carefully, and reached inside. Then she let dirt sift through her fingers into a tiny mound next to the marker. "I brought home to *you*, Papa—and now you can carry it close to your heart like all good soldiers who must leave the Motherland. I've had it with me ever since the day I was arrested in Moscow. And I brought you something else . . ." She laid a soft, colorful bundle next to the mound of Russian soil. "It's Mama's shawl, Papa—the one you sent to me. It kept me warm inside and reminded me of you and Mama."

She took a deep breath. "Rolf Schulmann said that your soul is still alive, Papa—and that because of what you did for me I'll get to see you again someday." She brushed at a stray tear. "I like that idea. It makes me think you might be happy where you are. And now you'll be warm while you travel to be with Mama again. That's what Rolf said—that you and Mama and my brother are going to be together again—and that someday I can be with you too! I'm so happy if that's true . . ."

She wiped at her cheeks. "Alex said he is going to take care of me. You would like him; he's kind to me. Thank you for allowing him to help me! And—and . . ." She struggled to continue. "Thank you, my dear Papa, for finding me. I *knew* you would find me. I will miss you."

Natalie stood off to one side with Ina in her arms. The baby whimpered and turned her head into Natalie's chest. Natalie let her own head rest on Hans's shoulder. She whispered, "Hans, you have no idea how Viktor has protected me." Natalie's eyes misted. "But oh, how I hated him! How I despised him for all that he did! His lies and deception shocked me, Hans. But even though many of the things he did were awful"—she swallowed, her pain evident as she struggled to say the next words—"I'm still grateful to him for saving my life." She kissed Ina's soft forehead. "And how much I owe him now!"

Hans held her close, and he contemplated whether he should ever tell her the awful truth—a truth he'd learned from Rolf as they crossed the Sea of Japan. He knew if he didn't tell her, it might forever remain a secret, forever buried in this grave—the dark shadow of a husband she never knew had been hers.

He kissed her cheek, the act as protective as it was possessive, and he realized that he never wanted her to find out what Rostov had forced her to do—even if the odious act had saved her life.

No. He didn't want to tell her. He wanted to let the dark secret die here, alongside the man who'd created the secret and then gallantly guarded it. Hans knew Viktor Rostov had loved her—the man's actions spoke of a love so deep that it had kept Rostov from breaking her heart. Hans wondered how God would judge such a man; would Viktor be condemned for stealing Natalie away from Hans? Or would Viktor be pardoned because his lies had ultimately protected her? Would God look at his actions or his heart?

Much about Rostov had been good. But would God forgive the rest?

It would be a long time before Hans could completely forgive Rostov. But he knew if he were to have the eternal marriage he'd dreamed of since before the end of the war, he would have to work on that forgiveness.

And he would read again about that Alma, in Rolf's Book of Mormon, who experienced a change of heart. Alma's experience had influenced Rolf Schumann to protect two missionaries before the war. Alma's conversion had become Rolf's own. And Rolf's change of heart had made Hans Brenner want to change *his*—and over time his own conversion had been accomplished, softly, gently, with none of the drama of Rolf's experience, but with a gentleness tailored explicitly to Hans's personal needs.

Viktor Rostov's heart had also changed, little by little, over a period of time, until the Spirit could find a way to whisper to him what needed to be done. Perhaps, Hans thought with a hint of amusement, Viktor was even now learning more about the God he'd stubbornly refused to acknowledge.

Rostov's heart. All along it had been Rostov's heart that influenced him. His heart's weakness had dictated what he could and couldn't do and had influenced the love he felt for a young American nurse that silently, secretly matched Hans's own. It was ultimately Rostov's heart that guided him, gave him courage, and then continued to function until he'd saved the young daughter who'd been the driving force behind his heart's motivation. Hans could learn a thing or two from Viktor Rostov. But first, Hans acknowledged, he would have to forgive him.

Hans felt Natalie's warmth in his arms, and his love for her overwhelmed him. He'd lost her, and God had returned her to him unharmed. Hans knew it was because of Rostov's courage that Natalie was alive today. Perhaps, Hans reconsidered, when his own heart had had time to heal, he would tell Natalie of the relationship she didn't know she'd had with that courageous man.

I would like to shake your hand someday, Viktor Rostov, Hans thought. *But I hope it's a long time from now, because I haven't forgiven you yet. I'll work to forgive you until that day comes.* Hans held Natalie and the baby close.

Rolf swung Alma onto his shoulders and took Marie's hand. Major Matthews walked with them to the vehicles parked at the edge of the road. Hans and Natalie soon followed.

Alex Reynolds moved close to Rostov's grave. "Lucya," he said gently. "Are you going to be all right?"

She nodded, silent, and rose to her feet.

Alex took Lucya's hand in his, gave it a comforting squeeze, and turned with her to move away from the grave.

For a few moments she walked with him, and then she slowed. "Wait, Alex—please wait." Lucya slipped her hand free and ran back across the snow. She knelt one more time, pressed her lips to the palm of her hand, and then laid her hand gently on the tiny mound of Russian soil. "I love you, Papa," she whispered. "I'm proud of you for the good things you did—for your country and for me."

And then, her voice barely reaching the threshold of a whisper, she bade him farewell one last time in his native tongue.

"Dasvidanya, Papa. Dasvidanya."

SUGGESTED READING

Applebaum, Anne. *Gulag: A History.* Great Britain: The Penguin Press, 2003.

Figes, Orlando. *The Whisperers: Private Life in Stalin's Russia.* New York: Metropolitan Books, 2007.

Kuranov, V., translated by Anatol Kagan. *The Trans-Siberian Express.* New York: Sphinx Press, Inc., 1980.

Tobien, Karl. *Dancing Under the Red Star: The Extraordinary Story of Margaret Werner, the Only American Woman to Survive Stalin's Gulag.* Colorado: Waterbrook Press, 2006.

Wettlin, Margaret. *Fifty Russian Winters: An American Woman's Life in the Soviet Union.* Canada: John Wiley & Sons, Inc., 1994.

CHAPTER NOTES

ONE

American CIG: (Central Intelligence Group) Established by President Truman in January 1946, it was a successor to the wartime OSS and a precursor to the CIA.

TWO

Lisunov LI-2: A Soviet-built passenger plane. Used during the war to transport Soviet military and government personnel, it was a Soviet version of the Douglas DC-3.

Yalta Conference: Held at the Black Sea resort of Yalta in Soviet Ukraine in February 1945. Among other things, the UN had its ideological beginning there, along with a ruling that all Soviet citizens should be repatriated, whether voluntarily or not.

THREE

MGB (MVD, NKVD)—On February 9, 1946, Stalin confirmed that there would be no change in the Soviet system of "discipline and sacrifice." During 1946 The NKVD was strengthened and then reorganized as two separate entities: the MVD and the MGB. The MGB was given mandate over foreign intelligence and counter-intelligence, while the MVD controlled domestic security and the Gulag system. However, Orlando Figes, in his book *The Whisperers: Private Life in Stalin's Russia*, explains that because domestic enemies were regarded as enemies of the entire Soviet system, MGB functions spilled over into the domestic arena as well.

Discerning between the responsibilities of the two entities is a highly complicated process, and as such could have become a deterrent to the storyline. Therefore, in *Trespass* the author has chosen to refer only to the MGB (which is the actual forerunner to the well-known KGB), although many of the actions taken by MGB characters in the story would have in fact been more likely functions of the MVD.

Great October Revolution Parade: Held on November 7 by the USSR to commemorate the day the Bolsheviks (and Lenin) came to power in Petrograd (now St. Petersburg); the first was held November 7, 1917.

Five

Housing cooperative/Communal apartments: A Soviet citizen was required to be a member of a cooperative in order to rent a room in a communal apartment. Stalin decided that one of the evils that must be purged from the People was the pride of personal possession and luxury. He established the communal apartment to teach frugality and equality. Several families—sometimes up to six or more—occupied the same living space, shared the same bathroom, and used the same centralized kitchen. A room to oneself was considered a luxury. A family might be lucky to have two. Single men were not necessarily separated from apartments with single women.

"You'd get lost in a forest with three pine trees.": This is based on a common Russian saying.

Six

Red Square: Considered the hub of Moscow and even all Russia; has the Kremlin on one side and an important shopping district on the other. The site of government leadership since the age of the Czars.

Seven

Young Pioneers: Almost like a Soviet version of Hitler's Youth. Members were indoctrinated in the Soviet ideal and worked closely with the Village Soviet to regulate affairs of a community.

Young Pioneers were awarded medals and received high praise for denouncing citizens of their community—including (and possibly especially) family members. Denunciation was seen as the highest, most courageous form of patriotism and was taught militarily in the organization.

Lubyanka: Headquarters of the MGB in Moscow, and later the KGB. Lubyanka also housed the most notorious prison in Moscow. Lubyanka was seized by the government after the Bolshevik Revolution and has been used by the Soviet secret police ever since.

Dzerzhinsky Square: Now known as Lubyanka Square, next to Lubyanka.

Izvinitye: Forgive me.

EIGHT

Spaso House: The actual residence of the American ambassador to the Soviet Union, located in Moscow as described in this story. General Walter Smith was the ambassador during this timeframe, and Chin and Tang were the actual longtime servants to ambassadors of that house. The chandelier described briefly in this scene was a central focal point of the home.

Malen'kaya: Little one.

NINE

Scorn for Regina's decision to have a baby: The character Regina is sad that she is seen by coworkers as irresponsible for getting pregnant and bringing another human into the world when there is so much suffering, but this attitude was normal during Stalin's time. Abortion was the birth control of Soviet Russia. Even today, a woman having a baby in Russia (or more than one or two) is often seen as either an irresponsible drunk or a poverty-stricken prostitute. A modern Russian woman may have an average of five intentional abortions during her childbearing years. Very few children are seen on the street. A negative Russian birthrate is one reason for Russia's intense reaction to the recent adoption-gone-wrong stories in the news.

ELEVEN

Samovar: An urn used to boil water for tea; also to keep tea warm.

Village Soviet: An administrative council in rural communities in the Soviet Union. The Village Soviet was the governing body and administered punishment and praise, passports, permission, and counsel. Nothing important happened in a village without the permission or knowledge of the Village Soviet.

Politburo: The governing executive branch of the Communist Party.

Kulaks: When Stalin began his collective farm experiments, he met with resistance to the socialization of all private farms by an affluent class of farmers/peasants called kulaks. These "more privileged" landowners were not necessarily rich, but they resisted what they considered the theft of their property by the State. The Gulags were soon overflowing with kulaks as a result, and children of kulaks were denied a whole array of privileges, ranging from basic necessities like food and shelter to the opportunity to attend university or learn a trade. (Unless, of course, they were the ones who had denounced their kulak parents to the Village Soviet.)

THIRTEEN

Enemy of the People: Opponent to the Soviet ideal; someone who has been denounced for rebellion (whether perceived or actual) against Stalin and/or the Soviet government.

FIFTEEN

Nazi hunters: Individuals and organizations often hunted Nazis for a bounty—or out of a sense of vengeance. Often they were hired by countries or organizations to hunt down Nazis or Nazi sympathizers so that they could stand trial for war crimes, as established by the 1945–46 Nuremberg Trials.

SIXTEEN

The Hole: Slang term for jailhouse or solitary confinement in the Gulag camps (Aleksandr Isaevich Solzhenit, *The Gulag Archipelago,* Westview Press, 1997).

Seventeen

Harijs Svikeris: A deputy of a Nazi collaborator named Victor Arajs, who helped the Nazis murder Latvian Jews. Svikeris hid in Great Britain after the war.

OSO: Office of Special Operations. In mid-1946, President Truman reworked the CIG and renamed it the OSO—another step in the transformation of America's intelligence organization to the CIA.

Twenty-one

Were Soviets religious enough to hold anything—like Lucya's bread—sacred? Even though few received formal religious training during the Stalin years, many believed in some form of God. In 1929–30, police recorded, among resistance to farm collectivization, "protests against closures of churches" (Figes, *The Whisperers,* p. 93). Also, for brief periods during the war Stalin was less vigilant in his denunciation of organized religion. A citizen might mention God in public and not necessarily face censure. However, in an attempt to minimize Western influence, Stalin clamped down again on religion at the close of the war as Soviets displaced by the violence returned home to their native countries. (Figes, *The Whisperers*)

Twenty-Two

Chort vozmi: *Chort* means "devil" and *vozmi* basically means "take it." The phrase, therefore, is a mild interjection that means "the devil take it."

Twenty-Three

Childbirth in the Soviet Union: In *Fifty Russian Winters,* Wettlin describes her experience giving birth in Moscow just before WWII. She describes it as one of the most violent, painful, humiliating, and frigid experiences of her life. They used no anesthetic—not even when there were complications and she had to have placenta scraped from her uterus. She gave birth on a cold steel table in the same room as five other women and had absolutely no privacy. She described that experience as "being gutted like a chicken for

broiling" and said that giving birth was like "losing your humanity."
(pp. 110–11, 131–32)

TWENTY-FOUR

Andre Sakharov: A brilliant physicist who spent two decades design-
ing nuclear weapons for the Soviets.

Arzamas-16: A closed town (meaning secret, like an ultra-high-security
military base) that Stalin established at an old monastery. It was used
as a secret laboratory to develop Russia's version of the atom bomb.
Arzamas-16 was functional in the Soviet Union from 1946 to 1991.

Shpagin: A type of Russian submachine gun named after its inventor,
Georgi Shpagin (1897–1952).

TWENTY-FIVE

Oppenheimer: A reference to J. Robert Oppenheimer, often referred
to as the "Father of the Atomic Bomb." Rima calls him a German
scientist, but he was born in the U.S. to German immigrants.

TWENTY-SIX

Prisoner riot: There actually was a prisoner riot in 1946 at Arzamas-16;
every prisoner who took part was eventually captured and killed.

TWENTY-NINE

Orlov Trotters: Considered the most famous Russian breed of horse,
known for its considerably fast gait. First bred by Alezei Orlov,
the breed was well known and well prized among Russians for its
beauty, size, and stamina. Breeding of the Orlov resumed after the
tumultuous years of WWII, and cross-breeding was forbidden by
Stalin.

THIRTY-ONE

"The Mustache": Anne Applebaum makes reference to this derogatory
nickname for Comrade Stalin in *Gulag: A History.*

THIRTY-TWO

Ford factory: Henry Ford actually did take advantage of Stalin's seasonal goodwill and establish a Ford factory near Gorky. He enthusiastically advertised in the United States for workers, and many who were feeling the pinch of hard economic times answered his call. (See Tobien, *Dancing Under the Red Star.*)

Collective farm: Also known as *Kolkhozes.* Part of Stalin's plan for the socialization of the farm system and the demise of the kulaks. Farmlands were seized by the government and added to a system of government-run farming organizations in order to increase productivity. Usually the results were exactly the opposite. (For more, see *The Whisperers.*)

Thirty-Three
Proshaitye: A more permanent form of "good-bye" than *dasvidanya.*
Detskidom: Children's home, orphanage.

Thirty-Five
Shapka/ushanka: Often used interchangeably; however, an ushanka oftentimes has earflaps, and a shapka might be used without earflaps. This is a rather generalized description of the difference between the two.

Thirty-Six
Krauts: A derogatory nickname for Germans supposedly inspired by the idea that Germans liked to eat Sauerkraut.

Thirty-Eight
Vtoraya Rechka: A Gulag transit camp near Vladivostok. Mostly utilized as a way station for prisoners on their way to the Kolyma mines in the Arctic Circle.
Kolyma: Here refers to the series of Gulag labor mines north of the Sea of Okhotsk in the Arctic Circle.
"Kolyma znachit smert!": "Kolyma means death." A common phrase whispered fearfully by those who knew of Stalin's most notorious cluster of Gulag camps. The Soviet people feared these camps more than any other. A family member sentenced to Kolyma was considered already dead.

Kolyma fleet: Old ships purchased from different countries (including the United States), remodeled and secretly used to transport "cargo" (prisoners) across the Sea of Okhotsk to the Kolyma mines.

Cossack murders: Several sources describe the tragic results of the Allies' agreement to return all Soviet-born citizens to their place of birth. Peasants of Polish and Ukrainian descent were forcibly returned, only to be slaughtered by Soviet troops as soon as they set foot on Soviet soil. For more information, run an internet search for Yalta Ruling, victims of Yalta, Cossacks, etc.

FORTY-TWO

Fedor Gusev: Soviet ambassador to London, 1943–46.

FORTY-FOUR

"Ey ty Durak!": "You are such a fool!"

FORTY-SEVEN

Leningrad Station at Komsomol Square; Yaroslavl Station: Train stations situated next to each other in Moscow. Leningrad station serves northern Russian destinations, while Yaroslavl was a trans-Siberian portal to the east and Siberia.

FORTY-NINE

Room for Mother and Child: In *Fifty Russian Winters,* Wettlin describes her family's escape from Moscow during the war, and also her joy, amazement, and relief when she discovered an entire suite of rooms in the Novosibirsk train station with a sign posted ROOM FOR MOTHER AND CHILD. The author has written of it here according to Wettlin's description.

FIFTY-THREE

Dzhurma: Formerly the SS *Brielle* built in the Netherlands, the vessel was purchased by the Soviets and added to the notorious Kolyma fleet. Its main purpose was to transport "cargo" from the transit camps (such as Vtoraya Rechka) to Magadan and the Kolyma mines. It was employed in Stalin's Gulags from 1936 to 1950.

In *Gulag: A History,* Applebaum explains that ships in the Kolyma fleet were required to winter of the Sea of Okhotsk, frozen into the ice. The outcome for all aboard is easily imagined.

FIFTY-EIGHT

Soil from the Motherland: A soldier or another traveler leaving the Soviet Union for any extended period of time might carry a handful of Russian soil with him in his pocket. It was a sentimental thing, along the lines of our saying "there's no place like home." They left it there until they returned home. Lucya would have carried Moscow soil with her as a reminder of her home. Placing the soil on her father's grave is a very Russian way of showing her hope that there might possibly be life after death—and if there was, then someday Rostov (and his family) might be able to return to his motherland.

ABOUT THE AUTHOR

Sandra Grey was born in Inglewood, California to a very large two-generation military family. Many of the ideas for her stories were inspired by her father's service during the Cold War. Her father is a retired air force major who trained to be a spy during that time.

Sandra has fond memories of an experience in Snowflake, Arizona as a child: One snowy winter morning her mother's cousin, Sanford Flake, showed up outside the family home with two horses harnessed to a sleigh. Sandra piled onto the sleigh with her siblings and cousins and hung on as he took them for the ride of their lives. It was adventurous and memorable enough to give Sandra a hint of what a troika ride behind three spirited steeds might be like for her characters.

Sandra graduated from Brigham Young University with a degree in humanities and has followed her insatiable curiosity and love of history on adventures from Asia to Alaska, Mexico to Europe, and Russia to Brazil. Sandra currently lives with her husband and their own large family in Arizona.

Sandra Grey won Best Novel of the Year at the 2008 Whitney Awards for her first novel, *Traitor*.